31/7/2018

Diane Allen was born in Leeds, but raised at her family's farm deep in the Yorkshire Dales. After working as a glass engraver, starting a family and looking after an ill father, she found her true niche in life, joining a large print publishing firm in 1990 and rising to the position of general manager. She is also Honorary Vice President of the Romantic Novelists' Association. Diane and her husband live in Long Preston in the Yorkshire Dales, and have two children and four grandchildren.

LIKE FATHER, LIKE SON

From birth, Polly Harper seems destined for tragedy. Raised by her loving grandparents on Paradise Farm, she is unknowingly tangled in a web of secrecy regarding her parentage. When she falls in love with Tobias, the wealthy son of a local landowner of disrepute, her anxious grandparents send her to work in a dairy. There she is instantly drawn to the handsome Matt Dinsdale, propelling her further into the depths of forbidden romance and dark family secrets. When tragedy strikes, Polly is forced to confront her past and decide the course of her future. Will she lose everything, or will she finally realize that her roots and love lie in Paradise?

Books by Diane Allen
Published by Ulverscroft:

FOR THE SAKE OF HER FAMILY
FOR A MOTHER'S SINS
FOR A FATHER'S PRIDE ×

DIANE ALLEN

LIKE FATHER, LIKE SON

Complete and Unabridged

CHARNWOOD
Leicester

First published in Great Britain in 2015 by
Macmillan
an imprint of
Pan Macmillan
London

First Charnwood Edition
published 2016
by arrangement with
Pan Macmillan
London

A catalogue record for this book is available from the British Library.

ISBN 978–1–4448–3026–2

Published by
F. A. Thorpe (Publishing)
Anstey, Leicestershire

Set by Words & Graphics Ltd.
Anstey, Leicestershire
Printed and bound in Great Britain by
T. J. International Ltd., Padstow, Cornwall

This book is printed on acid-free paper

For my sister Margaret, with love.
Our farmer in the family.

Also grateful thanks to all the hard-working
people within the Ulverscroft Group who
provide our libraries with an excellent
selection of titles for the visually impaired.

With a special thank-you to my
fellow workers at Magna Large Print,
who are like a second family to me.
Keep up the good work.

1

Garsdale, in the Yorkshire Dales, November 1886

Danny Harper looked back down the dale as he climbed on board the steam train that was standing at Hawes Junction. He was half-hoping that his father would come rushing up the steep incline of the station hill and beg him to come home. Or perhaps ask him to sit down in the cosy kitchen of Paradise Farm and talk it through, like two grown men, but he knew that was not going to happen. For one thing, it was still black as pitch, the late-November morning yet to open to the day's weak light; and for another, his father and mother wouldn't yet be out of their beds — let alone have had time to read the note waiting for them on the cluttered kitchen table. Danny wasn't proud that he was taking the chicken's way out, by not daring to face his parents, but at this moment in time he could see no other way out of it, without living a life of drudgery and toil, trying to make a living on a Dales smallholding while raising a family.

'Well, are you coming, mate? We can't wait any longer,' the guard on the early-morning mail train shouted, as the last bag of mail was passed into the stationmaster's hands for safe delivery to the postman.

'Aye, I'm coming — hold your horses.' Danny

1

stubbed out his cigarette and heaved his pack of possessions across his back, before climbing aboard the empty train, looking around quickly at the lighted signal box, afraid that the local signalman might recognize him as he gave a final glance around the dale of his birth, the only dale he'd known.

Old Bunce, the stationmaster, blew the whistle, and the jolt of the carriages told Danny there was no turning back. He'd done it now; he'd left. No matter what happened, this was the start of his new life. He listened as the engine picked up steam, as every shunt and blow of steam gave more haste to the engine's power. He felt for his most valued tickets in his pocket. This was only the first part of his journey. He knew this line like the back of his hand, but after he changed trains at Carnforth he wouldn't know the line at all.

The mighty port of Liverpool was his destination, and then over the sea to America — the land where dreams were made, and where Danny had decided life would be better for him. He'd thought about stopping at Liverpool. His mother had told him of his father's kin living there, of keeping cows within the city itself and grazing them on the local parks and football fields, so that the city dwellers could be supplied with fresh milk. He remembered laughing when she'd told them how they kept the cows in back yards, and even in spare rooms in their houses, just to make money and supply milk to the mighty city. He'd even helped his father send kits full of milk on the train, when his aunt had been short, for her to supply to the townspeople. But, thinking better of it, Danny knew that Liverpool was perhaps not far enough away from his family; he wanted a bigger adventure, and the thought of it made him feel sick with anticipation as he felt for the tickets in his waistcoat pocket.

His best friend Bill Sunter had helped him acquire the tickets, urging Danny not to get caught out with a wife and baby, like he had, and Bill had been all too happy to listen to how grand Danny's new life could be in the promised land. Bill and Danny had sat for many an hour dreaming and reading about a better life, and the opportunities that lay in the expanding new world of America.

'New York, United States of America.' Danny whispered the words with reverence. His destination wasn't just down the line, but over the great ocean. By, he didn't dare think about it. Perhaps he should change his mind and go home — it wasn't too late! Hitching a lift on the mail train was commonplace among the lads of the Dales. But to sail to America was a different matter.

He sat back in the corner of the carriage and listened to the clatter of the train as it picked up speed down the track. He felt a pang of guilt as he thought about what he'd done. His mother would be first up in the household. She'd probably find the letter after she'd lit the fire, put the kettle on to boil and then shouted to him and his father to get up. He imagined her tears as she read that he'd left, without giving any

3

explanation, and then he imagined his father's anger as he realized that not only had his son disappeared, but he'd taken all of his father's savings from the tin cash box that was always kept under lock and key in the oak corner cupboard of Paradise Farm.

Danny covered his eyes with his hands and ran his fingers through his blond hair. What had he done? He'd broken his mother's heart, and stolen from his father. He'd never be forgiven. He'd either have to make it big in America and come back the prodigal son or never show his face again. But most of all he thought of Peggy, the lass he'd thought he loved, up until a few months ago. But what a blow she'd struck him, when she said she was having his bairn. A baby, with him only twenty-two, and with so much to do yet that he didn't want to be tied down, with a father-in-law nagging at him and a bairn around his feet. There was no way he was going to wed Peggy; no matter how sweet her kisses and how soft her whispers, he knew she'd change as soon as they were wed. He'd seen it so many times: young lasses changing to old women nearly overnight as, with each year, a new baby came along, and with it more work and worry. His mate Bill was a prime example, with his missus nagging him and a baby crawling around his feet.

Nah! He was doing the right thing. Danny sighed loudly; the sooner he got to the Liverpool docks and on board the *Albion*, the better. He'd find work, perhaps make his way across the big new country, even find a bit of land and buy it

— make something of himself. It would be better than scratching about on a smallholding up Garsdale or Dent, just about managing to put food in his family's mouth from day to day. He'd send his father his money back, and more besides. His mother would forgive him — after all she hung on his every word; and Peggy . . . Well, it might not be his bairn anyway, for that Coates lad was always making eyes at her. Though it probably was his, now he thought about it.

No, he was doing right, Danny thought. He sighed and scrunched up his coat behind his head to make a pillow. Time to get his head down. By evening he'd be in the port of Liverpool and he'd have to have his wits about him, if he wanted to survive. God only knew what lay ahead of him, but he knew all too well what he was leaving behind.

★   ★   ★

Ada Harper shook as she stood, holding the letter that she'd just found on her kitchen table, tears running down her cheeks and her nose running freely, without care. The newly lit fire crackled as the kindling sticks took light, causing sparks to fly onto the pegged rug and singeing a hole in her home-made craftwork, before she had chance to put up the fire-guard to stop them.

'What's up, Mother? What are you crying about? I could hear the sobs as I came downstairs.' Edmund Harper tucked his striped shirt into his brown corduroy breeches and pulled his braces over his shoulders. 'What the devil's up with you? And where's our lad? Has the lazy bugger not got up yet? Danny! Get your arse down these stairs,' he bellowed, making Ada sob even louder.

'It's no good shouting, Father, he's not there — he's gone. Here, read this. What have we done to deserve a lad like this?' Ada passed the brief note to her husband and slumped down into the Windsor chair that was Edmund's, at the head of the table.

'I'll bloody kill him. He's buggered off, without bye nor leave. No explanation. Going to America! I'll give him going to America — I'll kick his arse. And, worst of all, he says he's pinched all our savings, and then said sorry and that we've to forgive him. I'll give him bloody 'forgive him', if I catch up with the bugger.' Edmund screwed up the scribbled note and stormed into the next room, where the cupboard that he kept his savings in hung on the wall. He strode back into the kitchen with the empty cash box, throwing it onto the table. 'Aye, my brass has gone. He's taken every bloody penny, all our savings — everything. For God's sake, stop snivelling, woman. Think — am I in time to catch him? I need my brass back more than I need him.'

'Oh, Father, stop it. He's my lad, why's he gone? He must be in bother, else he wouldn't have done anything like this — you know he wouldn't. How can he just walk out and leave us, with a note saying he's sailing for America and we aren't to worry. How can I not worry? He's

6

my only child, my Danny, and I love him. I just want him home!' Ada sobbed.

'He's been skulking about for bloody weeks, him and that Bill Sunter, when I think about it. When we went into Hawes the other day, he struggled to hold a conversation with me and jiggered off somewhere, not saying where he was going. I should have known then that something was afoot.'

'Well, he's gone, and I'll never see him again. You shouldn't have been so hard on him, Father. He's our only one, my baby!' Ada cried and sunk her head onto her chest.

'Shh now, lass, he'll be back by night. He'll think twice about running away, and I bet he's back by suppertime. He's never gone further than down the line to Settle — that's probably where he's gone.' Edmund patted Ada on the back. Any other man would have held his wife in his arms, but not Edmund. He didn't believe in showing his feelings, for it was a sign of weakness. Even though his heart was aching, he wasn't going to show it. He knew his lad had gone, and he'd gone a lot further than the nearby town of Settle.

30 January 1887

Bernard Dinsdale cursed as he lost his step on his steep decline of Dent Fell. The snow was falling faster now, and in another hour or two it would be nightfall, and he wanted to be back in the safety of his home, Lamb Paddock, in the

7

small dale of Cowgill. His jacket flapped in the sharp north wind and the snowflakes stung his weathered face as he gained his footing. He checked the safety of the bundle he was carrying. It was held in place with a piece of string tied tightly around his waist, and his coat was buttoned up to his neck, making a warm, safe place for the newborn baby that was his granddaughter. The snow was settling now, making it more urgent that he made his way down the outrake into the neighbouring dale of Garsdale.

The first sight of smoke rising from the cottages that followed the winding river of the Clough gave Bernard heart and he strode out faster, in the knowledge that in another few minutes he'd be at the doorstep of Paradise Farm. There he'd hand over the small body that he was carrying and be away to his wife Dora and her new ward, and back to the heartbreak that the birth of two babies had caused.

He swung open the wooden gate that barred the way to the rutted road that followed the course of the river down to the market town of Sedbergh, and looked across at the Wesleyan chapel. It had been a long time since he'd attended services there. He'd lost his religion when his mother died, and the more life threw at him, the more he knew that there was no God — or, if there was, he was a bloody cruel one. He peered down into the warmth of his coat and watched the small fingers of his granddaughter curl up around the knitted shawl that his wife had placed around her. Poor Dora, she hadn't wanted to part with the bairn, but he couldn't afford to bring up two young 'uns. Besides, when he was old enough, the lad would earn his keep.

He walked in silence, his heart pounding and his breath short as he passed the cottages on either side of the road, which he knew to be called The Street. Lamps were now being lit, and he could see the occupants of each cottage getting ready for nightfall. Finally he crossed the bridge that spanned the river and made his way up the path to Paradise Farm, knocking loudly on the weathered oak door inside the white-washed porch. He listened. He could hear chairs scraping as they were pushed back on the flagged floor of the kitchen, and the sound of voices, surprised that someone was visiting at this time of day and in bad weather.

'Now then, Bernard, what brings you knocking on our door at this time of day and in such weather?' Edmund Harper opened the door and frowned slightly at the visitor he knew to be Bernard Dinsdale.

'It's your lad, Danny; and it's a bloody good job he didn't open the door, else I'd have knocked his block off. Just let me in, Edmund. I need the warmth, and what I'm going to tell you isn't good news.' Bernard couldn't help how he felt; the bloody Harper lad had never been away from his lass, Peggy, and now he knew the consequences.

'Well, if it's our Danny you want, he's not with us any more. He's sailed for America, leaving us penniless and worried to death for his safety. We've not seen him since the end of November.

Our Ada here is heartbroken. What's he been up to, to make you come over in such a mood in this weather?' Edmund rubbed his head as Bernard pushed past him into the warmth and light of the Paradise Farm's small kitchen. The more he heard about his lad, the more he was wondering where he had gone wrong as a parent.

'Now then, Ada, you'd better sit down, pet. I've some news for you, and it's not pleasant.' Bernard's face looked troubled as he watched the stout form of Ada Harper drop into a chair, and Edmund Harper stand sternly behind her. He fumbled with the string around his waist, swearing as the cold made his attempts at untying the knot clumsy. He eventually managed to untie his coat without dropping the precious contents.

Ada gasped as the small form of a pink sleeping baby came out from under the coat, its eyes crinkled and its black hair still damp with afterbirth, completely unaware of the tragedy that she and her brother had caused.

Bernard Dinsdale stifled a sob and wiped a tear away from his forget-me-not-blue eyes. 'Our lass, Peggy, died in childbirth this afternoon, giving birth to twins. This is the lass; Dora's looking after the lad. Before she died, she told us that they are your bloody lad's. Perhaps that's why he's buggered off. At least I can't get hold of the bastard, else I'll be honest, Edmund: I'd kill the bugger! Not only has he not stood by his responsibilities, but he's killed our lass. My Dora's broken-hearted, as am I. I loved my Peggy, she was the apple of my eye.' Although he

10

was over six feet tall and solidly built, Bernard crumpled into a shaking mess as he spoke of his loss, and watched as Ada took the small body of his granddaughter.

Ada held the baby tightly and looked at her, searching out signs that would show her that the baby was her son's, before taking the shawl from around her and wrapping her up in a blanket. 'The poor mite is half-frozen. Aye, Bernard, I'm so sorry for you and Dora. What can we say, for we knew nothing of this. I wondered why our lad had to get away so quick. He not only broke your Peggy's heart, but he's broken mine, by going without bye nor leave. I knew there was something wrong.' Ada held the baby close and automatically rocked her back and forth, her mothering instincts returning as she looked at the small bundle in her arms.

'You can't blame our lad, for he's not here to defend himself. I'm sorry for your loss, Bernard, but them babies might not be his. Your lass could have gone with anybody.' Edmund Harper was thinking on his feet. The last thing he wanted was another bairn to bring up. They'd only had Danny, but that had been enough family for him.

'Father, think on what you are saying. Look at Bernard — he wouldn't come to our door with all this worry if it weren't true. You and I know that our Danny had been acting strange these last few months. Then, all of a sudden, he had to be up and gone.' Ada knew that what Bernard had said was true; the baby in her arms was Danny's, she just knew it was.

'Aye, well, he's made a good mess for us all.

I've no daughter, and my Dora's heartbroken, holding a baby that's no bigger than my fist, and then there's this 'un here.' Bernard nodded at the baby in Ada's arms. 'We can't cope with two of 'em, so I've brought her for you to fetch up, hoping that you'll share the burden that our two have made.' He put his head in his hands and looked down at the oak table with the white ring marks on it, where hot cups and plates had been placed, tracing them with his finger as his mind wandered back home.

'Course we'll share the burden. Not that it'll be a burden. It'll be grand to have a new life in the house. I don't know if I can do sleepless nights like, but we'll manage. It's the least we can do — it's both our children's faults, so it's only fair.' Ada smiled as the baby wriggled and clasped her finger with its small, perfectly formed fingers. 'Good job we've got a good milk cow. At least she won't go hungry.'

'Don't you bloody come to me, woman, when you are dead on your feet. You're forgetting how old you are. You're its grandmother, and it's a lass. She'll not even be any good around the farm in our old age. No son to look after us, and now a squawking baby.' Edmund Harper shook his head as he stoked the fire and looked out of the window at the snow, which was falling faster now. 'Do you want to stop the night, Bernard? You might have brought bad news to my door, but I wouldn't send a dog out into this weather. It will be wild up on that fell top.'

'No, I'll be away back to Dora. She'll not want to be left tonight, with Peggy dead in her bed and a newborn baby on her hands. Besides, like you, our cow will need milking; it too has a hungry mouth to feed now.' Bernard buttoned and tied his coat close to him. 'I'm sorry I brought bad news to your door. Your off-spring never grow into what you want them to. I had high hopes for our Peggy to be a teacher, and now she's gone.'

'I'm sorry, Bernard. We'll give this little 'un a good home, and she'll want for nowt. If our lad gets in touch with us, I'll tell him the outcome of his wanton ways. Give our condolences to Dora. We are so sorry to bring all these troubles to your home.' Ada looked at the heartbroken man as he bowed his head and reached for the latch on the door. 'Aye, well, you and Dora will fetch the boy up as your own, and hopefully nobody will remember any different in years to come.'

Bernard opened the door and the cold northern wind and snowflakes blew around him.

'Stop the night, man. You want nowt with walking back into Dent tonight.' Edmund might have been angry with the situation he'd been put in, but he worried for Bernard's safety.

'Nay, I'm off. It'll not take me long and I'll not get lost. I've wandered these fells both man and boy. I know them like the back of my hand.' Bernard shoved his hands in his pockets, nodded his head and stepped out down the lane, back the way he had come. 'Take care of yourselves and, if you hear from your lad, let me know.'

Edmund watched Bernard for as long as he could, but the blizzard began to wipe out any vision of him, and his footsteps, quickly and silently. He shook his head as he turned back into the warm kitchen. It was quickly being turned into a makeshift nursery, with milk warming in a pan on the fire, and a drawer being lined with blankets for the daughter that had been thrust upon them. 'Nay, Ada, I thought we were too old for this.'

'You're never too old for a baby in the family. Besides, she's our Danny's — our blood. Now what should we call her? Amy? Betsy? Lily? I know. Polly, we'll call her Polly, Polly of Paradise Farm, that sounds just right. Welcome to Paradise, Polly. I swear we will always be there to love you, and my lad will be made to do right by you, if we ever catch him.' Ada kissed her new ward gently on the cheek. 'Look at her, Edmund. She smiled, she knows she's home.'

Edmund grunted. 'It'll be wind, you daft old fool. She knows nowt yet.'

★ ★ ★

Dora Dinsdale sat around the dying embers of her front-room fire. It was dark outside. She couldn't even see to the other side of the dale, and the snow hadn't stopped falling since Bernard had left the house. Where was he? He should have been back hours ago. Perhaps he had stopped over in Garsdale. The day had thrown enough at her, without having Bernard missing. Above her, in the middle bedroom, lay the body of her daughter; and next to Peggy, in the old cot that had once been hers, lay her son, unaware of the drama of the day and content,

14

with his belly full of Jersey cow's milk.

Dora stopped a tear from falling. Where was Bernard? She pulled her shawl around her and put the guard around the fire, sleep calling her now to bed. She looked into her daughter's room and gazed at the corpse of Peggy, her skin pale and opaque in the candlelight, her black hair cascading over her shoulders. She then went to the cot and picked up her grandson. 'Come on, little man. You can't help what's happened. Come and share my bed until your grandfather arrives back.' Holding him close to her, she prayed for Bernard's safe return. 'Please God, let him be safe.' She then blew the candle out, before cradling the newborn baby close to her under the warmth of the bedclothes, sobbing herself to sleep.

★ ★ ★

High upon the very top of Dent Fell Bernard Dinsdale clung to the ridge of limestone escarpment that dotted the skyline. The snow was whipping around him as he took every step gingerly and with care. He made his way on, towards what he knew to be the drystone wall that led down into the valley. Following the wall, he made his way back down into Cowgill.

Exhausted and frozen, he made out the dark shape of the high barn in his top pasture. He'd take shelter there, and go the rest of the way in the morning. The smell of hay and tethered cattle hit his senses as he opened the barn door. The warmth from the cattle was welcoming. He closed the door quickly behind him and felt his way along the barn wall, to where he knew the hayloft to be. There he collapsed in a heap, pulling the dry, warm hay over him for warmth and cover. Down below he could hear the cows chewing on their cud, and the barn's resident cat made itself known to him, and, curled up next to him. He was home and alive. In the morning he would have to face the heartache of another day without his daughter, and grieve with Dora and the new baby. But for now he had to sleep. He'd deal with tomorrow's sorrows with the break of day.

2

Polly strode out across the wild moorland that led to the valley of Mallerstang. She'd been sent to look at her father's pregnant ewes, but the spring day had got the better of her and, instead of returning home, she decided to walk to the waterfall that gushed and fell at the head of the moody valley of Mallerstang. She knew it would be in full spate after the recent wet weather, and she couldn't wait to see the force of the gushing white water falling over the grey of the hard granite rock into the pool below.

Every footstep she took urged her on, with the smell of the earthy moorland peat filling her nostrils and a pleasant spring wind blowing her long dark hair. She stopped for a moment and breathed in the fresh moorland air and looked around her. How she loved to be up on the fell on her own, with not a soul in sight, and just the sound of the wind or the cry of a curlew or lapwing to break the silence. This was Polly's idea of heaven. Indeed, if she was to die tomorrow, she'd want her grave to be on top of Wild Boar Fell, which was looming in the distance, dark and foreboding, with many streams and rivulets running down its sheer, dark flanks. Polly caught her breath and pushed on with her walk; she'd have to reach the

17

waterfall soon, if she was to return home in daylight.

Mallerstang was a narrow dale dotted with white-washed farmhouses and walled pastures, running up to the sheer face of Wild Boar Fell and Mallerstang Edge. It was rich with legend, with stories of Dick Turpin jumping the deep gorge of Hell Gill on his trusty steed, Black Bess; and of the ghosts that walked Lady Anne's Way, the ancient pathway that ran along the rugged fell top of Mallerstang Edge. Polly had heard them all, on the knee of her father, as they sat around the fire in the kitchen of Paradise Farm. She savoured every minute of the tales, as her father puffed on his pipe and her mother's knitting needles clicked and her eyes got heavier as the night grew longer. Eventually she had to admit that she needed her sleep, before kissing her mother and father and then climbing the creaking stairs to her warm bed.

She was nearly there now. The railway that followed the curve of the dale was in sight and soon she'd see the waterfall. She started running as she came off the rough fell land onto the road that led to the market town of Kirkby Stephen, stopping short of the road bridge and looking to her left, at the marvel of the waterfall. As she sat on a damp bank's grassy mound, the water crashed and thundered down upon the wet, black, mossy rocks, and white spray covered the rushes at the edge of the river. Along its banks, marsh marigold was just starting to flower, along with some early forget-me-nots, and Polly thought how beautiful the blue and yellow of the

18

flowers looked together.

There, she'd got to her waterfall, she'd done what she'd wanted. Now to get home. It was a good three miles over rough moorland, and the sun was already beginning to sink. She stood up and turned quickly, only to see a young, dark-haired man sitting on his horse, watching her. How long had he been there, and what was he waiting for? Polly was unnerved. Why hadn't he made himself known? She picked up her skirts, put her head down and didn't dare acknowledge the dark gent as she walked past him.

'Good afternoon. I'm sorry, did I startle you? I didn't mean to. It's just that it isn't every day you come across a young woman sat next to a waterfall at the head of Mallerstang.' Tobias Middleton smiled down at the young woman, who was obviously startled by his presence. 'And such a beauty, too,' Tobias added as he watched the young Polly blush.

Polly didn't dare look up at her admirer, knowing that he wasn't just a local farm lad, by the way he spoke to her and the quality of the horse he was riding.

'I'm sorry, how rude — I've forgotten my manners. Let me introduce myself to you.' Tobias walked his horse to Polly's side, as she walked quickly past him, in a bid to get out of his gaze. 'I'm Tobias. Tobias Middleton. I live at Grouse Hall, down in Garsdale. I've just been visiting my new tenant, across there in the farm they call Intake.' Tobias pointed to the dark farmhouse nestling under the fell end. 'And you are?' He kept his horse moving with Polly's quick pace, until she stopped in front of the stile that led her back onto the rough moorland.

Polly was so close that she could smell the horse and the saddle leather, and hear the heavy snorting of the dapple-grey horse, which was her own height at its withers. She kept her head lowered as she listened to Tobias talking, knowing that she was vulnerable and on her own on the wild moorland, with, no one else in sight. Her mother had always warned her to be careful with men and Polly was heeding her words well, although this young man sounded the perfect gent so far. She climbed the stile and then, with the safety of the stile between her and Tobias, looked up at him.

'I'm Polly Harper, from Paradise.' She looked up at the dark-haired rider. He was smiling down at her, and his dark eyes shone with interest as she stood her ground behind the stile.

'I should have known that, aptly, you come from Paradise, Miss Harper. I never expected to meet an angel on top of Mallerstang Fell, but it seems I have.' Tobias grinned. He knew she meant Paradise Farm, although he couldn't help but tease.

'I meant Paradise Farm and, if you don't mind, I'll be on my way. My parents are expecting me back home.' Polly realized that Tobias was playing with her and decided that, no matter how handsome he was, she was best to make her way home.

'Indeed, it will soon be dark, and you don't want to be wandering up here by yourself. Can I offer you a ride home, up here on Bess, for she'll quite easily hold two?' Tobias held his hand out to Polly.

'No, thank you, I'll make my own way home. It doesn't take me long through the fields.' Polly turned, picking up her skirts, and started walking back across the tufted red-and-brown moorland grasses on her way home, not looking back at Tobias, who was watching her.

'Goodbye, Polly of Paradise. Perhaps I'll see you again soon?' Tobias shouted at the dark-haired beauty who had taken his eye, smiling as she struggled to walk between the tufted, boggy grasses. She belonged on the moorland, with her long, dark hair and her eyes of blue — like the pool of the waterfall that she had been looking into. His mother had introduced him to some beautiful women, but never one that had taken his eye like this young farm girl. He kicked the sides of his horse and cantered down the road, watching the disappearing form of Polly running down the fell side.

Polly ran as if her life depended on it, stumbling and reeling between grassy tussocks and peaty bog pools, until she knew she was safe and a good distance from Tobias. He sounded and looked the perfect gentleman, and she mused gently over his flirting with her, as she walked quickly down the greener fields of the valley floor. He did have devilishly good looks, with his collar-length jet-black hair and high cheek-bones, and he was obviously a man of wealth, if he owned a farmstead at the top of Mallerstang, as well as his own. Nevertheless, she realized just how foolish she'd been, wandering so far from home on her own; he could easily have raped her, and left her for dead on the bleak moorland, without anyone knowing where she was. Panting with haste, she reached the farmyard gate and untied the twine that held it closed.

'Where have you been trailing? Your mother's been worried to death, thinking something's happened to you.' Edmund Harper stood in the doorway of his barn, puffing on his pipe, waiting for Polly to return from looking at his sheep. 'I walked up around the top pasture — not a sign of you — so I want to know where you've been? It's coming in dusk; another half-hour and it'll be dark.'

As if to verify his words, a blackbird trilled its evening song and hurried into a safe nesting place in the nearby white-budded blackthorn bush for nightfall.

'Sorry, Father. It was such a grand day, I decided to walk over into Mallerstang. It's been the first decent day's weather we've had for weeks.' Polly's cheeks were flushed. She knew both her mother and father would have been wondering where she was, and she felt nervous as she explained her walk to her father, who seemed to be in a mood.

'Aye, well, while you've been trailing, that old ewe with the spotted face began to lamb, and she's lost both lambs. I found them dead behind the pasture wall. You can't have looked after them that well.' Edmund looked hard at the lass he'd grown to love like his own daughter. She was nearly a woman now — too old to be told the truth, and for her to know that she was their granddaughter, and not their daughter.

'I couldn't see her, Father. I know which one you mean. She's always stubborn and stamps her feet when you move her anywhere. I thought you must have moved her into another field.' Polly was distraught, for she must have missed the stubborn animal.

'Aye, well, she was just behind the wall, in the corner away from all the rest. You should have known they always find a quiet spot to lamb in. I thought I'd told you that?'

'You did. Sorry, Father.' Polly could feel tears welling up, at the thought of two dead lambs because of her wandering feet.

'Aye, well, I was young once and all. I couldn't resist a spring day, either. She's getting a bit long in the tooth now, anyway. I doubt she'd have had milk for twins. Come on, let's away in to your mother. She was going frantic wondering where you were.' Edmund knew the lass hadn't wilfully neglected her duties; she knew his flock as well as he did and was a good hand with the sheep.

'You two will be the death of me. You never tell me where you are going or how long you'll be. I swear there's gypsy blood in the pair of you!' Ada folded her arms and stared at both Edmund and Polly. 'Just look at the state of your skirt, our Polly. It's mucked up and drenched around the hem. When are you going to grow into the lady that I so wanted?'

Polly put her head down. She knew she was a disappointment to her mother, not bothering with the finery expected of a young woman, but she couldn't stand the simpering ways of some of her so-called friends. The way they acted and talked about the latest fashions, and who was courting whom, didn't interest her in the least.

'It's all your fault, Edmund Harper. You've brought her up like a lad. She's never been away from your side since the day she was born.' Ada slammed down the dinner plates as she laid the table for the evening meal. She was angry with worry; if anything had happened to Polly, she wouldn't have known what to do with herself. There was already a gaping hole in her heart, from when Danny had walked out of her life, never to be heard of again. She wasn't about to lose his daughter, Polly.

'It's best she's independent, lass. We aren't the youngest couple in t' dale. If owt happens to either of us, she can look after herself. Besides, you're as bad, woman — you've taught her how to run a house. She'll be right when we've both gone.' Edmund pulled up his chair to the table and took off his cap, throwing it onto the floor next to his feet.

'I don't know why you both think you are going to die. You're not that old. Besides, I might find a love of my own — someone who'll love and look after me — then I'll not be yours to worry about.' Polly's thoughts flitted to Tobias Middleton's smile and his teasing words.

'You'll not find a man that wants you, looking like a wild woman and with a streak of bog peat from one lug to the other,' laughed Ada. The lass obviously didn't know that her face was as black as the chimney-back.

'Oh, I don't know. Old Tim, the tinker that comes with his pots and pans every summer, might take her, Mother.' Edmund leaned back in his chair and grinned, as Polly rushed to the mirror next to the back door.

She was horrified. Had her face been that dirty when she'd been talking to Tobias? He must have thought her a common peasant.

'You could have told me earlier that my face was filthy,' shouted Polly as she scrubbed the dirt off it with a wetted end of her mother's tea-towel.

'We did!' both Edmund and Ada said together.

'And now my tea-towel is a black 'un.' Ada shook her head. 'Come and sit and have your supper, and then you can wash up for me. I'm jiggered tonight. While you've been out wandering I turned both feather beds over and gave them a good shake. Your father and me had started to roll into the middle of ours, with not much padding under us, so they needed a turn.'

'You should have waited for me, Mother. I'd have helped you shake them.'

'Nay, you are right. At least they are fresh, with clean sheets and blankets on them tonight.' Ada spooned the mashed potato onto the three plates, and then added slices of newly fried bacon. 'I've only made an easy supper tonight, so don't fret.'

'I'll have a day about the house tomorrow, Mother. Do you want me to clean the brasses or bake a pasty?'

Polly felt guilty, for her mother looked pale.

25

She shouldn't have made her worry.

'There was me, thinking you'd happen like a trip into Hawes tomorrow. It's market day, and I could do with seeing if anyone's got a pet lamb to suckle onto the ewe you missed lambing.' Edmund mashed his potatoes with the back of his fork, before pouring milk over them, a habit Polly could not quite get used to. He didn't dare look up at Ada or Polly, because he knew it was an offer that Polly would not want to refuse.

She said nothing. She swallowed her first mouthful of supper and waited for her mother to comment.

'Well, I suppose that's thrown pasty-making out of the window, because a trip into Hawes with your father wins every time. Am I invited on this trip, or is it just the 'men' of the household?' Ada pushed her plate to one side, with her supper hardly eaten.

'Aye, if tha wants to come, you can join us. I think we might just let you.' Edmund grinned at his wife. 'What do you say, Polly? Do you think she'll be any good at picking us a lamb?'

Polly smiled. There was often a bit of banter around the supper table, so she knew how far to go when she answered. 'Aye, go on, then we can. buy two, in case the one my mother buys dies.'

'I'll give you bloody 'die'. I was looking after and rearing sheep before you were even born!' Ada flicked the tea-towel around Polly's ear softly. 'Now, let's get some water warming on that fire and give you a bath. I'm not taking you into Hawes looking like that mucky family from further down t' dale. I've my pride, and so

26

should you have, Miss Harper. Father, when you've finished your supper, get the tin bath out from the outhouse and make yourself scarce for half an hour. Our Polly's getting too old for you to wander around or sit in the kitchen while she baths in front of the fire.'

'Do I have to, Mother? I'm not that mucky.' Polly hated the exposure of being naked in the kitchen, for she was always aware that anyone could walk in through the kitchen door and see her with nothing on. Lately she had been more aware of her feminine figure and the changes that she'd undergone in previous years, and felt awkward about her new body.

'Yes, you do — you could grow potatoes in the muck around your neck. I want you to help with the shopping, so I'm not taking a mucky tomboy around with me. I need some supplies from Sam Allen's, and I'm not having his hoity mother looking at us like we are a piece of dirt on her shoe.'

'Now, Mother, she's no better than the rest of us. She's just forgotten where she's come from. I remember when they hadn't a ha'penny to rub together. It was the building of the railway that made them. Old Elijah saw a good opportunity in supplying the navvies, and went for it, and you can't knock him for that.' Edmund belched loudly and rose from the table. 'I'll get this bath then. What's up with your supper, Mother? Tha's not eaten anything.' He nodded at the still-full plate, as Polly cleared the table.

'I don't feel like eating, that's all. Bacon and tatties isn't one of my favourites, and this year

27

our home-cured bacon's a bit fatty for me.' Ada reached out for the empty kettle and pan and put them under the cold-water tap that Polly was just starting to run, before washing up.

'As long as that's all. Tha looks a bit white to me. Go and put your feet up. Polly will bath herself. She's not a baby now, you know — she's sixteen, a grown woman. And you're right. The old pig last year was fed too well, so we'll have to keep her leaner for less-fatty bacon this year.' Edmund looked at his wife. She looked tired, and he knew how her heart hurt: sixteen years of not knowing if your son was alive or dead was a hard burden to carry. It had been Polly's disappearance that had made her fretful, but the lass were growing up. There'd be a man in her life before long — there was bound to be, with her good looks. And then she'd want a family of her own. Ada would have to accept it and make the best of it, for she must realize the day was coming. He went into the outhouse and came back with the galvanized tin bath, putting it down in front of the fire. 'I'll go and have a camp with Len down in The Street, see what gossip he has.'

'Don't you be coming home blathered. He always tempts you with his drop of whisky, does that one.' Ada bustled past him with a towel in her hand.

'Nay, I'll not be doing that. I'll just see what he knows and then wander back. See you in a bit, ladies.' Edmund dipped his head before going through the low doorstead.

'It'll be first time ever he comes back from

28

Len's walking straight, if he does.' Ada tipped the boiling water from the kettle into the tin bath. 'Now come on, lady, put some cold water in here and get into your bath, and I'll have forty winks in the parlour. I don't know why you've decided to come over all shy. There's nowt there I haven't seen before.'

Polly sighed. A bath on her own. Finally they'd realized how old she was. She put the washed dishes away into the Welsh dresser that stood against the main wall of the kitchen, and then poured the near-boiling pan of water into the bath, followed by a pan of cold water from the tap. She ran her hand in the steaming water of the bath: it was just right. On the side of the chair next to the fireplace Ada had placed the clean towel and a bar of carbolic soap, and over the wooden airing rack suspended from the ceiling hung a clean flannelette nightdress, in readiness for a cleaner Polly.

She slipped out of her clothes and shivered as she stood naked in the farmhouse's kitchen and tested the water with her toe, before lowering her young body into the warmth. The water's depth only reached halfway up her thigh, but it was warm and refreshing and, to be honest, she had needed a bath. She lay back and enjoyed the warmth of the water and the heat from the open fire, gently washing herself with the towel flannel and soap. Her thoughts wandered back to Tobias. She'd never been interested in a man before, but his dramatic good looks had got her feeling something she'd never experienced before. She closed her eyes and pictured his smile.

'Are you all right in there? You've gone quiet,' Ada yelled through from the parlour.

'Yes, Mam, just scrubbing myself clean,' Polly shouted back.

Just trying to forget Tobias Middleton, she thought to herself. But I don't know if I really want to, her heart replied.

3

The centre of Hawes was busy with market stalls, livestock and traders. Tuesday was the main market day, when all the Dales folk from Wensleydale and the surrounding districts came and got their shopping or bought and sold livestock. Outside the Crown Hotel and up to Townhead the cobbled pavements were filled with pens of sheep, tethered cows and wooden crates of clucking hens or geese. Further down the street, market traders and farmers' wives called out, selling fruit and vegetables, butter and cream, and home-baking ingredients.

'By heck, it's busy today, Father.' Ada held onto the side of the cart next to Edmund and looked down the street at the throng of people. 'Morning, Mrs Bentham. Morning, Agnes!' Ada shouted greetings at friends and neighbours, while Edmund acknowledged his friends with a tip of the head, or a gesture from his finger just tipping his cap. 'We'll go down to the butcher's first, then I need some cotton. And then, our Polly, you can come and help me carry what I want from Sam Allen's.' She turned round to give Polly, in the back of the donkey cart, her orders.

'But, Mum . . . I wanted to go with my father,' Polly whined.

'You're right. Our Pol, go with your mother. I've a bit of business to do, before I look for a

31

lamb.' Edmund skilfully drove his horse into a vacant space, to be tethered just outside the Crown Hotel. 'I'll meet you both here, outside the Crown, in thirty to forty minutes.'

'Would this business have anything to do with lifting your right arm, by any chance?' asked Ada to Edmund, as she climbed down from the cart.

'It's nowt to do with you, woman. Anyway, no doubt you'll be led astray by some of your old gossips. At least I find my news out in one spot, instead of chattering the length of Hawes.' Edmund tied the horse up securely and grinned at both Ada and Polly as they brushed their skirts down, before setting about their business. He knew forty minutes would be more like an hour and a half, by the time Ada had been in and out of the shops and had caught up with all the gossip. He watched as both of them strutted off down the busy street, not going any further than five yards before sharing some juicy morsel of news.

'She's growing up, is your lass, Edmund.' Len Brunskill slapped his lifelong friend across his back as he joined Edmund, and they both mounted the steps into the Crown.

'Aye, she is. I can't believe she's sixteen. It doesn't seem five minutes since Bernard Dinsdale brought her under his coat in a snowstorm. I didn't think we'd see her grow up, but both Ada and me are keeping fairly well. Aches and pains, but nothing to really complain about.' Edmund stepped up to the bar and winked at the serving lass. 'Pint, is it, Len?'

'Aye, go on then, you've twisted my arm.' Len

waited until both had been served, and then sat down in a quiet corner before he told his best mate his news. 'Well, you're doing better than Bernard Dinsdale, Edmund. I heard tell that he died, last week in his sleep, so Polly's brother has no father. Now, what Dora and the lad will do, I don't know? He's a bit young for taking on Lamb Paddock, where they live, and it will barely make them a living. It's not the biggest farm, up Cowgill.'

'Aye, that's bad news that you tell me, Len. I've never seen him since the night he brought Polly. I suppose he didn't want anything to do with us bringing all that grief to his door. But he wasn't a bad man. He's brought the lad up like his own, as we have Polly, and neither child knows any different than that we are their parents. It's for the best.' Edmund took a long sup from his pint glass and slammed it down. He was silently cursing Danny. He'd still not forgiven him for the grief he'd caused, on his disappearance.

'Have you still no word from your lad?' Len felt for his old schoolmate, for he was a good man and had stood by his commitments.

'Not a bloody word, from that day to this. We don't even know if he's alive. It's Ada I feel for. Some days you can tell she grieves for him. It would even be better if we knew he was dead — at least we could put closure on him. But we know nowt.'

'Aye, Edmund, I'm sorry. These bloody children, you bring 'em up best you can, but you still don't know what they're going to turn out like. You'll have heard that Dick Cooper's lad is trying to throw Dick out of his own farm, because he wants it for himself?'

'Never heard a thing, though it wouldn't surprise me. They think everything you've got is theirs, and bugger how long it's taken you to earn it.' Edmund shook his head and drank another sup.

'Here, drink up. I'll get next ones in, and I'll tell you all about it. Your women will be ages yet. Besides, there's a new stallholder down the far end, and he's selling lace and cotton and all the rubbish that women like.' Len winked as Edmund drained his glass dry and then wiped his lips on his sleeve.

'Aye, go on, we'll just have another. Old Clover knows her way home and, besides, Polly can handle her, if I sit in the back of the cart.'

* * *

'Just look at this, Polly, isn't that the bonniest piece of lace you've ever seen? So delicate.' Ada ran the intricate piece of lace between her fingers and showed it to Polly, who wasn't in the least bit interested.

'It's Nottingham lace, madam, made especially for me, in the homes of a group of ladies that excel in their skills. It would look beautiful around the edge of a handkerchief, or perhaps on a collar on a spectacular dress, for your beautiful young daughter.' The stallholder smiled a sickly grin at Polly and, as she looked at him, she couldn't help but be reminded of a fox

34

showing its teeth before killing its prey.

'How much is it?' Ada fumbled for her purse from underneath the sausage and rolled brisket that she'd just bought at the butcher's.

'To you, madam, one shilling. Would madam like any ribbons, thread, pins?' The Fox, as Polly had now called him, waved his hands over his stall of goods, lingering over the gaily tartan ribbon that Ada was eyeing next.

'A yard of that tartan ribbon and all, and then that's it.'

'One shilling and sixpence, please, madam.' The Fox measured out the tartan ribbon along a wooden rule, snipping it off with his shears — just like the snip of his teeth — as he pocketed the coins from Ada.

'Well, he was a pleasant man. I think you took his eye, our Polly,' exclaimed Ada as they made their way across from his stall to the shop doorway of Sam Allen's.

'I didn't like him, Mother, he reminded me of a fox.'

'You are a funny lass. How can he look like a fox? Sometimes, Polly, your imagination runs away with you.' The doorbell jingled as they entered Sam Allen's grocery shop.

'Morning, Mrs Harper. Morning, Polly.' Sam Allen smiled at two of his regular customers as he stood waiting for their order over his spotlessly polished counter.

'Morning, Sam, can you put this order together, please? It isn't a big one; just one or two things we've run out of.' Ada passed Sam her shopping order across the counter, and he

35

went about the business of putting the order together.

Polly stood next to her mother and waited. She loved the smell of Sam Allen's. It was a mixture that fused with her senses: the smell of freshly ground coffee, a real luxury that she had never tried; freshly baked bread; and, in the far corner, paraffin, which reminded her of last spring's chicks, which she had reared around a paraffin heater for warmth.

'Everything all right, up at Paradise? Have you started lambing yet? At least the weather's decent.' Sam was making conversation as he worked his way through the list.

'Aye, we've started lambing — that's why we're here. Edmund wants to see if anybody has a spare pet lamb. One old ewe lost hers yesterday. He wants to mother one onto her.' Ada watched as Sam weighed six pounds of flour out of the huge flour bins and folded it up into a crisp, new brown-paper bag.

'He'll get one. I heard some bleating coming from the pens this morning, and Mrs Blades from over Buttertubs was in earlier, telling me there's a lot of triplets being born this year. I suppose, if they are an old ewe, they can't manage to feed three.' Sam checked the list against what was in front of him. 'Is that all then, Mrs Harper?'

'Aye, that's grand. What do I owe you?'

Sam passed her the list with the prices next to each item, and the total at the bottom.

'Price of sugar's gone up, Sam. I'm sure it wasn't that last month.' Ada counted her money out and handed it over to a blushing Sam.

'Aye, well, I can't control price of sugar. It's something we don't grow in this country. Everything keeps going up, I'm afraid.' Sam placed his money in the till and passed some of the groceries to Polly and the rest to Ada. 'Here, I'll get you the door, seeing as your hands are full.' He rushed to open the door, allowing Ada and Polly right of way out of the shop. Just as they left, Tobias Middleton met them in the doorway.

'Tobias, your mother's in the back, with my father. She'll be glad to see you.' Sam stopped Tobias in his tracks, to allow Ada and Polly out of the shop.

Polly's heart missed a beat. It was him again, and there she was, with her arms filled with shopping.

'Good morning, Polly from Paradise. I see your hands are full. May I help you?' Tobias smiled at the blushing young woman, and then realized that her mother did not look at all happy with his offer.

'We are fine, thank you, Mr Middleton. We can manage quite well on our own. Come on, Polly, follow me.' Ada stepped out with determination, without looking round at Polly, expecting her to follow.

Polly looked up at Tobias and gave him a slight smile. He was so handsome.

'Polly — now!' Ada stopped in her tracks and waited for Polly to follow her, watching as Tobias Middleton removed his hat to her. Polly's comments about the stallholder came back to haunt Ada. Now that was a fox, and Polly was the chicken!

'How does he know you? You want nowt flashing your eyes at the lad. He doesn't come from much. He might own Grouse Hall and a few more farms, but his father was a wrong 'un, and he's like him because he has his looks. As for his mother — well, she married Sam Allen just to get her hands on his shop. She wasn't even married when she had Tobias.'

'I met him on my walk over to Mallerstang. We just exchanged pleasantries. So, Mother, you do know him?' Polly nearly had to run to keep up with Ada as she stepped out across the street.

'Aye, me and your father know him. He was treated no better than a dog when he was a lad, until his mother claimed him, after the death of his father. And now he's worth a bit of money and thinks himself something, with his fancy waistcoats and posh ways. You listen to my words, Polly Harper: keep away, for he'll only bring heartache, and you can do better than that for a man.'

Ada and Polly reached the horse and cart and deposited the groceries in the back.

'I see your father isn't here. He'll still be inside with his old cronies.' Ada nodded at the Crown. 'Damn, I've forgotten the cotton I wanted! Polly, run back to that stall and get me a bobbin of white cotton, while I stir your father. I thought we'd come for a pet lamb, not a drinking session.' Ada passed Polly some coins and pulled her skirts up, as she climbed the steps into the Crown. 'Mind you don't talk to anybody, especially that Tobias.'

Polly looked at the money in her hand. She'd not go back to the stall, as she didn't like the man that had served them. She'd go to the draper's next door to Sam Allen's. That way she could dally a little outside the shop window, just in case Tobias was there. What did her mother know? Tobias might not be like his father; and if he was, he couldn't have been all bad! She rushed across the street and entered the draper's, quickly asking for what she wanted, then glanced across at the horse and cart to make sure her parents weren't waiting for her. All clear! Polly gazed into the full windows of Sam Allen's, trying to peer between the advertising posters and jars of sweets in the window, but there was no sign of Tobias in the shop, just of women going about their daily shop. She sighed and hung her head, before crossing the street back to the horse and cart just in time to catch her mother and father coming out of the Crown.

'Give over, woman, I've only had a couple. To hear you talk, you'd think I'd drunk the beck dry.' Edmund was standing his ground while Ada chastised him for drinking more than he should.

'That Len Brunskill always was a bad influence on you. I can never forgive him for making you late on our wedding day.' Ada never forgot anything.

'That was forty years ago, woman, and it wasn't his fault. My horse threw a shoe and went lame — nowt to do with Len! Anyway, are you two done? Let's be away and buy this pet lamb.'

Edmund strode out up the street, with Polly and Ada following him, without waiting for Ada to answer back.

'When your father gets his awkward head on, there's no making sense of him,' grumbled Ada to Polly, as they leaned over the first pen of sheep and lambs and then moved on to the next one, not seeing anything that took their fancy.

The next pen was full of bleating Swaledale lambs, some only a day old and still unsteady on their legs. The lambs all rushed to the pen edge, bleating and crying for their mother, or at least a bottle of warm milk to fill their empty stomachs. Polly bent down and held each one's head in her hands. Their pitiful cries nearly made her want to cry. She couldn't imagine life without her mother. The lambs tried to suck her outstretched fingers as she caressed their bony heads and looked into their pale-blue eyes.

'Well, which one is it to be? Don't pick a tup; we want a gimmer, then at least we can have lambs out of her.' Edmund Harper stood back and watched his lass pick up each lamb and inspect it.

'Mind they don't pee on you, our Polly. That dress is clean, and I'm not washing it again for a while. Father, can't you pick one? It's a man's job, not a lass's.' Ada was aware of Josh Metcalfe and a few of his cronies watching Polly looking at the orphaned lambs that they were selling, and she didn't like the way they were grinning at her. They were Yorkshire Dales men, and a woman belonged in the kitchen, not out in the fields with the animals.

'Let her be, Mother. One day Paradise will be hers, and she's got to learn how to judge animals.' Edmund leaned on the railings and watched his daughter. She was more of a son than Danny had ever been. Danny had never shown any interest in the farm; he'd never stopped on the fell top and gazed around him in wonderment. He'd seen Polly do that many a time and knew just how she felt. There was nothing like a good spring breeze on your face, and the cry of nesting lapwings and skylarks as you gazed at the green shoots of spring erupting from the frozen earth. Aye, he was proud of her; and they could laugh at her, but she'd sort the best pet lamb out, of that he was certain.

'How about this 'un, Father?' Polly lifted a bleating lamb clean over the railing by its front two legs, then tucked it under her arm for her father to inspect. The thin body of the day-old lamb wriggled, trying to escape, but Polly held it fast.

'Aye, it looks all right. Now go and ask Josh Metcalfe how much he wants for it, and what he'll give you for luck?' Edmund watched Polly hesitate for a moment.

'For luck — what do you mean?' Polly struggled to hold the squirming animal as it tried to escape the tight grip it was under.

'Aye, Polly, I've told you before: folk will give you a price, and then he'll either knock something off there and then, or he'll give you a bit of something back when you pay for it. That's called 'luck money'. Bloody animal might die next day, if it frets. That's why you always give luck money.'

41

Polly stomped off with a determined look on her face, and Edmund watched Josh's face change as she spoke to him just like any man would, before coming back to him.

'It's a shilling, but he'll not give us any luck money, 'cause he says it's a strong lamb, so it won't need any. We've got to have her Father, she's the best one.' Polly rubbed her cheek against the lamb, which smelt of damp wool and lanolin.

'Here, I'll talk to him. He's got an old broken-tooth Herdwick sheep in this next pen; she's only fit for the knacker's yard, but looks like she's in lamb. I've always fancied Herdwicks, but they always want to go back to where they were born. They are devils for trailing, and can climb any wall in their way, but she's too old for doing that. I'll offer him something daft for the pair — he'll probably be glad to get rid of them.' Edmund walked over to the group of men. Ada and Polly watched as they joked and laughed, and a deal was reached, ending in Josh Metcalfe spitting into his hand and clenching it into Edmund's.

'What the heck your father's going to do with a Herdwick, I don't know. It'll be off back up the Lakes, where they come from, as soon as you can say 'Jack Robinson'. And that lamb you've got there will need a feed of bottled milk, before it's mothered on. More work!' Ada sighed, as Edmund came back, smiling.

'Well, we've got a deal. You've got your lamb, and I've got my Herdwick. Now let's see if we can keep them both.'

'Aye, and I've a lump-head of a husband, and a daughter who acts like a lad. And just how are we getting this menagerie back home?'

'Stop wittering, woman. Polly will hold onto the lamb, and I'll lift the old lass in the back of the cart and tie her to the boards. She'll not move so fast. After all, it's not far to home.'

'Father!' Polly's face was as straight as a poker. 'That's no way to talk about my mother. I think she may resent being called an 'old lass'.' Polly grinned.

'You silly bugger, you know what I meant.' Edmund flicked Polly with his cap and then, grinning, went to gather his sheep.

'You're as daft as your father. No wonder my hair's white,' grunted Ada. 'Oh! Polly, look what that lamb has done down your skirt. I just give up.'

Polly looked down at her newly washed skirt. The lamb had urinated down it.

'Sorry, Mam, she couldn't help it.'

'No, but you change as soon as you get home, and you must have a good wash.' Ada shook her head, as Polly loved the lamb even more.

★ ★ ★

The barn smelt of last year's hay and was warm and comforting to the senses, as Polly and her father dealt with their new additions to the farm.

'Now then, Pol, watch what I do.' Edmund got one of the dead twin lambs and cut his way through its skin, deftly skinning it and making the new pet lamb a jacket from the dead one's woolly coat. 'Look, I've left part of the legs in, so that we can feed your lamb's legs through them. Here, pass me her over.'

Polly passed the pet lamb over to her father. She'd nearly retched as she'd watched her father skinning the dead animal, but knew that without the overcoat made from the dead lamb's skin, the bereaved sheep would not accept the pet lamb as her own.

Edmund put the newly made jacket on the bleating lamb, bending its legs into the holes he'd cut, for a snug fit. 'It'll only be for a day or two, lil 'un, just until your new mother accepts you.' He then rubbed the lamb's head with blood from the dead lamb. 'That'll just make sure she thinks you are hers, and that she can't smell our Polly on you.' He got up from his bent knees and walked over to where the bereaved mother sheep was held within a tight pen. 'Now then, old lass, let's see what you make of this 'un. We can't be seeing you without a baby of your own, can we, Pol?'

Polly watched as her father put the foundling lamb into the pen, and held her breath as the wild-eyed sheep sniffed at the intruder in her space. The first few minutes would tell if she was willing to accept her new baby, or if it was a life of being bottle-fed in the kitchen of the Paradise. Edmund and Polly stood back and watched. They couldn't interfere. Even as the mother sheep butted the little lamb out of her way, they couldn't step in that early, for it would take a minute or two for the lamb's hunger for milk — and the sheep's instincts to mother — to kick in.

'Well, she's trying her best, bless her. She keeps making for the old ewe's udder.' Edmund leaned on his walking stick as he watched the pair.

'She can't keep butting it — the poor thing's ribs will get broken.' Polly wanted to reach in and rescue her ward, but knew that she had to give them time.

'Here we go, it's found milk. Look at that lil lamb's tail go.' Edmund grinned at Polly as the old ewe admitted defeat, and nudged and bleated lowly at the new baby, which was helping itself to her milk.

Polly's eyes were filled with tears. She'd seen the same thing happen nearly every year, and every year it astounded her, and made her feel a sense of awe that a mother's feelings could be so strong.

'Aye, lass, it's only a sheep, don't fret. We will leave them in this pen overnight, just to be acquainted, and then we'll let them out into the high pasture. Now, let's have a look at this old devil.' Edmund turned to the darkest corner of the barn, where he had placed the elderly Herdwick sheep. 'She's an old thing, is this 'un. Her teeth are nearly worn down, but she looks as if she's carrying twins. She's got milk for them, though, so that's good enough.' Edmund bent double over the wooden fence that held her, a decent space next to the dry barn wall. 'She's enjoying that bit of hay you gave her, Polly.'

'She's like a teddy-bear, Father. I've never seen anybody with her sort around here. Look at her face: it's all white and curly, not like our

45

patterned Swaledales.' Polly admired the old Herdwick sheep, which was very different.

'She's a bit of a way from home, wherever Josh has got her from. She must have come from above Kendal — that's Herdwick country. They like the rugged mountains up there. They are hefted to where they are born, so they always want to go home. We'll have to watch her like a hawk. You know, when she has her lambs, they will likely as not be black. They always are. Then they go lighter every year until, like this one, they are as white as snow.' Edmund watched Polly as she looked at the sheep, eating happily. He'd teach her everything he knew, and then it was her choice what she wanted to do with her life. 'Some folk say they came when the Vikings invaded these shores, and others say they were washed up on the Lakeland shores, when a Spanish ship sunk on its way to Ireland. Whatever is right, they are an old breed, and they've been about longer than we have.'

'That long, Father — that's amazing. Can I have her? I'll make sure she doesn't roam.' Polly watched the sheep eating. It looked docile enough, and she'd recognize it anywhere.

'She can be yours, our Polly, but Lord help you, because she'll keep you on your toes. But for now let's close this lot in the barn, and be away in for our supper.' Edmund leaned on his stick. His knees ached; rheumatism was no friend of his. Too many days in the past kneeling on damp grass, delivering lambs and climbing up fell sides, checking that sheep had caught up with him. Good job he had Polly. She'd be his

46

stick, and in another year she'd be old enough to take on a few more jobs. Aye, everything would be all right. Edmund felt content as he closed the barn doors and placed his arm around his lass whilst he walked across the cobbled farmyard. The weather had taken up for the better, lambing was going well, and there was a good smell of supper coming from the kitchen. What more could a man ask for?

4

Tobias Middleton leaned over the gate of Grouse Hall, remembering that his so-called father had clouted him around the ear for swinging on it, even though it had been nearly off its hinges when he was a youngster. Now it was freshly painted in verdant green, and was the gateway to a perfect cottage garden filled with traditional border flowers, which his mother loved to tend when she was not busy fussing around him. He gazed down the valley and watched the morning sunrise over the fell end. It was going to be a good day; the warmth from the early May sun already told him that, as he watched the narcissi nod their beautiful white heads in agreement along the paved path to the hall.

'Now then, Master Tobias, you're up early this morning.' Jed Mathews, the shepherd Tobias employed to look after his flock, wished him good morning and then leaned against the wall to exchange a few words, before going about his business.

'Now, Jed, how are we doing? What are we waiting to lamb now?' Tobias stood up and looked at the old man. He was well into his seventies, but as fit as a whippet, and wasn't happy unless he was dealing with sheep. His weathered, tanned face told the tale of the dale, every line made by the strong northern winds and the hail and snow that battered the northern fells. His strong, straightforward manner matched his looks.

'Nearly-finished for another year, just a few stragglers left down yonder in the bottom pasture.' He pointed to the pasture that ran down to the main road leading to Hawes. 'You've had a good year, Tobias, you've got some strong lambs. They'll fetch a good price this autumn when you come to sell them.'

'Well, it's all thanks to you. You've put a lot of hours in, and I appreciate it, Jed. In fact, come into the house and have breakfast with me. Agnes always makes too much for me on my own, and I can smell the bacon from here.' Tobias stood up and beckoned the old man through the gateway. 'Come on, man, I don't bite. And you've no one at home cooking for you.'

Jed was hesitant. It wasn't right to eat with his employer. You'd never have seen Tobias's father ask his shepherd into the house; his grandfather, happen, but not the devil that had been his father.

'Aye, I don't know, you'll not want me at your table. Look at me: I've got muck on my knees, and the lambs have peed and dribbled on me. It wouldn't be right, now that Grouse Hall is all done up.'

'Get yourself in here. I'm not that posh and snobby that I can't reward my hardest worker with a good warm breakfast.' Tobias put his arm around the shoulders of Jed and urged him into the kitchen of Grouse Hall. He'd never forgotten the hunger that had been in his belly as a young boy, hiding under the kitchen table like a wounded dog. 'Now then, sit here, next to the fire. I know it's not that cold this morning, but I bet there's a bit of a nip in the wind on that fell top. Agnes!' Tobias shouted to the resident cook, who was clattering plates in the pantry. 'Put another egg in the pan — we have a guest.'

Bacon and eggs were already cooking on the newly fitted Yorkshire Range, and Agnes came running out and put another egg into the frying pan.

'Your grandfather wouldn't recognize this spot now, Master Tobias. You've done it proud.' Jed looked around the kitchen with its new range, pot sink and warmly decorated walls.

'And my father would have cursed me under his breath. Let's not waste words, for he was not a man close to anyone's heart, Jed.' Tobias leaned back in his chair and watched Agnes plate up two helpings of bacon, egg and fried bread. He thanked her as she placed them on the table in front of them.

'Aye, but your grandfather was an honourable man. When he said it was a deal, it was a deal, and he was always true to his word. You take after him and your mother. She's a good gentle soul. She's put up with a lot from the gossips, over the years.' Jed nearly dribbled onto his plate, looking at his portion. He'd want nothing else for the rest of the day.

'Well, it was my mother who got us out of those dark days, and I'm eternally grateful to her. I'm thankful that she raised me up well and, when I couldn't make the decisions for myself, she was there. Now tuck into your food, Jed, it's going cold. There's tea in the pot. Help yourself.'

'Thank you, sir. Breakfast looks grand.' Jed lifted his knife and fork and cut into the perfectly fried egg, making the yolk run into the crisply fried bread.

'Jed, do you know the family at Paradise Farm, further down the dale? Harper, I think they are called. Have they been here long?' Tobias watched as the egg yolk dribbled down Jed's stubbly chin, and smiled to himself as Jed wiped it away on the back of his ragged jacket sleeve, before answering.

'You'll mean Edmund, his wife Ada and the lass — now what do they call her? I haven't seen her since she was a baby. They're a bit protective of her, what with her father doing what he did.' Jed wiped the remains of the egg with the buttered bread from the plate that had been placed in front of him, then started on the bacon.

'What do you mean by 'her father'? Aren't Edmund and Ada her parents?'

'No, she's their lad Danny's, but he buggered off before she was born, and Edmund and Ada have brought her up as their own. She'll not know that, because I don't think she's ever been told; best not to. Least said, soonest mended, and she's not wanting for owt.' Jed watched Tobias as he listened with interest to his words.

'And where's her mother? And does nobody know where her father is?' Tobias wanted to know more about the dark-haired beauty he had come into contact with twice in the same number of days.

'She died giving birth. I think she had twins,

51

but I'm not sure. I do know they were born out of wedlock. I think the girl's Polly — aye, that's her name, now I think about it. Her father, Danny, is in America, but you never hear him talked about. He robbed his father of his savings, when he jiggered off. Ada and Edmund never mention it. He broke their hearts, but they worship his lass.'

'Another black sheep. It seems my father wasn't the only one who didn't face his responsibilities.' Tobias leaned back in his chair and put his thumbs in his waistcoat pocket; he'd found out a little of what he'd wanted to know.

'Talking of black sheep, Edmund's got a Herdwick with triplets, in his bottom pasture. The lambs are as black as night, bonny things, but I bet he doesn't keep them long. They are fond of wandering.' Jed leaned back and looked at his clean plate. 'That breakfast was worth a king's ransom, sir.'

'Agnes is a good cook. She keeps me well fed; perhaps a little too well fed. You say the Harpers have Herdwicks. What on earth does he want with them?' Tobias grinned.

'I think the lass has taken a fancy to them. Like I say, they do anything for her.'

'So she likes her farming, then?'

'She'll match any fellow, when she gets a bit older. Edmund's taught her everything. Paradise Farm will be hers after their day, and it's a good farm.' Jed rose from the table.

'Will she now? Well, fancy that. Are you leaving me, Jed?' Tobias stood up and looked at the spotlessly clean plate of his guest.

'Aye, I'd better go and walk this breakfast off. I'll take a last look at them late lambers and then get myself home. I'll be back in the morning. Can you keep an eye on them this evening, sir?'

'Of course, Jed, you know I like to keep an eye on everything. Get yourself home. I'll have a wander down to the bottom pasture myself, now that we've got the worst done. A few stragglers, as you say, is nothing to worry about. Besides, it's a lovely day. I might make a start on tidying the barn, ready for hay-time. It'll keep me out of mischief.'

'Right, sir, see you in the morning perhaps. And thank you again for filling an old man's stomach.' Jed tugged on his cap as a sign of respect.

'See you in the morning, Jed. Glad Agnes has filled you.' Tobias watched as Jed closed the garden gate and disappeared down the rough pathway. He'd finish his cup of tea and then have a wander and inspect his sheep, all the while thinking of Polly at Paradise.

★　★　★

The grass was growing fast for early May. Tobias was thankful it had been a mild spring and winter was now a distant memory. Soon it would be time to turn the stock out of the bottom meadows and let the lush green grass grow, for the coming winter feed. He walked slowly around the few remaining sheep left to lamb. All were grazing contentedly, none showing signs of being ready.

His mind returned to thinking of Polly. He'd never seen a prettier thing, and she had a farm to her name. Bad luck with women had always dogged him — not that there had been many. Those that he had managed to get interested in him had soon vanished, once their parents told their daughters of his parentage, and how he was conceived. He hated his bloody father with a vengeance so fearful that it would probably take him to his grave. How his mother could be so saintly about him, Tobias didn't know; he'd have seen him hanged for being such a bastard. What she must have gone through to be raped by him, then outcast from her family, he couldn't comprehend. And to be told your child was dead was cruel enough. But then to find that her parents had lied to her, and that her child was alive and had been living like a dog under the table at Grouse Hall, must have been too much for Daisy. He could still remember the day his father had died, and the sheer relief when that horrible man had brought him back, lying over his saddle, dead. And the warm feeling of Daisy's arms around him as he cried, half with relief over his father's death, and half with fear of what the future held for him.

He needn't have worried about his future, for Daisy had turned out to be his mother, and his grandfather had made sure that Tobias, rather than his wayward son, had inherited Grouse Hall. After that, his life had gone from strength to strength: good schooling; a loving home with his mother and her husband, Sam Allen; and, most of all, he'd learned farming with a passion and a skill that had earned him three farms in Garsdale and Mallerstang within his twenty-five years. The only thing missing in his life was the love of someone of his own, someone to share his life with. Good horses, good food and fine clothes weren't to be taken for granted, but it was time he found himself a wife — someone like him. Polly Harper seemed to have taken his eye, and now he knew that she came from a farming background and was unwanted by her natural father, like himself, she seemed even more appropriate. How could a father walk out on his children, or treat them roughly? If he had children, he'd nurture and love them with every breath in his body, because without love, a child was nothing.

Tobias gathered his thoughts. He'd have to think of a plan to get to know Polly and her family. Unfortunately he had no reason to go and knock on the door of Paradise Farm, and he probably wouldn't get a warm reception anyway. All the dale knew him, or knew of his upbringing, and thought the worst. He'd think it through and see what he could do. There must be a way to get to know Polly better.

★   ★   ★

Polly stretched and snuggled down deep into her feather bed, pulling the sheets and blankets up to her chin. She watched the dappled shadows of sunlight bursting through her window onto the ceiling, and listened to the swooping, screeching swifts and swallows as they excitedly went about their business of making new nests under the eaves of the farm building. She didn't want to get out of bed, for she was comfortable and relaxed, and she just wanted a day to herself, to do whatever she wanted. She was tired of knowing how to dose sheep for fluke-worm, or how to calve a cow. In fact she was fed up of farming, full stop, but she just hadn't the heart to tell her mother and father. All the lads her age looked at her as if she was abnormal, when she strode about the market with her father; and as for the lasses — well, apart from her best friend, Maggie, they didn't give her the time of day. She loved the land, but wasn't ready to be tied to it. She wanted to have a bit of fun, like Maggie was having with Ralph Bannister, her most recent admirer, and the latest one in a very long line.

'Polly, are you up yet? Your father's waiting. He says you've the hens to feed, and the calf-shed wants mucking out,' Ada shouted from the bottom of the stairs, trying to rouse her snoozing daughter.

'Yes, Mother, I'm coming.' Polly sighed and pulled the covers back and sat on the edge of her bed, looking out of her bedroom window. Well, at least it was a good day, and she wouldn't get soaked to the skin or freeze to death while looking after the new spring lambs. She untied her nightdress and pulled on her dress for the day. Even her dress had seen better days. No wonder she couldn't catch a boy's eye. She looked in her wardrobe mirror as she brushed her long, dark hair. It was her crowning glory, and she knew it. Falling nearly to the middle of her back, it was thick and glossy, with a slight curl, instead of being lank and drab. Along with the bright blue of her eyes, she knew that her looks — if she put on the right clothes — could be striking.

'Oh well, another day on the farm, waiting for Mr Right to come along. Although he never will, not while I'm stuck cleaning the calf-sheds out. But if he does come along, please don't let him be a farmer,' whispered Polly to herself. She tidied her bed, plumping up the pillows and straightening the blankets and quilt, before opening her bedroom window to let the fresh spring air into the room. She looked down to the bottom pasture, where she usually saw her father's gift to her: the Herdwick ewe and her three lambs. That's funny, she thought, they're not there. Her father must have moved them this morning, but the rest of the flock were still there. Perhaps they were down near the gill's edge. The lambs always went where their mother went, so they'd be with her. She pulled her hair back over her shoulders and made her way down the narrow, creaking stairs to the kitchen.

'I thought you were never going to get up. It's eight o'clock, and your father's done a day's work already. He should be on his way back from the station, after dropping off the kit of milk to Evie that she asked to be sent to Liverpool. He expected you to go with him.' Ada banged the cup of tea down in front of Polly.

'I just wanted a lie-in, Mam. I was tired.' Polly drank her tea and took a bite from the bread and jam put in front of her.

57

'Aye, well, we are all tired. It's a hard life, but if you want to keep food on the table and a roof over your head, you've got to work for it. And lying in bed thinking daft thoughts, like that Maggie Sunter puts in your head, does neither. She's all right, for her father owns that new dairy they are building, so she will never have to lift a finger. They're made of money, that lot.' Ada sat across the table from Polly and looked at her. 'You want nowt with listening to her. She's not like us, Polly. We're farming stock, and her mother's from off the stage in Bradford. She caught Bill Sunter's eye when he stopped a night after delivering some milk, and before he knew it she said she was having his baby. Poor bugger was caught, with a baby that probably wasn't his!' Ada sighed and folded her arms. She was worried about Polly. Edmund hadn't seen it, but since winter had turned into spring, Polly had become restless and not as interested in the farm. She prayed that Polly hadn't been given her father's wandering feet and that she was about to lose her, too.

'I don't think Maggie would thank you for talking about her like that, Mother. She's a good friend to me. In fact she's the only one I've got.' Polly was nearly in tears. She couldn't suit her mother at the moment, whatever she did.

'Well, just don't listen to her daft tales, and make sure to keep your feet on the ground. I listened to Maggie the other day when she was on about that Bannister lad. I just thought to myself: thank heavens our Polly is not that fickle. We brought you up with values, and I know you

58

are a daughter to be proud of. Come on, Polly, I'm not that cross.' Ada smiled at her pride and joy as she wiped a tear away from her cheek.

Ada had been wanting to get that off her chest for a day or two. She'd been horrified with what she'd heard and didn't want Polly to go the same way. With Edmund being out of the house, it had given her chance to raise the subject.

'You know men are always wanting something they shouldn't have. Until you are married, you make them wait for it; and then, when you are married to them, you've to endure it, whether you want it or not.' Ada blushed; sex was never talked about in the Harper household and she felt uneasy with the subject.

'Mother, I wasn't born yesterday. I've seen plenty of tupping sheep, and I'm not that daft.' Polly sniffed and put her head down. She didn't know who was the more embarrassed of the two of them. Changing the subject, she coughed and lifted her head up. 'Has my father moved the Herdwicks? I couldn't see them from out of my bedroom window.'

'He never said he had done, and he hasn't had time this morning.' Ada got up from her seat and was glad of the opportunity to change the subject to something more comfortable.

'I'll go and feed the hens and then, before I start on the calf-shed, I'll have a look down in the bottom pasture. They are probably down the gill side.' Polly drank her tea in one gulp and then stood up, making for the door. 'Stop worrying about me, Mother, I'm not that daft. And Maggie is a good friend, but hasn't a lot of sense, as you say, when it comes to men.'

'I just worry, Polly. You aren't our baby any more. You're all grown up, and your father doesn't realize this.' Ada watched as Polly left the house and went across the yard and into the barn. She was the spitting image of her real father and that spelt trouble, she was sure of it.

Polly threw out handfuls of yellow corn kernels to the greedy clucking hens pecking at her feet in their eagerness to eat their daily ration. 'Out of my way, you clucking, mucky things.' Polly hated the hens. She hated climbing in the hen-hut and putting her hand into the straw-lined laying boxes to pick up the eggs. She'd guarantee that there would be hen-muck on some of the eggs and that she'd put her hands into it, in the dim light of the hut. She always thought about that when her mother boiled her an egg for her breakfast. Mucky things! She gazed down over the field. She still couldn't see the Herdwicks and hoped to God that they hadn't decided to wander. She went into the hut, collected the eggs without incident and then left them in the porchway of her home, before walking down into the bottom pasture.

The day was glorious, the sun warm and, in the wood behind Paradise, a cuckoo was singing its signature song. It echoed around the dale. Polly ran her hand through the cow-parsley and buttercups that were flowering in the pasture and lifted her face to the sun. She loved its warmth. It made her feel so much better, after the long, cold, grey months of winter. Looking around her, there was no sign of the missing sheep. She wandered down to the gill side and followed it as far as the road, but there was still no sign of the missing foursome. They must have got out under the gate and onto the road — her father had warned her that they were escape artists. Polly opened the gate and walked onto the road that led in one direction to Hawes, with the other way leading to the market town of Sedbergh. Which way to take? She decided to take the road to Hawes and walked over the river bridge and through the narrow cluster of houses known to the locals as The Street. Len Brunskill, Edmund's friend, was standing outside his house as Polly walked past.

'You've not seen a sheep with three black lambs, have you?' Polly stopped.

'Nay, lass. You've not lost the Herdwick and its lambs, have you? I told your father he'd not keep 'em.' Len grinned, showing his toothless gums. 'I've not seen them go past this last hour, and nobody's said anything to me. I'd try the other way, if I were you.' Len yawned. 'I didn't sleep right well last night. I was woken with a noise about midnight. I looked out of my window and there was a grey horse on the bridge. I've been trying to think whose it was all morning. It looked like a ghost-horse in the moonlight.' He wandered away with his thoughts as Polly half-listened, wanting to carry on with her search.

'All right, thank you.' She turned around and made her way back over the river bridge, getting to her field gate just as she heard a horse and cart coming up behind her.

'Open the gate, our Polly,' her father shouted as his cart clattered over the bridge.

Polly ran quickly and opened the gate for her father to ride up the path to home.

'Whoa, Clover! Do you want a lift up home? What are you doing down here?' Edmund pulled his horse up as Polly closed the gate behind him.

'I'm looking for the Herdwick and her lambs. She's gone missing.' Polly looked flustered.

'Eh! She could be miles away by now, bloody animal. Come back up home with me. I'll just have a bite to eat and then we'll go out with Clover and the cart, unless somebody brings her back first. Don't waste your energy looking for her on your legs — she could be anywhere.'

Polly didn't need to be told twice. She didn't fancy walking the roads on her own and climbed in next to her father.

'Don't worry, I knew she'd not settle. We'll find her and, when we do, I'll hobble her front legs together — that will stop her trailing.' Edmund urged Clover on and the cart made its way back home.

'I don't know why you bought them. All we've done since she lambed is watch her like a hawk, and she's still managed to escape,' Polly moaned.

'I thought you liked her and her lambs?' Edmund was surprised by Polly's outburst.

'She's only a sheep. They are all a bit thick, and always do what others do.' She got down from the cart as Edmund brought Clover to a standstill. 'I've got better things to do with my time than chase daft sheep.'

'And what's that then, lass? Had you

62

something in mind for today?'

'Seemingly, cleaning the calf-shed out, or so my mother tells me, a real ladylike job.' Polly couldn't bite her tongue. She knew she was being sarcastic.

'Aye, well, we all have to pull together. I don't suppose you wanted to be up by five this morning to catch the express train with the milk, did you? So think yourself lucky, Miss, and we'll have less of your cheek.' Edmund tied the horse up and watched as Polly flounced into the home, picking up the abandoned hens' eggs as she entered the kitchen. There was no pleasing that lass at the moment, he thought.

'Have you found them?' Ada came downstairs after hearing their voices and looked at the sulky face of Polly.

'No, they are out on the road, Father says. He'll go and look for them with Clover when he's had a bite to eat.' Polly slumped in a chair and waited for her father to enter the kitchen, regretting her hasty words.

'Well, they'll turn up somewhere. Everybody knows whose they are, up and down the dale, so there's no need for that long face. It'll stop that length, if the wind changes, you know.' Ada could see that Polly was in a mood and tried to make light of it.

'I'll go and clean that calf-hut out and get out from under your feet.' Polly jumped up and made for the door, hoping to meet her father before he came in. But it was too late, for he was just entering the porch as she opened the kitchen door.

'Where are you off to, and what's with the bad mood?' Edmund stopped Polly in her tracks.

'I'm off to clean the calves out and I'm just a bit fed-up.' Polly wanted to say, 'I want a different life', but she daren't, not to her father.

'Aye, well, everybody gets days like that. But the sun's shining and we are all well, and that's all we can ask the good Lord for.' Edmund looked at his wild-eyed daughter. He'd seen that look in Dan's eyes, just before he left.

Polly went past him and didn't answer as she walked across the farmyard to the calf-shed, grabbing the pitchfork and brush that were against the entrance, before disappearing from sight.

'Aye, Mother, we've got another wild 'un on our hands. She's just like her father, God help us.' Edmund sat down to his drink of tea and the bread and dripping that Ada placed in front of him.

'She's at that age, Father, and being friendly with that Maggie Sunter doesn't help. But we can't wrap her up in cotton wool, and she's to grow up sometime. That's where we went wrong with our Dan. We mollycoddled him too much. Happen now she's left school she could do with working for someone a few days a week — someone we know?'

'But there's enough to do here. She wants nowt with working for someone else.' Edmund wasn't going to let Polly out into the wider world. She was his life, his hope of carrying on the farm.

'Aye, but she's a lass, Edmund. Sheep and

cows are not the be-all and end-all of everything. Besides, she could bring a bit of money in as well. Have a think about it, and then we'll talk to her. It'll make her think how lucky she is living here — when she has to get up at seven in the morning and won't finish work until perhaps as late as seven in the evening. Two days a week with someone else will be just the thing to bring her back into the real world.' Ada sat back and watched Edmund finishing his breakfast with a scowl on his face. She knew she was right. Polly was bored, and if they didn't do something about it, they were heading for disaster.

★　★　★

The calf-shed had never been cleared with such fervour. The old rush bedding had been thrown out into the barrow in the yard, and the cobbles on the floor were being brushed to within an inch of their life, as Polly took out her frustration on the job she hated. Bloody animals, bloody farm — she hated the lot at the moment. The only thing she did like was wandering over the fields and watching nature in all its glory. But she knew she couldn't do that all day.

She stopped in her tracks as she heard hooves come into the yard and the snort of a horse as its rider alighted. She put her pitchfork down, rubbed her brow and went to the doorway. It was him! What was Tobias Middleton doing at her house? She watched as he tied the grey dapple to the wooden railing of the kitchen garden and then brush himself down, without noticing her presence. Polly was full of panic. He mustn't see her or smell her like this; she'd just cleaned out the filthy calf-shed and must look an awful mess. She turned and hid around the corner of the barn, accidently knocking the brush over, sending it clattering to the floor.

'Hello, hello, Polly!' Tobias caught sight of her striped dress as she fled around the side of the barn. 'Polly! Polly, can I have a word?' He took off his riding gloves and started walking over to the group of buildings that he had seen Polly vanish behind.

'Can I help you, Mr Middleton?' Edmund came out of the porch upon hearing the arrival of a horse in the yard and then a man's voice calling for Polly. He was surprised to see the flamboyant form of Tobias Middleton in his yard, and even more surprised that he knew Polly's name.

'Hmm, yes. Mr Harper, I presume . . . ?' Tobias held out his hand to shake.

Edmund stared at him. He'd heard plenty about the lad who stood in front of him, but up until now he'd had nothing to do with him. His father had been a wrong 'un, but his mother and the lad who stood in front of him seemed to be hard workers. Albeit a different kind from the quiet living that Edmund and his family were used to.

'Aye, that's me, what can I do for you?' Edmund shook Tobias's hand and looked at the neatly dressed young man. From the way he was dressed, he would never have thought Tobias was a farmer, if he hadn't have known otherwise.

'Mmm, I believe I have something that belongs to you, Mr Harper. Are you missing a Herdwick with triplets?' Tobias waited for an answer, while trying to keep in his periphery the farm buildings and the skirt that he could just spy, hiding at the side of the shed.

'Aye, I am, lad. Have they made their way up to you at Grouse Hall? They must have run like the wind to have gone that far.' Edmund couldn't believe they had walked so far, especially the lambs.

'Well, Jed Mathews tells me that they are yours, so I've penned them in my barn, until it's convenient to pick them up.' Tobias watched the elderly man, as he thought about the distance between farms and the probability of the sheep being his.

'Oh! Well, if Jed says they are ours, he'll be right. He knows his sheep, does old Jed. Does he still shepherd for you then? He must be a good age — he's older than me, is the old devil.' Edmund smiled.

'Yes, he's a good man. Bit of rheumatism in his knees, but he's a good help. I'd have been lost without him this lambing time. I've taken on a bit too much, I think.' Tobias leaned against the garden wall and looked around him. 'You've a grand farm here, Mr Harper. Lovely position, and it's got a stunning view across the valley.' Tobias smirked as he saw Polly's face quickly glance around the side of the building.

'Aye, I'm lucky fifth-generation here. It does us proud. We manage to keep our heads above water anyway, and that's more than a lot can say, in this day and age. Now, about these sheep, do you want me and our lass to come and pick them up?' Edmund thought it was only right that he offered to bring them back home.

'If you could. I'll keep them in the barn until you have the time. They aren't any bother to me.' Tobias walked to his horse.

'Polly and I will be along this afternoon. Did I hear you shouting her name? She was cleaning the calf-hut out.' Edmund questioned the young man as he mounted his horse.

'I think you must be mistaken. I don't think I've had the pleasure of meeting your daughter yet, Mr Harper. I look forward to meeting her later in the day.' Edmund pulled on his gloves, tightened his reins and kicked his dapple into motion. 'See you later, sir!'

Edmund watched as the landed gent made his way down the path, and he watched as Tobias opened the gate without bothering to dismount, before he crossed the bridge. How the hell had the old sheep, along with its three lambs, managed to walk nearly five miles in such a short time? It was a marvellous animal, if he was telling the truth.

'You can come out now. I can see you hiding by the side of the shed,' Edmund shouted to Polly. 'What are you skulking for anyway? He was shouting your name, wasn't he?' Edmund watched as Polly walked with her head down across the yard.

Polly blushed.

'How do you know him?' Edmund asked as she brushed past him.

'I met him when I was on my walk up

Mallerstang. He only asked my name and wished me a good day.' Polly looked shyly at her father.

'Aye, well, keep it that way. I'll have to take you to help with these sheep, but don't you encourage him. He's not like us. He's been brought up different, our Polly, and he perhaps wouldn't treat you right.' Edmund put his arm around Polly's shoulder.

'I know, my mother said,' cried Polly as she entered the kitchen with her father.

'Mother, you never told me that the Middleton lad had been talking to our Polly.' Edmund's voice was raised.

'Cause there was nowt to tell. He only wished her the time of day. It must be over a month ago now. Anyway, I told her not to bother with him, that his father was a bad 'un. So don't you yell at me, Edmund Harper.' Ada put her hands on her hips and glared.

'I only said hello!' Polly sat down in the chair and looked at Ada and Edmund.

'We know, lass. We are just looking after you.' Ada put her arm around her shoulders. 'Your father and I are too protective, perhaps.'

'Mmm! Well, don't encourage him when we pick them sheep up. In fact, keep in the cart until I fetch them out. I don't trust him an inch.' Edmund still didn't believe the sheep had travelled that far. Something was amiss.

★   ★   ★

Polly had to hide her excitement as she sat next door to her father on the way up to Grouse Hall.

69

He was still in a bad mood and Polly was grateful for the silence between them, just in case her enthusiasm for her visit to Tobias's house showed. She'd changed her dress and washed while humming to herself privately in her bedroom, coming to a sombre mood as she climbed up into the cart with her father. She'd never been to Grouse Hall, but it wasn't that she was bothered about; it was Tobias — the one everybody was warning her of — that was sending the blood pulsing in her veins. They reached the bottom of the track to Grouse Hall and her father turned to her.

'Now, think on. You say nothing, and you stop in the cart until I pass the sheep and lambs to you.' Edmund looked at his daughter as she nodded in compliance.

As they reached Grouse Hall they could see that they weren't the only visitors to the house. The horse and trap that belonged to the police sergeant from Hawes was parked outside the garden gate, with one of its officers seated in the trap.

'Afternoon, sir. I'm afraid Mr Middleton is being questioned by the sergeant at the moment.' The officer got down from the trap and held the reins of Edmund's horse. 'He's not receiving visitors.'

'But I've come for my sheep, which strayed onto his land. A Herdwick with its three lambs. He asked me to pick them up this afternoon. I'm not going back without them, and it'll be nothing to do with what you're talking to him about.'

'And you are, sir?' The officer looked at him questioningly.

'I'm Edmund Harper from Paradise Farm, and this is my daughter, Polly.'

'Just a minute, sir. Wait here until I get my sergeant.' The officer walked off, entering Grouse Hall and leaving Edmund cursing Tobias Middleton, and swearing to Polly that he took after his father.

Tobias and the two policemen came out of the hall, with Tobias shouting and cursing in front of them.

'I told you I hadn't stolen the sheep. That silly old fool down in Garsdale must have been seeing things. Why would I go and tell a man I was holding his sheep, when supposedly I'd stolen them?'

'Mr Brunskill said he'd seen your horse on top of the river bridge and that he'd heard noises, and subsequently there was a sheep and her lambs missing from Paradise Farm. What were we supposed to think, when we found the sheep and the lambs he described in your barn?'

Edmund climbed down from his trap after hearing the conversation.

'I'm sorry, Sergeant Meadows. Mr Middleton came this morning to tell me he was holding my old Herdwick and her lambs. I think Len — Mr Brunskill — has perhaps let his imagination run away with him. If you'd spoken to me first, none of this need have happened.' Edmund looked at the red-faced sergeant and his embarrassed constable. 'I don't think you'll find there's been any sheep-rustling here, and anyway they're not worth a lot. The old ewe's nearly on her last legs.'

'Thank you, Edmund. I've been trying to tell them that.' Tobias Middleton sighed in relief.

'Well, we had to follow the report through. There's been a lot of sheep-rustling down Maller-stang, and we don't want it creeping into our patch.' The sergeant motioned to his constable to get into the trap.

'Perhaps it was a case of giving a dog a bad name. Nobody in this godforsaken place can forget what my father was like. I am not him, and never will be,' Tobias yelled at the police as they got into the trap and set the horses in motion.

Tobias, Edmund and Polly watched as the police went out of the yard, barely believing what they had all been a part of.

'Thank you again, Edmund. They had accused me of stealing, and I'd never do that.' Tobias sneaked a look at Polly as he spoke. 'Would you both like to join me for tea? It's the least I can offer you, for proving my case.'

'It's 'Mr Harper' to you, lad. And no, we'll not be having tea with you. Just point us in the direction of my sheep and we'll be away.' Edmund didn't know why he'd spoken up on behalf of Tobias Middleton, as he knew damn well that the old Herdwick hadn't wandered that far away from home without help.

'Of course. I'm sorry, I'm forgetting my manners. And good afternoon, Miss Polly, I'm sorry if this has caused you distress.' Tobias looked up at Polly. His plan hadn't quite worked out the way he had planned it, but it was worth it, just to get a glimpse of those sparkling blue eyes.

'I'll give you a good afternoon, if you don't get me the sheep and lambs. You needn't look at my lass like that. She's not for you, and never will be, so just think on!' Edmund stormed off to the barn's doorway. 'Now get on with it. The sooner we are away from here, the better for everyone.'

★ ★ ★

Polly lay in her bed and thought about the day. She could hear her mother and father talking quietly in the next-door bedroom. No doubt they were talking about her and Tobias Middleton. Her father had been so angry, but Tobias had still dared to look at her. And how her heart had fluttered at his sultry good looks. She'd felt herself blush as his eyes read her deepest thoughts. She had hoped her father would accept the offer of tea at Grouse Hall, just to be neighbourly, and for her to see how Tobias lived. But he wasn't falling for Tobias's pleasantries. Her father seemed to see straight through the young man's charm offensive and was putting a stop to them seeing each other, making his feelings as clear as the crystals that adorned Sam Allen's shop shelves.

Polly hugged her pillow close to her and thought of his dark, swarthy looks and fine clothes. Somehow she would see Tobias again — she had to. She knew for sure that she loved him.

5

'Look at this letter, Mother. What do you think?'
Edmund tried to pass Ada a letter that had been
delivered by the postboy as he was walking out of
the door. 'He's offering a ha'penny a pint. It's
picked up here, and he'll supply the milk-kits.'

'Who's offering what?' Ada had sweat running
down her nose as she stirred her weekly wash in
the dolly tub with the wooden three-legged posser.
Doing the washing was hard, back-breaking work
and she could have done without the interrup-
tion. She reluctantly stopped for a moment to
glance at the letter that Edmund wafted under
her nose.

'That Bill Sunter and his new dairy. He's
saying he'll pick up the milk from all the
surrounding Dales and take it to Hawes, to make
into butter or cheese, and he'll pay a ha'penny a
pint — like I said, if you'd been listening.'
Edmund waited for her response.

'Well, are you going to take him up on it? Evie
in Liverpool will be disappointed if you stop
supplying her when she wants the occasional kit.
But I'll not complain; it seems good money, and
it saves me from making as much butter with the
spare milk.' Ada stood with her hands on her
hips and watched as Edmund read the letter again.

'I don't know. I'm not keen on Bill Sunter.'
Edmund put the letter down on the table and
stood thinking.

'You're not keen on anybody at the moment, Edmund. It seems to me that it'd be a good thing, especially when winter comes. You'll not have to trail up to the station when our Evie asks for an extra supply, but you'll still be paid just for putting it in his kits. He's all right, is Bill. It's his wife that's the flighty one, and that Maggie, their lass. Bill's a worker, else he wouldn't be doing this.'

'I'll think about it. In fact I might go into Hawes and ask him about it. I'd rather do business face-to-face than through a letter.' Edmund had been curious for a while to see what was going on at the building of the dairy, and this was his chance.

'Aye, go from under my feet. I want to get on with this washing, and you aren't helping by rabbiting on about the price of milk.' Ada pummelled her clothes again, as steam from the dolly tub filled the kitchen. 'Take our Polly with you, she could do with a look out.'

'Polly!' Edmund shouted up at the bottom of the stairs. 'Polly, do you want to come into Hawes with me? I'm off to see Maggie's father about his new dairy.' Edmund listened to footsteps racing down the stairs and waited for the beaming Polly to appear.

'Aye, I thought you'd be quick down them stairs when there was an outing to be had. I wish you'd show as much enthusiasm over hanging this washing out.' Ada smiled.

'Are you off to Maggie's? Can I go in and see her while you look around the dairy?' Polly's day had suddenly improved.

'Aye, if you want. I'm sure you'll have plenty to talk about — all rubbish, I'm sure.' Edmund picked up his cap and the letter, placing it safely in his jacket pocket.

'Mind what you're doing, Missy. No daft talk about lads and, if you walk into Hawes, behave yourselves. At least it's a weekday, and that Bannister lad that Maggie's sweet on will be at work at the lead-mines.' Ada wiped her brow as she watched both Polly and Edmund go out through the kitchen door. At least she'd have a bit of peace with them out from under her feet. She might even be lucky and be able to have forty winks after she'd hung the washing out to dry.

★ ★ ★

Edmund and Polly stood on the cobbled bridge over-looking the river in the centre of Hawes and looked upstream at the gushing of the fosse and the mill-wheel that was attached to what now was becoming the new dairy.

'I remember when that wheel never stopped. Old Ben Chapman had it then. It ground corn into flour, and now Bill's making it into a dairy. It needed using, it was beginning to look a bit dilapidated.'

'That must have been a long time ago, Father. I can't remember it ever turning.' Polly looked at the whitewashed lettering on the three-storey building, telling the world of its new ownership.

'Aye, it was Polly, well before your — ' Edmund stopped in his tracks. He'd nearly said,

'Well before your father was born', but had realized just in time. 'Looks like he's making a splash: *Bill Sunter, Milk, Cheese & Butter*. Well, you can't miss where he's at, with lettering as big as that. Let's go and have a look inside, and see if I like his set-up.'

'Now then, Edmund, what brings you to my doorstop?' Bill Sunter stood with a clipboard in his hand and a pencil behind his ear. 'Have I tempted you with my new scheme?' He grinned and ran his hand through his greying slicked-back hair. He knew damn well that Edmund must have been tempted to have a look, else he wouldn't be standing in front of him. 'If it helps, the Aldersons, Thwaites and Lunds have all signed up, from down Garsdale, so I'll be passing your gate every morning and night. They seem to think it's a good idea. There's a market out there for Wensleydale cheese and butter. Folk are visiting all the time, now the train lines have opened these Dales up. What's better than taking a bit of Wensleydale cheese back home, to remind you of Hawes and your visit?' Bill was a true salesman and knew his patter off by heart.

'Aye, no doubt you are right, Bill. It's just that I send our Evie milk occasionally to Liverpool. To back up her supply. I maybe couldn't supply you all the time.' Edmund glanced around the whitewashed walls of the dairy. There were huge wooden trays waiting to hold the milk, and for rennet to be added, before beginning the process of cheese-making, and equally big butter-churns ready to be turned into action.

'I tell you what, Edmund. Come and have a

look around with me, and I'll convince you that if you sign up with me, it'll be the best thing you can do. Polly, Maggie's in next door, and this will only bore you to death — it's men's business. Do you want to pop your head in and say hello?' Bill put his arm round Edmund's shoulders to guide him around the building, while he winked at the bored Polly.

'Can I, Father?' Polly was relieved that Bill Sunter had suggested that she visit Maggie, as she wasn't really interested in the dairy, when a gossip with Maggie was in the offing.

'Well, I thought you might want to see how it's all going to work. After all, one day it'll be your milk that comes here.' Edmund looked disappointed as he saw that his daughter was more interested in seeing her friend.

'Edmund, let her go, it's not women's business. And besides, I've a suggestion I want to make to you first.' Bill watched as Polly was torn between her friend and her father's wishes.

'Go on then. I'll shout to you before I go home.' Edmund turned to Bill. 'Come on, show me how it works.'

Polly couldn't get out of the dairy fast enough, away from the talk about milk and cheese and butter. She knew how to make it, as she'd churned the milk often enough, helping her mother to make butter. And she knew how it made her arms ache, turning the paddles that battered the creamy milk into butter. She ran down the dairy's steps and knocked on the cottage that stood next door to it. The sound of the gushing fosse filled her ears as she stood waiting for an answer to her timid knock. She knocked louder when nobody came to the door, and watched the beer-coloured water rush down under the bridge as she stood there, feeling awkward, on the doorstep.

'I said, 'Come in', didn't you hear me?' The red-haired Maggie came to the door, opening it wide to let her friend in. 'You must be deaf. I shouted from upstairs.' Maggie never minced her words, which could be a good thing, but at the same time could be hurtful, if she was that way out.

'I didn't hear you because of the waterfall. The river's full because of last night's rain,' said Polly as she stepped into her friend's home.

'What are you doing here anyway? It's not market day or Saturday, and they are the only days you are usually in Hawes. My mother said she saw you with your father as you walked up to the dairy. I didn't think you'd be allowed to see me, after your mother heard me talking about Ralph. I can still see her face — she's a bit of a prude, isn't she?' Maggie giggled and brushed back her long ginger locks, revealing a nose covered with freckles and a pair of green eyes, which hinted at a little wickedness.

'We are here because of your father and his dairy. My father is thinking of supplying him with milk. And don't call my mother a prude. She's just set in her ways, and you wouldn't shut up in front of her about kissing Ralph. So she got mad. How is he, anyway?'

'Oh, he's been and gone. He's always up at Gunnerside at that blinking lead-mine. He doesn't have time for me. When he does have time, he's only after one thing, and I'm just not that kind of girl.' Maggie fell backwards into one of the huge easy chairs and laughed again. 'Plenty more fish in the sea, especially now that my father is employing most of the eligible young men in the district.'

'You are so shallow, Maggie Sunter. I thought Ralph loved you.' Polly sat in the chair opposite her friend and looked at her, as she twiddled with hair around her fingers.

'You've got to kiss a lot of frogs before your prince arrives. That's what my mother has told me. It's what she did before she met my father.'

Polly remembered what her mother had said, about how Maggie's mother had cornered Bill, and thought to herself that it could just be true. 'Yes, but you have to take care. You don't want a reputation,' she said thoughtfully.

'Well, it's better than just looking at them and dreaming your life away, like you are with that Tobias Middleton. Of all the men in the dale, why do you admire him? Everyone knows he's a wrong 'un, just like his father — that's what I hear.' Maggie was making fun of her friend.

'He isn't, he's just misunderstood; he's always been a gentleman to me, and he's so handsome.' Polly blushed as she thought of her secret love. She knew that perhaps Tobias was dangerous, but that was part of his attraction.

'Look at you blushing, and you haven't even kissed him. Your father won't let you anywhere near him, since the stint with the sheep, and you know it. Do you want a drink of tea? I'll go and ask my mother to make us some.' Maggie stood up and looked down at her friend with what seemed to be almost a sneer on her lips.

'If you want one.' Polly watched as Maggie went into the adjoining room to ask her mother for some tea. If it had been her, she'd have had to make it herself and wouldn't have expected to have her mother running after her. As the only child, Maggie was a bit spoilt by her parents; her every whim was adhered to, and the trouble was that she'd become so accustomed to this that she expected it from everyone else. Polly sighed. Sometimes she wondered how Maggie and she were friends. Whilst they were both only children, they were from completely different backgrounds. She also knew why Maggie was popular with the male population — not only was she generous with her affections, but her father was also extremely well off. Maggie would be a good catch for any aspiring young lad.

'Here you go, Polly love. Maggie said you and her would like some tea, and I've brought you a slice of cake on a plate as well. I bought it at Sam Allen's this morning. I don't like baking myself — too messy.' Jenny Sunter placed a tray with willow-pattern china and slices of cake on a table between the two chairs. 'I'll leave you two girls to it. You must have plenty to talk about. I know I had at your age. What a life I had, back then in Bradford. I had men flocking at my feet.' Jenny gazed wistfully as she remembered the good old days. 'And then I met your father.' She paused. 'Still, never mind.' She smiled as Maggie sat back in her chair, and then she disappeared back into the kitchen.

'Does your mother miss Bradford? It must have been a bit strange, coming to live here after being in such a big city?' Polly looked at the shop-bought cake. Her mother would never have considered buying such an easy thing to bake.

'Don't know. She talks a lot about it, but she never goes back there.' Maggie stirred her tea and put the slice of cake on her plate, before biting into it.

'Do you not have any relations there? I know I have an Aunty Evie and Uncle Albert in Liverpool, but I've never seen them. Polly mused on the idea of her relations — and the lack of them, in Maggie's case — as she tucked into her cake.

'Nah, just me mother. My father's got his brother, Uncle Steven, at Bainbridge, but that's it — don't need anybody else. This is good cake, isn't it?' Maggie took a long sip of tea and sat back in her chair.

'Yes, it's all right,' Polly replied, thinking it wasn't a patch on what she and her mother could make at home.

'So, is your father thinking of bringing his milk to our dairy? It'll be less work for him, and money coming in on a regular basis. My father says the locals will be fools if they don't sign up with him.' Maggie sat askew in her chair, wiggling her legs carelessly under her long, expensive chiffon skirt.

'I don't think any of the farmers will be fools, and that's probably what's worrying your father. If it's a good deal, they'll take it; if he's robbing them blind, they will soon find him out. He needs them as much as they need him.' Polly wasn't having the local farmers called fools. In times of hardship they were always there to support one another, and if Bill Sunter thought they were fools, he was going to be in for a surprise.

'Listen to you! When did you become interested in commerce? I thought you were a farm girl, only interested in sheep and if the grass is growing,' Maggie scoffed.

'There's a lot you don't know about me, Maggie Sunter. And I thought we were friends. Stop making fun of me!'

'I am your friend. That's why I told my father that if there's an offer of a part-time job in the dairy, you'd be interested. I thought it was time we got you off that farm and into the real world.' Maggie suddenly sat up straight and grinned at Polly. 'I suggested we could both work at the shop counter that he's opening. He knows we both have the looks, and you'll soon learn the patter. It'll be a laugh. And besides, Pol, every farm lad in the district will be coming through those doors. Forget your Tobias — he's had his chance!'

'Oh, Maggie, you didn't. I don't think my father will ever agree. And besides, I don't know if I want to come and work for your father. How would I get to work? How would my mother and father manage without me? They are not as young as yours.' Polly was torn, but it would be a lot more interesting working in a shop in Hawes than mucking out a stable.

'Of course you want to. Now I think about it,

how come your parents are a lot older than mine are? Your mother must have been ancient when she had you — well past you-know-what, I'd have thought! Do you never think about that?'

'Maggie, do you mind! Sometimes I can't believe what you come out with. No wonder my mother warns me about you. I don't think she will want me to work with you, as she already thinks you are a bad influence.' Polly grinned at her best friend while she finished her tea.

'She's not seen anything yet. If we work together, it'll be a laugh a minute,' Maggie smirked.

'We'll see. It will be up to my father, and whether he brings his milk to be processed.' Polly secretly hoped that he would agree, giving her the best of both worlds. A comfortable home life on the farm, while enjoying the fun of working in a shop.

★ ★ ★

'I don't know, Father. I heard that Maggie talking the other day and she's nowt but a brazen hussy, stringing all the lads on, playing with their hearts.' Ada pulled the bedclothes up to her chest and put her arms out of bed. 'Her mother was just the same.'

'I take it you don't have a high opinion of the Sunter women?' Edmund turned to Ada and looked at her, as she scowled at the thought of Polly going to work for the Sunters.

'No, I don't, and I'm not keen on our Polly as a shop lass. Couldn't we get her a bit of a cleaning job at the vicarage, or up at the big house down the dale? That's more to her breeding.' Ada folded her arms in defiance.

'She'll get picked up in the morning with the milk, and the same bloke will bring her back at night, when he picks the evening milking up. She'll be under the watchful eye of Bill all the time she's at work, and he's offering her a decent wage for two days a week. That's better than scrubbing floors at any vicarage or big house. You know yourself it was no job being in service.' Edmund was finding it hard to persuade Ada that Polly should work at the dairy, but after seeing the new business Bill would bring in, he knew Polly wouldn't get anything much better.

'And what about hay-time? We'll need her to do some of the raking and gathering in.' Ada was thinking of every excuse to stop Polly from going.

'That's another two month off yet. The grass is no higher than my ankles, and by then she might be bored of it anyway. And we still have her the rest of the week, so there's no problem that I can see of.' Edmund could sense he was winning the fight.

'If Bill Sunter swears that he keeps his eye on her, and if her hours don't change — because I can't manage to rake all those hay-meadows myself — then she can go.' Ada was tired of arguing and was in need of her sleep. She rolled over onto her side.

'It'll be right, lass; it'll be the making of her, you'll see. We can't keep her under our wing forever. Besides, there will be plenty of good solid lads who go to that dairy. We could do with a son-in-law to inherit the farm, 'cause our lad's not coming home, and well you know it.' Edmund regretted the words as soon as he'd said them.

Ada turned round sharply. 'That's just it, Edmund Harper. What if she finds out she's not our daughter, but our granddaughter. There's many a gossip in Hawes, and it's Bill Sunter's dairy — he knows exactly who she is, else I'm a monkey's aunty.'

'Hold your noise, woman. Nobody's said anything in these last sixteen years. Folk have nearly forgotten whose daughter she is. Nothing will be said, and she'll be more content than pacing about like a caged animal, here with us two old crones.' Edmund pulled the covers over him and turned away from his wife.

'On your own head be it, Edmund Harper. I can see this being nothing but trouble.' Ada turned over and pulled at the covers.

'Well, she's off to work there, and that's an end to it.'

★　★　★

Polly once again lay in her bed. She could hear the muffled words through her bedroom wall, and knew the subject was yet again her, and the job at the dairy. Her mother had not looked happy when her father had come back with a glowing report of what Bill Sunter was going to do, and what promises he had made for the delivery of milk to him. But she had been even more unhappy when the pair of them told her of Polly's job offer. It seemed there was no pleasing her at the moment. Polly could see no problem. She could easily get there and back, she had a promise of good pay from people she knew — what more did her mother want? She pulled the covers up around her chin and listened to the raised voices, and then to the silence that followed. Somebody must have won, but was it in favour of the job, or against?

Maggie would be laughing at her worrying. Nothing seemed to bother Maggie, but then again she was selfish, and Polly knew it. Could she work with Maggie? That was the next question. She was the boss's daughter, and she'd know it and abuse her position. Polly lay awake, watching a moth fly around her room in the pale moonlight. She felt a bit like that moth, trapped in a life that she didn't really want. She was alone, so terribly alone, with no one to talk to and no one to understand her.

6

'Well, did she get her lift? And who was it that picked her and the milk up, from the lane end?' Ada dried her hands on the tea-towel and waited for the report from Edmund as he pulled up his chair to eat his breakfast.

'Aye, she's gone. You know, I felt full of pride, and nearly bawled. She looked so bonny in her black-and-white dairy uniform. She's grown up so quickly.' Edmund tucked into his breakfast.

'And . . . ' Ada knew he had more to say.

'Oh! Aye, it was Oliver Simms from Buttersett that picked her and the kits up. You know him — he has that big family and preaches at Chapel on a Sunday. She couldn't be any safer than with him, so stop fretting.' Edmund was getting tired of the constant ear-bashing from Ada, but was still adamant it was the right thing for Polly.

'Oh, well, I don't have to worry about him, It's who else she works with that might be the problem.' Ada continued to wipe the pots.

'Will you stop bothering. She'll be all right. Bill will look out for her. He owes it to our Danny, because I'm sure it was Bill that led him astray.' Edmund ventured to mention his son's name, fearing a reaction from Ada.

'Aye, and look what he did to this family last time. I tell you, Edmund, I'm worried to death. I don't mind you supplying the dairy, but when it comes to our Polly, I wish she wasn't working there.' She could nearly have cried.

'You didn't see her face, Mother, as she waved goodbye. She'll be right — it's only two days a week. She just looked so happy.'

'Well, I hope that you are right, for all our sakes.' Ada sighed. How she wished she had never encouraged Edmund to supply the dairy with milk.

★ ★ ★

Polly sat next to the man her father had called Oliver and waved to the farmers she knew, as they picked up kits full of fresh milk. Oliver, she gathered, was a man of few words, not bothering to pass pleasantries about the weather, or ask if she was nervous about starting her new job. If he had asked, she would have told him she was petrified, and that she had never worked for anyone other than her father, and didn't class that as work really. He had said, 'Now then, Edmund', when he loaded the two kits onto the back of the cart, but that had been over half an hour ago. And now they were passing through the tiny hamlet of Appersett and were nearly into the town of Hawes.

'You'll be wanting a lift back tonight, Mr Sunter tells me. I'll be round the back of the dairy at six. Don't be late. I want to see something of my missus and kids before she puts them all to bed.' Oliver talked drily as he focused on the bobbing heads of his horses.

'If that's all right with you? I believe that's what was agreed between Mr Sunter and my father.' Polly smiled and turned her head to look at Oliver, hoping to strike up a conversation on the last mile into Hawes.

'It'll have to be right — I've no say in it. I just get my orders and hope I get paid at the end of the week, else my family goes hungry.' Oliver still kept his gaze on the horses and the road ahead, not turning his head to acknowledge Polly.

'I see. Well, six o'clock it is, and I won't be late.' Polly thought she wouldn't dare to be. Oliver might completely blank her if she were to be or, worse still, might refuse to take her home.

The cart shook as it made its way through the streets of Hawes, with kits clanging together from the rattle of the chains that held them in place. Polly felt herself sway with every uneven cobble and flagstone on the road, and was thankful as the cart came round the corner and down the track that led to the back entrance to the dairy.

'You get out here. Go through them doors and ask for Miss Swaine. She'll show you where to go and what to do.' Oliver jumped down from the front of the cart, without any offer to help Polly alight. Instead he went round to the back of the cart and started to undo the chains from the milk-kits.

Polly sat for a second and then slowly swivelled her bottom to the edge of the high seat and made a tentative step down onto the ground, feeling her skirt get caught on a piece of metal bar just under her seat. She blushed, as she knew she was showing her ankle. She quickly turned round and tried to free herself before anyone noticed, silently cursing to herself as she hastened to undo the material.

'Here, let me help.'

Polly looked up and noticed a young man of about her age coming to her rescue.

She blushed. 'It's all right, really, I can manage.' She tried again, but the material had become wedged between the two pieces of metal, and the more she moved her body, the tighter it caught.

'Don't move, I'll pull it free while you just keep still . . . There you are, free to go, but I'm afraid you look a bit grimy where it was caught.' Her rescuer smiled, his eyes twinkling with amusement at the embarrassment of her plight. 'Oliver, next time offer Miss Harper a hand. It's a big step down off the milk cart for a woman,' he shouted as he smiled at Polly with a knowing look.

'Yes, sir. Will do, sir.' Oliver was quick to talk now.

'You know my name. Thank you for your help.' Polly flattened her skirt down and looked up at the young man, who must be of some importance, judging by the way Oliver had jumped to attention.

'I do indeed. Maggie has told me all about you, and that you are to be looked after, in her absence. She also told me to warn you that Miss Swaine can be a bit of a tartar, and to watch yourself. Anyway, she'll be waiting, so I'd get a move on. Miss Swaine's a stickler for time-keeping.'

'Thank you. I'd expected Maggie to be here.

91

I'd better get a move on, in that case.' Polly stared at the good-looking man in front of her.

'Oi, you watch them kits — the lid nearly came off that one,' he shouted, as another wagonload of milk came into the yard and the delivery man roughly unpacked his load. 'Excuse me, I'll have to go.' He rushed forward to have words with the delivery man, shouting as he crossed the yard.

Polly watched for a second and then realized she didn't know his name. 'What's your name?' she shouted.

'It's Matt. Matt . . . ' The clatter of the milk-kits drowned out his last name and she watched as he squared up to the delivery man, who was swearing at him.

So that was Matt. Maggie had told her all about him and his winning ways. He obviously had manners, because he'd saved her from more blushes as she'd tried to free herself from the cart. Polly looked at her skirt. It was torn and wrinkled, with red markings of rust halfway above the hemline. Thankfully it was at the side of her skirt, so perhaps no one would notice. She brushed it down again and quickly walked the few steps to the wooden doors that led into the main dairy. Immediately the smell of cheese and souring milk assaulted her nostrils, nearly making her stomach hurl. She liked to drink milk, but when it was on the turn, there was no smell worse. The huge empty wooden troughs and baths were now filled with curdled milk, and an army of women was chopping the curds up and draining the whey into buckets for the nearby piggery. Polly held her nose while she watched, as the curdled milk was then salted and put into round wooden tubs lined with fine cheesecloth, then squashed between presses to make a firm cheese.

'So, you've decided to show your face. You were supposed to report to me straight away, not gape at those women making cheese. And you'll have to get used to the smell, if you are to stay working with us.' The tiny form of Beattie Swaine looked at her new employee. 'What have you done to your skirt? You'd think the first day in your employment you could look a bit smarter. You're on the shop's counter: the customer expects you to be smart, and it's our reputation that you are maintaining. It doesn't matter so much for the lasses back, if they aren't smart, but you have to set the standard.' She looked Polly up and down, scrutinizing every inch of her.

'Sorry, Miss Swaine. I got my skirt caught on the cart and . . . ' Polly tried to explain.

'I don't want excuses — excuses mean nothing to me. Now come on through here and I'll show you what I expect of you today.' Miss Swaine obviously didn't listen to anything she didn't want to hear. Her small body set off at a quick pace, past the women making cheese and the huge vat of milk that was supplying them, and through the double doors that led to the shop frontage. 'Right, this is your world for two days a week.' She folded her small hands on the top of her stomach and looked around her and at Polly. 'I presume you know how to churn butter, like all farm lasses do?' Beattie nodded to two huge butter-churns. They were bound wooden barrels on a pivot, with a handle that had to be turned

93

when it was full of cream, until the butter had separated from the buttermilk.

'Yes, I make it for my mother, but only in a small glass churn with wooden paddles that turn when you turn the handle.' Polly looked at the churns; this was going to be back-breaking work, as the churns must hold more than a gallon of cream at a time.

'Well, you get your cream from out of the area we have just walked through. Churn it in one of these, drain the buttermilk from the butter when you know it's separated, and add salt, just like at home. You only need to do this when your stock is low. I then expect you to weigh the butter into pounds, pat it and pattern it, and wrap it in our greaseproof-paper wrapping, which you find under the counter here.'

Beattie Swaine lifted a pile of wrappers out from under the serving shelf. They were all thin leaves of greaseproof with the lettering *Bill Sunter's Finest Yorkshire Butter — the very best from Wensleydale* on them.

'Now, look, this is how you fold them.' Beattie reached for a pound of butter ready-wrapped, from the pile that was at one end of the counter, and nimbly unfolded it from its wrappings and refolded it again. 'You unfold it now — see if you can do it — and then we'll open the shop door. It must be nearly eight.'

Polly nervously held the butter, unwrapped it and wrapped it again. It was easy practising on an already-wrapped packet, as the creases had already been made, but she was sure she would get the hang of it.

'Aye, you look as if you'll make a do of it. Now put yourself an apron on, from behind the door, and you can go and unlock the door.' Beattie put the pound of butter back on the pile, and watched Polly as she put her apron on and walked across the empty shop floor to unbolt the door and turn the sign on the door to 'Open'.

Polly felt nervous. She'd never been under such scrutiny, and she had expected Maggie to be there with her. She climbed the two steps that separated the shop floor from the counter and the way into the dairy, and stood next to Beattie, waiting for her next instructions.

'That churn's full of made butter. I made it myself last night. Now I want you to add some salt to it. I'm not going to say how much — I want you to judge it for yourself. Then I want you to weigh out a pound in weight, pat it with these Scotch hands, and pattern it with the dairy's name with this stencil.' Beattie held up a pair of wooden butterpats and a piece of wood with the name *Bill Sunter* carved in relief on it. 'And then wrap me it, ready for sale. If I'm satisfied, I'll watch you serve a customer.'

Polly looked at her instructor. It was only what she had done at home a thousand times for her mother, but this strict little old woman was putting her off her stride.

'Go on then. Salt's in the barrel, over there. You'll need that big basin on the back shelf, and you can wash your hands with the water in the sink.'

Just then the shop bell rang and the first customer of the day entered the shop. Beattie greeted her, and Polly decided to make her move. She got hold of the heavy earthenware basin and put it on the floor under the churn. Turning the handle so that the churn lid was nearly level with the bowl, she unscrewed the lid and pulled the greasy yellow butter into the bowl, before lifting it up and putting it onto the back shelf. It weighed a ton, and she could hardly lift it. She then made a hollow in the middle of the butter, added a good scoop of salt from the barrel and began to blend it in.

'And how's your old man? I hear he's not been so well. His lumbago's been playing up again, I hear.' Beattie was busy talking, as well as keeping an eye on her new ward.

'Aye, he's not been so good, but it's what you expect at our age.' The customer leaned on the counter and watched Polly, as well as passing the time of day. 'Got a new worker then, Beattie?'

'I have. This is Polly, she's just working for us two days a week. Polly, this is Mrs Ward, she lives over the bridge across from the fosse. If you leave that butter now, I'll have a taste, before you go any further'. Beattie smiled as she watched Polly wash her hands under the tap and Polly acknowledge her customer.

'I don't envy you, Beattie, training a young lass. They have minds of their own nowadays. Young lasses are not like we used to be when we were young. The world's gone mad!'

'It has indeed, Mrs Ward. Do you need anything else this morning?' Beattie waited patiently as Mrs Ward reached for her purse.

'No, that's it, thank you. I'll see you another

day, Polly. Miss Swaine will keep you straight.' After paying for her goods, Mrs Ward made her way out of the shop.

'Thank you, Mrs Ward.' Beattie watched as she closed the door behind her. 'Now, let me sample this butter.' She put a small piece on her finger end and then placed it in her mouth.

Polly held her breath. Had she given it the right amount of salt? She waited while Beattie looked at her with a straight face.

'Aye, that'll do. Your mother's taught you well. We'll keep you for another day. Now let's get it packaged.'

Polly smiled. It was only a little thing, but she was glad she'd proved to the strict Miss Swaine that she could be trusted. She cut and weighed a pound of the rich, creamy butter out onto the scales, and then patted it into shape with the ridged wooden butterpats that Miss Swaine had called 'Scotch hands'. Then she carefully indented the butter with the wooden stamp bearing the name *Bill Sunter* on it, before wrapping it tightly in the greaseproof paper.

'A bit tighter on the corners, but not bad for a first attempt. You'll pass. Now, the price list is here in this drawer. We don't give tick, if anyone asks, but we can deliver. If you run out of cheese, go and ask for Ruby in the back dairy, and she'll bring you more out. You cut and weigh the cheese, just the same as the butter, and wrap it up in greaseproof. If somebody wants cream, they bring their own jug and you measure it out in that quart ladle hanging up above the barrel. What's left in your barrel on an evening you put

97

into the churn to make butter with the following day. Nothing is wasted, and the biggest rule to remember is: the customer is always right.' Beattie rattled off all the dos and don'ts, showing Polly where everything was kept. Polly followed her like a trained dog, nodding her head in agreement to all she said. 'Right, I think I've shown you everything. Anything you want to ask?' The beady-eyed little woman looked at Polly and waited.

'Miss Swaine, I thought Maggie was going to be working with me. Is she not here today?'

'What — the boss's daughter, working in here! Lord help us, we wouldn't have a customer left, she's such a mouth on her.' Beattie laughed out loud. 'She'll be showing her face, no doubt. She likes to make her presence known to the young men in the yard. If she comes in here, you can talk to her, but not for long, mind. And only if we have no customers in. Have I made myself clear?' Beattie looked at Polly's long face.

'Yes, Miss Swaine. I thought she was going to be working with me. I must have misunderstood.'

'Aye, well, happen she led you on. She's not keen on work, isn't that 'un. Takes after her mother, not her father. But there's me, talking out of turn. I shouldn't happen have said that. Now can I leave you to make the rest of that butter into saleable pounds, stack it on the counter, like the rest? If you've time between customers, keep on top of keeping the floor clean. It just looks better than being greeted with muddy footprints.' Beattie looked at the young lass as she closed the door behind her. She'd be all right on her own; a lot better off than working with that flibbertigibbet Maggie. That would never have worked.

★ ★ ★

Polly looked at the shop around her, now that Miss Swaine had gone. It wasn't that big, and the window looking down to the bridge gave her a clear view of customers on their approach to her. The floor was wooden, but freshly varnished, and the walls were whitewashed and clean. All that she wanted was there: butter wrapped and ready for sale, and Wensleydale cheese in huge rounds, ready for cutting or selling whole, in the cabinet on the wall. The only thing that wasn't there was Maggie. Polly was going to have words with her the next time they met, that she was sure of. She set about weighing the butter and patting it into shape, but was soon interrupted by the shop bell tinkling and her first customer.

'Oh, you are a new one. It's usually Beattie that serves me.' Her customer eyed Polly over, as she asked for half a pound of Wensleydale cheese. 'Now whose lass are you? I bet I know your father and mother. I've lived here all my life, and I'm seventy-five now.'

'I'm Polly — Polly Harper from Paradise Farm, down Garsdale.' She cut and weighed the cheese and parcelled it up, smiling at her first customer.

'Now would you be Edmund's lass? But no, wait a minute — they had a lad and he'd be older than you. I'm sure it was a lad?' The old woman looked at her, with her head to one side, reminding Polly of a sparrow about to attack a worm.

'Yes, I'm Edmund's. And Ada's my mother. But I'm definitely not a lad, and I'm the only one.' Polly smiled, passed over the cheese and took her change.

'Aye, it's me, lass. The mind plays tricks when you get to my age. I remember your mother well, now you say her name; she was a right bonny woman when she was younger. Remember me to her. I'm Mrs Ewgill — Edna — she'll know who I am.' The old woman put her cheese in her basket. 'I could have sworn she had a lad,' she muttered, while shaking her head. 'Thank you, dear.' And she closed the door after her.

Polly returned to her butter-packaging, thinking to herself that she never wanted to get to that age, when everything became confusing. Her mother and father had never had a son and, as for her mother being bonny, she had always been covered with wrinkles. Mrs Ewgill must have been thinking of someone else.

The morning went by quickly, with no sign of Maggie, but with Miss Swaine popping back and forth between the dairy and the shop, checking up on Polly's progress. Customers were plentiful, some coming for the first time since the opening more than a week ago, and some returning for a fresh supply of butter, cream and cheese, which Miss Swaine said was a good sign. It was soon lunchtime, and Polly turned over the 'Open/Closed' sign hanging in the shop window with

100

relief. She had half an hour to herself before starting the afternoon shift.

She reached for the battered tin that held her mother's lovingly prepared sandwiches and decided to go and sit out in the early summer sunshine next to the bridge and eat them. She closed the door behind her and walked the short distance to the river bridge, then leaned over watching the foaming waters below, before opening her sandwich tin. Cheese-and-chutney sandwiches; she couldn't believe it. She was sick of the sight of cheese already, and she had only been there for half a day. She smiled as she took a bite, but found the smell of the curdling cheese in the dairy reminding her that she was eating soured milk. She doubted if she'd ever eat cheese again, as she tore her sandwich up into crumbs for a family of ducks below her in the foaming waters.

'Now, my mother would call that a waste.' Her rescuer from earlier in the morning caught her by surprise, as she watched the ducks fight over the last remaining crusts. 'Let me guess: they were cheese, and you couldn't face them?'

'How did you know?' Polly turned round, embarrassed that she had been found throwing away good food, when it was hard-earned.

'Because it's the good, staple diet of all us farmers. That and eggs, I don't know which I hate the most: the smell of cheese in the making, or that of stinky boiled eggs. You'll get used to the smell of curds and rennet in a bit, and think nothing of it, then soon go back to eating cheese. How are you finding your first day then? Beattie

101

got you working hard?' The tall blond man smiled and lit a cigarette.

'Aye, she has that, but at least she leaves me to it, so I must look as if I can be trusted. She speaks her mind, though, doesn't she? I don't think she reckons much to my friend Maggie, even though she is the boss's daughter!' Polly looked at her companion. He was about her age, but acted as if he was a man of the world, in his smart tweed suit and polished brogues. She watched as he smoked his cigarette and leaned back on the arch of the bridge.

'So, you're friends with Maggie. Well, don't boast about it to old Beattie. She can't stand the lass, and calls her a trollop out of earshot, because Maggie's always flirting with the fellas. That's all she does, like. They wouldn't dare touch her, with her being the boss's daughter.'

'And what do you think of her . . . ? Er, I'm sorry, I didn't catch your name this morning, for the noise of the kits being unloaded.' Polly watched as he stubbed out his cigarette butt under his foot.

'Just call me Matt — everybody else does. Your mate Maggie's all right, just a bit forward. Fellas prefer their women shy and modest, or most of us do.' He looked at Polly and noticed her blushing, as he explained what he thought men wanted.

'Well, I wouldn't know. But Maggie does have a mind of her own. And she told me she was going to work with me, and she's nowhere to be seen. I'm a bit cross with her really. She said she would be working with me.' Polly was trying hard to forgive her friend for not being that honest with her.

'Never mind, Polly. It's her loss. Look, we are having a good natter and getting to know one another — that's what counts.' Matt leaned over the bridge and looked down into the water. 'By, the ducks are hungry buggers. Do you think anyone would miss one of 'em, if I caught it for me and my gran's dinner?' Matt leaned on his elbows and smiled at Polly, who was leaning over the bridge right next to him.

'You can't do that — they are too bonny. Besides, you'd never catch them!' Polly was horrified.

'Don't ever say 'no' or 'never' to me. I don't know the meaning of either word, and it's like a red rag to a bull, especially coming from such a bonny lass as you.' Matt grinned at Polly's horrified face, showing his sparkling set of white teeth, which matched his fresh good looks.

'Well, you'd better not go near them, else I'll tell Beattie. And if that doesn't work, I'll tell Bill Sunter.' Polly looked crossly at him, a frown puckering her brow.

'Do you really think I'd go down there and wring the neck of a duck, for my supper? Nay, I'm not like that. I was joking, Polly. I'm a soft lump really. Besides, they'll be as tough as old boots, they will. I bet they've been here since this bridge was built.' Matt grinned at his new friend with the temper; she was a bonny lass, with her long dark hair.

'Oh! I don't know why I've bothered talking to you, you're just a tease.' Polly picked up her

103

packing box and started walking back towards the shop, as her half-hour had nearly finished.

Matt ran after her and caught her arm. 'Share dinner with you tomorrow — same time, same place — Polly?' He brought her walk to a halt as he tugged on her arm, and smiled as she turned round.

'I don't know. Why? But yes, go on then. At least you are someone my age to talk to, and not nearly knocking on death's door, like half my customers have been this morning.' Polly sighed, but secretly she was smiling on the inside. She'd found a friend, and it was without the help of Maggie, who she knew would be furious with her, for making a friend without her.

'See you tomorrow then, and if it's raining I'll meet you in the shop's doorway. All right?' Matt grinned.

Polly nodded. 'Yes, but let me go now, else I'll be late, and I don't want to suffer the wrath of Miss Swaine.'

Matt watched as Polly turned the shop sign around and closed the door behind her. She was a grand lass, and that show of ankle had just enthralled him this morning, making him want to know Polly Harper a little better.

★   ★   ★

'I turn my back one minute to go shopping with my mam, and you chat up the best-looking fella in the dairy. It just isn't right, I've been after him since my father took him on, last month.' Maggie was furious, and her faced showed it, as she

104

scowled at Polly from the other side of the cheese counter.

'It's not like that. We are only going to meet and share lunch. Besides, you told me a whopper when you said you were going to be working here, so you needn't look so innocent.' Polly carried on with weighing out the butter she had churned earlier, slapping it down into the paper wrapper with force, as she started to lose patience with her friend's annoyance over her new friendship with Matt.

'Aye, but I had to tell you that, or else you'd never have left your mother's apron strings. And I could see that you were slowly going mad on that godforsaken farm. So I was thinking of you, and then you go and nick my Matt!' Maggie pulled a face at Polly and then placed a small square of cheese in her mouth, from the complimentary samples on the counter.

'Hey, those are for customers! I haven't nicked him, and besides I didn't see a label around his neck saying, 'I'm Matt, I belong to Maggie.'' Polly was going to stand her ground on this one, as she knew just how jealous Maggie could get.

'Listen to you. Only been here a day and a half and already telling me, the boss's daughter, what to do! Anyway I'm not bothered. There's plenty more fish in the sea, and he's only a farm lad anyway, I need someone with their own business and money.' Maggie leaned on the counter and idly placed another square of cheese in her mouth, smiling at the perplexed Polly. 'There's a dance at the end of the month in the market hall. Will your mother and father let you come, or will you have to stay at home like a good little girl?' Maggie taunted her friend, and knew that her words would get the right answer.

'I'll do what I please. I might come. Now that I'm working, I'm old enough to make my own mind up. I don't have to ask my parents for everything,' Polly spat back.

'Well, if Mummy and Daddy give you permission, you can stay at ours,' she said sarcastically. 'Then we can stay there until the band stops playing. They are blinking good. It's the Beresford Band — they play all the best songs — and you could ask Matt!' Maggie smiled sweetly at Polly. There was more than one way to catch her man, and Maggie knew exactly how to do it.

'I'll see.' Polly wasn't going to be bullied. The thought of going to her first dance excited her, but she wasn't going to let Maggie know that. She could just wait. Besides, Maggie was only using her to get at Matt, and well she knew it.

'When you young ladies have finished arranging your private lives, this floor needs a sweep, Polly. And while you are at it, clean the windows. You'll find a cloth under the counter.' Beattie stepped into the shop from out the back of the dairy and gave a disdainful look at Maggie, who was admiring herself in the reflection of the glass windows.

Polly quickly picked up the sweeping brush and set to sweeping the floor, after acknowledging her orders.

'And what can we do for you, Miss Sunter? Or have you just come to pass the time of day with us?' Beattie gave Maggie a cutting smile, which told her in no uncertain terms that she was not welcome.

'I was just on my way, Beattie. I'd just come to see how the new girl was doing. I thought I could report my findings to my father. I'll be going now.' Maggie smiled at the tartar of an old maid, before opening and closing the door behind her.

'That girl is such a madam. Spoilt, that's what she is. Calling me 'Beattie'. You always respect your elders. I'm Miss Swaine to the likes of her. Think on, Polly. Manners cost nothing.'

'Yes, Miss Swaine.' Polly stifled a giggle as she watched Maggie pulling faces outside at Beattie, whilst she cleaned the window.

'She's common, that one is, just like her mother.' Beattie looked around the shop and, finding all in order, stepped back into the dairy.

Maggie pressed her nose against the shop window and shouted, 'Don't forget to ask your mother and father about the dance. It'll be a right laugh!'

Polly nodded as she quickly wiped away a smear. It would be lovely, but would her parents agree? She'd never been to a dance before — let alone out in Hawes of a night, without her parents. But it sounded exciting, and perhaps Matt would be there. And, even more enthralling, perhaps Tobias Middleton would be there, the charming dark-haired man who had taken her heart, from the day she'd talked to him along Mallerstang Edge.

7

'Aye, I don't know, Father. She'll be with that Maggie, and you know what her and her mother's like.' Ada stood at the kitchen sink, gazing out into the yard, worried to death about the fact that she and Edmund had given in to Polly's pleas, and that Polly was to attend the dance in the market hall at Hawes that evening.

'Now, Ada, how many dances did you attend when you were younger? I remember seeing you at many a village hall, dancing the night away. In fact we met at Lund's School Hall. Do you remember? You'd only be a bit older than our Polly. Such a bonny lass you were, you caught my eye straight away.' Edmund cast his mind back to his early years when things seemed simpler.

'Aye, and my father warned me of you; said you were a wild 'un, and that I could do better for myself.' Ada smiled as she wiped the breakfast pots and thought of the dances she'd attended and the hearts she could have had.

'Aye, well, he would say that. Fathers always think their daughters should have better. Anyway, your father was an awkward old stick. I would do nowt, and even that would be wrong.' Edmund supped the last dregs of his tea and passed Ada his cup.

'And my mother worshipped you. That got my father even more narked, especially when you used to come to Sunday dinner and he had to sit and look at you holding my hand.' Ada smiled, remembering how that had seemed so risky, in her parents' company.

'Aye, so you see, Polly has to start somewhere. And she's a lump older than we both were, when we started going to dances. She'll be right, our lass. Maggie and her will stick together, and Bill Sunter says it's right that she stops with them the night.' Edmund stood in the doorway, watching Polly hang out the washing in the summer sunshine in the small adjoining paddock. The sheets and shirts flapped in the wind, along with her long black hair. 'I take it she's learned to dance?'

'Aye, we've hummed tunes together and I've taught her the basic steps. She's quite light on her feet.' Ada joined him at the doorway.

'And a frock? Has she got a frock?'

'She's going in the one your Evie sent her from Liverpool. That green taffeta one that sets off the colour of her hair.' Ada linked her arm through Edmund's.

'She'll look right bonny in that. Our lil lass is growing up, Mother. Her first job, and her first dance. Next thing we know, a lad will be coming courting. It's been on the cards for some time now.' Edmund watched as Polly turned and smiled at them both.

'I know. I just hope he doesn't break her heart. Although you have to have your heart broken, before you know you have the right man for you. Mine was broken several times before you turned up, and it didn't do me any harm; just

made me more determined to find the right one.'
Ada squeezed Edmund's hand tight.

'Give over, Mother. Anybody would think we
were still courting, not married these last forty
years.'

'Edmund Harper, you never were one for
showing your emotions. No wonder I nearly ran
off with Fred Turner — you always were slow to
kiss me.' Ada pulled her hand away.

'Whisht, Mother, our Polly's coming back in.
And besides, Fred Turner wasn't up to much.
Your father would never have put up with him.'

'That's what you think, Edmund Harper.
Maybe I regret being married to a miserable old
devil,' Ada teased.

'Nay, tha doesn't. You wouldn't have all this, if
you'd have married him.' Edmund held his hand
out and looked around the homely kitchen.

'And I wouldn't have had the worry.' Ada
stopped in mid-conversation as Polly came into
the kitchen, bringing the smell of the fresh
summer's day back in with her basket of
washing.

'What worry? You're not both still worrying
about this dance? I'll be fine. How can I not be?
I'm only stopping at the Sunters'.' She put the
empty wicker washing basket back on the kitchen
shelf and smiled at her parents. She couldn't hide
her joy at the thought of attending her first
proper dance.

'Just as long as you're careful, our Pol. Don't
let that Sunter lass turn your head. She's such a
devil for the fellas,' said Ada.

'She'll be fine, Mother. She's got a sensible

head on her shoulders, has our Polly.' Edmund patted her. 'I'll take you up to Hawes about six, Polly. I'm just going to weed some thistles out in the top pasture, before they flower and go to seed. I wish the hay-meadow was growing as quick as them weeds. Stuff never does as it should.' Edmund left his two women in the kitchen. He knew that Ada would be feeding Polly with dos and don'ts all day. The poor lass would be glad to be out of earshot, by the time evening came along.

★　★　★

The day couldn't go quickly enough for Polly, but it was finally time to climb up beside her father, with her overnight bag on her knee, and set off in the horse and gig to Hawes. It was a beautiful summer's evening as the old horse trotted at a decent pace along the open valley. The sun shone on the vivid green of the early summer leaves, and insects buzzed busily, collecting pollen before the onset of night.

'By, you don't often get many evenings like this, but when you do, it feels grand to be alive.' Edmund flicked his whip, hardly touching the flanks of his faithful horse, Clover.

'It is — it's a lovely evening. The sun's still warm on my face.' Polly smiled and closed her eyes, soaking up the warmth of the day.

'Aye, and there are you, all excited at your first dance, and looking as bonny as anything I've ever seen. Now, I know your mother will have lectured you all day, but you watch what you are

111

doing tonight. It doesn't take much to egg us fellas on and, before you know it, you are in trouble.' Edmund felt embarrassed, but it was his duty to say something.

'Father ... I know! My mother's never stopped telling me all day. I'm not daft, you know.' Polly could feel herself blushing. Her father never talked of womanly things. Neither did her mother really, so she knew they were worried about her.

'Well, you just have a good night then, and I wish I was as young and had a bit of a thing like you on my arm. I'd be as proud as punch.' Edmund slowed Clover down as they climbed the slight incline into Hawes, passing the road to Dent Head and the school, making their way past an already busy market hall, down the cobbles to the house next to the new dairy where Maggie lived. 'I'll not come in. I'm sure you lasses will have plenty to talk about. Think on what I said, and I'll pick you up in the morning.' Edmund helped Polly down from the gig and watched as she knocked, heaving a sigh as she entered the house, giggling with Maggie. He knew they couldn't keep her forever, but for tonight, Lord keep her safe.

'Just look at you, Polly, don't you scrub up well?' Maggie added blusher to her cheeks and pulled at her neckline, revealing a little bit too much, as she admired herself in the mirror. 'Where did you get your dress from? It's not my colour, and the style is a bit ... let's say out of date, but it suits you.' She squeezed her lips together and added another layer of lipstick while Polly sat on the edge of her newly made-up bed.

'I don't bother with all that stuff. You don't need it, when you are our age.' Polly watched Maggie preening herself. She wasn't going to let her friend's sarcastic remarks get her down tonight.

'Clearly you don't. If you want to attract the men, you've got to show them you are on the market.' Maggie giggled.

'I'm not on the market, and I'm not bothered about a man. I just want to have a good time.' Polly played with the strings of her little draw-string bag, which held her purse and her essentials for the night ahead, and ignored Maggie's comment.

'Exactly, let's show them men what they could have, Pol. I'm going to dance the night away with every man in Hawes. I'll show that bloody Ralph what he's missing, because he's bound to be there tonight. Come on then, stop playing with that bloody bag and let's go get 'em. It's eight o'clock — the church clock's just chimed. We've only got four hours of dancing.' Maggie pulled on Polly's hand, dragging her off the bed, and ran with her down the stairs, slamming the front door behind them as they both ran giggling up the cobbled street to the hall.

Maggie and Polly ran up the small set of steps and reached into their bags for entrance money, as the man on the door asked for payment in return for a ticket. He watched the two girls impatiently, as they giggled and looked around the hall before passing over their money. The hall

113

was packed full of Dales folk, who had all come to dance and listen to the local Beresford Band, who were popular with everyone. There was a division in the hall between the couples, the single women and the single men. The single men looked bashful, standing at one side of the hall, and the single women stood giggling at the other. Both eyed one another up, but didn't dare make a move this early in the night.

'Come on, Polly, let's get a drink, and then we'll sit over there and see who's here.' Maggie pulled on Polly's hand, leading her across the partly empty dance floor, making Polly feel uncomfortable, as people on both sides of the room watched the two young women. 'Did you see Matt? Matt's here, he's talking to Joe Fothergill. I saw him looking at us when we crossed the floor.' Maggie dipped a small glass cup into a large bowl of punch and passed it to Polly.

'What's this?' Polly looked at the cup of drink that had been given to her.

'It's like fruit juice, but it makes you giggle and dance better — you'll enjoy it.' Maggie grinned and sipped a big mouthful, while wiggling her bottom in time to the music, casting a glance over to Matt and his friend.

'Uh! It's terrible.' Polly took a mouthful of the punch and shuddered at the taste of alcohol in it.

'Don't be such a baby. And drink up, the first mouthful is always a shock, and then it gets better.' Maggie took another swig of hers and then waved candidly to Matt, who ignored her completely.

Polly took another mouthful. It did go down better, but she still wasn't convinced that she'd feel better for drinking it. She then looked over at Matt and his friend Joe, who were both looking at her, not Maggie. She felt herself blush as Joe smiled at her and then waved enthusiastically, before whispering something to Matt.

'Suit yourself, snooty Matt, you'll want me before the night is out.' Maggie took another big mouthful of punch and pulled on Polly's arm to join her. 'Come on, we'll stand halfway down the room, so we can see everything. Just look at the lead singer, isn't he handsome in his dinner suit? I think he farms over in Hubberholme.' Maggie flashed her eyes at the lead singer as he gently finished singing 'The Boy I Love'.

'And now, ladies and gentlemen, to save my voice for the rest of the evening, would you kindly find your partners for the St Bernard's Waltz.' The singer made his way down from the stage as the band played loudly and with style, and both sides of the room came alive in a frenzy to find a partner for the easy waltz.

'May I?' The singer from the band held his hand out to an eager Maggie, who giggled and left Polly without a second glance.

Polly looked at the good-looking man, with his slicked-back black hair and small, dark moustache that turned upwards with his dashing smile, as he whisked Maggie onto the floor. She could hear Maggie laughing above the music, and the traditional stomp of the feet that the rhythm and dance determined. She knew this dance would be Maggie's highlight of the night, and that she'd talk of nothing else the next day. She sat down in one of the hall's little wooden chairs and watched the couples dancing. She felt like a wallflower; she hardly knew anybody here and her dancing skills were limited. Her mother had taught her the basics in the front room of home, but everyone looked as if they had been dancing for years, as she sat and watched the neat footwork of the dancers. She glanced up as she noticed Matt coming towards her.

'Has she left you already? She's a flibbertigibbet. Just look at her making eyes at Tom Beresford. He'll have danced with every young lass in all the Dales — and he has a wife with three bairns at home.' Matt bent down, squatting on his knees, as he talked to Polly.

'She's just Maggie — she's always got her eye on a man.' Polly took a drink of her punch and looked at Matt. He was a good-looking man, and even more so tonight, with a crisp white shirt tucked into his tweed trousers, and a brass collar stud that caught the light from the numerous candles around the hall. She blushed, as her thoughts for the man beside her got the better of her, and the warmth of the alcohol made her feel aglow.

'You don't want too many of them — you'll feel sick as a dog in the morning. I'm sticking to my bottle of beer. At least I know what's in it.' Matt chinked his bottle next to her small glass of punch and smiled, before taking a long swig out of the bottle that he held in his hand.

'Don't worry — I won't. I don't even like it. I'm only drinking it because Maggie gave it to me.' Polly nearly had to shout above the sound of the people dancing and the music, and Matt leaned nearer to hear what she was saying. It was the closest she had ever been to a man, besides her family, and she felt her heart flutter as he shouted in her ear.

'Do you want to dance? I've two left feet, but you can't go wrong with a waltz.'

Polly nodded her head and stood up, holding Matt's hand tight, and he put his arm around her waist. 'I've two left feet as well,' she apologized, as the first few steps were taken and toes were stood upon. She ran her hand over Matt's shoulder and smelt the familiar scent of the washing soap that his mother must have used to wash his shirt, and wondered what his home was like. She felt like a princess in his arms, and he was her prince, as they made their way around the dance floor of the market hall. Matt's arms were strong and his voice gentle and, contrary to his confession of not being able to dance, it was like being whisked around the room on a cloud. He kept smiling at her, and Polly blushed at his every word as one dance followed another. She could dance to anything, with him on her arm; and dance all night, if she had to. Polly cared nothing for the crowd that was watching them, as they waltzed and foxtrotted the hours away. She was enjoying herself with Matt, and that was all that mattered.

Out of the corner of her eye, as she floated around the hall, she noticed the unmistakable face of Tobias Middleton. His brooding stare watched her as she danced a circle of the hall, happy in the arms of Matt. Polly's heart sank as she saw the frown on his forehead when she twirled past him, and saw on the next lap that he had disappeared. She tried to smile at Matt as he whispered something in her ear, but her heart felt heavy. Tobias held a spell on her, whether he knew it or not, and even Matt's safe arms could not break it.

'Polly, I have to go. I promised my grandmother to be home by eleven. She'll be waiting for me, and she'll only worry if I'm not on time,' Matt whispered in her ear as the music ended, only for it to start up again with another, louder number. He held her hand tight and lingered a bit, before relinquishing his hold on her fingertips. 'Will you be all right? I can't see Maggie. Happen she's in the ladies' room.'

'I'll be fine.' Polly could have cried. Up until that moment she had hoped to see the night out by dancing with Matt, and now she was left the wallflower again. And as for Maggie, she'd hardly seen her all evening.

'I'll have to go, Pol. My grandmother's on her own, and she'll no doubt worry. I'll see you at work on Monday.'

'Yes, you go. Don't worry about me, I'll be fine.' Polly squeezed his hand in thanks and smiled at the beautiful blue eyes that she'd gazed into all night.

'See you then. Behave yourself.' Matt grinned and then pushed his way through the dancing crowd, leaving Polly standing alone in the corner of the dance hall.

She'd expected a kiss on the cheek at least, or

would that have been too daring for a first night? She put her head down, feeling a tear welling up, as she felt abandoned. Stupid woman, she said to herself, get on with it and get yourself another drink. You hardly know Matt, so why should he stay with you until the end of the dance? She looked at the doorway, half-hoping for Tobias to be standing there, beckoning her to join him in a dance. She sighed, feeling like such a hussy; she was going from the arms of one man and hoping to be held in another's. Her mother would be ashamed of her.

'Some friend you are, dancing with Matt all night. I saw you making eyes at him, when you know I fancied him something rotten. Besides, you can't have . . . ' Maggie pulled on her arm, as Polly helped herself to another small drink of punch from the nearly empty serving bowl. Maggie's words drifted away on the air as the band played louder.

'You were dancing with Tom Beresford. Besides, Matt and me are only friends — there's nothing in it.' Polly looked at her red-faced friend; Maggie's complexion matched her hair, and there was spite in her voice.

'Nah, you did it to get back at me, for not working in my father's poxy shop. I watched you, all lovey-dovey, smiling at one another. You needn't think you are coming home with me tonight. You can go to his place to sleep.' Maggie was angry with jealousy and drink, and her eyes blazed as she pushed Polly's arm off hers.

'Don't be stupid, Maggie, I'm coming home with you. Where else can I go?'

'To hell, perhaps. Now bugger off and leave me alone.' Maggie wasn't listening to sense, as she struggled to walk straight across the dance hall.

Polly watched as Maggie went up onto the stage and pulled on Tom Beresford's sleeve to join her. He didn't take much persuading, and she walked out of the dance hall on his arm. She looked around the dance hall. People were staring at her, wondering what the commotion was about. What a night!

And now where was she to go? She looked up at the huge clock face that hung on the wall of the whitewashed hall. It was a quarter to midnight. She didn't want to see the last dance, with no one on her arm and no bed to go to. It was time to go home. She'd walk back home — the moon was bright enough to see her way back down into Grisedale. It would only take an hour to walk back down the dale.

She went past the couples dancing and made her way down the steps, giving a backward glance at the market hall as she walked through the street of Hawes. Leaning against the outside of the market hall she could see her friend Maggie in a tight embrace with Tom Beresford, his hands placed where no honourable man would place them. No good would come of that night's work, Polly was sure of it.

Climbing up out of Hawes, she stood for a moment and listened to the floating lyrics of 'After the Ball is Over' and thought how true they were, as she hummed the next line: 'Many a heart is broken, after the ball.' At least she now knew that Maggie was no friend, or at least not to be trusted when she'd had a drink. She bent down and took her tightly laced heeled shoes off. She could walk faster without heels on her feet. The dark shape of Stagg's Fell stood in front of her, and an owl hooted as she hummed to herself to keep her spirits up. It was darker than she had expected and there was a sneaky chill in the air. Perhaps she should turn back and go and knock on Maggie's parents' door? But pride and stubbornness set in. No, she wasn't going to be treated like that. She'd walk home, no matter what; she would not go snivelling to Maggie Sunter. She picked up her skirts, rubbed her feet and set out, more determined now. It was just as she approached the halfway houses that she heard the sound of horses coming down the road. She stood to one side to let them and their rider past.

'Whoa there!' a voice called out to the pair of horses that were pulling a dimly lit carriage. It pulled up next to Polly, causing the dust from the dry road to catch in her throat. The carriage door flew open and the driver alighted.

'I saw you at the dance. But why are you walking home on your own, at this time of night?' Tobias Middleton stood next to her, blending into the night as if he belonged to it.

'I didn't see you. I didn't know you were there.' Polly coughed, trying to hide her lie. For the second time she felt herself vulnerable and alone in the presence of Tobias.

'Clearly you didn't, as you only had eyes for the young man you were dancing with. I left to go and have a drink at the Crown, I was so disappointed to see you in his arms. He, however, can't be a gentleman, else he wouldn't let you walk this road at this time of night.'

'He is a gentleman, but he had to go home to his grandmother. And Maggie, my friend, was jealous and wouldn't let me stop at her house. That's why I'm walking home.'

'Well, it's not safe for you to be on this road at this time of night. Let me take you home. Get in the carriage.' Tobias held out his hand to Polly.

Polly hesitated, not wanting to be rude by saying no. But the rumours about Tobias's father were still strong in the dale, and it was said that Tobias had surely inherited his ways.

'I'm fine, thank you. I'll make my own way home,' she said politely.

'What, with no light, no shoes on your feet and another good three miles to walk, and plenty of drunken fools roaming the roads? Do you think that wise?' Tobias stood and held his horse's reins, waiting for an answer.

'I prefer to walk.' Polly picked up her skirt and started to walk past the side of the impatient horses.

'Then I'll walk with you. It will give us time to become acquainted. And perhaps, by then, I will have convinced you not to believe the wagging tongues of the local gossips and you'll find me the perfect gentleman. Perhaps you'll realize that I just want to know you as a friend.' Tobias pulled on the lead horse and walked beside Polly.

'You are impossible! You needn't walk all the way home with me. And I don't listen to gossip.

'I've learned that it is only half-true, no matter what anyone says.' Polly stopped in her tracks.

'Only half-true, Miss Harper? Well, how about I whisk you away — home, may I hasten to add. And leave out of tonight having my evil way with you. You know, I really don't take after my father, no matter what people say.' Tobias smiled and held out his hand for Polly to climb into his carriage.

In the dim light of the carriage Polly saw Tobias's smile and realized that, no matter what she said, he was going to see her home — safely, she hoped.

'Very well, I give in. I'll take you up on your offer of a lift home, but I alight at the bridge. You've no need to take me all the way home.' Polly took his hand and felt her heart flutter as Tobias gently helped her into the carriage, remembering the first time she had met him and seen his dashing good looks.

'Believe me, Polly, I have no wish to meet your father in the cold hours of early morning with a shotgun in his hand, accusing me of abducting his daughter.' Tobias closed the carriage door. 'I'll sit up aloft, and then you'll know that you are safe. Half an hour and you'll be home and safe in your bed.' The carriage swung as Tobias climbed onto the driving seat, and then the team was whipped into action.

Polly sat back in the darkness of the cab. She could be being taken anywhere, and she wouldn't have known from the darkness outside. But now she trusted Tobias. She even felt sorry for him. People were so fast to judge you by your family, and he was nothing at all like his father. Still, she wouldn't tell her parents how she had arrived home. It was best they didn't know. She'd tell them she'd walked, and suffer the consequences of that.

★　★　★

Polly opened the kitchen door. The house was silent, the warmth from the banked-up coal fire hitting her as she warmed herself by its light, before climbing up the stairs to bed. Her head was full of the night's happenings: memories of being swept off her feet by Matt; and of Maggie and her horrid, spiteful ways and her loose morals when it came to Tom Beresford. No wonder men thought of her as a tart. And then of the gallant Tobias, who had saved her aching feet, and perhaps more. She'd edit what she told her parents in the morning. What they didn't know wouldn't hurt them, and it was bad enough she had to say why she was home. She yawned and pulled on her nightdress. It was good to be home. She snuggled down into her feather bed and smiled. Now, which man was the best? No doubt time would tell her, but at that moment her head was filled with thoughts of both of them.

8

'Aye, that Maggie — she'll get herself in bother yet.' Ada listened as Polly told her how Maggie had been the worse for drink, and so she had decided to walk home.

'I don't think she knew what she was drinking, Mother, that was her problem. She thought it wasn't an alcoholic punch. Else I'm sure she wouldn't have been in such a state.' Polly folded the tea-towel and looked innocent as she tried to excuse her friend's actions, knowing all too well that Maggie had known what she was doing.

'She's like her mother. I'm just glad you walked back home, and that you were safe. It was a bit of a daft thing to do, but you came to no harm. You don't bother with that lass again, do you hear?'

'No, Mother, she went too far this time. It's a good job she isn't working with me tomorrow, else it could have been embarrassing. I'll have to pick up my overnight bag from her house, though, so I'll have to talk to her.' Polly felt sick at the thought of having to knock on the door of Bill Sunter's house, but she needed her few possessions back. 'I'll go in my dinner hour.'

'Aye, and if her mother asks why you didn't stop, tell her straight. Maggie's not too big to get away from having a good hiding. It's what she's been short of.' Ada sat down and gasped slightly. Just lately she had been feeling under the weather, and a niggling pain down her arm would not go away.

'Are you all right, Mother, you look a bit white?' Polly watched her mother as she caught her breath and sat back in the kitchen chair.

'Aye, I'm all right. I think I've pulled a muscle or something, when I was gardening the other day. I keep getting a pain in my chest and down my arm. Old age, Polly — I forget how old I am. It'll go in a minute.' Ada smiled at Polly as she pulled out the stool and placed her mother's legs on it. 'You're a good lass, I don't know what we'd do without you.'

'You'd be a lot better off, I bet — a lot less worried — if I weren't about.' Polly passed her mother a cup of tea and placed it by her side.

'Nay, lass, never say that. You were a shock to us when you landed, but we'd not send you back now.' Ada smiled and closed her eyes, thinking of the day that Polly had arrived underneath the thick overcoat of Bernard Dinsdale in a snowstorm, while Polly thought of the shock of her mother giving birth when she thought she was well past the age of having children.

Polly looked at her mother, with her eyes closed. Her grey hair was almost white now and she looked so tired. Lately Ada seemed to have lost her fight. A few months back she would have wanted to know everything about Polly's night. But this morning she had got off lightly with the inquisition, which she was thankful for.

★ ★ ★

126

Monday morning came quickly, and Polly's stomach was churning with the thought of the possibility of seeing the fierce Maggie. Adding to her anguish were butterflies at the thought of seeing Matt, after their night of dancing together.

After entering the dairy's yard, she climbed down from the cart; she'd given over expecting a hand down from Oliver Simms, and jumped down the last few inches on her own.

'Pol. Pol! Did you have a good night? I'm sorry I left you, but I'd to get home to my grandmother. She doesn't like being left on her own at the moment — it's not long since my grandfather died. I live with her, you see.' Matt came running across the yard, his jacket flapping as he hurried to talk to Polly.

'I had a lovely night, thanks, Matt. You don't have to explain. You did right to go back to your grandmother. Family is precious. My mother's not so well at the moment. My father is trying to convince her to go to the doctor tomorrow in Hawes, but she's not having any of it.' Polly looked up at Matt, remembering the way he'd held her, and the smell of him as she'd placed her head on his shoulder.

'I'll make up for it. How about I take you home tonight? I'll tell Simms I'll do his evening run. He'll appreciate a few more hours with his family. I hope your mother's all right. Your father does right to take her to the doctor.' Matt held Polly's hand tight. 'I've thought of nothing else but you all day yesterday. My gran thought I was drunk, because I kept smiling so much.' His eyes

127

twinkled as he watched Polly blush.

'Polly, have you come to work or to catch up on your social life?' The voice of Beattie Swaine yelled across the yard for all to hear, making everyone look at the couple in their intimate moment, as their hands parted with reluctance.

'Coming, Miss Swaine.' Polly looked back as Matt whispered, 'Tonight, I'll be waiting' and then ran quickly through the dairy doors.

Matt stood watching Polly as she disappeared. It was true; he'd thought of nowt else but the lass in his arms that he'd danced the night away with, and her long, black hair hanging down her back, cascading onto the emerald green of her swishing dress. The way she smiled, the way she talked . . . He was bewitched and was determined not to lose her to anyone else, ever.

★ ★ ★

The morning dragged for Polly. Her arm ached from churning a full churn of milk, and the shop had been so busy, but finally her lunchtime came and she turned the 'Closed' sign on the door for her half-hour break. Her stomach told of her nerves as she knocked on the door of Maggie's house and waited for a reply.

'We wondered if you would have the nerve to show your face on our doorstep, you little hussy.' Maggie's mother answered the door and stood on the doorstep making her less-than-cordial greeting. 'If it had been up to me, Bill would have sacked you this morning. Leaving our Maggie alone all night, after getting her in such a state. If I was your mother, I'd be ashamed of you. Our Maggie's been sick all yesterday with crying over you.' Jenny Sunter's face was fuming. 'My poor little darling, she doesn't need friends like you.'

'I'm sorry, Mrs Sunter, but it wasn't like that. I think if you ask her again, you'll find it was more the other way round, and that's why I walked home.' Polly wasn't going to be accused of doing something she didn't do, no matter how distraught Mrs Sunter was.

'Walked home, walked home — you didn't walk home. Maggie told me you stopped the night with one of our yardmen, you little slut, leaving her all alone. Here, take your bag of stuff, and don't bother calling on our Maggie again.' Jenny reached inside the room and passed Polly her bag from the nearby table. 'My Bill might employ you, but I'm fussy who comes into my house.' With her last parting words Jenny closed the door in Polly's face, leaving Polly nearly in tears as she held her small bag of overnight possessions.

She clutched her bag to her and clenched her knuckles until they turned white. She was no slut! Maggie, however, was. She'd been there at the side of the hall with her skirt around her waist, enjoying sex with a married man. How dare she turn this around on Polly, without taking any blame.

A tear welled up in her eye, but she wouldn't let it fall. She knew the truth. Matt had never even kissed her, let alone tried to do anything else. She wiped her face, and walked away for what she deemed to be the last time from the Sunters' house. She didn't need friends like Maggie. And besides, she had Matt now and, what's more, Maggie didn't.

★   ★   ★

'What's up, Polly?' Beattie had watched her protégée struggle at work all day. The butter had nearly been slapped to death with the Scotch hands and the customers hadn't had a smile all day. 'It's nearly home-time now. I hope you come back in a better mood with yourself tomorrow.' Beattie covered the cut cheese and placed it under the glass counter, ready for the next day.

'I will, Miss Swaine. It's just that Maggie . . . ' Polly started to explain her mood.

'Don't mention that lass to me. Anything she says or does is always too outrageous for me to think about. If you've fallen out with her, forget about her. She's nothing but trouble, like I keep telling you.'

'I know, but she's told her mother and father I've done all sorts that I wouldn't even dream of, let alone do.' Polly untied her apron and hung it up behind the door. 'If folk believe it, they'll think I'm terrible.'

'If you haven't done owt, you've nothing to bother about. Let folk think what they want. And her father knows Maggie. He'll have taken with a pinch of salt all that his flighty wife and that spoilt Maggie say. He's not a bad man, is Bill Sunter, so give over fretting and get yourself

130

back home. It'll be Tuesday in the morning and the shop will be heaving, so let's have a smile back on your face.' Beattie watched as Polly pulled on her shawl and picked up her bag, which she'd collected from the Sunters'.

'I'll be fine tomorrow. I just don't appreciate so-called friends that lie.' Polly smiled.

'No, lass, I don't either, so she's a fight on with two of us. I hear that Matt, out of the yard, is taking you home tonight, so get yourself home with him. And you just take care with him. A young lad's fancy sometimes gets the better of him.' Beattie watched as Polly blushed and pulled the door behind her.

Beattie had heard the gossip that Maggie had spitefully spread, but she knew it was wrong. It was Maggie who had wanted Matt in her bed, and instead he'd made eyes at Polly. She was a spiteful bit of stuff, that one; and she'd told Bill Sunter that, when he'd asked about Polly's moral values. She'd told him to look at his own lass, before preaching about others. Polly was worth two of Maggie, and well he knew it. Still, there must be a bit of something between her and Matt, as Oliver Simms had made it common knowledge that Matt was taking her home tonight. She smiled. They'd make a lovely couple. She hoped they'd be happy together, and that life would treat them kindly. Sometimes it was hard being a dried-up old spinster. Perhaps, if she had her life over again, there would be a Matt for her somewhere. Instead, it was home for her, supper for one and a saucer of milk for the cat. She closed the door and pulled her shawl on. The dairy was still at work, but her day was done.

★ ★ ★

Polly climbed up onto the milk cart next to Matt, who offered his hand in help. She smiled at him as she wrapped her shawl around her and he jolted the horses into action, without a word said between them until they left the prying ears of the dairy. All the way down the dale they talked of their day, and of how much they had enjoyed one another's company; of how upset Polly had been with Maggie, and how Beattie had stuck up for her. The sun shone on the young couple, and the buzz of bees and dragonflies from the nearby stream filled the air as a gentle summer wind blew on their fair faces. They were a couple who were quickly falling in love with one another, and they both knew it.

Their arrival at the bridge came all too soon, as Matt brought the horses and cart to a halt.

'Right, here we are, Pol. I'll drop you off here, as Oliver does, and then your parents will think it's him that brought you back.' Matt jumped down from the cart and held out his hand for Polly to alight.

'I wish we could have carried on to Sedbergh, just you and me. This last half-hour's gone so fast, and there's so much I still want to tell you.' Polly lingered on Matt's outstretched hand and then realized that the people behind the twitching curtained windows of the small row of houses called The Street could see their every

132

move. No doubt they would be reported to her father, especially by Len, who didn't seem to miss a thing, and added on what he didn't know.

'Aye, it's been a grand ride out. I don't call this work at all: picking up and delivering kits with a bonny lass by my side.' Matt ran his hand through Polly's hair and smiled.

'Don't! One of my father's mates lives over there, and what he doesn't know he invents.' Polly stopped Matt's hand and held it tightly in hers.

'Well — here, I'll give him something to really talk about.' Matt dropped her hand and put his arm tightly around her waist and kissed her passionately on the lips.

Polly felt like she was going to faint, but she wanted him to kiss her again and again. It was the first time anybody had kissed her in that way, and she hoped it wouldn't be the last. She stood back and looked at her Matt.

'I meant to do that on Saturday night, but there were too many people about, and I didn't know how you'd take it.' He smiled, seeing the look of astonishment on Polly's face. 'You didn't mind, did you? I mean, you didn't put up much of a fight.' He looked worried for a minute, thinking he'd perhaps gone too far and too fast for Polly.

'No, no. I just wasn't expecting it, and I can't believe you'd want to kiss me. I'm just Polly from Paradise, as my mother calls me — a plain farm lass — and you could do so much better than me.' Polly looked at the row of houses over the bridge, worried that they were being watched.

'Aye, I think you have come from Paradise, and you are more than a plain farm lass to me. You're the lass with the sparkling eyes and the jet-black hair; the one I can't wait to see of a morning; and the one I think of as I go to sleep on a night. I know we haven't known one another long, Polly, but it's as if I've known you all my life.' Matt held her hand tight and watched as she blushed deeply in front of him. The colour in her cheeks made her beauty even greater to him.

'Matt, stop it. I feel the same about you, but I'm frightened. I've never felt like this before.' Polly looked into his blue eyes, but at the same time her mind raced to the gentlemanly Tobias, whose dark, mysterious side attracted her with a fascination she couldn't understand.

'I'll take it slowly, Pol. Let's see how we feel over this summer. I'll keep bringing you home of an evening, and if it doesn't work out, then we'll just have to say and be honest with one another.' Matt let go of Polly's waist, sensing her uneasiness at being watched by prying eyes.

'Aye, let's do that. I've loved this evening, and I do have feelings for you, Matt, I really do. I just don't want my parents worrying about me. My mother isn't well, and my father has enough on, with it coming up to hay-time and me working two days a week at the dairy.'

'I used to love hay-time when we were up at the farm. It was the hay-field teas I used to love, a time when we all sat together in the hay-field, with the family and helping friends. My grandmother would bring a big basket out filled

134

with tea, sandwiches, pasties and cake, and we'd all sit down and have a natter, before going back to either scale the hay or load it up onto the horse and sledge. There's nothing comes close to the taste of a cup of tea in a hay-field. I think it must be the added flavour of the grass seed that you always find floating in your cup.' Matt recalled happier days back on his family's farm and sighed.

'You see, I didn't even know you farmed. There's so much to know about one another yet, Matt. Do you miss your farm? Why did you have to leave? And why do you use a sledge for hay-time?' Polly had a hundred and one questions about Matt that she wanted to ask, and she was only just beginning.

'Aye, we farmed up Dent until my grandfather died, and then my grandmother thought we'd be better moving into Hawes. The farm was only rented, and my grandfather was struggling to make a living before he died, so she decided to call it a day, without even asking me what I thought. I'd have liked to keep it on, but my grandmother wouldn't hear of it. And as for a sledge, it is exactly what it sounds: a huge wooden sledge that a team of horses pull, and the dried hay goes on it to be taken to the barn. It's more stable than a cart, if you have a hilly meadow — that's why we used a sledge. I loved that bloody farm. I knew every nook and cranny of it.' Matt shook his head and bowed it.

'Aye, I love Paradise, although my father will treat me like a lad, and sometimes I just want to be treated like a lass. That's why I like working in

135

the shop for two days. I'm sorry you didn't have the chance to take your farm on yourself. But what about your parents: where are they now?' Polly felt sorry for Matt, for she knew how much the land under her feet meant to her; and she'd die for her home, rather than have to leave it.

'My mother died giving birth to me, and I never knew who my father was. I've always been brought up by my grandparents. I've never known anybody else. But don't worry — it's not your headache. Now get yourself up home, else they'll wonder where you are.' Matt smiled at Polly, as she looked so sorry for him.

'I'm so sorry, Matt, you must have had it hard. But aye, I'd better go, else I'll be in bother. I'll see you tomorrow.' Polly looked at her crestfallen suitor as she opened the gate up to her lane. She stopped for a second, then ran back and pulled on his shoulder, before giving him a quick kiss on his cheek. 'See you tomorrow. I'll be counting the minutes.' Polly laughed and quickly closed the gate behind her and started up the lane.

'Aye, and I, Polly Harper, will be counting the seconds,' Matt shouted to her as she waved him goodbye.

★   ★   ★

'Now you're sure you'll not come and see the doctor with me this morning?' Edmund looked at Ada. She must not be feeling well, for it was market day at Hawes and, along with saying no to the doctor's visit, she'd also said she wasn't going into town with him.

136

'There's nowt wrong with me that an hour's peace on my own wouldn't put right. You'll manage with the list of things I need. Besides, by the time you've picked up your new hay-rake from Heseltine's, the joiners, and had a natter with Len Brunskill, I'll be fed up of waiting for you in that cold market place.' Ada gave Edmund her list of supplies for the week ahead and sighed as he screwed it up, putting it in his jacket pocket.

'It's not cold today, Ada, it's a grand day. Just look at that bottom meadow — it's growing so fast in this bit of good weather. I'll happen think about starting to mow it this weekend.'

'It might be warm in the sun, but there's always a sneaky wind as I stand outside the Crown Hotel, and that's where I'd have to wait, if you have a pint with Len.' Ada sat down in her chair.

'I don't know why you don't come in and join us. Nobody bites in there.' Edmund made his way to the door. 'Come with me. Get your coat and come with me. The day out will do you good.'

'It'll be a cold day in hell before you get me in a pub. Decent women don't go into suchlike. Just get yourself gone, and leave me be. I'm going to have forty winks while you are out.' Ada wanted a bit of peace; she was tired of Edmund telling her to go to the doctor, and there always seemed to be something to do nowadays.

'All right, if you're sure. I'll not be long, I'll get what you want on this list. Anything else you want?' Edmund lingered with his hand on the kitchen door-knob.

'Will you get yourself gone. It'll be midnight by the time you get back, if you don't get gone,' Ada snapped.

'Right, I'm gone.'

She stood up and watched Edmund go down the track, from the kitchen window. He was right, it was a glorious summer's day. The cow parsley in the bottom meadow was gently swaying against the beautiful yellow hues of the meadow's buttercups, and the smell of the flowers blew into the house through the open windows. She would have enjoyed the ride into Hawes, but she felt so tired. It was better that she had an hour in bed, in peace, while the house was empty. She climbed the stairs and went into her bedroom. Lying on her bed, she looked up at the dancing reflection on the low bedroom ceiling of the leaves from the apple tree that grew next to the house. She listened to the bleat of a sheep up on the fell side, calling for its wayward lamb. The peace was glorious. She closed her eyes and gently found herself drifting asleep.

★　★　★

'Edmund, I don't know how to tell you this, and I don't want to cause any bother, but I think there's something you should know.' Len Brunskill lifted his pint to his lips and looked at his lifelong friend.

'What are you on about? You've never caused bother for me yet, so get it spitted out, man. It'll be right, whatever you've got to tell me.'

138

Edmund looked at the worried face of his best friend and wondered what it was that he'd been building up to tell him for the last half-hour.

'Now I know part of it is true, because I've seen him myself, but the other might be a load of rubbish.' Len took another sip of his pint as he summoned up the courage to carry on with his news. 'Your Danny's son is working at the dairy with your Polly. That Bill Sunter's taken them both on. He always was good mates with your Danny; he'll think he's doing him a favour. He'll know that they are both his children, and it wouldn't surprise me if he kept in touch with your Danny — thick as thieves them two were, when they were growing up. But I don't have to tell you that.'

'He's what? I thought the lad, and his grand-mother, were over in Dent. Where are they living? The stupid, bloody fool. Bill never did know when to stop meddling in our business.' Edmund went white with anger. He'd always tried to act right with Bill Sunter, but he always suspected that Bill knew where Danny was.

'The lad is called Matt. He lives with his grandmother up Gayle. They moved here just after his grandfather died, just in time for the dairy opening. Bill Sunter took him on as his yardman. He's in charge of the milk deliveries, and he's damn good at his job, from what I hear.'

'I don't give a damn about what he does; it's if he knows our Polly, and what the Dinsdales have told him as he's been growing up.' Edmund looked into his pint.

'Aye, well, that's the other bit of news. The

lasses at the dairy say Matt's sweet on her. In fact a bit more than sweet on her, if you believe the gossip. But it may all be nowt, you know what women are like. Our lad did see them dancing together, though, at that dance last weekend. I don't think either of them have the faintest idea that they are brother and sister, but you'd better do something before there's a disaster.' Len withheld the worst bit of gossip he'd heard: that disaster had already happened, if there was truth in the young couple sharing a bed. It was that news that he'd taken as pure gossip, for he couldn't see Polly being easy with her affections.

'Jesus Christ, it gets worse. For sixteen years we've brought her up as ours. She never had an inkling that she was our lad's dirty secret, and that he'd walked away from it, along with walking away from his family. And now I'm going to have to tell her everything. It will break her heart, and my Ada's. I hope to God this lad isn't our Danny's, and that you have it wrong.' Edmund stroked his white hair and felt that he could have shouted his anger for all to hear.

'I'm not wrong, Edmund. He's Bernard and Dora Dinsdale's grandson. He even looks like your lad — more than your Polly does, because she takes after her mother. He's the spit of Danny. No matter where your lad is, his image is in Hawes, and I think he's courting his sister.'

Edmund stood up and gulped the rest of his pint down, slamming his glass on the varnished table.

'Where are you off to? Now, think of what you

140

are doing. Folk might have got it wrong. There might be nowt between them.' Len looked up at his usually placid friend and regretted telling him the news.

'I'm going to our Polly, and will see for myself if this lad is who you say he is.' Edmund wiped his mouth with the back of his sleeve, before putting his cap on.

'And then what are you going to do? You can't tell your lass at work, and if you tell Matt, he's going to blame you for all those years without a father. He won't understand that it wasn't your fault. Wait until she comes home and then sound your Polly out; it's no good going in hot-headed.' Len tried to calm his best friend down.

'Nay, Len, save your words, I'm off down to the dairy now. It needs nipping in the bud, right now.' Edmund walked out, banging the door behind him. He was on a mission, and he had an uneasy feeling about meeting the grandson he'd never known.

★   ★   ★

Polly was busy serving in the shop as she watched her father come in through the door. He looked angry and then frustrated, as he saw the shop was extra-busy with demanding market-day shoppers. When another group of shoppers entered the shop, he waved his goodbye, in frustration at not being able to talk to her alone.

It can't have been important, Polly thought, as she filled the basket of her customer. Father would catch up with her at home.

141

Edmund walked around to the yard of the dairy and stood watching the loading and unloading of the milk and kits. He knew most of the men working there, but in the centre of the activities stood one whom he guessed to be Matt Dinsdale. Len was right: the lad was the image of Danny, his father. It was as if life was replaying itself, as Edmund watched the young man giving orders to the workforce. He was a fine-looking lad, there was no doubting that, but why did he have to be working there?

Edmund watched Matt doing his job and remembered how Danny had broken his heart, and how he could never forgive him. Now was he to break Matt's heart, and turn his world upside down, by saying the lass he had his eye on was his sister? Edmund cursed under his breath. He couldn't tackle Matt at the dairy and bring his life to a halt in front of the workers. He'd see what Polly had to say for herself when she got home. It wouldn't pay to be too hasty, and they might hate the sight of one another, if the gossips had got it wrong.

9

'Ada, Ada, where are you, lass?' The house was silent apart from the ticking of the grandfather clock at the bottom of the stairs. 'I've brought the shopping. Where are you?'

Edmund looked in the pantry and shouted through to the sitting room, before making his way up the creaking farmhouse stairs. 'Aye, lass, you're not still asleep — you must have been jiggered.' Edmund walked across to Ada, who was laid out on top of the patch-work-quilted double bed that had been in their bedroom since they had been married. She didn't stir. Her hand hung over the edge of the bed and her chest was still. 'No, no, not my Ada. God, please. No, don't have taken the only woman I've ever loved, not yet! I need her, I need her more today than I've ever needed her.'

Edmund rushed to the bed, sat down beside his wife and gently rested her head on his knee, trying to feel for a pulse in her wrist. He found none. 'Aye, Ada, what am I going to do, my love? You are my rock, I can't face life without you. And what do I do about our Polly?' He stroked Ada's white curly hair and kissed her still-warm brow. 'Well, at least I don't have to break your heart, like our Danny did all those years ago. You've never been the same since that day. Damn that lad, the selfish bugger.' Edmund stroked her hair and a tear fell among the silver

143

locks of the woman he had loved all his life. Why did life always hit you hardest when you were already down. Without Ada, he would be lost.

He continued to stroke her hair and sighed. He'd loved her so long — so long that he'd forgotten how to tell her just how much he loved her. They had been like a comfortable pair of shoes that you walked around in every day, and then suddenly realized one day that they were old and tattered, but you still loved them anyway. How was he going to live without his rock, his friend and, most of all, Polly's supposed mother? There was going to be a lot to explain, but now he would have to send for the doctor and see to an undertaker. And then break his heart again, when he looked Polly in the eye.

* * *

'Now then, Polly, get yourself down from that cart and come up home with me.'

Since the doctor had been and gone, Edmund had waited in the sunshine and had sat on the newly built milk-kit stand at the bottom of the lane from Paradise, waiting for Polly to come home. The doctor had handed him the scrap of paper that told Edmund his way of life had changed forever. He'd not noticed the birds singing, or the heat of the sun, or how the river gurgled its way down the valley. All he'd thought about was breaking to Polly the news that Ada had died, and then having to tackle the subject of Matt Dinsdale. He'd watched as the young couple on the cart had come down the road, giggling and chattering to each other, and instantly knew that the gossip was true. Polly and her brother were in an unhealthy relationship, and he'd have to tell them both the truth.

'Polly's got some bad news waiting for her at home. Can you tell Bill Sunter she'll not be coming to work any more.' Edmund watched as Polly looked at him.

'What do you mean? You can't do that just because I've come home with Matt. You can't stop me from seeing the people I work with. I've got to go to work, Father.' Polly had known this day was coming, as soon as her father had heard she wasn't coming home with steady old Oliver Simms. And she wasn't going to take it — he couldn't rule her life any more.

'Did you not hear, lass, you've heartbreak waiting at home. I'm sorry, but you aren't listening, and I'm not making myself clear. Polly, you lost your mother this afternoon. She died in her sleep, while I was at Hawes.' Edmund nearly broke down as he said the words to the young couple that he now knew both to be his grandchildren.

'No, you are wrong — she can't be dead, not my mam.' Polly dropped her apron and ran up the farm path, not looking back at her father, who was standing with Matt. She had to get home, she had to see her mother.

'And, Matt lad, I need to talk to you and your grandmother, after we've laid my Ada to rest. There's something we have to sort out.' Edmund looked up at the blond lad, who was obviously heartbroken for Polly, as he watched her running

145

into the farmyard of Paradise. 'Perhaps you'd like to come to the funeral. It's next Thursday at the church in Garsdale, 2 p.m. The undertaker has just confirmed and is coming back later with a coffin; he only lives across at The Street.' Edmund found himself rambling with his thoughts as he looked at his grandson. He had every right to be at his grandmother's funeral, if he did but know it.

'If it's about me and Polly, I've been honourable, sir. I'd never be anything else. I'm so sorry for your loss. Please tell Polly I'm there for her.' Matt looked down from the cart at the heartbroken old man. What did this man need to see his grandmother and himself for? He'd never lay a finger on Polly, so there was no need for him to see his grandmother.

'Aye, well, Polly and I will come up to your house at Gayle on Friday afternoon. Tell your grandmother that Polly's mother has died, and that we are coming to see you both. She'll know what it's about.' Edmund closed the farm gate after him and walked slowly up the track, the weight of the world on his shoulders. It was best that all was out in the open. With the death of Ada, and Polly and Matt's burgeoning romance, the truth had to be faced and secrets could no longer be kept.

Matt watched Edmund climb the track to his farm, and the sorrow that it held within. How he wanted to go and comfort Polly. She hadn't even said goodbye, else he would have given her words of comfort. He'd be there for her at the funeral, it was the least he could do. Perhaps by then he'd know why Edmund Harper was to visit his home, and why his grandmother would somehow know why to expect him.

★ ★ ★

Polly knelt at the side of Ada's bed, stroking her cold hand. Tears trickled down her cheeks and Edmund could hear her sobs from the bottom of the stairs.

'I loved you, Mother, and I always will. I should have known you weren't well yesterday, when I put your feet up on the stool. I shouldn't have gone to work today. All I was thinking about was myself, and enjoying Matt's company.' She sobbed into the quilt and blew her nose on the edge of it, as she realized her face was covered with snot and tears. 'What am I going to do without you, and what is Father going to do, now he's on his own?' Strands of her long black hair fell onto her face and she caught her breath as she heard her father's footsteps climbing the stairs.

'The undertakers are coming up the path, Polly. Mr Raw is going to take her into his chapel of rest until the funeral.' Edmund put his hand on Polly's shoulder. 'It's time to say your goodbyes, lass. You know how much she loved you, and she wouldn't want to see you upset.' Edmund slipped his arm around Polly's waist and lifted her up onto her feet. 'She didn't suffer, that's the main thing, Polly love; she just went in her sleep.' Edmund hugged the distraught Polly next to him and stroked her long hair. 'Life's cruel, lass, and if I could take the blows for you,

147

I would. But we are all the better for having had my Ada's love, and she will always be in our hearts.' Edmund couldn't stop a tear from falling as Polly shook with sorrow. What would he do now, with his Polly? She had always confided in Ada, and now he was going to have to be mother and father to the lass, and be responsible for telling the deeply buried truth.

'Edmund, are you up there?' Bob Raw yelled up the stairs as he and his apprentice pulled up outside the farmhouse with a coffin on the back of his cart.

'Quiet now, lass. Tidy yourself up and stop crying. Bob Raw's here to take her away.' Edmund kissed Polly on her cheek and urged her to stop sobbing. 'Aye, up here, Bob. We've said our goodbyes.'

Polly felt her chin wobbling again as she whispered, 'I love you, Mother', before rushing out of the bedroom and brushing past Bob Raw and his help. She had to get away, get some fresh air in her lungs and think about what the day had thrown at her. She looked at the coffin on the back of the cart. Her mother would soon be in that, deep down in the dark earth, where no light and no air could get at her. What if she wasn't dead, what if she was just asleep? Happen her father had got it wrong.

Polly ran back into the house and flew up the stairs and into her parents' room. 'She isn't dead, she can't be dead — check she's just asleep!' But she knew she was wrong, as soon as she realized that they had dressed her mother in a burial shroud.

'Polly, Polly, you can't bring her back. Your mother's gone.' The three men looked at her, their hearts breaking with her cries.

Polly ran down the stairs. She ran past the coffin, through the farmyard and up to the high meadow. The long grass caught in the buckles of her shoes, and her skirts tangled around her knees. Her breath ached in her lungs, and her heart pounded as she threw herself onto the hard ground when she could run no more. There she lay, looking at the setting sun and running her fingers through the long ears of the seeded grass and clover. She sat up and looked down towards the farm path and the bridge that she had crossed so happily a few hours ago. A few hours that seemed like a lifetime now. She watched as, down the path and along the road to The Street, the coffin with her mother in it went with Bob Raw to his chapel of rest. Tears filled her eyes as she pulled on the stalks of grass, filling her hands with their seeds, only for her to discard them in a heap next to her skirt. Lying back down in the long grass, she listened to the woodland birds singing their evensong and felt the chill wind of night encroaching on her face. She smelt the scent of clover and buttercups in the long hay-meadow and watched as a late-evening bumblebee made its way home between the long grasses.

'I thought I'd find you here. You always hid here when you were a lil 'un. Any bother and we'd find you up here in the top meadow, watching the world go by.' Edmund bent down and sat next to Polly. 'Everybody's got to die sometime, Pol. Some just sooner than others,

149

and your mother was getting a bit weary of this old world. I knew there was something up, but I just didn't realize how ill she was.' Edmund looked down upon the dale that he had grown up in, and thought of his beloved Ada and the hours they had shared together.

'I know, Father, but I just didn't expect it yet — not yet — and I loved her so much.' Polly sat up and snuggled against Edmund's jacket.

'Aye, well, we both did. It's a bit like your old Herdwick over there in that pasture. She has her three babies with her now, but come September we'll have to take them off her. She's loved them, done the best for them, and now they've to grow up and have their own life. She might see another winter or she might not, but life will go on, no matter what, and we can't stop it. But don't forget we'll always have your mother here, in our hearts, and that will never change.' He held Polly tight. 'Come on now, lass, let's be away down home. The night's drawing in and it's been a long day for us both.'

Polly stood up and offered her hand to her father, whose knees were stiff from too much fell-walking and damp days of kneeling on wet grass helping sheep, lambs and cows calve. 'Yes, let's go home, Father. I'll make supper and stoke the fire. I'll not let my mother down — she'd want us to carry on, wouldn't she?'

'That she would, lass, that she would.' Edmund put his arm around Polly. Their hearts were going to be broken yet again after the funeral, but for now he had to be strong for his Polly.

* ★ ★ ★

It was Thursday, the day of the funeral.

'Chin up, lass, she wouldn't want us bawling over her. She never was one to make a fuss, was your mother.' Edmund smiled at Polly. Her face told him everything. Tear-stains ran down her cheeks, and her nose was red from being blown. 'I was only six when my mother died. My oldest sister brought both me and Evie up. I remember as clear as yesterday, her clouting me around the ear for dropping a jar of jam she'd just made. Looking back, I don't blame her. The sugar would have cost the earth, and she'd have spent all day stirring the huge jam pan over the hearth. By, she'd a fair temper, had our Meg; you were a brave 'un if you took her on.' Edmund cast his mind back to his childhood. 'She jiggered off with a salesman from Newcastle as soon as Evie and I were old enough to look after ourselves, only to die of influenza the next year, and that was that. I was left with my old father here, at Paradise, and when Evie married Albert, and I've been here ever since.' Edmund spat on the black shoes he was polishing and gave them a final buff with the shoe brush, before lacing them up and putting the brush away.

'Do you remember your mother?' Polly was curious, for her father had never talked of his family before.

'No, I can hardly remember her face, poor woman, but what I do remember is her smell — she always smelt of violets. I can be walking past the bank of primroses and violets that flower

151

above the wood in spring, and thoughts come flooding back to me of when I was a bairn. Thinking about it, she must have worn violet perfume.' Edmund leaned against the kitchen window and looked out down the field. 'Well, we'd better walk down to the church. Dick is waiting for us by the bottom gate. I can see him. Len said he'd take us up to the funeral tea at the Moorcock and bring us back. He's a good man. I've known him both man and boy.'

Polly took her father's arm and swallowed deeply. She wasn't going to cry; she'd hold her head high and think of the good days she'd had with her mother. Her father pulled the kitchen door to, and they walked through the farmyard and down the rough farm path bordered by the tall grasses of the hay-meadow.

'We'll have to mow this next week, if the weather holds,' Edmund said as they reached halfway down the field.

'I'll have to help keep the house going,' Polly replied.

'Aye, that'll be grand, lass. We'll manage it between us.' He hesitated as he opened the farm gate and saw the coffin on the undertaker's cart.

'It's too fine a day for a funeral, Bob. Is the good Lord not going to welcome her with a drop of rain?' Edmund shook Bob Raw's hand and nodded to the bearers, who stood on either side of the cart.

'Doesn't look like it today, Edmund. She'll be welcome anyway, will Ada. She was a good woman.'

'Aye, that she was. Let's be off. Folk will be

152

waiting, and my lass here looks a bit faint.' Edmund took hold of Polly's hand as the cortege made its way over the small narrow bridge and up the road, past the houses along The Street, with their curtains drawn as a sign of respect, and on for a further few hundred yards to the small Norman-built church that served the people of Garsdale.

Polly thought it was the longest walk she had ever made, as she entered the church porchway. The bearers lifted the dark oak coffin onto their shoulders, on the instructions of Bob Raw, and the vicar said words of blessing as he walked in front of the funeral party. She sat down on the front pew, next to her father, aware of the church being nearly full with Dales people who had come to pay their respects, yet not daring to look at who was actually there.

'I am the life . . . ' The vicar turned and stood in front of them.

'Oh, Mother, why did you have to die? There was so much I wanted to tell you. There were so many times I should have said sorry, or helped more.' Polly could only think of what she hadn't done, and her heart ached as she listened to the service and sang the hymns that she and her father had chosen in the kitchen of the Paradise with the vicar a few days ago.

'You all right, Polly?' Edmund squeezed her hand after the service, as they followed the coffin out into the churchyard to be interred. 'She's had a full church — she'd be proud to know that she was well liked.' He smiled at his daughter; she was bearing up well.

'Yes, I'm fine.' Polly wanted to scream how she really felt, but knew her father must be hurting in just the same way.

She followed and copied her father, as he took a small handful of earth from the box that Bob Raw offered him and threw it down onto the coffin that held Ada. She looked down into the deep, dark hole where her mother lay, and filled up with tears as she threw the damp earth clay, watching it splatter over the coffin, before walking away from the hole, and from her mother.

'My condolences, Miss Harper. You must be heart-broken at the loss of your mother.' Tobias Middleton stood in front of Polly and looked truly upset for her loss.

'Thank you, Mr Middleton. I am at a loss, I'm afraid.' Polly wiped her eyes with her hand-kerchief and looked up at Tobias.

'Please — it's Tobias. We know each other too well to stand on ceremony. If there is anything I can do . . . '

'We'll be fine, thank you, Mr Middleton. But thank you for your concern.' Edmund came to Polly's rescue, once he saw the attention she was getting from one whom he thought a cad.

'Again my condolences. It must have come as a shock to both of you.' Tobias bowed his head.

'It did, and thank you for coming to the funeral. I'm sorry, but will you excuse us? I believe both Polly and I are needed by the vicar.' Edmund took Polly's arm and escorted her onto the church path and away from Tobias. 'I cannot take to that Tobias Middleton. He's got such a

154

look like his father. Mark my words, he's a wrong 'un.'

'He was only saying his sympathies, Father.' Polly wanted to defend her Tobias.

'Nay, it was more than that, lass. I know that look he gives you. You keep away from him, do you hear? He's nothing but bad news. He never even met your mother, so why is he here?'

'He's here like most of them, Father. When someone in the dale dies, everyone shows their respect. I don't know half of the folk here today.' Polly looked around her, and her heart missed a beat as she spotted Matt standing under the yew tree at the edge of the graveyard. He lifted his hand and waved gently at her as she smiled at him.

'And that 'un — the sooner I go to see his grandmother, the better,' Edmund muttered, as he saw the first smile for a week on Polly's face.

'Can I go and talk to him, Father? I never said goodbye the other day,' Polly pleaded.

'Aye, go on, but I've got my eye on you both.' Edmund couldn't say no, for the lass needed a friend and, besides, all would be settled by the next day.

Polly nearly ran to talk to Matt, but thought better of it, as folk watched her cross the churchyard towards him. They seemed to be showing interest in the friendship between them, and she could tell that some were even whispering about them, as she smiled and greeted Matt.

'How are you keeping, Polly? I'm sorry for your loss. You'll miss your mother.' Matt looked

155

at Polly. The high-necked black dress suited her, especially as her long black hair was neatly plaited on her head, making her look even more beautiful.

'It's my father — he's going to be lost. They were so close and had been married so long.' Polly wanted to throw herself into Matt's arms and cry her heart out, but knew she had to keep herself respectable.

'Do you know what he's coming to see me and my grandmother about tomorrow night? When I told my grandmother, she went as white as a ghost and just muttered that she knew the day would have to come, some day.' Matt leaned his arm on the old yew tree and watched the mourners as they talked to one another and then, one by one, made their way out of the churchyard, apart from the group that was congregating around the church porch.

'He's not said anything, but I don't think he likes us two being friends. He nearly curses when I say your name.' Polly lowered her eyes. She felt uneasy telling Matt the truth about her father's reaction to her closeness to him over the last few days.

'Aye, well, you want to tell him there's a lot worse than me. At least I work, and I'm saving up for my own farm. My grandmother and your father should let us be. We aren't hurting anyone.' Matt was angry, and his voice told everyone that. Polly's father didn't even know him, so how could he judge him?

'Are you all right, Polly?' Tobias Middleton had been watching the couple with interest, like the other mourners next to the church porch, when he heard Matt's raised voice. He looked at Matt and then stood next to him, coming between him and Polly.

'Yes, I'm fine, thank you.' Polly blushed. 'Matt was just voicing his opinion on something.'

'As long as that was all it was. This is not the time or place for raised voices.' Tobias stood back. He looked at the proud blond-haired lad, who was obviously smitten with Polly, and wished that he'd disappear. Polly was going to be his, and Tobias would stop anyone who stood in his way.

'What's it got to do with you, what I say? Who are you anyway? You don't look like family, in them flash clothes.' Matt didn't like the look of the preened peacock who was coming to the aid of Polly, after just a few raised private words.

'You can say I'm a friend of the family, and I was just concerned for Polly. She looked upset.' Tobias could feel his anger building, as Matt sneered at him and grabbed Polly's arm, so that she was beside him.

'Well, bugger off! Pol's fine. She's with me, and you shouldn't have been eavesdropping.' Matt turned his back on Tobias and linked his arm into Polly's.

'I'm sorry . . . ' Tobias started, only for Matt to turn around.

'I told you to bugger off, but you wouldn't listen.' Matt lifted his fist and hit Tobias squarely on the chin, sending him wheeling into a crowd of mourners and making Edmund turn round from talking to the vicar, to see what the commotion was. 'She's my lass, so stop bloody bothering us.' Matt stood over Tobias, who was now being dusted down by the crowd.

'That's it — stop it! By God, you are like your father. He broke his mother's heart, and now you are spoiling her funeral day.' By the time Edmund had said the words, it was too late to retract them.

Matt stood still, his fists still raised over Tobias. 'What did you say? What are you on about? How do you know who my father was? And how can Polly's mother be related to me?'

'Aye, God, what a bloody carry-on. Polly, come here — come into the church; and you, Matt, put your fists away and listen to what I've to say as well. I'd better finish what I've started. Vicar, can you tell everyone there's a bit of tea up at the Moorcock, while I sort my family out.' Edmund looked at the shocked Tobias and shook his head. 'You just bugger off. You always seem to make trouble for me and mine.' Edmund put his arm around the crying Polly. 'I didn't want you to find out like this. I was going to sort it out tomorrow night.'

Edmund saw the vicar shaking hands with the departing mourners and watched as Tobias mounted the white horse that was tethered at the gate. He'd have smiled at the lad thumping him, if it hadn't been under such terrible circumstances. Tobias probably deserved it. Edmund sighed and went into the dark interior of the small church with his arm still around Polly.

She sat next to Matt on the back benches of the little church, sobbing into her handkerchief.

She didn't understand. What had her father meant by saying that Matt was like his father, and that he'd also broken her own mother's heart? Had the sorrow of the day made her father not think straight?

Edmund ran his fingers through his hair and sat down in the pew next to them.

'I've asked the vicar to give us ten minutes before he locks up. What I'm going to say is going to hurt us all, and I'm just glad that Ada isn't here to hear, and that she didn't see that outburst in the churchyard. She'd have been broken-hearted to think someone was fighting at her funeral.'

'I'm sorry Mr Harper, it was my fault, but he had no right listening into our conversation.' Matt dropped his head. 'So, who's my father then? You obviously know?'

'Aye, lad, that I do. And, Polly, I'm so sorry — we've not been truthful to you all these years, but it was easier to bring you up as our daughter. You've got to understand.' Edmund reached for Polly's hand, which he took and held, shaking. 'Your father's our son, Matt. Our Danny. He got your mother in the family way and hadn't the guts to stand by her. I'm ashamed even to say his name. But what he didn't know — and what you partly don't know — is that when your mother, Matt, died in childbirth delivering you, she didn't just give birth to you. She had twins that night.' Edmund stopped and looked at the faces of Matt and Polly, who appeared dumbstruck. 'Aye, and you've guessed the rest. Polly, here, is your sister. Your father came over from Dent with her in a blizzard, and we brought her up as ours.' Edmund hung his head and then lifted it up to look at the young couple, who obviously loved one another. 'It's been hanging over our heads for the last sixteen years, and we were just hoping that we would never have to explain. Ada was so proud of her granddaughter, Polly, and I tried to protect you as much as I could, lass, but we couldn't coop you up forever.'

Polly shook with grief. She didn't know what to think. She'd just buried her mother, who was really her grandmother, and she was sitting next to the man she thought she loved, but who now turned out to be her brother. Her thoughts were confused, and her heart was confused. Where, then, was her father, and why hadn't she ever met him?

'No, no, this can't be right. Matt isn't my brother. I've kissed him as a lover — you can't do that with your brother!' Polly shook. 'You'd have pictures of my father. I've never seen him — he's never once been mentioned. Besides, where is he? I can't believe you!' Polly cried hysterically.

Matt looked at Polly and grabbed her other hand. 'Polly, it could be worse. At least we've got one another now. And I now know who my father is, and that I've got a sister that I know I love, albeit in a different way now.' He turned to Edmund. 'And our father: where is he then? Do you ever hear from him?' Matt asked a heart-broken Edmund the question that was on the lips of them both.

'I've never seen him since the day he stole my

life savings and got onto a train at Garsdale station. He never wrote to his mother — no Christmas or birthday card, nothing. He just disappeared. He broke everybody's heart that day he left the dale, the selfish bastard, and I'll never have him back in my house. That I do bloody swear by. Your mother was a lovely lass and deserved better than our lad. It was the least we could do, to raise you, Polly, as our own. I hope you understand. We knew that you'd be all right, Matt, with Bernard and Dora, for they were good folk. Good folk that my lad treated like muck. He left a lifetime of heartache behind him.' Edmund squeezed Polly's hand tightly and patted Matt's knee. 'Polly, we have always loved you as our own — you know that — and we always will. And now that Matt has made himself known, I'll treat him like the grandson he is.'

Polly sobbed and looked at Matt and her grandfather. 'It's all been one big lie. At least Matt knew that his mother had died, and never knew his father. But I've had my whole world torn apart. I've lost my mother — grandmother — and found out that my real father is a bastard, all in one day. And you expect me to smile and take it.' Polly sniffled and wiped her red eyes with her handkerchief.

'Polly, it changes nothing. I love you just the same as I've always done. You are still my flesh and blood, and you know Ada worshipped the ground you walked on. She must be turning in her grave to think that, on the day we have buried her, I'm having to tell you both this. If that bloody interfering Bill Sunter hadn't taken

161

you both on at the dairy, none of this need ever have come out into the open.' Edmund couldn't help but curse, even though the setting wasn't congenial for such language.

'Does Bill Sunter know we are brother and sister?' Matt asked quickly.

'He might, or he'll have a good idea. He was our Danny's best mate. I have my suspicions that it was Bill who persuaded him to leave the dale, or at least frightened him out of married life.' Edmund looked at Matt.

'I always thought he took me on without bothering about what I'd done in the past. But the fellas at work think he favours me. I just thought I was good at my job. He even took me to one side the other day and gave me a father-like lecture, about behaving myself with women. Now it all makes sense. His lecture was about you, Polly, as he knew you were my sister.' Matt smiled at Polly.

'Well, he could have said something to me. I'll be the laughing stock of the dairy: flirting with my own brother and dancing with him all night.' Polly blew her nose and played with her handkerchief in her hands.

'Will he know where our father is?' Matt looked at Edmund. Now that he knew whose son he was, he wanted to track Danny down.

'I don't know, lad. He's never said anything to me. Don't go looking for him, but if you want to know what he looks like, just you look in the mirror. You are the spitting image of him. My Ada would have been all over you, if she were still alive.' Edmund sniffed and breathed in deeply. It hadn't been the funeral he had planned, and the funeral tea would be in full swing now at the Moorcock Inn further up the dale.

A discreet cough made the family of three turn and look towards the shaft of light coming through the open doorway.

'Do you still want that lift, Edmund? Vicar says just pull the door to, when you've finished; and if you need him, he's at the vicarage.' Len Brunskill twiddled with his cap as he waited for a reply.

Edmund tapped the hands of Matt and Polly. 'Are we up to seeing your grandmother off with a drink, and her friends?' His face looked pained as he waited for an answer from the young couple.

They looked at one another and then nodded their heads in agreement.

'Aye, we are coming, Len. I don't think you've been introduced to my grandson, Matt. Doesn't he look like his father?' Edmund put his arm through Polly's and squeezed her tightly as they walked up the aisle.

'As long as he isn't such a pillock as his father was,' Len muttered, as he walked down the churchyard path.

'Nay, I think this 'un's a grand lad, and I'm glad he's one of mine. Did you see how he chinned that Tobias Middleton?' Edmund made light of the incident in the churchyard.

'Everybody saw that. The poor devil was left reeling,' said Len.

'He deserved it. He was pestering Polly.' Matt

163

was quick to defend himself.

'He wasn't pestering me; he was making sure I was all right. He's a gentleman, and you were just jealous.' Polly closed the churchyard gate behind her, before Len helped her into his trap.

'How could I be jealous? I'm your brother, it seems. I'll look out for you even more now — he doesn't stand a chance.' Matt bowed his head and frowned.

'You'll do no such thing. I like Tobias Middleton.' Polly looked quickly at her grandfather's face.

'We've had enough upset for one day. The less I have to hear about your liking Tobias Middleton, the better. He's a bad lot, and I keep telling you that.' Edmund climbed up into the trap between his two grandchildren.

Polly bit her tongue. After being lied to all her life, who did her grandfather think he was, to tell her how to run her life? She'd see Tobias if she wanted to, and he wouldn't stop her.

10

Polly stood with the hay-rake in her hand and looked down the dale. The sun blazed, drying the two-day-old mown grass to a crisp and filling the air with the fragrance of hay-meadows filled with buttercups and daisies. Sweat ran down her brow and she swept it and her hair back with a flick of her hand. It was hot, not quite midday, but the sun beat down on her as she shook the clumps of drying grass out with her hay-rake. This was the first time she had been asked to do this, but with her grandmother dead and only her and her grandfather on the farm, it had to be done.

She swished the rake back and forth, getting air into the grass that was still green underneath, in order to dry it into hay fit to place in the barn for the coming winter. The prongs in the rake pulled on the grass, and her arms ached from tossing the grass into the air. Along with the blisters from the coarse wood of the rake-handle, she was becoming short-tempered as she finally finished the last swathe of grass on the steep hillside of the top meadow.

She sat down in the hay-field and put the rake down beside her. The short grass stubble prickled her legs, and she wrapped her skirt around them in order to stop them from itching. She frowned as a school of midges danced around her, and wiped them away with the back of her hand. Sighing, she looked around her. The dale lay like a patchwork quilt before her, the summer meadows mown and cleared, ready for the onset of winter, some with grass still standing and other pastures filled with the white dots of grazing sheep. There was a warm haze over the dale and, if she hadn't been in such a mood with herself, she would have probably smiled and appreciated the beauty of the day. As it was, she hadn't time to appreciate the delights that nature had thrown at her feet, and was angry at the world and at the plight that she was in, through no fault of her own.

Things had not been the same since her mother's funeral — or, as she kept having to remind herself, her grandmother's funeral. She'd not been back to the dairy, partly because she felt embarrassed to face everyone and partly because she hadn't the time, as she'd taken the place of her grandmother and had a house to run and a farm to look after. She looked down into the farmyard under the hillside and could just make out her grandfather letting the last sheep out of the pen, where he had been inspecting them for foot-rot, and parting the now-grown lambs from their mothers. He'd want his dinner and expect it on the table at twelve-thirty, just like her grandmother had done, every day of her life.

Edmund's life hadn't changed much since her death, but Polly's definitely had, and not for the better. Matt had become part of her family, but only when he wanted; and he now made more fuss of his grandfather than of Polly, leaving her feeling rejected and unloved, as Edmund showed Matt around the farm and shared a cigarette or a pint with him. Polly sighed. She'd never escape from the farm — she didn't have the time or the transport. She pulled herself up, using her hay-rake as a prop, and made her way down the field to the farmhouse.

'You finished scaling that meadow then? We'll cart it all in tomorrow, if the weather holds.' Edmund looked up from sweeping the yard of lost sheep wool and droppings, as he noticed Polly walking down by the side of the house.

'Yes, it's done for the day. Looks like good hay, this year.' Polly stood in front of her grandfather and looked at him as he brushed his boots clean with the yard brush.

'I'm ready for my dinner, Polly. What have you got for us?' Edmund grinned at her and walked after her to the open farmhouse door.

'I left some potatoes from last night in the side-oven in a bit of fat. They should be warmed through, and I thought we could finish the cold brisket off with them. And there's still some apple pie left.' She had planned dinner as much as she could. Surely he couldn't expect the top meadow to be scaled and to have a full lunch?

'Mmm, I suppose that will be all right. You'll be baking this afternoon, will you? Just in case we have some helpers tomorrow.' Edmund sat down at the table and waited for dinner to be served.

'Oh, aye, and I'll wash the bedding, mend your socks and sing the National Anthem, just to keep me busy,' Polly snapped as she laid place-settings for them both.

'Now then, Polly. We didn't bring you up to be sarcastic, and there's no need to snap at me. It's just your mother — '

'What! My mother died sixteen years ago — something you all forgot to tell me. And now I'm nothing more than a skivvy.' Polly threw the tea-towel down on the table, turned her back on Edmund and sobbed as she held onto the sink, then looked out of the kitchen window.

'Polly, I'm sorry. I'm asking too much from you. But it's hard for me, too. Your grandmother ran this house with one hand tied behind her back, and I forget how young you are. Look, when we've got the hay in, go and have a day in Hawes. Buy yourself some material for a dress from Margaret Milburn, or perhaps she would run you one up — I don't know what you womenfolk do.' Edmund put his hand on the shaking shoulders of Polly and bowed his head.

Polly looked out of the window and sobbed. 'I'm doing my best, Grandfather, but everything's altered and I feel so trapped. Even if I go into Hawes, folk will be talking about us. I feel such a fool.'

'Aye, lass, folk will always talk. They did when your father left. But, by the following week, there was something else to take their fancy. Now come on, sit down and have your dinner. I'll get these tatties out of the side-oven. Is the brisket and pie in the pantry?' Edmund made for the door.

Polly turned and faced her grandfather. 'I'm sorry. I'm just lonely and tired, and life is all wrong. I'll make the dinner.' She wiped her eyes and gave a wan smile.

'I know, lass. Life's been hard this last week or two. You've done a good job in that top meadow. It's worth a new frock, I think.' Edmund smiled.

'How do you know I've done a good job? You've not been up there. You're too busy with your favourite old sheep.' Polly smiled.

'Those blisters between your thumb and fingers tell me you've done it. Make sure you put something on them.' He grabbed Polly's hands and held them in his. 'You know I love you, lass. I've never told you that before, because I'm an old fool and I never say how I feel. After my day, all this is yours — you do know that?' His eyes nearly filled with tears as he looked at his beloved Polly and reflected how to do right by her.

'Give over, you'll be with us for years yet. And I don't need to know whose Paradise is. You might change your mind. My father might come back, and Matt might want half, so I don't even want to know.'

'No, Paradise should be yours. The solicitor in Hawes knows that, and losing Ada has made me realize that I should tell you. So now you know. Your father will never come back, and Matt was not brought up as ours, so he doesn't enter into it. So look after it, Pol. Every inch belongs to you.'

'Sit down, Grandfather, sit down and eat your dinner. I'm not going anywhere, and neither are you. Now, let's hope the sun shines tomorrow. And then I will have a day in Hawes and, yes, you can buy me a frock in payment for my blisters.' Polly walked into the whitewashed and slate-shelved pantry and put the beef and pie in her hands. She sighed. How could she lose her temper with the old man seated at the kitchen table? He'd lost just as much as — and more than — her, and she should learn to bite her tongue.

★ ★ ★

The following morning dawned bright and warm, and Polly breathed in the early morning air that was heavy with the smell of hay, as she stood at the kitchen doorway. The oven was already full with a gooseberry pie and a dozen small plain buns, in preparation for a day spent in the hay-field. She'd fry some bacon and eggs later and place them into sandwiches, and then neither she nor her grandfather had to worry about dinner until nightfall. She'd felt guilty all night, tossing and turning, and going over the words she had said in haste to her grandfather.

'I thought I could smell something in the oven.' Edmund came down the stairs and yawned as he reached the kitchen. 'There was no need to get up this early, lass. We'd have made do with what we already had. After all, there's only me, you and old Clover.'

'I thought if I filled the basket like my grandmother used to do, we could be up in the meadow all day. You don't know how long this weather will last.' Polly poured a cup of tea and watched as Edmund pulled on his boots.

170

'Aye, well, we need the dew to be taken off the grass first. No good taking it into the barn damp, but it looks like the sun will soon do that fairly fast.' Edmund sipped his tea and stood in the doorway. 'Looks like I might have to eat my words. I hope you've enough in that oven, Polly. We've got visitors.'

Polly went and stood behind Edmund and peered over his shoulder.

'Well, that's Matt, but who's with him on the other horse?' Edmund stared at the two men riding up the lane from the road.

'It looks like Joe Fothergill, Matt's best mate. His father has the joinery on the street behind the market hall. You'll know him, when you see him.' Polly went and stirred the porridge that was simmering on the fire. 'I hope they've had their breakfasts, else I'll have to make some more porridge. Come and sit down, and then we've had ours, even if they haven't.' Polly poured two dishes of porridge out, and Edmund pulled his chair up to the table.

'Are you two only just having your breakfasts? Me and Joe here have had ours, and ridden down from Hawes, and even caught a trout in the beck for our suppers. Here, you can have mine, if you like.' Matt held the slippery brown-spotted trout in his hands and teased Polly with it, opening its mouth up and down in front of her, as he strutted into the kitchen and leaned upon the back of her chair.

'Give over, Matt. I hate fish — they are better off in the beck.' Polly quickly spooned her porridge into her mouth and then got up from the table. 'Where's Joe?'

'He's stabling the horses. I left him to it, as he's better with horses than me. I take it you won't say no to us both giving you a hand with getting your hay in? Here, Pol, put these fish in the pantry; they need to be cool.' Matt pulled up a chair and sat across from Edmund.

'I could just eat a trout — it's years since I had one, so I'll not say no to it. And, aye, you'll be more than welcome to help get in the hay. I never said owt to Polly, but we'd have struggled without your help.' Edmund leaned back in his chair.

'We'd have managed. I hate slimy fish!' Polly washed her hands under the cold-water tap and watched as Joe Fothergill crossed the yard and knocked on the kitchen door. His hair shone nearly white in the summer's sun, and Polly wondered why she hadn't noticed his blond good looks before.

'Come in, lad, we don't stand on ceremony here.' Edmund looked at the lanky lad who stood in his doorway. 'Now I know who you are: you're Bob's lad. I picked my hay-rake off you the other week.'

'That's right, Mr Harper. My father and mother have asked me to pass on their condolences. They couldn't get to the funeral, I'm afraid.'

'It's all right, lad, don't worry. Polly, make them a cup of tea, and then I'll go and put old Clover into harness. Sit here, Joe. Tell Matt to shift his feet; you'd think he owned the place.' Edmund pulled a chair out for Joe, not noticing the quick glance between friends with a secret, as he made his way out of the kitchen.

'Are you all right, Polly? I haven't seen you since the dance in the hall the other month? Matt here danced you off your feet. I didn't get a look-in, but of course that was before he knew you were his sister . . . ' Joe's conversation trailed off, knowing that he had hit on a delicate subject.

'I'm fine, thanks, Joe. Sorry I didn't get a chance to talk to you, but this one here wanted my attention. And then I fell out with Maggie.' Polly smiled at Joe, who had turned a shade of pink as he tried to cover his words.

'Hey, Polly, that reminds me: you'll not have heard the latest. Maggie, your so-called best friend, is off to live in Bradford. Rumour has it she's having a baby. Her father's going mad, and old Beattie Swaine is going round the dairy saying it's only what she expected from her.' Matt changed the subject quickly.

'She isn't! Poor Maggie. Who will she go to in Bradford? I didn't think she had anyone there!' Polly stopped in her tracks as she cleared the table. 'I can't believe she is in the family way; all she seemed to want to do was give herself to a fella. I couldn't believe it, when I saw her with that man from the Beresford Band.' It was Polly's turn to blush now, remembering that she didn't know Joe that well and shouldn't be talking that openly.

'Aye, she's a bit outgoing, is Maggie. I think there will be a few men in Hawes wondering if it's theirs.' Joe looked wistful. 'She's not my sort of lass. You couldn't count on her looking after your house and bairns.'

173

'Oh aye, Joe, so you're thinking of having a house and bairns, are you? Bloody hell, man, tha's only twenty — life's for living! You don't want to be tied down with all that.' Matt mocked his friend, just as Edmund caught the tail end of his conversation as he came back into the kitchen.

He looked at his grandson. Matt was the image of Danny, and those words could have been Danny's — he was his father's son all right.

'There's nowt wrong with having a steady lass on your arm. They are worth ten of any flirty thing, so you think on, Matt. Else you'll land yourself in trouble, just like your father.' Edmund looked at Polly. What was she thinking, having fallen for this lad, until she found out that he was her brother? And now Matt was being so flippant with his thoughts.

Polly looked at her grandfather. She could see he was not happy with the way the conversation had gone. The words that Matt had said made her wonder why he'd been so attentive to her. If he wasn't ready for a proper relationship, why had he persisted in being so close to her? In truth, his words hurt. She'd been just a game to him, she could see that now.

'I'll walk your horse and cart up to the top meadow, shall I?' Joe made for the doorway, sensing that the atmosphere in the kitchen was tense and realizing all too well what his best mate had just said.

'Aye, all right, lad. We'll be with you before long.' Edmund patted Joe on the back. At least he was sensitive to the stupidity of Matt's words.

Matt watched Joe walk out of the doorway and then sighed. 'I'm sorry. I was stupid to say that — I wasn't thinking.' He put his head in his hands, then looked at both Polly and Edmund.

'That's the trouble, lad; neither did your father. And that's why Polly means everything to me. If she's ever hurt like that again, you'll have me to, answer to.' Edmund turned his back on Matt and spat into the kitchen fire.

'It's all right. I know he didn't mean it. I'm not bothered, Grandfather. We are brother and sister, so it isn't of any consequence to me any more what Matt thinks of his women.' Polly was trying to ease the tension.

'Thanks, Polly. You know I didn't mean to hurt you. I'd best catch Joe up.' Matt rose from the table and looked at the old man standing over the fire. He was going to have to watch what he said to the old bugger; Edmund was sharper than he thought. Bill Sunter had told him that Edmund was an old stickler, when Matt had talked to him about finding out that Edmund was his grandfather and Polly his sister. Bill had been a fount of knowledge, telling him how his father, Danny, had worked at the family farm for little or no money. Matt had laughed when Bill told him that Danny had loved his women and used to climb out of his bedroom window late at night, in order to go courting without his parents' knowledge. Bill had also planted a seed of thought in Matt's head. If anything happened to Edmund, the farm of Paradise should go to his next of kin, which — as it stood — would be Polly, as Edmund would definitely not be leaving

175

anything to his lad. There and then Matt had decided that he was going to worm his way into the family. Paradise would be just right for him. After all, it should rightly be his, for he was the male of the family!

'I know he's your brother, but — by, Matt's got a side of him I don't like. He's too bloody much like your father, and he took after my grandmother, and she was a hard woman and all.' Edmund stood in the doorway, watching Polly take the pie out of the oven. 'Are you all right? I'm away up to the top meadow.'

'I'm fine. Matt was only showing off in front of Joe.' Polly put the pie down quickly on the kitchen table, as the juices from the gooseberries spilt over the edge of it, bubbling and falling in a sticky gloop on the paved floor.

'Well, as long as you are, lass. Do you want to see this Maggie, before she goes? She'll need a friend, and now she'll know what comes of not keeping herself to herself. I'm going to the dairy next week to cancel them taking my milk. I'm going to start sending it to your aunty again, in Liverpool. That Bill Sunter knew what he was doing when he took both you and Matt on — clever bugger. I bet he knows where your father is, but won't let on. Well, he can bloody well do without our milk, and without you in the shop.' Edmund swore as he thought about Bill Sunter.

'If you are going in, yes, I'll come with you. I know Maggie isn't much of a friend, but I can't turn my back on her in that state.' Polly wiped the floor clear of her spillage with the floor-cloth

176

and smiled at her grandfather.

'Aye, she'll need you all right, lass. We'll go on Monday. Right, I'll go and sort those two headstrong young lads out. That Joe's not a bad lad; he seems to have his head screwed on. Are you coming up and helping, when that lot is ready?' Edmund nodded at the oven.

'I'll be up before long. I'll just fry some bacon for sandwiches. You can manage without me, now you've two lads.'

'Perhaps I can, but one of 'em's not got much sense; let's hope he makes up for it in strength.' Edmund, grinned. She was a good 'un, was Polly. She was worth ten of her brother, from the bit he had seen of Matt.

★   ★   ★

Polly turned the sizzling bacon in the pan and then filled the large wicker basket with her newly baked buns, the gooseberry pie wrapped in a tea-towel, two bottles of home-made lemonade and the cutlery, cups and utensils to enjoy a hearty lunch in the hay-field. She then placed the cooked rashers of bacon onto some newly baked bread and covered them with a tea-cloth, before placing them in her basket. She filled two empty bottles with newly brewed tea. It would be almost cold by the time the men drank it, but nothing quenched the thirst better than a cup of tea in a hot hay-field. As she did this, she remembered the conversations she'd had with Matt, and the memories he had shared about his time on the farm in Dent. She should have known that he'd come and help with getting the hay in. What a shame the day had been spoilt by his stupid, thoughtless outburst. Because that's what it had been: an outburst of male ego that had shown the worst side of him.

She put her arm through the basket's handle and hooked it over her arm. It was surprisingly heavy, and made her realize that in years past her grandmother had never been helped in bringing it up to the hay-field. Closing the kitchen door behind her, she made her way through the farmyard and opened the low pasture gate that led to the top meadow.

The smell of chickweed and groundsel from beneath her feet filled the air as she closed the gate behind her. It was now a perfect day: the sky was blue and the sun was beating down; although only mid-morning, its rays were strong. Polly walked slowly up the pasture, the basket handle weighing on her arm and making welt-marks in the pattern of the cane-weave. She rested for a while next to the wild dog rose that was growing in the hedge, and looked down the dale. It was beautiful; she was lucky to live in such a place. The trouble was that she didn't always feel lucky. She looked up to the high pasture. She could see all three men loading the flat cart with mown hay, and then urging old Clover on a few yards further to the next hillock of dry hay. At least the cattle wouldn't go hungry this coming winter, for they would have enough to eat. She picked up her basket and started on the last leg of her journey, the short stubble of the hay-field making her walking easier.

'So you've joined us then? We've nearly cleared the bottom half. It's grand hay, really dry.' Matt leaned on his pitchfork, while Edmund and Joe carried on loading the cart.

'I just had to wait until everything was out of the oven.' Polly put her basket down next to her feet. 'Do you want a drink of lemonade?' She offered Matt a bottle from her basket, and watched as he wiped away with his hand the sweat that was trickling down his brow. He'd long since abandoned his jacket, and stood in front of her in a collarless striped shirt, with his braces hanging around his waist. He took a long swig from the bottle neck and grinned at Polly. 'I'd forgotten what hard work this is. Now I know why I like working for Bill Sunter.'

'Aye, well, at least it's honest work, and you can have the pleasure of knowing none of our stock will be going hungry this winter.' Polly looked at Matt. She was trying hard not to notice how handsome he was without his jacket on, and fought back her feelings, reminding herself that he was her brother.

'Give us a swig of that, Matt. I'm fair gasping — these hay seeds get stuck in your throat.' Joe came over and grabbed the partly drunk bottle from out of Matt's hands, gulping the tart lemonade down quickly, until more than half the bottle had gone.

'Hey, leave some for my grandfather.' Polly looked at the blond Joe, gulping back the lemonade, and reminded him that it wasn't all for him.

'Sorry, Pol. I was desperate. That sun's

stronger than it looks, when you're loading this hay up.' Joe grinned and passed back the nearly empty bottle.

'Aye, well, it'll soon be dinnertime, and we'll all have a sit and something to eat then.' Polly put the near-empty bottle back in the basket and made her way over to her grandfather. 'Want a drink, Grandfather?'

'Nay, I'll not bother.' Edmund lifted his full fork of hay and threw it onto the piled-high cart. 'You can tell those two this load is ready to go. I'm leaving the hard work to them two. Why keep a dog and bark yourself? These old arms are feeling their age,' grinned Edmund.

'I'll put this basket in the shade under the hedge, and then I'll go and tell them. Is there anything else you want me to do?' Polly strode off with the basket and left it in the shade, before returning to Edmund.

'If you can rake out the hay from the top corner of the field — it's still a bit green and not dry enough yet for loading — that would be a help. I'll take that bit in, in the morning. We might as well get all of it in.' Edmund watched Polly walk off and tell the two lads to take the cartload of hay to the barn and put it up in the hayloft. She then picked up a hay-rake from next to the cart and walked up to the top corner of the meadow, to where the cut grass was still a bit green and in need of a few more hours of sunshine on it, then to be turned one more time.

Joe walked over. 'Next year, Mr Harper, Matt has asked that I make you a hay-sledge. It won't be as much work for you, as they are lower to the

180

ground and not as likely to tip over as your cart is, on this steep hillside.' He grabbed the horse's reins and chivvied it into motion.

'Aye, that might be an idea, lad. My father had one, and I've always used the cart. But I'm not getting any younger, for throwing forks full of hay around.' Edmund caught his breath as he watched the young lad lead old Clover to the barn to unload.

Matt slapped Edmund on his back. 'It's a good job we came. You and Polly would never have managed all this.' He walked behind the horse and cart.

Edmund watched. He didn't reply, but he knew he and Polly would have managed. It might have taken them two days, but they would have done it. They'd done it in the past without help and they'd do so again.

Lunchtime came around fast and the group of four hay-timers sat down on a grass bank and waited until Polly had spread her wares around them. Each got an enamel mug of semi-warm tea, and was told to help himself from the bacon sandwiches and the baking laid out on the checked gingham tablecloth. The men and Polly ate hungrily, the fresh air and hard work making them all have healthy appetites, with hardly a word said between them.

Afterwards Matt and Joe lay out in the long grass of the bank and lit a cigarette, breathing in deeply, before exhaling the smoke.

'That was grand, lass. Ada would have been proud of you. She taught you well. That gooseberry pasty could have been hers, if I didn't know better.' Edmund tipped the last dregs of his tea out into the grass and passed Polly his empty cup as she cleared away.

'Aye, it was like old times. It was like I was at home up Cowgill and helping my grandfather there.' Matt sat up, wrapped his arms around his knees and legs and looked across at Polly. 'Polly, you remember me saying that I loved the hay-field tea — there's not a better taste? I miss helping my grandfather on t' farm. It's a pity we only rented it. I'd have liked to have still been there.'

'Well, it's only over that fell, Matt — you're not that far away.' Joe sat up next to him. 'And you are helping here, so nowt's changed, except you've got a fresh grandfather and a sister. You're bloody lucky, from what I'm seeing.' Joe smiled at Polly, making her blush slightly.

'No, but it's not the same when it's not your own. One day I'll own my own place, and then I'll not be working for nowt.' Matt emptied his cup out and stood up, stretching his legs and arms, as he got ready to start loading the last few loads of hay onto the cart.

'I'll see you right for today, if you are wanting some brass.' Edmund looked at Matt, who couldn't have hinted any harder that he didn't expect to give his day's help for nothing.

'I didn't come for money, Mr Harper. I just came to help.' Joe stepped in quickly and jumped up from his seat.

'No, and I didn't. I came because I knew Polly and you would struggle getting this in, especially as my grandmother's barometer gives it bad weather for tomorrow. But if there's some beer-money in it for tonight, that will be grand. I'll be ready for a drink before the day is out.' Matt grabbed hold of the pitchfork and looked at his grandfather.

'Aye, your father used to like a drink. I like an odd 'un with Len Brunskill, of a market day often enough, to catch up with the gossip and set the world right. But you should never let it control you — else that farm you talk about will never be yours.' Edmund looked at the brazen young lad who stood in front of him.

'I will never let that happen. And I will get my farm one day, of that I'm sure. Come on, Joe, let's get a move-on. Another hour and we'll have cracked it.'

11

Polly sat on the sofa in Bill Sunter's drawing room. She watched as Maggie wrung her hands in despair and mopped the tears from her cheeks with her lace handkerchief.

'My mam says I've got what I deserve — that I've brought shame to the family. That if I was going to get into this state, I should have made sure he was single, or at least had plenty of money to keep me and the baby in a fitting lifestyle.' Maggie sniffed and stifled another sob.

'But where are you going, Maggie? Can I come and see you?' Polly watched her friend. Maggie was obviously heartbroken.

'Nah, my father's paid for me to go into a place that takes in unmarried women in my condition. When I've had the baby, they'll find someone to adopt it and, if I'm lucky, then my mother and father might have me back.' Maggie gave a quick glance at Polly.

'What about its father — doesn't he have a say?' Polly couldn't help but think of her own father, who might or might not know she existed. She thought this baby should at least have the chance of knowing its parents.

'That's just it. I don't know who the father is. If it's anyone's, I think it could be the singer from the Beresford Band; but I don't know, because it could be Ralph Bannister's and all.'

'Oh, Maggie! What did you think would

happen? You were so loose with your favours. I know it's hard, but you shouldn't let fellas have their way. You only get a bad name or end up like — '

'Like this, you mean, with this bloody thing growing in me every day? I wish I were dead, Polly. I really do wish I were dead. So don't you start lecturing me. I know what I've done.' Maggie's bloodshot red eyes looked at Polly as she crumpled her handkerchief up into a knot.

'I'm not lecturing. I'm hardly in a position to lecture. The man I loved turned out to be my brother, and my father is my grandfather. And all's to hell in my life as well. Even Joe Fothergill asked me out the other day: now do I trust him or not? And then there's Tobias. I know I shouldn't feel this way, but I do think nobody understands him. He's always been kind to me.' Polly had missed talking to her best friend, and so much had happened to her since the quarrel in the market hall. She just wanted to tell Maggie everything.

'Just listen to yourself. I'm like this, and you're prattling on about this lad and that lad. Well, aren't you the lucky one? You always have been, but didn't know it. Just like you didn't know who your mother and father were. All along I knew your deep, dark secret. My father told me — he knows all about your lot. How your grandfather drove his lad away because he was so self-centred and stingy. Just like you: only thinking of yourself.' Maggie got up from her chair and stood behind Polly, as she let fling her usual cutting remarks in defence of her own actions.

'Maggie, stop it; you don't mean what you are saying. Why do you always come out with all this hurtful rubbish, when things are not going your way? I know your father was my father's best friend. It was him, my grandfather says, who made my father go away, just like he's making you leave now. No matter what you say, you can't hurt me any more, because everything is out in the open. I just can't understand why you hate me so much, when all I am is a friend to you.' Polly's eyes filled with tears. Maggie's tongue was caustic, and the vulnerable young lass of a few minutes ago had vanished now.

'I hate you, Polly Harper, because no matter what you are, you are loved. I used to watch your grandmother and grandfather looking after you — making sure you were home on time, that you knew how to look after yourself — all the while knowing they weren't even your parents. Whereas my mother can't cook, clean, or anything. She's only good for one thing — that's what my father says. Now he knows that I am the image of her and shouldn't have been born, just as he's always keen to remind me. The slight problem is that, unlike my darling mother, I didn't catch a fella with money; and now nobody wants me, nobody in the whole wide world.' Maggie was crying and nearly screaming with anger and fear. Unlike Polly, her family was a sham and always had been. Money had earned Bill Sunter respect, but behind closed doors his family was just going through the motions of looking like a respectable middle-class family.

'Maggie, come here — stop all this. I love you.

You are my friend and always will be, never mind our families. I bet there isn't a family in the dale that doesn't have a skeleton in their cupboard. Unfortunately, ours are a bit open to gossip at the moment.' Polly stood up and wrapped her arms around the now-sobbing Maggie.

'I'm sorry. I shouldn't have said all those things, and I've a spiteful tongue in my head when my temper gets the better of me,' sobbed Maggie into Polly's shoulder. 'My mother says it's the Irish in me, but don't ask me where that comes into it, because I'm damned if I know!' She sniffed and let go of Polly's tight hug.

'Aye, well, we are a mixed-up bunch. It's a wonder we all survive, the way we hurt one another. Are you all right now?' Polly stood at arm's length to Maggie and looked at her. Maggie looked pale and worried.

'I'm fine. I'm sorry. Happen I should have told you about your father, but my father told me not to. And you were so blissfully happy, and then Matt started making eyes at you and I didn't know what to do. I knew he was your brother.'

'I thought you were jealous. I thought you wanted Matt for yourself.' Polly looked at Maggie.

'I did at first, and then I heard my father talking about your father, Danny, saying that he did right to leave and that Matt reminded him so much of Danny; that once his mind's set on something, he'll not give in until he gets it. And I watched Matt bossing some of my father's staff around, grinning if he'd got the better of them, or making them look small in front of other folk.

187

It was then that I realized I didn't really care for Matt, he has a side to him that you don't know, Polly, so you take care.' Maggie grasped Polly's hand tightly with shaking fingers. 'I think he's after something from you, but I don't know what. He's friends with no one unless it benefits him. I've been watching him.'

'Maggie, you don't have to tell me. I think I know what he's after. I've watched him talking to my grandfather, trying to sweet-talk himself into his good books and making him feel guilty for knowingly having nothing to do with him all these years. I know what Matt's after.' Polly stood up and looked out of the window of the Sunters' parlour onto the business of the dairy. 'He's after Paradise, my home. He's trying to worm his way into my grandfather's will and to block me out!' Polly turned and watched her friend's face as she sank into a chair and gasped at the words she had just heard.

'He can't do that. Paradise is your home. You know it like the back of your hand; you would farm that place just as well as any fella, and your grandfather knows that. Besides, it isn't anyone's until after his day.'

'Aye, but he's a lad, and they always come first. Women aren't supposed to farm. Even though my grandfather has told me Paradise is mine after his day, I know that having a male heir means everything to him, though he will always be heartbroken over my father walking away from home. Do you know the most terrible thought I've had of late?' Polly hung her head and waited for Maggie to ask what was troubling her.

Maggie shook her head and waited for Polly to continue.

'I think, when he was making eyes at me, and kissing me and laughing and flirting, I think he knew that I was his sister. And that I was the stepping-stone to get to what he wanted: my farm.'

'Oh, Polly, he couldn't use you like that. Surely that would have been too wrong!'

'I don't know, but he doesn't seem to have been as shocked as I am. He's strutting around without a care, and I'm feeling used, dirty and confused. He's making himself indispensable at Paradise, although Grandfather doesn't seem to take kindly to some of Matt's phrases. I think Matt's too much like my father. But, anyway, this isn't about me. I came to see you, so I'm going to shut up. As you say, I like the sound of my own voice.' Polly smiled. She was glad she had aired her thoughts with her friend, but they were nothing compared to bringing a baby into the world on your own.

'I didn't know you had all these worries. At least I know that even when I've had this baby that's growing inside me, I can always come home. I know my father's got plenty of brass, and that he's always there for me. Pol, you watch your back with that Matt. Don't let him make Paradise his. He may be your brother, but he's no right to your home.'

'Come here, Maggie, let's give one another a hug. We've always got one another. You will keep in touch, won't you, when you're in Bradford?' Polly held her arms out and squeezed Maggie

189

tightly as she shed a tear on her shoulder.

'Course I will. And I know I'm not one to give advice, but I'd be looking at Tobias Middleton — at least he has brass and isn't in anybody else's pocket. I just think he's a bit creepy and dark; he looks so moody.'

'That's what attracts me. I'm curious about him, and I still think that the theft of my Herdwick and her lambs was planned,' grinned Polly.

'He's a dark one, for sure. Perhaps I should say he's the father of my baby. At least it would have some money behind it.' Maggie grinned.

'You didn't . . . you haven't?' Polly was horrified to think that Maggie had slept with Tobias.

'No, I didn't. What do you think I am? He's not my sort. This baby is either a Beresford or a Bannister. Either way, when you think about it, it's a little B. A little B that's got me into a lot of bother!' Maggie sniffed while she fought back the tears again.

'I'm going to miss you. You keep your chin up and just count the days until the baby is born, and then come home. I don't know how you'll manage to walk away from the baby, once you've seen it.' Polly thought of the child that was about to be born, unloved; she couldn't just walk away and leave it in an unknown person's arms.

'I'll just have to do it, Pol. No one wants a woman with a bastard baby on her apron strings. Just think of all the tales we have heard about your Tobias. I'm not having that said about mine.'

'He's not *my* Tobias. And he wasn't wanted by his father, and his mother didn't know he'd lived. Are you sure you couldn't tell Ralph Bannister that it is definitely his? He's not a bad lad. There's no shame in marrying a lead-miner; they are hard workers, and your father will always support you all.' Polly was still thinking of the baby being left with a family in Bradford, not knowing where it really came from.

'No, he's not come near me, and he must have heard by now that I'm this way — all of Hawes seems to know. He'll be thinking, like the rest, that I'm just a common slut. I'm so frightened, Polly. I don't know if I can handle childbirth, and I'll have nobody I know with me.' Maggie started to sob again, and Polly comforted her with another hug.

'Don't cry, Maggie, you'll be all right. Things will turn out fine, I promise you. It's only a baby; folk have them every day — you'll manage it.' Polly held Maggie close; words were easy to say, but she wouldn't be in Maggie's shoes for all the tea in China.

★　★　★

Edmund waited outside the draper's as Polly took her time ordering the dress that he had offered to pay for. He sat with the reins in his hands, watching the folk of Hawes go about their business. His mind was wandering to the conversation he'd just had with Bill Sunter, and he was regretting that his temper had got the better of him. The bloody fella had always been a pain in his side, so he'd decided to stop supplying milk to him. Evie in Liverpool would take it again, although it meant getting up at an unearthly hour to catch the train. Tah! That Bill — the bloody cheek of the man — trying to tell him how old he was, and that he wouldn't get the same price as he gave him.

Edmund spat on the pavement. Bill might be right on both counts, but at least he wasn't in that bloody man's pocket, and that counted for a lot. He should have listened to Ada from the start, and then none of this would have happened. He sighed. What was that lass doing? Surely it didn't take this long to be measured and choose material for a new frock? He looked across to the solicitor's offices. If he'd known Polly was going to be this long, he'd have called in and seen old Winterskill. It was time to put his affairs in order. Ada hadn't needed a will, for all that was hers was his, but now it was time to put things down in writing, square things up, for after his day. He wanted to do right by the folk he loved, the way it should be.

The tinkling of the draper's shop bell brought him back from his thoughts and he sighed with relief as Polly climbed up next to him, beaming from ear to ear in excitement at the thought of her new frock.

'Well, have you spent my brass, and is she making you what you want?' Edmund stirred Clover into action as Polly told him the colour and fit, and that it would be ready in a week's time. 'I'm glad you are happy with it. My Ada never had one made; she always made her own.

She'll be looking down and saying I'm spoiling you,' grinned Edmund.

'I know. You are spoiling me, and I'm really grateful.' Polly leaned over and gave him a kiss on the cheek.

'Aye, well, I've only one woman in my life now. I'd better look after her, because she's growing up fast and turning the heads of all the young men in the district.' Edmund clicked his tongue, making Clover go into a trot.

'Don't know what you mean, Granddad,' Polly smirked.

'I think you do, Missy. I think there will be hearts broken when that new dress is worn.'

★   ★   ★

It was the week after Polly's visit to the Sunters' when her grandfather shouted to her as she was busily making the beds and dusting the dressing table. 'Polly, have you seen who's coming up the track?' he yelled up the stairs to her. 'I think it's yon Sunter lass, Maggie, with a fella next to her. I thought she'd been sent to Bradford in shame?'

Polly ran down the stairs and stood in the porch at Paradise, then watched as the red-haired Maggie and a determined-looking Ralph Bannister came up the track in a little gig, pulled by a piebald horse that had a mind of its own as it snorted in defiance of the reins.

Edmund stood behind Polly as she waved to them both, whilst Ralph tied the headstrong horse to the ring next to the saddling steps at the side of the barn. 'It's got a mind of its own, has

193

that horse. He'll have to be careful, especially with her in that condition,' commented Edmund, as he watched Ralph help Maggie down from the gig.

Maggie, flushed with colour, and a hesitant Ralph made their way across the yard to the porch where Edmund and Polly stood waiting.

'I thought you were in Bradford?' said Polly, as Maggie reached the porch.

Maggie beamed. 'No, I've come to tell you my news — or should I say *we* have come to tell you our news.' Maggie reached round and grabbed Ralph's hand, making him blush in front of the sombre Edmund Harper. 'Ralph and I are to be married. He proposed to me the day after you came to see me. I couldn't keep my news to myself. I had to come and see you.' Maggie grinned from cheek to cheek as she stood in front of Polly and her grandfather.

'Congratulations, Maggie. Congratulations Ralph, that's wonderful news. I'm sure you will both be very happy.' Polly smiled and bent down and kissed Maggie on the cheek, before beckoning them to enter her home.

'Aye, it's good that you've done the honourable thing, lad. Sometimes you've to stick by your commitments, no matter how hard they'll try you.' Edmund drew on his pipe and watched the excited couple make themselves at home in his kitchen.

'Thank you, sir. I don't look upon it as being too hard a task. I've always been sweet on Maggie here. And a baby — well, it will be somebody to look after us when we are old and grey.'

'Aye, tha's a long way off them days, lad. But a baby will always bring happiness. Look at our Polly here — she keeps me young. Her grandmother worshipped the ground she walked on. From the day she entered this house she filled it with love and hope, and I'll never forget that. Anyway, enough of my wittering. I'll leave you lot to it; you don't want an old codger like me about the place.' Edmund placed his pipe in the side of his mouth and decided to make himself scarce.

He made his way across the farmyard and heard the two girls giggling as he leaned over the pasture gate. It reminded him of when his beloved Ada and her bridesmaid, her cousin Winnie, were planning their wedding, and of how excited she had been. Her cheeks had been flushed. They were like roses next to her black hair, and her laughter had been infectious as she'd smiled at him with love in her eyes. How he'd loved that lass; how he still loved her now. He didn't know how he'd survived the last few weeks without her. It was just as well she wasn't alive to see and hear her family being gossiped about.

Ever since last week, when he'd gazed across at the solicitor's office, Edmund had been in a quandary. He'd always promised Paradise to Polly, but now Matt had made himself known, and hadn't been away from the place since he'd found out that Edmund was his grandfather. He should do right by the lad and leave him half, after his day, but something was stopping him. He didn't like Matt's attitude — he was too

195

much like his father. Perhaps he'd just bide his time and see what happened. If Matt was like his father, then farming would be too steady for him.

Another ring of laughter made Edmund smile as he gazed down the valley, watching the smoke from the early-evening fires rising from the houses of the dale. It was good to hear them being happy. He didn't think much of the Sunter lass, but the baby would need a father, and perhaps a baby in her arms would steady her down. Perhaps it was time for Polly to find someone. That Joe Fothergill seemed keen; he was always finding an excuse to visit with Matt. She could do worse than him, and there'd always be need of a joiner, so she'd never be short of brass, even if she didn't farm Paradise. No doubt whatever he thought, he'd be wrong. Best just to say nowt and keep his thoughts to himself, Edmund thought, as he took in the evening rays and puffed on his pipe.

⋆　⋆　⋆

'I was just getting into my father's trap. I'd even packed my bags and said goodbye to my mother, when Ralph here comes running hell for leather down the street. He nearly fell over when he got to the cobbles, he was in such a rush to see me.' Maggie giggled and squeezed Ralph's hand. 'Anyway, to cut a long story short, he'd never heard of my predicament until that morning. But as soon as he realized he was going to be a father, he'd hitched a lift out of Swaledale with a drover and decided to make an honest woman of me. Another ten minutes and I'd have been on that train on my way to Bradford.'

'Aye, I don't think your father's that suited that I caught you in time. I don't think he thinks I'm good enough for you.' Ralph looked sheepishly at Polly.

'Well, I'm just glad it's ended in good news, and that the baby is going to have a pair of loving parents.' Polly smiled. She'd done her bit towards bringing them together when she'd written her note telling Ralph of Maggie's plight. That was a secret between her and Ralph, else Maggie would never have agreed to his hand in marriage, thinking that he was only giving it out of pity.

'And I'm trying to rent us somewhere to live. Boggle Hole has been empty for years, but it's near where I work, and with a bit of attention it will make a good home. I'm determined to show your father, Maggie, that I can support you and our baby.' Ralph looked lovingly at her; she was the woman of his dreams, and now she was his.

'The wedding's a bit rushed, and a quiet affair. My father says not to make a fuss, after all the gossip. We are trying to make the wedding for the last day in September, if the vicar can fit us in on time. You'll come to the wedding, won't you, Pol?' Maggie sat on the edge of the chair and waited for an answer from Polly.

'Maggie, I'd love to. Is the wedding at St Margaret's in Hawes?'

'Yes, but only our parents are invited, along with a few other friends. And you, of course; and

Ralph's brother, Bert — he's to be best man.'

'Don't forget we've got to invite Tobias Middleton, if I can rent Boggle Hole from him. He sort of invited himself, when I was telling him I was to marry you. I don't suppose we can turn him down, with the rent he was initially thinking of charging us,' Ralph added quickly.

'You are renting a house from Tobias, and he's coming to the wedding?' Polly was surprised.

'Oh, Ralph, I forgot to tell you. Polly has a strange fascination for Tobias. In fact I think it is more than a fascination.' Maggie giggled.

'Well, she'll meet him at our do, if I can rent the house, that is. He looked at me as if I was wrong in the head, when I said I wanted it. All the locals say it is haunted. That's why it's called Boggle Hole. A boggle is an evil sprite, but I don't believe in such rubbish.' Ralph sat back and laughed.

'Nah, it'll be all right. Just don't tell me father until you've got it. And you, Polly Harper, you should have a good day, with the man of your dreams to hand. What more could you wish for?' Maggie winked, for she too had been planning. There was no way she was going to move into a godforsaken haunted house up on some remote hillside, but if it got Polly within talking distance of Tobias, then it was worth playing along with. Her father would buy her and Ralph a good house in Muker, and well she knew it.

Polly smiled. A whole day with the dark and handsome Tobias, with no one to stop them from talking together. Maggie's wedding couldn't come quickly enough.

12

Polly walked through the churchyard gate, and on to the graveside of her grandmother. She had visited the grave at least once a week since Ada had died, placing fresh cut flowers in the jam jar and saying a silent prayer for her grandmother's safekeeping. Today she placed the vivid orange blooms of the calendula on the grave, before entering the church to help the local women decorate it for the harvest festival, in thanks for another fruitful year of good crops and healthy stock.

The sun shone down. It had been a good summer, but soon the autumn winds would be blowing and the rain would never cease, and the days would be long and dark as the winter months drew in. In her other hand Polly held a basket full of home-made jams; a cabbage from the small garden that Edmund spent many an evening in; and lengths of rosehips, picked from the nearby hedges and then thread onto cotton by her. They shone like a precious necklace of rubies, ready to be hung from the candleholders and pews of the church. She'd spent the last two nights with a darning needle in hand, threading the hips, just as Ada had shown her, ever since she was old enough to be trusted with a needle and thread. It was a tradition that she supplied the threaded hips, and this year was not going to be any different.

'Polly, it's good to see you, my love. We didn't know if you'd make it or not, this year.' Mrs Armitage, the churchwarden's wife, welcomed Polly as she entered the church, while the other farmers' wives and women of the district smiled and waved to her.

'I couldn't let you down. My mother — sorry, I mean my grandmother — would never have forgiven me.' Polly blushed at her honest mistake, as Molly Armitage took her arm.

'We were all saddened about Ada, my love. We didn't think, this time last year, that she wouldn't be with us now. Are you and your grandfather managing? He must be missing your grandmother terribly, and it must have been a shock for you to find out in such a terrible way about your real father and mother. I saw your brother hit that Tobias Middleton. They were always trouble, that family. I bet that Tobias takes after his father. 'Neither a fighter nor a gambler be' — and he was both.' Molly shook her head and then shouted at the woman placing the flowers on the altar, telling her to centre them more.

'Actually, Tobias wasn't doing any wrong. Matt was just being over-protective. That was before he realized we were sister and brother.' Polly leapt to the defence of Tobias and watched as the frustrated Molly yelled out some more instructions to her army of helpers.

'Still, my dear, you don't want to have anything to do with him. It was unpleasant business, the way he was brought up. Now, what have you got in your basket? Let's find a place for them. I'm so glad that you have strung some hips together — they look so lovely draped around the brass candleholder at the end of the nave. Oh, Winnie, will you stop moving that vase of flowers! Excuse me, Polly, I'm going to have to sort Winnie out. She has no eye for balance, and that's what a good decorated church is all about.' Molly bustled off, hands in the air and posh voice on; after all, she was in charge of the whole operation, whether her fellow helpers knew it or not!

'Eh, I bet you're glad she's shut up. Is she bossy or what?' Len Brunskill's wife Martha came and helped Polly to empty her basket, placing the jams and cabbage in one of the church's windows. They were to be displayed throughout the coming Sunday's service, and then to be auctioned off the following night, for church funds.

'She is just a bit.' Polly smiled.

'Aye, and she's a nosy old bugger. Reckons to know it all, but knows bugger-all,' whispered Martha Brunskill, grinning. 'Are you all right Polly? The news of you having a father and mother, other than Ada and Edmund, must have come as a shock. And then to find the fella you like is your brother must have really hurt.' Martha looked at the young lass, who was running her hands through the string of beaded hips, and knew she was hurting.

'I just get upset sometimes. My world has been turned upside down, and I've no one to talk to.' Polly fought back a tear. She'd known the kindly Martha since she could toddle and loved her like an aunt. 'Everyone else knew the

201

truth, except me. I wish someone had told me, stopped me making a fool of myself with Matt.' She sniffed.

'Aye, lass, sometimes thing are better left buried. You were loved, and still are. Ada loved the ground you walked on, and Edmund would lay down his life for you. As for Matt turning up like a bad penny, you'll have to learn to love him like a brother; happen it's better that way. From what I hear, he'll not be the marrying kind. Sounds like he's a bit like your father in that respect.' Martha patted Polly's hand.

'Martha, did you know my mother? I've no one to ask. I don't want to upset my grandfather. What did she look like? Do I look like her?' Polly's eyes pleaded with Martha for the much-coveted information that had been on her mind since she'd heard about her conception.

'Come on, let's go and sit on the bench outside where prying ears can't hear us. We'll come back and hang up those hips in a minute.' Martha placed Polly's basket down on a pew and made for the brilliant sunshine outside, with Polly following her.

'Now then, lass, what do you want to know? I know exactly how things happened, and how much heartache your father caused. And, aye, I remember your mother. She was a young slip of a lass. She was a bonny thing, with long black hair and forget-me-not-blue eyes. And, yes, you are the image of her. She was shy and quiet, yet the lads were round her like bees around a honey pot, but she had only eyes for Danny.'

Polly smiled as she thought of her mother as a

young woman just like her.

Martha carried on with her story. 'The trouble was that Danny was never one for commitment. He was spoilt by Edmund and Ada, being their only child. And he hadn't the courage to tell his father when he got your mother in trouble, so he left the dale like a dog with its tail between its legs, and robbed your grandfather of his savings. Edmund should have followed him, brayed him around the lugs and brought him home, but he's a proud man, is your grandfather. Besides, at the time he didn't know why Danny had left, until Bernard Dinsdale turned up on the doorstep of Paradise in a blizzard, with you wrapped up under his coat. I remember the first time I ever saw you, a little bit of a crinkly thing, with a huge tuft of black hair and the bluest eyes! No wonder Ada and Edmund brought you up as theirs; they'd never think they were doing any harm. You were loved, lass, and that's all that matters.' Martha held Polly's hand and smiled. 'Everybody meant well, lass. No one wanted you hurt.' She raised her face to the sun and sighed deeply.

'And my father? Does anyone know where he is?' Polly looked at Martha.

'Aye, your father — I wish I did know where he was. I thought he might turn up at Ada's funeral, but he never did. Bill Sunter once said he'd gone across the sea to America. They were best friends, you do know that?'

Polly nodded.

'I can't see him going there myself. He hadn't the guts to do anything on his own.' Martha looked at Polly. She was the image of her mother

— she'd not told her a lie there. 'I hear that Joe Fothergill is sweet on you. He's not a bad lad; a bit steady, but will not make anything of himself, apart from being in business with his father. Life's what you make it, Polly. If you want something, or somebody, go for it, just as long as you don't hurt anyone on the way.'

Polly blushed. 'He's all right, but he's Matt's friend.'

'All right isn't good enough. Now that Tobias Middleton has the world at his feet, and he's not a bad lad, no matter what folk say about him. And he was going to fight for your honour, if I remember.' Martha grinned.

'You know Tobias?' Polly was shocked.

'Aye, I know his mother, Daisy, the kindest woman you can ever meet. Now his father was a different matter, wild as a mountain hare. But Tobias hasn't a bad bone in his body; he's just judged because of his father, and because he looks like him. Don't tell your grandfather, or my Len, I spoke highly of him. They don't understand us women.' Martha let out a loud laugh. 'It's good to look at the mantelpiece, when you are stoking the fire.'

Polly blushed; her grandmother would never have been so crude.

'Are you two here to help or to gossip?' Molly Armitage shouted from the porch of the church, squinting in the sharp sunshine.

'Just catching up, Molly. We are on our way,' Martha shouted back. 'Any suggestions where to wrap those strings of rosehips, Polly? I have one, if you haven't!' She laughed as she made fun of the bossy Molly Armitage.

'I think I could think of one.' Polly was glad to have found an ally.

★ ★ ★

'Are you not going to the harvest festival, Polly? You know I think nowt of going to church, but I thought you'd have gone.' Edmund looked at Polly, who was sitting next to the fire, darning his socks.

'No, I can't go. I don't feel there's anything to celebrate this year. I will go to the sale tomorrow night, though. I enjoy the harvest sale.' Polly wrapped the darning wool around her fingers and broke it off from the darned hole that she had mended, then examined her handiwork.

'Ada would have liked you to have gone.' Edmund placed the Sunday paper down and looked at Polly over the top of his reading glasses.

'I'm not going. Just for once I'm stopping away. That Molly Armitage only looks at me like I've got two heads, and I don't want to face the vicar. I still remember his face when there was all that carry-on outside the church at the funeral.' Polly put her sewing things away and sighed.

'All right lass, if that's what you want.' Edmund shook his paper and started reading the news of the day.

'I think I'll go for a walk, up the side of the gill. I'll look if there's any nuts on the hazel trees along the bank, although it's a little too early to pick them yet.'

'All right, lass. Do you want me to do anything while you are away?'

'No, all's done for the day. I like my Sundays — at least they are nice and quiet.' Polly reached for her shawl and smiled, looking at Edmund with his feet up, engrossed in the paper and enjoying his pipe. The smell of the tobacco filled the air, and Polly loved the heavy fragrance of Kendal Twist. 'I'll not be long,' she shouted as she closed the kitchen door behind her.

She made her way to the back of the house and followed the gill up through the pastures and onto the fell side. Every so often she stopped to examine the gnarled branches of the hazel trees that lined the gill side. It was going to be a good year for the sweet little nut that both squirrels and humans liked. The trees were covered in clusters of nuts that grew in twos and threes, still coated in their little green-frilled jackets, and not yet quite brown and ripe enough to be gathered. She pulled a single nut from off its branch, shelled it from the green jacket and then tried to crack it between her teeth. She pressed her teeth hard onto the nut, finally deciding to crack it between two stones, to save her from breaking a tooth. The shell splattered, revealing a small white kernel inside the shell. Polly picked it up and placed it in her mouth; the nut tasted milky, with just a hint of what it was going to taste like if left to mature. No, the hazel nuts needed another two or three weeks yet and then they would be just right.

She liked this time of year, for wherever she looked there was an abundance of free food. Her gaze fell upon some wild mushrooms in a ring, among an especially green tuft of grass. She'd pick them on her way back down and place them in her shawl. They'd be good for supper with a slice of bacon. Ever since she was small she had been taught which toadstools and mushrooms were safe to eat, and to take care not to pick the poisonous ones, so identifying them was no problem.

The line of hazel trees following the beck soon gave way to the open fell side and Polly strode out over the long moorland reeds and grasses, picking her way through the patches of sphagnum moss that squelched under her feet. The late-summer breeze blew, with a hint of a chill in its breath, making Polly grateful she had her shawl with her. Polly climbed to the very edge of the fell land that belonged to Paradise: to the stony limestone outcrop that ran along the top of the fell ridge. There she sat under the protection of the limestone ridge and breathed in the peaty fell air and basked in the late-summer sun's rays. A skylark bobbed up and down above her, singing its familiar tune and, far down in the valley, she could hear the church bells calling for everyone to attend the harvest festival and give praise for another year.

She felt it more appropriate that she shared her thoughts with her God on the fell top, out of sight of some of the hypocrites who went to church. She sighed. What a year! Who could tell what was going to happen in the coming months? Ada's death had shaken Polly, making her feel less certain about the future. But she knew she was not going to be content with just living from day to day, going through the motions of running a home for her grandfather. That thought made her feel guilty; she was selfish and should be grateful for what she had, but all the same, there must be more to life surely? Tomorrow night she would attend the harvest sale. Everyone in the dale usually attended and it was a good social evening for young and old alike. She'd always gone, since being a toddler on her grandmother's knee, enjoying a 'Jacob's join' supper and then bidding for the produce up for sale for church funds. It was a night for meeting old friends and making new ones.

And then there was Maggie's wedding to look forward to. Tobias would be there and she would be wearing her new dress, and without anyone to tell her how to behave. A smile played on her lips. That would be the day to talk to him again, to remind him that she was free and available, no matter what her brother and grandfather thought.

★   ★   ★

Polly placed her bacon-and-egg flan out onto the already-laden long table that held all the neighbours' offerings for the 'Jacob's join' harvest supper. She then placed down her apple pie and a jug of fresh cream for dessert. The church was full with neighbours and friends, and Edmund and Polly could hardly get a word in edgeways, with people welcoming them and asking how they were keeping.

'By, they've got a good turnout, Pol.' Edmund bit into a cooked sausage and looked around him. 'Have you seen them dahlias that old Bert has grown — they'll look grand in a vase up at home. I'll bid for them when they come up in the auction.'

'They do look lovely. I think we should have a go at growing some next year.' Polly blushed when Joe Fothergill waved at her as he entered the church and made a beeline to her.

'I think I'd better make myself scarce. I'm not going to cramp a young lad's style. I'll be over there with Len, if you want me.' Edmund sipped his tea and grinned at Polly's embarrassment. Young Joe must have gone out of his way to be halfway down Garsdale on a Monday evening.

'I was hoping you'd be here, Polly. Matt said you would be, so I thought I'd come down and see you, and grab a bit of free supper and all. It's a good spread, isn't it?' Joe placed a whole delicate brawn sandwich in his mouth, making him unable to answer for a moment, as Polly asked if Matt had come with him.

'Nope, he's got business with Bill Sunter. God knows what, at this time of night. It isn't as if it's his own business, to be working them hours.'

'It's a wonder he's not here. He seems always to be swarming around my grandfather nowadays. He hardly ever talks to me.' Polly watched as Joe made his way down the table, picking out a bit of this and a bit of that, and finally finishing with a dish full of apple pie and cream.

'Well, he's embarrassed, isn't he? Fancy falling

for your sister!' slurped Joe between a mouthful of pie.

'Is that it, or is there more to it?' Polly wanted to see what Joe thought.

'Don't know what you mean, Polly. Course it's only that, and that he likes coming to Paradise — he says it's his new home.' Joe looked at Polly, who was frowning at his answer. 'He's just glad he's found where he's come from, that's all,' Joe added, sensing that he'd said something wrong.

'If you say so.' She made little of his answer, as she still doubted her brother.

'Come on, Polly, sit next to me. The auction's about to start. What do you fancy buying? I'll treat you.' Joe tugged on her arm, pulling Polly down next to him in a pew nearly at the front of the church.

Polly sensed people were watching them and commenting that they made a lovely couple. It was true, they did; but she felt nothing for Joe, even though she knew he was sweet on her. She sat and looked around her as the local auctioneer rose to the lectern to take the forthcoming bids. His assistants were Martha Brunskill and Molly Armitage, who stood on either side of him, smiling proudly at one another, dressed in their Sunday best and holding the first piece of fruit and veg to be auctioned. The room went quiet as the auctioneer lifted his hammer to start the auction, and winked at the local farmers that he knew from his farm auctions.

'Now then, ladies and gents, let's dig deep in our pockets this evening for funds for this lovely church. God might work in mysterious ways, but

I haven't seen him putting slates on any of his buildings as of yet, and this church needs some reroofing.' His audience of potential bidders laughed. The portly auctioneer then started. 'Right, Mrs Armitage, what have we got there then?'

Molly shouted up to him 'Onions' as she lifted up a string of beautifully presented onions for everyone to see.

'Any liver to go with them? There's nowt better than liver and onions. My old lass makes me it regular. Now how about tuppence for the onions. Tuppence, anybody? Come on, a penny ha'penny then.'

A shout went out. 'Aye, here, penny ha'penny.'

'Any more offers?' The auctioneer knocked the first lot down to the bidder and then proceeded with the next lot, gathering speed as the produce was held up for sale.

'Now then, here's one for all you courting couples. Kiss-me-cake. My old lass used to make this when we were first wed. How she knew I'd a sweet tooth, I'll never know.' He patted his ample stomach and laughed. 'Mrs Brunskill has just told me she baked it this morning, so it'll be good.' Martha Brunskill glowed with pride as she held a plate of the sweet jam slice in the air.

Joe looked at Polly and then shouted out, 'A penny', before flushing bright red at the sound of his own voice and the glance that Polly gave him.

'A penny bid. Any more?'

'Aye, threepence,' came another voice from the back of the church.

Joe frowned and shouted out again. 'Fourpence.' He was determined to buy it and give it to Polly.

211

'Sixpence,' the other bidder shouted.

The auctioneer stopped and looked at Joe, who was busy trying to see who was outbidding him. 'Well, is she worth another offer?'

Joe looked determined and shouted, 'Sevenpence.'

'And you, Mr Middleton, are you counter-offering, for your fine lady?' yelled the auctioneer, as heads turned and looked at Tobias Middleton and the beautiful woman on his arm.

'Aye, a florin for the cake.' Tobias smiled at the auctioneer as the church buzzed with excitement and amazement at a few pieces of kiss-me-cake making such a price.

The auctioneer looked at Joe, who shook his head, crestfallen that he could not compete at such a price.

'Sold to Tobias Middleton and his lovely lady. That buys us at least a few slates. God bless you, sir.'

'Bloody show-off,' Joe whispered to Polly. 'I wanted to give that to you.'

'Doesn't matter, Joe. It was silly money that he paid. Who's the woman he's with? I can't see from here.' Polly was unconcerned about Joe's feelings, but she did want to see who was with Tobias. She hadn't realized that he was there. She peered through the faces behind her, but still couldn't see Tobias and his mystery woman.

'I don't know, probably someone who's after his brass. Why else would she be with him? Let's face it, he doesn't have many charms.' Joe scowled at Polly. He knew that she had feelings for him.

Polly went quiet. Tobias had a girlfriend, yet she thought he'd had eyes for her. He'd probably bring the woman to Maggie's wedding, and Polly would be there like a wallflower. How could he do this? Didn't he know she was his, if he'd only ask?

'Joe, do you want to come with me to Maggie's wedding? I'm sure she won't mind if you come with me.' Polly would show Tobias that she, too, could attract the opposite sex.

'Are you sure? Does this mean we are courting?' Joe grabbed her hand.

'If you like. Everyone seems to think that we are already anyway.' Polly looked towards the back of the church again, as Joe beamed with delight.

'I'll buy you these flowers. You can take them home from me.' Joe looked excited as the auctioneer started the bidding for the flowers that Edmund had previously admired.

'No, don't. Listen, my grandfather's bidding for them — he said he would.'

'Bloody hell, I can't buy anything for you. The next bunch is mine, no matter what,' Joe exclaimed.

★ ★ ★

Polly lay in her bed. The smell of the russet-coloured chrysanthemums in the vase next to her hung in the air. Joe had bought them and walked her home, with Edmund watching them from the doorway as they said goodnight at the gate. He was a good lad, an honest lad, but

213

Polly knew Joe was not for her. Her grandfather might wish it so, but she still had her eye on someone more intriguing, and her heart had sunk when she'd heard that he had a love of his own. Joe was just a cover-up; she had no intention of falling in love with him. It was out of spite that she'd asked him to the wedding, and well she knew it, though she wasn't proud of herself for playing with Joe's feelings.

She pulled her pillow around her head and replayed the evening's events in her head. Why had she been fool enough to ask him to Maggie's wedding? It was out of jealousy at discovering that Tobias would be there with someone else on his arm. She was kidding herself, and she knew it.

13

'Right, lass, I'll leave you here. I've a bit of business to do in Hawes, while you are enjoying yourself at this wedding. I know Joe's bringing you home, so the pair of you behave yourselves.' Edmund pulled on Clover's reins and watched as Polly climbed down from the trap. 'Looks like rain, lass, so don't get that bonny new dress of yours wet. Get yourself up the hill and into the church quickly.' He looked up to the heavens as a heavy drop of rain fell.

'Oh no, surely it could stop fine for Maggie. I can't see it being one of the brightest weddings as it is, with her parents not liking Ralph.' Polly reached for the umbrella she'd brought as a precaution against the inclement September weather, and pulled her best shawl around her shoulders.

'It'll be all right. They'll only have eyes for one another, from what I can see, so the weather won't matter. Get a move-on, lass. I can see Joe waiting in the church doorway.' Edmund watched as Polly walked through the church gate and up the steep incline to the church. She touched Joe's arm and smiled at him. They made a handsome couple, and Joe was a good catch. Happen not a farmer, but did that matter, in the new scheme of things. 'Gee up, Clover. I'll do my business another day, let's get home before this weather sets in.' Edmund placed a blanket around his knees, flicked the reins and started out for home. He was looking forward to an hour or two on his own, perhaps having a snooze in front of the fire and enjoying having his home to himself. The solicitor could wait for another day. Besides, he had no intention of dying just yet, so his will could wait.

Polly looked at Joe, who looked very smart in his pinstripe suit and brogues.

'You look beautiful, Polly.' He smiled as they waited in the vestibule of the church.

'You don't look too bad yourself. You scrub up real well,' grinned Polly. 'Do you think we should wait here or go into the church? I really want to see Maggie coming up to the church. It's a pity she's not got any bridesmaids. I'd have liked to be one, or at least her maid of honour.'

'I know. I thought she'd have asked you, but I think Bill's a bit disappointed at her only marrying a lead-miner, and they've put the cart before the horse, if you know what I mean. Let's go and sit down. It may not be a big wedding, but you'll want to see when he puts the ring on her finger.' Joe pushed open the vestibule door and led the way into the church. The door creaked as the couple entered the historic Norman-built church with its strong arched pillars, making the congregation turn to see who was entering. The vicar was standing next to the entrance and welcomed them quietly, passing them over to the warden, who discreetly asked them, 'Bride or groom?', in order to seat them behind the appropriate family. The organist looked at the young couple, wondering whether to play the wedding march for them, until the vicar made it obvious that they were not the couple everyone was expecting. Joe grinned, finding it funny, while Polly hit him silently on the knee, as she bowed her head in a minute's reverence.

'Your mate's on his own,' Joe whispered as he quickly looked around the church. 'She soon got rid of him, whoever she was, because he's sitting by himself over there.' He held Polly's hand tight, claiming what he now thought was his.

'What do you mean?' Polly whispered back.

'Tobias Middleton, he's come on his own!' said Joe.

Polly looked across to Ralph's family and there, at the back, sat Tobias. She felt herself blush as he smiled at her, with his dark eyes belying his feelings. Polly was thankful when the organist started to pump the organ and play, as Maggie and her father entered the church and walked down the aisle, with the vicar now in place, waiting to greet them. Why had she brought Joe? she thought. Tobias was on his own; she could have been sitting next to him. Polly watched as Maggie floated down the aisle, her arm linked in her father's and smiling at everyone, as they admired her dress and bouquet. She watched as Maggie passed her flowers to her sobbing mother, and then looked lovingly into Ralph's eyes as she said her vows. Polly brushed a tear away from her eye. She was happy for Maggie. Whether Maggie would be happy, up Swaledale, being a lead-miner's wife, was another matter. But Polly knew she'd miss her tempestuous best friend; although no more than fifteen miles away, it might as well be in another county, for the road was that bad to travel.

'You all right, Pol?' Joe squeezed her hand.

'I'm fine, just happy that the baby's got a father and that they love one another. I'll miss Maggie when she goes to live in Swaledale.'

'Never mind, Pol, you've got me now. You can share all your thoughts with me.' Joe smiled as she brushed away another tear.

Polly nodded. What could she say? She didn't think she'd ever feel comfortable telling Joe her thoughts and, at that moment in time, he'd certainly not want to know what she was thinking.

He smiled and squeezed her hand tighter as the couple made their way through the wedding vows, while the families of both sides looked on. Ralph's family was made of tough, no-nonsense, hard-working folk, who partly farmed the wild, rugged landscape of the Dales as well as mining the lead in the fells, while what there was of Maggie's family were more gentle shop owners and business people. Polly looked around her. It was a funny clash of occupations and personalities, but perhaps the marriage would work, if they all gave their support to one another. She watched as the couple kissed, once Ralph had put the ring on Maggie's finger, and a pang of jealousy made her feel uneasy at her own emotions. Maggie had got her man, a house, and a baby on the way, and what had she herself got? Nothing compared to Maggie, and everything seemed to be slipping away, no matter what she did.

Polly felt disgusted with herself. She had a good life and she should stop thinking that she hadn't. The trouble was that she always wanted more than she had, and she just couldn't help it.

★ ★ ★

'So are you two courting then?' Bill Sunter didn't hold back with his questioning as he ate another salmon sandwich and looked at the young couple seated across from him. He'd paid for the wedding breakfast and he was going to have his fill.

Joe stuttered and blushed. 'Yes, Mr Sunter, Polly and I are walking out together.'

'Well, bloody well make sure there's none of that how's-your-father, else old Edmund will shoot the head off your shoulders.' Bill leaned back in his chair and grinned as Joe blushed, and Polly looked down at her feet in embarrassment. 'She's told you, has she? Our Maggie. I've bought them a house in Muker. Couldn't have them living in the hovel he was going to have them living in; it wasn't fit for a dog.' Bill leaned back further in his chair and watched Polly as she nodded her head. 'Well. I might as well spend some of my brass to set them up proper, because his side haven't a ha'penny to rub together. Look at them, I don't think they even have running water in their houses. They all look like they need a bloody bath.'

Bill nodded his head at Ralph's family, who were smart and clean enough, in Polly's eyes, but obviously not so for the outspoken Bill Sunter.

219

'And that bloody Tobias Middleton, sitting over there on his own, he'll make money out of anybody's disadvantages. The place he offered to them to live in needs knocking down. Why that so-called son-in-law thought my lass would live there beats me. Bloody Middleton, he still has the cheek to turn up at our Maggie's wedding, even though I told him he wasn't welcome, after cancelling all his farm's milk supply to me. He's another stubborn bugger, just like your old fella. Seemingly they can live without my dairy, or so they think. What's the silly bugger doing with all his milk, or don't you want to tell me?' Bill took a long slurp from his glass of beer and summoned the waitress to fill it up again, grabbing her by the waist as she did so, while waiting for Polly to reply.

'He's back taking it to the early-morning train, to send it to my Aunty Evie in Liverpool.' Polly felt sorry for Maggie's mother, as she watched Bill pat the waitress's bum and nearly dribble his mouthful of beer, as she smiled at him and tripped away giggling. Bill Sunter could have anything he wanted, because money talked, and well he knew it.

'He's a silly old bugger, if he's getting up at that time in the morning and trailing up to Hawes Junction with a few gill of milk. He'd have been better stopping with me. After all, there was no harm done. The whole of Hawes knew who your father was, and I did nowt wrong with taking your brother on. He always was a bit cobbed — that's why your father left.' Bill took another long drink and glared at his wife, sitting at the next table. 'That and not wanting to get landed with something like that!'

'I think we'll go and have a chat with Maggie and Ralph, if you'll excuse us, Mr Sunter.' Joe had heard enough of Bill Sunter's drunken talk and decided to save them both from any more insults, sensing that Polly was on the brink of tears.

'Aye, go and see the loving couple. Get some tips, lad. Or perhaps it's our Maggie that can learn you a thing or two, but I seem to remember the dairy being full of gossip when you worked there, lass, so perhaps you don't need them.' He stared at Polly.

Polly rose from her chair. What an obnoxious load of rubbish Bill Sunter was. She would have liked to have given him a piece of her mind, if it wasn't Maggie's wedding and he hadn't been old enough to be her father.

'Don't let him upset you. My father warned me he couldn't hold his drink. I think, even for all his money, he's not a happy man.' Joe led the way to where Maggie and Ralph sat with his parents.

Maggie stood up, hugging Polly tightly, and kissed her on the cheek. 'I'm so glad that you are here, Polly. This is my new family, Ralph's mother and father and his two brothers.'

Ralph's family nodded their heads in recognition of Joe and Polly, and smiled as Maggie sat down with her best friend and Joe talked to Ralph. 'And has my father told you he's bought Ralph and me a cottage in Muker.' She hardly stopped for breath. She'd wanted to tell Polly her

221

news and introduce her to her new lifestyle in Swaledale.

'Yes, yes. You are very lucky. You've everything now, Maggie, I'm so pleased for you.'

'But you're going out with Joe now.' Maggie smiled and then whispered into Polly's ear. 'He's so good-looking.' She giggled and glanced at Joe and Ralph, who were talking business, even though it was the wedding day.

'Mmm, I know.' Polly smiled, feeling really ungrateful for the good-looking man on her arm.

'I can feel that there is a but, and I know just where he is standing,' Maggie whispered as she glanced over to Tobias Middleton, now standing talking to Ralph's brothers. 'Polly, let me introduce you to my brothers-in-law. You must meet them. Besides, listen to these two old men of ours. Who wants to talk about how to extract the best quality of lead? That's boring.' Maggie giggled and pulled on Polly's hand, taking her next to the window that overlooked the market square, where Tobias and Ralph's two dark-haired brothers stood. 'I thought I'd brighten the day up for you three single gentlemen and introduce you to my best friend, Polly Harper. Although, Tobias, I do believe you already know her.' Maggie giggled, and watched as Tobias turned in surprise towards Polly, who was standing next to him.

'Oops — excuse me, I think my mother wants me.' Maggie smiled, making an excuse for leaving her friend, knowing full well what she was doing, and leaving Polly embarrassed that she had been so obviously dumped on Tobias.

'Miss Harper, or may I call you Polly?' Tobias smiled and noticed the flush of colour in Polly's cheeks. 'I was just saying to Ted and Frank here that the price of land is going to rise this coming year. Do you think I'm right, Polly?'

Polly looked at Tobias and felt like a dumbstruck schoolchild as he gazed upon her. 'I don't know. I leave such like to my grandfather, but if you feel it might, I'm sure it must be correct.'

'Indeed, I aim to buy whatever I can afford, when it becomes available, of course. The world is changing and there is only one thing that holds its value and worth, and that is the fields and the fells around us.' Tobias drank from his glass and smiled as the two Bannister brothers gave their apologies; talk of finance and bragging of money matters was not for them.

'So, Polly, how are you? Now that we have lost our unwanted company, I see you have a new suitor on your arm, though I don't think he's quite strong enough for the likes of you.' Tobias smiled.

'I think I'll be the judge of that. Joe is thoughtful and sweet, and a gentleman.' Despite knowing that Tobias was right, Polly wanted to show some loyalty to her new love.

'Aye, but he'll never make you happy. You are a woman of the wild fells, not a dreary carpenter's wife. I'll never forget the day when I first saw you up near Mallerstang Edge: your hair was wild and as tangled as a gypsy child's, and those blue eyes flashed with a hint of fear, but also with a hint of curiosity.'

'Tobias, be quiet — folk will hear.' Polly bowed her head.

'Well, let them hear. I've decided that from now on I'm going to have what I want, and to hell with folk. I know what they all say about me: that I can never be any good because of my father. Well, perhaps they are right.'

'Aye, perhaps they are right about you, because what about the poor woman on your arm at the harvest supper? Have you got fed up with her already? You spent enough money on buying courting cake for her.' Polly's hatred of the woman who had won Tobias's favours tumbled out, before she could stop them.

Tobias looked stunned and then let out a hearty laugh. 'You mean my mother? You are jealous of my mother? Did you not see who it was on my arm? I bid it up for her. She always loves kiss-me-cake, as it reminds her of her time in Leeds. The only person to eat it was me and old Jed, my shepherd, when we had our morning break.' Tobias grinned. The look on Polly's face told him everything. The lass was smitten with him, and well she knew it.

'I thought you had a girlfriend on your arm. I couldn't see, from where Joe and I were sitting.' Polly was feeling foolish. She'd used Joe for nothing, and now she was stuck with him. Tobias had already guessed how shallow her friendship really was.

'Never mind, Polly, I'm sure you are happy with your new conquest. If you do feel like a change, meet me next Saturday afternoon on Mallerstang Edge, next to the waterfall. It can be our meeting place,' Tobias whispered in her ear as he watched Joe make his way through the crowd. His laughter had alerted Joe to the fact that Tobias was talking to his girlfriend.

Polly blushed as Joe grabbed her arm.

'Are you all right, Pol?' Joe looked at Tobias and puffed his chest out like a bantam-cock.

'Of course she's all right. Polly's just been telling me all about you. What a perfect partner you are, and how lucky she is to be with you today.' Tobias patted Joe on the back.

'You said all that, Pol? I didn't realize that you felt all that.' Joe smiled and looked at Polly.

'All that and more, my man.' Tobias grinned as he moved away.

Joe's face burst with pride.

Polly smiled angelically. Now she'd have to go to the waterfall this coming Saturday, just to give Tobias a piece of her mind, if nothing else.

★ ★ ★

The October wind was bitter as Polly trudged up over the fell, but that wasn't going to deter her from seeing Tobias. She'd thought of nobody else since the wedding, and now the day had come and nothing was going to prevent her from seeing the man who made her feel light-headed and utterly wicked. Thankfully, Matt had turned up like a bad penny and she had been able to leave him and her grandfather talking, while she made her way through the waist-high rushes and squelching sphagnum moss of the fell over to Mallerstang.

The low cloud clung to the dark shape of Wild Boar Fell and there was a smell of rain in the air. Polly's long black hair whipped across her face, and the bottom of her skirt was wet and muddy as she climbed over the stile onto the Mallerstang road. She remembered the first time she had seen Tobias there; how she had been fearful of him, but even then had felt an attraction. Now she was nearly running in her urgency to see him, her breath heavy and pounding in her chest as she came within sight of the waterfall. The force of the wind was pushing the water from it backwards, making a spectacular white shower at the head of the fall, as well as the usual frothing cascade, and the laden rowan tree at the side of the bank creaked with the wind's strength. Polly pulled her shawl around her and brushed back her straggling locks of hair, taking shelter at the foot of the fall, under the hillside. She looked down the valley at all the smallholdings dotted along the dale, and at the rivulets and streams like white ribbons, which flowed down the side of each fell to the river in the valley bottom. It was a wild landscape, but one she loved.

Ahead lay the market town of Kirkby Stephen and, beyond that, the wide plains of the Eden valley leading up to the Scottish borders. Over these lands, in times past, battles had been fought between invading Scottish tribes from the north and the hardy Dales folk. Border reivers had swept down under the cloak of night, stealing cattle and sheep and taking them back over the border, but still her ancestors had stood

226

their ground. Hers was a heritage to be proud of, and Polly knew it.

She pulled her shawl tighter around her, hoping that Tobias would not be too long. Her ears were pinned for the noise of a horse's hooves on the cobbled road. An hour or more passed, and still Polly sat waiting. She was chilled to the bone and shivering with cold. Where was he? Soon the heavy grey afternoon would give way to dusk and she would have to go home. The first spot of threatening rain fell, and Polly knew it was time to go back. Had Tobias been playing with her heart-strings again? Perhaps he had no intention at all of meeting her; perhaps he was the cad everyone said he was.

Polly sobbed as she made her way back into Garsdale. She was frozen, soaked to the skin and broken-hearted. Tobias Middleton was a bastard. Everyone kept telling her so, so why didn't she believe them?

★　★　★

'Where the hell have you been, lass? Look at you — you are sodden to the skin and mucked up.' Edmund looked at Polly's sorry state.

'Don't . . . just don't. I got caught in the rain. I went out for a walk, because you were talking to Matt, and I just got wet.' Polly stood soaked to the skin, her hair dripping and hanging like rat's tails down her back. She struggled to keep the disappointment out of her voice, and if her grandmother Ada had still been alive, she would have broken down in tears in front of her. But

Edmund was different, and he'd play hell with her, if he knew what she had been up to.

'Well, you'd better get up them stairs and change, before you catch your death of cold. You can't hide from Matt all your life, you know. He is your brother, whether you like it or not!' Edmund scowled at Polly. She had a jealous streak in her sometimes.

'I didn't go because Matt was here. I went because I fancied a walk,' shouted Polly from halfway up the stairs.

'Aye. well, I worried where you'd gone. Matt says to tell you Joe's coming by tomorrow night.' Edmund stood on the bottom step of the stairs and received no reply from Polly. He heard the floorboards creak above him as she walked into her bedroom. She was sulking. He didn't know what about, but he did know that the dark, scowling look upon her face meant that she wasn't happy.

★ ★ ★

Tobias stood in his stable, stripped off to the waist and steaming with sweat. He wiped his damp hair with his shirt and looked on, as the foal took to its legs. He smiled as it took its first unsteady steps towards its mother, and milk. The bloody animal, he thought, of course it would decide to foal today and have a difficult birth. But he couldn't leave his favourite mare for a lass who might not be waiting for him anyway. He smiled again as the mare gently nudged the little filly, urging the newborn to fill its empty

228

stomach with protecting milk. It would be a grand horse when it got older, having its mother's markings.

Even though he'd been looking forward to seeing Polly, being at the birth was worth missing her for. Besides, Tobias hoped she'd understand. He pulled on his shirt, tugged up his braces and looked back at the mother and daughter, before making for the closed door of the stable. He opened it to find that the weather had changed. He hadn't noticed because he'd been so involved in the birth. He stood at the stable door and watched as the eaves above the barn and stable overflowed with the rain, which was coming down in torrents. Grouse Hall looked grey and brooding, fitting into the dark, moody Dales landscape and the wet October day. He leaned with one hand on the door, his shirt sleeves billowing in the cold wind as he looked across the farmyard and down the valley to Garsdale. His thoughts were now with Polly. Had she waited for him? Was she still there? Surely not, for dusk was nearly falling and she would be at home now. He should have gone; he should have gone and left the mare with Jed. If only her grandfather was more receptive to him, he could tell him why he hadn't been there for his granddaughter, the next time he saw Edmund at the station with his milk-kits. As it was, the old man would be more likely to threaten him with a shotgun than let Polly even talk to him. It was a shame that some memories were not buried along with his father, and that some folk would never forget.

Tobias watched as the torrent from the eaves trough became worse, and felt his mood change with the day. He too felt dark and miserable. He was tired of being alone, and all he wanted was someone to love.

★ ★ ★

'Polly, my lass, what's wrong?' Edmund came rushing into Polly's bedroom in his nightshirt and carrying a candle. 'I can hear you in my bedroom. Are you having a nightmare?'

The old man leaned over the iron bedstead and looked down at his granddaughter, whose brow was covered with perspiration. Even by candlelight he could see her burning cheeks.

'Aye, lass, you've caught a chill from trailing out in that weather. You're burning up.' Edmund's voice was full of panic as he pulled the cover up around Polly's chin and sat down beside her.

'No, Matt, don't hit him!' Polly sat nearly up in bed and then lay back down again and mumbled something that Edmund couldn't make out, before fighting an imaginary demon that was tormenting her, lost in her delirium.

Even though Edmund knew Polly couldn't hear him, he talked to her. 'We've got to get your temperature down. I'll get some cloths and a dish of cold water, and place the cloths on your brow. I'll have to go down to the kitchen and get them. Don't you move.' Edmund lit the candle on Polly's chest of drawers and quickly made his way down to the kitchen, returning in a flash with cooling towels and extra candles for light. 'I don't know what you were doing out in such weather, and you'd next to nowt on — no wonder you are so poorly tonight.' He wrung out one of his cooling cloths and placed it on her burning brow.

Polly tossed, turned and flayed her hands out, mumbling gibberish as Edmund soothed her.

'Aye, lass, if owt happens to you, I've nobody. I think the world of thee, you do know that, don't you?' Edmund patted Polly's head and stood over her. 'You were all me and our Ada lived for, after your father left. So you're not leaving me now.' He patted and cooled his granddaughter and pulled up a chair next to her bedside. He drew back her bedroom curtains and looked out into the dark night, as he listened to his Polly rambling. 'My Ada would have known what to do. I'm just a useless old man. I'll get the doctor in the morning, if we make it through this night.' Edmund gazed out into the night, noticing the stars twinkling over Rise Hill. 'Thy mother lived over there, lass. Bonny bit of a thing she was, caught our lad's eye straight away. Can't say I blame him, and you look a lot like her.' He got up and changed the damp cloth from her head. 'I'd have kicked his arse, if I'd have known what he'd done to her.'

He looked down on Polly, who tossed and turned with fever. 'Here, take a sip of this water.' He lifted her head up from the pillow and tried to trickle some water into her parched lips. 'Perhaps if I just wet your lips instead. Oh dear, I'm spilling it all down your nightdress.' Edmund laid Polly's head down and wet her lips with

231

some water on his finger. 'Aye, lass, what are we going to do? Don't leave me. I know there's Matt, but I never watched him growing up, and I don't feel the same about him as I do about you.' His eyes filled with tears as he held her hand and prayed for the fever to break. The night was going to be a long one, and morning just couldn't come quickly enough.

★ ★ ★

'You'll not leave her, will you, Joe?'

Edmund had never been so grateful in his life for the sight of Joe Fothergill entering the yard of Paradise, just before lunchtime the following day.

'I'll look after her, Mr Harper. You go and get the doctor.' Joe sat in the chair next to Polly, with a furrowed brow and a worried look on his face.

'And you'll behave yourself with her — you know what I mean? It isn't right conventional, leaving a young man alone in a woman's bedroom.' Edmund frowned.

'Mr Harper, who do you think I am? Polly's ill. And besides, I respect her!' Joe was clearly insulted that Edmund had even considered that he might take advantage of Polly, for the thought had never crossed his mind. All he was worried about was Polly's health.

'Aye, I'm sorry, lad, but I had to say it. Right, I'm off. I'll be back as soon as I can.' Edmund took a long, lingering look at Polly as she mumbled words under her breath, and Joe patted her forehead. Old Clover would have to pull out all the stops and get him to Hawes double-quick.

Joe sat next to Polly and watched as she tossed her head back and forth, muttering to herself while the pillowcase became drenched with her sweat. What had she been doing to get so cold and wet, out on the top of the fell? It hadn't been fit for a dog to be let out yesterday afternoon, let alone someone out for what should have been a pleasurable walk. The look on old Edmund Harper's face had told him how harrowing the night had been. Joe had thought the old man was going to break down and cry, as he'd entered the house. Polly meant everything to Edmund — everyone knew that — and she was beginning to mean a lot to him too, despite Matt's disapproval.

He patted Polly's hand and thought about Matt. He was a secretive one, that was for sure. Joe hadn't quite worked out what Matt was after at Paradise, but he did know that Matt was trying his best to worm his way in with Edmund. Perhaps he was just glad to have a grandfather and to know where his roots lay, but Joe knew Matt better than that. He was a schemer and didn't do things without a reason.

'Shh, Polly, I'm here.' He calmed Polly as he bathed her head, whilst she yelled out for Martha and then muttered something that stopped him in his tracks.

'Tobias, Tobias, I love you. Why didn't you come?'

Although said in a delirium, the words that Polly yelled out cut like a knife through Joe's heart. So that was why she had been out in the rain and wind. She'd been waiting for Tobias!

She'd always be waiting for him, and Joe knew it. They were alike to the colour of their hair and the blue of their eyes; both fatherless, both wild like the fells themselves. Joe had hoped that Polly would grow to love him, but he'd seen her at Maggie's wedding, talking to Tobias. He'd seen the twinkle in her eyes, the coy look she gave him and the playful finger that curled her hair as she spoke to him. He himself was playing second fiddle, and always would be, no matter how much he loved her.

★ ★ ★

'So she'll be all right, Doctor?' Edmund sat at the kitchen table with Dr Spence from Hawes and watched as he closed his bag.

'I've given her something to bring her temperature down and to make her sleep. Keep giving her those powders, and she should be fine in a day or two. She's fit enough, and it could have been a lot worse — we could have been looking at pneumonia. As it is, I think she just has a severe chill. You need some sleep yourself, Edmund, you're not getting any younger.' Dr Spence looked at the white-faced old man over the top of his spectacles. 'Do you not think of selling up and retiring to Hawes?'

'I'll be right. When I leave here, it'll be in a box, Doctor. This is my home and always will be, and after my day, it'll be Polly's.' Edmund wasn't going to be told by a town-dweller what to do with his ancestral home. After all, it was nowt to do with the doctor and, besides, he hadn't enough brass to sit back with his feet up, like a toff.

'Well, don't be doing too much. I want no early-morning train-catching with that milk of yours — that's a young man's game. Go and make peace with Bill Sunter, and let him pick your milk up from the bottom of the lane.' Dr Spence knew he was overstepping the mark with his advice, but it was common knowledge that words had been said between Bill Sunter and Edmund Harper.

'When I want your advice, I'll ask for it. Tha came to look after Polly, not to tell me how to do my business. Now I'm grateful for that, but if you'll excuse me, I've some stock to look at, while she's asleep.'

'I'm only telling you that you're not as young as you were, Edmund. I didn't mean to interfere.' Dr Spence made for the door.

'Aye, well, happen so, but I keep my own council. It's better all round, and perhaps you should try it.' Edmund held the door open and glared at Dr Spence, who up until then he'd thought of as a friend.

'If Polly gets worse, you know where I am. But she should be all right now, as her fever's broken. Good day, Edmund.'

Dr Spence shook his head, once outside the house. Edmund could be a stubborn old devil, once his mind was set.

Edmund slumped in his fireside chair and stoked the dying embers of the fire into life, watching as sparks crackled when he added some dry kindling sticks, before adding a shovel of coal from the bucket that he kept next to the fire. Today he felt his age. The doctor was right. He'd watched young Joe Fothergill mount his horse, without a creaking limb, and had wondered where all those years had gone. He was thankful Joe had visited. By the time he'd returned from Hawes with the doctor, Polly had started to improve. It must have been Joe's soothing ways. But it was funny how the lad couldn't get away fast enough, once he and the doctor arrived. You'd have thought he'd have wanted to know what the doctor said, Edmund thought. Still, perhaps his father needed him. After all, Joe had stopped a good length of time, and the joinery business didn't run itself.

He put the kettle on the fire and waited for it to boil, walking to the bottom of the stairs to hear if Polly was making any noise, before making himself a cup of tea. There wasn't a murmur. She was asleep, thank God. What a night it had been. The doctor was right in a way: too many such nights and he wouldn't be delivering milk up to Hawes Junction four times a week for the good people of Liverpool, whether his sister wanted it or not!

14

Polly sat in the chair next to the fire and listened to the bleating of the sheep and lambs as Matt and her grandfather herded them out of the yard and down the home field, then onwards to be sold at the market at Hawes. She had always hated the day when the year's lambs, and some of the older sheep, were sold to bring in much-needed income for the winter months. But this year it seemed worse. She'd not helped Edmund with the decision about what sheep to keep and what to sell; Matt had. And her disappointment had been made worse by knowing that the old Herdwick ewe that she'd encouraged Edmund to buy in the spring was amongst the sheep for sale. It would probably end up with the knacker-man now. Poor thing, she thought, it was only being sold because it was long in the tooth and past its best. Polly couldn't help but think it was a good job the same thing didn't happen to humans, or else there would be nobody alive past the age of forty.

At least her grandfather had heeded her pleas for him to keep the three lambs, despite how troublesome they were proving to be, as they tackled the limestone walls with their escape tactics, causing gaps to appear and a cursing from her grandfather. They were bonny little sheep and easily spotted from down in the valley, with their nearly black fleeces. It was the fleeces that made them so loved, along with their sweet white faces.

Polly yawned and stretched out in front of the warmth of the fire. Usually she would have walked the road behind the herd, along with her grandfather, but since catching the chill she had felt so weak and her legs were still a little shaky. It had been five days since she was so ill that she could hardly get out of her bed, but now her strength was returning, along with her spirits. Since Tobias's failure to show for their lovers' tryst, she had been in a dark place with her moods, but now — with the love shown by her grandfather, and the bed rest that he had insisted on — she'd decided that she could live without the teasing Tobias. He wasn't going to get the better of her, with his promises of unkept meetings and his flattery. He was playing with her feelings and, like a fool, she'd nearly died because of his games.

She listened to the grandfather clock ticking. The house was silent. The only noise was the constant tick. It was heaven to be alone with her thoughts in front of a warm fire. She closed her eyes and tried not to think of past events, but she couldn't help but remember her grandfather saying that Joe had looked after her while he fetched the doctor, and that she should thank Joe for his care. But how could she, when he hadn't been near her since her recovery? She'd asked Matt this morning if he'd seen Joe and hadn't got a straight answer, just a mumbled 'No', as if he was hiding something. No doubt Joe would turn up like a bad penny when he was ready.

She'd thank him then, and make sure she treated him with a bit more respect. He was, after all, always there for her, which made him twice the gentleman that Tobias was.

Polly yawned, her eyes filling with water, and brushed the tears away. Another few hours in bed wouldn't go amiss, she thought. After all, it was only seven-thirty in the morning and no one else was around. She placed the fire-guard around the fire, yawned again and then climbed the stairs to her bed. There she climbed in under the patchwork quilt made by her grandmother and curled up in a ball, in the comfort of her feather bed. Within minutes she was asleep, without a thought for Joe, Tobias or Matt.

★ ★ ★

Matt stood with his grandfather near the pen that held the fifty or more sheep and lambs that they had patiently walked down the road from Garsdale. It had taken at least two hours, with the sheep stopping to nibble at the verdant grass borders, and the lambs taking scare at the slightest movement. Both Edmund and Matt were glad when they had passed the Halfway Houses that heralded the run into the town of Hawes, and then went up the slight incline into the main street and the awaiting pens. There auction staff waited at the road-end leading over to Widdle, flapping their hands to ensure the meandering sheep went in the right direction, and then into the wooden pens that lined the main street, finally then into the night

239

holding-pen, called the Penny Garth.

'I'm glad we've got them here, Matt. It's a bloody hard job moving them, and this old lass is getting past her best, a bit like me.' Edmund ruffled his sheepdog's head as it panted for breath, its tongue dripping with saliva. 'She's crippled with rheumatics. Polly usually does the dog-work, so it's a good job you offered to help.'

'Aye, well, I knew you'd never make it on your own. And the weather will be getting worse before long, so you're best getting them sold, and then you're all right for the winter.' Matt leaned over the pen, looking at the mixture of Swaledale sheep and lambs, and wondering what they'd fetch at auction. 'Last time I did this was when my grandfather died in Dent. We had to pen them up at his farm sale. It broke my heart, it did, to see all the stock sold. But there was nowt I could do about it.' He leaned back on the wooden pen, with one foot resting on the slats, and gazed across the road at the auctioneer selling his first lot, as Edmund pulled his cap down over his brow.

'Aye, there's nowt worse than losing a farm. I was sad to hear it, when I found out that Bernard had died. He was a good man, was your grandfather, as straight as a die. Your grandmother must miss him.' Edmund spat as he heard the auctioneer banging down his hammer at a lower price than he'd expected.

'She does, but what can you do? And she depends on me to keep a roof over our heads. She pulled a face at me this morning when I said I was coming to help you, instead of going to work with Bill Sunter. But it's like I said to her: I couldn't see you stuck, not with Polly being so poorly, and you being my new family.'

Edmund could hardly control the smirk on his face. He'd wondered when the hint of payment for the day was coming. There was one thing he'd learned quickly about his new grandson: he didn't do owt for nowt, and today was not going to be an exception.

'Aye, well, we'll see what this lot makes. Have a beer in the Crown and then I'll pay you what I think you've earned. How's that?' Edmund leaned and looked at his flock, as the auctioneer moved closer. The farmers and landowners of the district were swarming around him as he shouted in a rhythm of quick bids, as the farmers let him know in their own secret way of bidding. Some touched their caps, some stroked their noses, others just held their finger up or nodded their heads slightly. All their signs meant the same thing: that they were bidding for that particular sheep, or pen of sheep. The auctioneer had to have a quick eye and know the farmer well to recognize his style, quickly registering the bid and then finally knocking his gavel down at the last bid.

'Excuse me, Mr Harper, I wonder if I could discuss a little business with you?'

Edmund turned to see Tobias Middleton standing behind him.

'What do you want?' Edmund didn't mince his words, as he noticed that Matt had come quickly to his side.

'I wondered if I could interest you with an

241

offer for your flock? I'd pay a fair price, and it would save the hassle of the auctioneer. Jed, my shepherd, says that they are in decent shape, and I need to restock a farm I've just acquired.' Tobias looked nervously at Matt. He disliked the man, even more so since the episode in the graveyard.

'Aye, I saw Jed Mathews looking at my lot. I thought they were for him, else I'd have stopped him. I don't think I'm interested in selling them to you.' Edmund leaned over the fencing, not looking at Tobias as Matt stepped forward.

'You heard my grandfather — he's not interested.' Matt stood a few inches from Tobias, in between him and his grandfather.

'Edmund, I thought thou was a reasonable man. Tobias here is a good man; he's not like his father — he's a bloody good farmer, for all his airs and graces. They'll not get a better home.' Jed pulled on Edmund's arm. 'He's all right, is the lad.'

'I'll give you ten shillings a head, and half a crown for the old Herdwick. That's more than the auctioneer's sold the last three lots for, and you'll have no commission to pay.' Tobias stepped forward, only for Matt to stop him going further.

'It's not bad brass, Grandfather, but you'll have to make your mind up. Our pen's the next to be sold.' Matt's love of money soon made him change his mind.

'He's right, Edmund. It's a fair price and he'll buy them all, even the old lass that should be in the knackers' yard.' Jed looked at Edmund, who

242

wasn't saying anything.

The auctioneer and the crowd gathered around Edmund's pen now, pushing the debating party as they looked at the pen of sheep.

'From Paradise Farm, Garsdale: forty-five Swaledale lambs, five hogs and a Herdwick that's a bit long-in-the-tooth. What am I offered?' The auctioneer lifted his gavel and waited for the first bid. 'I can split into lots!' He paused.

'Threepence for the old Herdwick,' the knacker-man shouted from the back of the crowd. And the farmers laughed.

Edmund breathed in deeply and stood on the wooden fence around his sheep. 'These sheep aren't for sale. I'm withdrawing them from the auction.' He scowled at the auctioneer and looked around at all the farmers he knew. 'Bugger off to the next pen! I've decided not to sell them today.'

The crowd muttered and swore, discontented, as they moved on to the next pen.

'Mr Harper, this is most irregular. You can't just withdraw from the sale,' the auctioneer growled.

'I bloody can, and I just have. You'd better get a move-on — they are waiting for you.' Edmund spat out his mouthful of saliva and turned to Tobias. 'Tha can have 'em, providing that old Herdwick lives out its days in peace. Our Polly loves the bloody old thing, and she didn't want to part with it. It's only because she's poorly that she's not with me today, and it would break her heart further if she knew it had gone for dog-meat.'

Tobias and Jed breathed out a sigh of relief.

'Of course I'll look after the old thing. I presume you prefer cash? I hope Polly is not too ill?' Tobias delved into his pockets, producing a wad of money, which Matt nearly gasped at, when Tobias counted it out into Edmund's hand.

'She nearly died from a chill. She got sodden over a week ago when she went for a walk. She's only just getting her strength back.' Edmund counted the notes that were in his hand, and noted the hesitance of Tobias's count, at the news of Polly being ill.

'That's not good news. Can you pass on my best wishes to her, if I'm not being presumptuous?' Tobias smiled as the last note was counted, but in reality he was worried about Polly. She must have been caught in the downpour when he was with his mare.

'She'll be all right, don't you worry,' Matt butted in.

'I'll tell her, lad.' Edmund watched the cloud that passed over Tobias's face. 'She's a good lass, is my Polly. I'd never want anyone to hurt her.'

'No, I understand. She is precious to you.' Tobias watched Edmund as he studied his face.

'Aye, she is. She's my life, and I live for her.'

Matt sighed; no matter what he did, Edmund would never think the same of him as he did of Polly.

'This one's the new one in my life. He's to prove himself to me.' Edmund patted Matt's shoulder, hearing him sigh. 'But Polly we raised as our lass, and she's special.'

'I know how you feel, Mr Harper. And now Jed and I will take your sheep home. Thank you for doing business with me.' Tobias had read the message well. Polly was to be respected, or else!

'Are you not coming for a drink for luck with us, to the Crown?' said Edmund to Tobias and Jed, as he and Matt stepped away from the pen of sheep.

'Not today. I'd rather get these home.' Tobias untied the pen's string fastener and watched as Jed walked the sheep out of the pen.

'Another time then, lad.' Edmund smiled as he strode out down the street. That had been a good morning's work, and happen he'd been wrong about Tobias Middleton.

★   ★   ★

'I don't like that cocky bugger.' Matt sat in the corner of the taproom of the pub and said what he thought about Tobias Middleton.

'Tha'll like his money, though. Here — here's two quid to put in your pocket. That'll keep your mother quiet.' Edmund pushed two pounds into Matt's hand, as he watched Len get in the drinks at the bar. 'I hope our Polly's all right at home on her own. We'll only have these and then I'll get myself home.'

'He's sweet on her, you know Tobias Middleton — you should watch him.' Matt was grinning as he placed his easily made money in his pocket.

'Who's sweet on who?' Len asked, as he placed three pints on the table next to them.

'Tobias Middleton and our Polly. I can't stand him, flash bugger!' Matt slurped a mouthful of

245

beer and sat back in his seat.

'Tobias — he's a grand lad, once you get to know him. My Martha is friends with his mother. Martha worries about him, because folk judge him to be like his father.' Len looked at Edmund.

'He seems all right,' said Edmund. 'He's just bought all my flock. Happen I've perhaps been a bit hasty in the past, judging him. But he wouldn't come here with us for a drink. I'd have bought him one for luck. I'm not keen on loners, or people who think themselves better than us.' He sat back and looked around at all the farmers doing extra business over a shared pint.

'You'll not get him in here. He doesn't drink. Saw too much of it when he was a little 'un. You know what his father was like: a right wrong 'un; would drink until he fell over, that 'un. If anything, it's made Tobias go the other way.' Len looked at Matt and Edmund.

'He never said that. I didn't know.' Edmund sighed.

'Aye, well, give a dog a bad name and it sticks. The poor bugger has had it hard. He's pulled himself up, and he's making something of his life. I hear he's just bought Blue Bridge Farm at Appersett. He must be worth some money — he works every hour of the day. Believe me, there's a lot worse out there than Tobias. Not all sons are like their fathers.' Len sipped his pint.

'Aye, and some are, worst luck.' Edmund sighed and glanced at Matt, who was too busy counting his money to listen.

★ ★ ★

Polly lit the oil lamp and placed it in the window. She'd put a mutton stew on the hearth, which was now simmering gently. The meat was nice and tender, ready for eating. She'd also found the strength to milk the two cows and cool the milk, ready for the delivery up to the station the following day. Where was her grandfather? He didn't usually take this long selling the lambs.

She opened the kitchen door and stood in the porchway. A strand of gloriously red Virginia creeper hung down over the porch roof, and the late-afternoon light shone through its leaves with a beautiful transparency. Another quarter of an hour and the sun would have set. She watched as bats started to screech their way out of the barn, catching the last of the day's insects in the dying sun's rays. As he made his way through the bottom field gate, she could just make out the form of her grandfather, stumbling and fighting with the gate-fastener. So that's where he'd been: in the Crown with his old cronies! He'd regret it in the morning when he had to get up to take the milk. She smirked to herself as he wandered from one side of the track to the other, his gait all over the place, finally making it to the farmyard.

'Well, I take it you've had a good day?' Polly tried to keep a straight face as her grandfather nearly tripped over the porch step and grinned like an idiot at her stern face.

'I have, lass, I've had a right good time. Did I ever tell you that you've a look of your

247

grandmother, when tha gets vexed?' Edmund swayed and made his way to his favourite chair, where he undid his shoes and slumped.

'I suppose you've been in the Crown with our Matt and Len Brunskill? It looks like you've drunk them dry, between you.' Polly picked up his shoes and put them to one side and then stirred her stew and stood, looking at her grandfather, with the ladle in her hand. 'Did you not think I might be a bit worried?'

'It was right, lass. I walked home with Len as far as The Street. And, anyway, it's your fault I'm in this state — tha can't blame anyone else!' Edmund hiccupped and smiled.

'Well, I don't know how you came to that conclusion. I wasn't behind the bar pouring beer down your throat. Now, are we going to have some supper, and did you get a fair price for the lambs?'

'Like I say, it's all your fault. If that Tobias Middleton hadn't bought the whole lot for nearly double the price, I wouldn't be in this state. And we all know why he bought 'em off me . . . Because I'm your grandfather, and he's got his eye on you.' He pointed his finger at Polly and grinned again. 'He's worth some brass, is that lad. Here, take this from out my pocket and put it in the tin box in the corner cupboard.' Edmund pulled some crumpled notes and coins out of his jacket pocket. Some fell to the floor as he pushed them all into Polly's hands.

Polly grasped the money and then looked at her grandfather. She couldn't believe what she'd just heard.

248

'I'm beginning to think you could do worse than setting your cap at Middleton. For a fella, Len says he's all right. I'll think about it in the morning when I'm more sober. My head's spinning.' Edmund held onto his armchair and stood up. 'I'm off to bed, Polly, it's been a long day and I'm buggered.'

With her hands still full of money, Polly watched as Edmund made his way across the flagged kitchen floor and up to bed. She'd never seen him in such a state. The silly old devil. Len and Matt had a lot to answer for. She unfolded her armful of money and counted it on the kitchen table. It was just short of twenty pounds. Her grandfather was right, Tobias had been generous. Her heart skipped a beat as she thought of him, and the fact that her grandfather was warming to him. Still, she couldn't forgive Tobias for not meeting her, and then causing her nearly to catch her death, due to his failure to appear.

She walked into the parlour and unlocked the oak corner cupboard, reaching up for the ancient tin box that held all the savings and deeds to the farm. She placed the money carefully at the bottom of the box under the title deed, stopping as a tide of curiosity came over her. She'd never looked at deeds before, and she fumbled as she unfurled the document before her. There it was: generations of Harpers all written down neatly on the deeds, father-to-son for five generations, ever since Paradise had been built. She smiled and quickly folded it back up. It wasn't hers to look at, but one day it would be, she knew that for sure, because her grandfather had always promised her it.

Polly sniffed the air. A smell of burning wafted through from the kitchen. It was the stew — her supper! She ran through to the kitchen to save it. It was burnt. That just served her right for looking at things that weren't hers, she thought, as she scraped the charcoaled remains of mutton and tatties from the pot and sat down to supper on her own. She could hear her grandfather snoring in his bedroom above. The likelihood of the milk being delivered tomorrow was very slim. She'd have to make butter with it and see how her grandfather was when he finally awoke. Nothing worried her at the moment. Tobias was beginning to be accepted; they had enough money for the winter and she was feeling better. What more could she ask for?

15

'Oh, my head!' Edmund sat with his head in his hands, feeling sorry for himself as Polly pushed a cup of tea into his hands.

'Here, there's a fried egg on bread for your breakfast.' She placed the fizzling fried egg, with the yolk split and oozing out down the bread, on the table next to him.

'You are a hard woman, Polly Harper. How do you think I'm going to eat that, in this state?' Edmund lifted his eyes to look at his granddaughter, who was standing in judgement of him.

'You'll eat it. It'll bring you back to your senses. My grandmother would have made you, so I'm standing in her shoes.' Polly watched her ailing grandfather as he lifted his fork and poked at the offensive breakfast. 'I've skimmed the cream off the milk and churned it into butter. I'll make a milk pudding with some of the rest, and try to do something with what's left. The cows are milked, and today's milk is kitted ready for tomorrow's delivery, so all you've got to do is apologize to Aunty Evie and her clan, for her standing freezing on Liverpool station waiting for this morning's delivery of milk.' Polly was curt with her words, but really she was laughing inwardly at the state Edmund was in. She watched as he attempted to eat the greasy fried egg, nearly retching as he swallowed it down. 'So, I take it Len Brunskill and Matt will be in the same state? That'll not go down well with Bill Sunter, if Matt's working at the dairy with a hangover.' Polly folded her tea-towel and waited for a reply.

'Nay, Matt went home quite a while before us. He took a dislike to Len singing praises about Tobias.' Edmund swallowed the last piece of egg and bread and took a long sip of tea. 'Did you know he's got four farms now, and everybody says he's a good landlord. He must get his brains from his mother, because his father hadn't any.' Edmund leaned back in his chair, before reaching down for his boots. He struggled to fasten them, as the acid from the night's drinking, mixed with the fried egg in his stomach, made him belch.

'By, I do feel bad — never again. I should have taken a leaf out of that Tobias's book and not bothered with that drink. Do you know he's told Bill Sunter where to put his milk-kits and all? Len says Tobias reckons nowt to the prices Bill's paying, and he's going to be joining me, selling his milk in Liverpool. In fact, when I think of it, he might have been doing that for a while, because the farm man from Blue Bridge has been there in a morning, but I never thought anything of it.' Edmund stood up and looked at Polly scowling at him. 'Are you feeling all right this morning, lass?'

'Never mind about me. I'll have to be all right, otherwise nowt would have been done this morning. A few months ago Tobias Middleton was the devil incarnate to you, and now you won't shut up about him. You've never even thanked me for all I've done this morning, even though I was nearly at death's door last week. Did you see Joe? He's not been to see me since I were ill. I thought he'd have been by now.' Polly was annoyed at her grandfather. When she'd had feelings for Tobias, her feelings hadn't been allowed. Now, once Edmund knew he was worth a bob or two, the tables had turned. Had he been blind when they went up to Grouse Hall? Had he not seen how it looked, and how Tobias dressed?

'Oh! Sorry, lass, I forgot. I did see Joe. He came into the Crown and asked me to give you this.' Edmund rummaged in his waistcoat pocket and pulled out a crumpled envelope with her name on it and passed it to Polly.

Polly looked at the scrawled handwriting, as if a spider had dragged its legs over it to write her name, and then quickly tore it open to read the contents. She stood holding the kitchen chair, as she read the letter that told of Joe's feelings for her:

My Dearest Polly,
I've thought about this for a long time, and my heart ached seeing you so ill the other day. In fact, like your grandfather, I feared that we could have lost you, if the good Lord had wished it. As it was, he wanted me to hear of your true love, when you were in the depths of delirium. My heart broke when you called for Tobias Middleton, when it was me that was patting your forehead and praying for you to live. I'll never hold the key to your heart,

and I'll never be the man that you want,
but you will always have a part of me, and
I wish you well. However, this is where
our friendship must end. I'm not prepared
to play second fiddle to a man I cannot
compete with.

I wish you well, my dearest, and that
one day you catch the man of your
dreams.
Joe

'Well, what's he say — is he wanting to get wed?'
Edmund looked at Polly, who sat down quickly
in the kitchen chair, her face telling a story.

Polly's eyes brimmed with tears, and she
wiped them away quickly and blew her nose on
her pinny. 'No, Grandfather, it's the other way.
He says he doesn't want to see me again.' She
screwed the note up and sniffed, while her
grandfather patted her on her back.

'Tha's better off without him. If he hasn't got
manners to tell you to your face, then you can do
without his kind. He wasn't a farmer anyway;
knew a bit about horses, but nowt about sheep.
Somebody bigger and better will come along,
mark my words. Tha's too bonny a lass for them
not to.' Edmund was uncomfortable talking to
Polly about matters of the heart, for that was
women's stuff. 'I'll go and look at the stock, get a
bit of fresh air. Don't you be crying over that
Fothergill lad — he's not worth it.' He walked
over to the kitchen door and stood for a second,
his hand on the door latch, before walking out
into the yard and closing it behind him. He lit

254

his pipe and looked down the dale. It would never have worked between Joe and Polly; she was too strong-willed for him. Besides, he was Matt's best mate, and Matt had made it as clear as the nose on his face that he wanted Paradise. Well, he wasn't going to get it, not even over his dead body. So they could think again!

★　★　★

Polly sat and reread the words that Joe had written down. She must have called out for Tobias when she was ill. Why hadn't Tobias come that afternoon? He must think of her just as a foolish girl, and be using her for his amusement. She screwed the letter up tightly in her hand and threw it on the fire, watching the orange flames curl around the burning paper, and the fire-fairies of burning soot glow at the back of the chimney. The tears weren't for the loss of Joe's love; they were for Tobias. What made it even worse was that he would probably meet with her grandfather's approval, now that Edmund knew more about him. Would she have a chance to meet him again before spring? She doubted it. The winter months were nearly upon the Dales, and with them came snow and rain. It would soon be time for the weekly visits to Hawes to stop, halting any fleeting chance of bumping into Tobias.

Already she had been busy preparing jams and preserves to see them through the winter. Bacon flitches hung from the hooks in the pantry ceiling, and the flour barrel was full for the oncoming winter months. Her grandfather might deliver the milk to the station, but other than that, nobody stirred far in the winter months. All were self-sufficient at home, warm and dry. Polly sobbed. A few weeks ago she had the choice of two men, and now she had none. Instead she was stuck at Paradise, with only her grandfather and her scheming brother, whenever he wanted something. Even Maggie was over in Swaledale and could no longer be visited. She was happily building her new home and planning her family. Polly felt a wave of loneliness sweep over her. How she wished Tobias had come to her. Why hadn't he come to her?

'Polly, Polly, here, this is for you.' Edmund opened the kitchen door and held a parcel in his hands. 'The delivery lad from Sam Allen's has just given it to me, at the bottom of the lane.' He handed over the brown-wrapped parcel with no writing on it, to a swollen-eyed Polly. He watched as she peeled back the plain brown paper, his heart beating as fast as hers as she came to the contents.

'Well, what is it?'

'It's some courting cake from the shop: six pieces.' Polly looked at her grandfather and then noticed the note that was wrapped in with the cake. She quickly unfolded it and read it, in front of her grandfather, who was peering at it:

> Grouse Hall
> 15th November 1903

> Dear Polly,
>   Forgive me for being so presumptuous,

256

*but your grandfather said you'd been ill. So
I thought I'd send you this, in the hope that
it will help you get your strength back. May
I also ask for the first dance at the Boxing
Day Ball at Hawes? Although I know it is
quite some time away, it will give us both
something to look forward to, and this time
I will attend, I promise.*

*Please tell your grandfather that his sheep
are doing well, and I enjoyed doing business
with him.*

With fondest wishes,
Tobias

'Well, what does he say?' Edmund leaned over
her shoulder and tried to read the wording.

Polly folded the letter up quickly, not wanting
her grandfather to see the invite to the dance.
'You must have told Tobias Middleton I was ill.
He's sent the courting cake for me, and says to
tell you that all the sheep are doing well.' Polly
looked up at her grandfather, who stood staring
at her with an inquisitive look on his face.

'Well, that's good of him, lass. But I think
there's more to telling me the sheep are all right.
I think that lad has his eye on you, lass. You
know, I didn't think a lot of him up until the
other night, but I've seen another side of him
now, and he'd be good for you.' Edmund rubbed
his chin with his hand and studied Polly's face.

'All right, I'd better tell you, he's asked me for
the first dance at the Boxing Day Ball, down in
Hawes.' She lowered her head, for she couldn't
lie to her grandfather.

'That's a while away yet. He must be keen, if he's thinking that far ahead. Well, lass, you go and meet him there. If Len Brunskill says he's all right, that'll do me. You'll never go hungry with that 'un on your arm, so that's a big thing in this life.'

Polly stood up and hugged her grandfather, putting her arms around his neck. 'Thank you, Grandfather. I think he's a good man, too.'

'Aye, well, time will tell. I still remember his father, and I wouldn't want anything like him in my family.'

16

The wet and windy days of November blew the autumn leaves from the trees, leaving them looking bleak and black against the dying grasslands of the Dales. They were long, dreary days of pouring rain and biting winds, with the sheep standing huddled next to the limestone walls and the cows being thankful of the warm, hay-filled barn.

Edmund lifted his oil-filled storm lantern and stepped out into the darkness of the farmyard, while the wind howled around him and the rain poured down in torrents. This was no way to make a living at his age, he thought, as he slapped the reins over old Clover's withers and set off on his three-times-weekly visit to Hawes Junction, to meet the connecting train to Liverpool with his kits of milk for his sister Evie. Perhaps he should rethink and go back to Bill Sunter's dairy.

The rain dripped down his neck and through to his vest, making him shiver as he made the long haul up Garsdale to Hawes Junction. The junction was used for the Wensleydale line, and as the main line for the Midland Railway to go through Westmorland and over the Scottish borders up to Glasgow northbound, and south to Leeds. As he neared the station, he passed the small shop that all the locals used. The curtains were still drawn and in darkness as he climbed the hill steadily, before crossing over the bridge that strode the track and then making his way onto the platform. The yellow glow of the lit gas lamps welcomed him, as he rolled the full milk-kits off the back of the cart and placed them on the edge of the platform, ready for the train to halt for them.

'Now then, Edmund. Shit of a day, isn't it?' Bunce, the stationmaster, came over the sleepered walkway across the track and looked at his watch. 'You're in good time this morning, Edmund, it isn't yet six.'

'Aye, well, I thought I'd better come in good time. I didn't know what the weather was going to do.' Edmund pulled his collar up and stood under the dripping eaves of the waiting room.

'I haven't lit the fire in there yet, else I'd say go in and get warm. Once the Scotch express has gone through, I'll put a match to it. It's late, is the express, by five minutes, by my watch. Tom Moorby's set the signal, so it's on the way.' Bunce looked at his watch again, agitated that his railway was not working on time. 'Hey up, here's your mate from Blue Bridge with his milk, coming down into the yard, and here comes the express.' Bunce leaned over the platform and listened as he heard the distant rumble of the Scotch express coming out of Ais Gill summit, and he sighed a sigh of relief.

'Morning, Edmund. It's days like this that make you wonder why we bother with this milk. My old woman is complaining like hell at these early mornings; says I should get Tobias to bring it himself, then he'd soon back down with his ideals.' Bob Brown pulled at his full cart of ten kits, downloading them next to Edmund as the fast-moving express whooshed past them, not stopping on its way over the border.

Bunce walked up the platform, looking for the southbound train, and glanced up at the lit signal box for the next train to be pegged, in readiness for the milk to be loaded onto it.

Edmund shivered and looked at Bob. 'Nay, you can't knock the lad; he knows when he's being ripped off. That Bill Sunter's making fools out of most folk, but not us. You got to give Tobias his due.'

'Aye, but it's not him freezing his bollocks off on this platform in the pitch-black, with a wife still nice and warm in bed and needing some attention.' Bob grinned at Edmund and then wished he'd not said anything, as he looked at the stony-faced old man.

'Aye, well, she's not got much longer to wait — the train's here. Look, I can see the lights of the carriage coming over Dandymire viaduct. We'll soon be home, and then tha can get to your bed.' Edmund stood by his kits and waited for the jolting train to pull up at the platform. He didn't think much of Bob Brown; he was a bit common, with his talk of his private life. Like all the young, he'd no respect of age, so Edmund was glad the train had been on time.

Edmund and Bob rolled their milk-kits onto the goods carriage with the help of the guard. It was a routine they did most mornings of the week. The guard expected them and knew where the milk was bound. They went through the same motions each morning. The carriage door slammed shut, Bunce blew his whistle, and the train made steam and shunted away from the platform into the slight glimmer of the dawn.

'Right, let's get away. See you again, no doubt.' Edmund climbed up onto his cart and urged Clover into motion. All he wanted to do was get home out of the rain, then dry out in front of the fire at Paradise. His bones ached, and it was on mornings like this that he knew his age. Now the weather was cooler, the milk kept better, which was a blessing. Perhaps he should consider sending two-day old milk for delivery to Liverpool. The folk of Liverpool didn't know any difference; they were just glad of a doorstop delivery from Evie every day. By the time she'd mixed it with her cow's milk, it would taste no different, and it gave Polly the chance to skim off the cream the night before, to make into butter.

Edmund thought about the way his sister lived, and her lifestyle, after marrying her husband Albert, a docker from Wallasey. Even though she'd brought up six children in the back streets of Liverpool, she'd not lost her roots in farming, keeping two cows in an outhouse and supplying the streets around her with milk. She was quite the businesswoman, grazing her cows on any green spaces that the establishments in Liverpool would allow her to use. She reminded him of Polly in a way; once she got something in her head, she wouldn't let it be, until she'd sorted it to her liking. But on mornings like this, Edmund wondered if it was worth the hassle of delivering the milk and receiving the small payment that Evie sent him every month. Perhaps he should just keep the one cow for themselves. If December and January brought snow, then he'd think about it. As it was, at the moment all he wanted to do was get dry and have some breakfast.

★ ★ ★

Polly stoked the fire and looked out of the small-paned kitchen window. It was just breaking light, but you could hardly tell. The surrounding fells blended in with the dark grey of the rain-sodden skies, and heavy clouds lay on the highest peaks, threatening to keep the rain there all day. She hated days like these, days when you couldn't leave the house, and the grandfather clock in the corner of the kitchen reminded her of every dragging minute. She watched as her grandfather entered the yard, dismounting from the cart in his sodden oilskins, unharnessing Clover and then leading her into her stable. He'd get the horse dry before himself, which was always his way, knowing that without Clover in good health, nothing would be done.

Polly put the kettle on the fire to boil and turned a warming pair of socks, some trousers and a shirt on the fire-guard, in readiness for her grandfather to put on. He was a stubborn one. He'd rather get sodden most mornings than make his life easier and have his milk picked up by one of Bill Sunter's men. On a day like this, she'd like to be working in the dairy rather than watching time with her grandfather, but she daren't raise the subject.

'Christ, lass, it's wet, it's not fit for a dog out this morning.' Edmund slung his sodden cloth cap on the floor and shook himself out of his dripping oilskins.

'There's a change of clothes over the fire-guard, and I've some porridge in the pot. Go and get changed, and I'll put your breakfast on the table.' Polly picked up the soaking clothes and hung them up in the back porch to drip.

'I've been thinking, lass. In the New Year I might not bother with milking any more, apart from keeping a cow for milk for the house. If you were a lad, it would be different; you could take it some mornings. But as things stand, it isn't worth it.' Edmund picked the warm, fresh-smelling clothes up from the fire-guard and walked towards the stairs.

'I could take it up to the station. Why do you think I couldn't? I'm strong enough — happen not at the moment, with being ill last month, but give me another week or two and I'll be right.' Even though Polly didn't agree with her stubborn grandfather, she wasn't going to see him defeated.

'Nay, you can't. It's a man's job, and you are nobbut a slip of a lass. And I'm a stubborn old bugger, who should know better than to be trailing in the dark with two kits of milk to be delivered to our Evie. It was all right when I was younger, but I'm old, and it's time I realized it.' Edmund put his hand on the banister and climbed the stairs. All his life he'd brought Polly up to be as strong in her ways as any man, but she was

264

built like a woman now, and heaving heavy milk-kits was not woman's work. Evie had three lads to help her; he hadn't any. Life was a bugger, there was no two ways about it.

★   ★   ★

The grey, wet days of November gave way to the frost and snow of December. The dale glistened and shone in a crystal covering of winter's white blanket. The skies were clear blue through the day and freezing cold through the night, with stars and moon that shone like diamonds in the sky. Christmas was beckoning, and with it in Polly's heart came both sadness and joy. Christmas was about family, and this year the main family member was missing. Her grandmother had always made sure that the plum pudding was made, the cake was baked and everyone had a present. However, it wasn't just about the gifts of Christmas; it was her love that would be missing, and Polly knew that, as she took her first batch of mince pies out of the fireside oven.

Along with the heartache were sudden flurries of excitement as she thought about the Boxing Day Ball and her promise to Tobias. Christmas Day couldn't get over fast enough, she thought, as she placed her mince pies out to cool. She longed to see Tobias and to be swept around the dance floor of Hawes market hall, with her grandfather's blessing. Tomorrow morning it would be Christmas Eve, and her grandfather had promised to take her into Hawes after he had delivered the milk at the junction, to enable her to buy Christmas presents and to have dinner with Matt and his grandmother at Gayle. The thought of having an hour or two to shop in Hawes compensated for having to have lunch at what she now called her 'new grandmother's home'. She'd only met the woman twice and had taken an instant disliking to her, as she was sharp with her words and very offhand when it came to sparing any feelings for her new granddaughter, Polly. Matt had barely been seen since the winter months had crept in. He was too busy at the dairy, and the weather had added to his excuses for not coming to see his grandfather and Polly. Polly had passed the long nights of November knitting him some gloves and embroidering a pair of handkerchiefs for their grandmother, which were now wrapped and waiting for delivery in the morning.

'They smell good, lass.' Edmund entered the kitchen with the goose that he'd just necked, plucked and cleaned, ready for their Christmas dinner. 'There's plenty of meat on her, our Polly, she'll make us a good dinner.' Edmund lifted the dead bird up to show her, before taking it through to the pantry to hang from one of the bacon hooks.

'I'm glad to see the back of that goose. She did nothing but make a noise around the farmyard, even when you were feeding her, the ungrateful bird. I'm sure she knew she was only here for our Christmas dinner.' Polly spooned another table-spoon of mincemeat into an uncooked pastry case and then wiped her hands, before putting the pastry tops on.

Edmund leaned over the kitchen table and pinched a hot mince pie from the cooked pile, juggling it in his hands as he realized they had just come out of the oven.

'Bloody hell, I nearly burned my hands.' Edmund sat in his favourite chair and blew on the hot pastry, before placing it in his mouth.

'If you'd have asked, I would have put one on a plate for you and made a drink of tea, instead of you pinching it from my pile.' Polly laughed at her grandfather acting like a small boy.

'They are always better if they're pinched. But aye, make me a cup of tea, and then I'll go and milk the cows and filter it into the kits, ready for the morning. Are you all right going that early? It just saves me coming back down Garsdale to pick you up.'

'It's early, but it will be all right. I've quite a bit of shopping to do in Hawes, and I want to call in at the dairy and wish Miss Swaine a happy Christmas. She was always all right with me.' Polly put the next batch of pies in the oven, while her grandfather pulled a face at her, not happy that she was going to the dairy. 'It's all right — I'll not talk to Bill Sunter, but I would like to know how Maggie is. She's only got a few more months and the baby will be born.' Polly reached for the kettle and pulled it onto the fire.

'It'll be a shock for her, having to look after something of her own. It'll be the first time she'll have had to do that. She should have behaved herself at the dance last summer.' Edmund watched Polly as she passed him his cup of tea. 'It'll be the Boxing Day Ball before you know it.

267

Is your frock ready? Let's just hope there's no snow over Christmas, or a certain fella's going to be disappointed.' Edmund took a long sip from his tea and noticed a flush come to Polly's cheeks.

'You don't have to tell me to behave myself, Grandfather, if that's what you are getting at. I don't want to end up like Maggie — not yet anyway.'

'Aye, well, your grandmother would have wanted me to say it, so I'm just doing my duty. As long as that Tobias behaves himself.'

'He will, he's a gentleman.'

'That I've yet to discover, our Pol. Time will tell, no doubt.'

★　★　★

It was pitch-black and freezing when Polly and Edmund climbed up onto the cart, after locking the door of Paradise and backing up the fire, in readiness for their return. There was nothing worse than returning frozen from the biting winter winds, to a cold house. The two lit storm lanterns swayed with the motion of the cart as they made their way up the Dales road to Hawes Junction, throwing ghost-like shadows along the hedges.

'I doubt it smells like rain, Polly, and it's so bloody cold it could even be sleet.' Edmund pulled the thick horse-blanket around their knees as they climbed the hill up to the station. 'I hope old Bunce has lit that fire in the waiting room this morning. I don't fancy standing out on the platform for long.'

'I don't know how you do this, week in, week out. You are right: after Christmas, tell Aunty Evie you are giving up sending her milk. We'll manage without the money. I'll get a part-time job.' Even though Polly had four layers of clothes on, she was frozen to the bone and could barely talk, for fear that her teeth would chatter.

'We'll see. Get Christmas over and then we are into a new year. Bloody hell, Bob Brown's here before me this morning. Who would have thought it, on Christmas Eve? At least he'll have tomorrow off.' Edmund urged Clover next to the horse and cart from Blue Bridge, jumped down from the cart and started to unload the kits. 'Get yourself into the waiting room. The fire's lit, the smoke's clouding down from the chimney, so Bunce must have just recently put a match to it. Bob's unloaded his kits, so he must be in there getting warm.' Edmund watched Polly as she slowly climbed down from the cart and entered the double-fronted doors of the waiting room with its welcoming gas lights.

She was glad to feel the heat of the blazing fire as soon as she was inside the small room. It was painted in whitewash, with a large oak table in the middle of the room and claret-coloured benches for waiting passengers to sit on. Standing next to a guarded fire, in the centre of the northern wall, stood the person she understood to be Bob Brown. He was warming himself with outstretched hands, rubbing them to get the circulation back into them, with his back to Polly. Polly coughed to acknowledge her presence and to make him aware that she'd like to share some of the warmth. The figure turned, and in that moment Polly's heart missed a beat. In front of her stood Tobias Middleton, wrapped in a thick overcoat, looking as frozen as she was.

'Polly, what are you doing here at this time of day?' Tobias moved away from the fire and held out his hand. 'Come stand here and warm yourself — it's perishing out there.'

Polly took his hand and lowered her eyes, not daring to look into his face. She knew her cheeks were blue with cold, and she shivered as he urged her to stand next to the fire.

'My grandfather's catching the train with our milk, and then we're going on to Hawes for some Christmas shopping.'

'But you are frozen, Polly. Here, let me warm your hands in mine.' Tobias held Polly's hands in his and looked into her blue eyes with care and concern.

She relished the moment. Tobias's words were nearly as warm as the fire's flames, and she smiled at him as she let him rub her hands hard to help her regain some feeling in them. That was until the handle of the waiting-room door lifted from the outside, announcing Edmund's entrance.

'What's thou doing here, lad? It's usually Bob I see in a morning.' Edmund stepped in to the waiting room just as a goods engine shunted slowly past on its way to Carlisle. He walked over and joined the couple, lifting his jacket up and warming his backside next to the fire.

'I've given him the morning off. I thought he'd appreciate it, with having three children and it being Christmas Eve.' Tobias distanced himself from Polly and looked at the old man warming himself.

'Well, that's good of you. I hope he appreciates it? I'm sure our Polly does, by the look on her face.' Edmund grinned at a blushing Polly. 'Where's old Bunce, and what was that goods engine that just went through? There's never usually anything on that line at this time of the morning. They keep it clear for the express. Unless it's been through already? But I can't see that happening, because it's not quite six.'

'Can't help you with either, I'm afraid. I take it Bunce is the stationmaster? I think he's across in his office. I lit the fire because I was bloody frozen. No wonder Bob Brown curses me under his breath — it won't be his favourite job of the day. Now I know what a miserable job it is.'

'Whisht, lad, is that the express coming? I bloody hope not, because that goods engine won't have cleared the Dandymire viaduct yet. If the points haven't been switched, they are right on top of one another.' Edmund's ears pricked up as he heard the familiar noise of the express making its way up the line.

'The signalman will know what he's doing, surely?' Tobias was unconcerned as Edmund made for the door and the express flew past, with all its carriage windows alight with the glow of the gas lights for the early-morning travellers. Edmund snatched at the door handle and walked out onto the platform and watched as the last carriage vanished into the darkness.

'Bloody hell — oh my God! What's Dawson

doing in the signal box? They are both on the same line!' Bunce, the stationmaster, yelled across the track at Edmund and looked up at the signal box. 'Come on: quick, we've got to catch up with it. There's going to be a disaster.'

No sooner had Bunce shouted out the words than there was a screech of brakes, and the sound of metal tearing and bending on metal, from down the line, followed by screams and the shouts of people fighting for their lives. Sparks lit up the sky as the first carriage of the second train lifted up into the air like a screaming monster.

Tobias and Polly hurried to Edmund's side and then, along with Bunce, they ran down the side of the platform and onto the track bed, guided by the still-burning lights of the express.

'Mr Bunce, Mr Bunce, I've wrecked the Scotch express.' Dawson, the signalman, called down from his lit signal box, shocked by the dire consequences of his lapse in concentration.

Bunce ran past the bottom of the signal box and shouted up to Dawson, who was obviously in shock. 'Block the line, lad. Stop any other trains and send for help. You've done enough bad work tonight. At least you can stop it from getting any worse.'

Tobias and Polly ran ahead, with Edmund stopping to catch his breath alongside the portly Bunce.

'Polly, you should prepare yourself for the worst. There could be folk dead in the wreckage, or people with dismembered limbs.' Tobias reached the first carriage with Polly not far behind him.

'It's all right, Tobias, I'm not frightened.' Polly watched as people made good their escape out of the last few carriages, with blood dripping from them, screaming and moaning in pain.

'You look after the people out of these carriages. Get them away from the wreckage — take them up the line — while your grandfather, Bunce and I look at the rest of the carriages.'

Polly nodded and aided a young woman with a damaged leg, by lending her an arm to lean on, and telling the injured around her to follow her up the line to the station. She looked back as Tobias waited for the out-of-breath Edmund and Bunce, urging the passengers who could walk to follow Polly up the track to safety.

The three men walked down to where the express had overridden the carriages of the goods engine. They were amazed by the sight that met their eyes. The steam and coal fumes coming from the smashed engines assaulted their sense of smell. The carriages had risen in the air and screamed with steam from the engine pistons and boiler, and the cries of dying and injured people could be heard all around. A small fire was burning in the front engine, and Tobias looked around at the undamaged carriages with their gas lights still burning brightly and watched as people fled from them, following Polly up the line.

Bunce, Tobias and Edmund scrambled to pull people from the wreckage. They could hear moaning in the carriages and were aware that the situation was dangerous, as sparks flashed around them, raising the risk of fire. The scene surrounding them was horrendous; people with smashed legs and arms and cracked skulls were all trapped within the first three carriages, with the express-train driver not having stood a chance. He would be dead in his cabin, along with the stoker. The sweat poured off the three men as they passed the injured to one another, all aware of the fire that was spreading upwards from what had been the coalbox of the engine.

'I'm going into the second carriage. I'm sure I heard a baby crying.' Edmund looked at the flames starting to engulf it. 'I'd not live with myself if I couldn't save a baby.'

'Don't be daft, man. Let me go in there.' Tobias pulled at the old man's sleeve.

Edmund looked for a second at the lad standing in front of him. 'Look after my Polly, if I don't make it.' And, with that, he pushed Tobias down onto the floor, pulled his overcoat over his head and climbed into the already alight carriage.

'Edmund, Edmund, you silly old bugger!' Tobias got up from his knees and he and Bunce watched as the man's shape dashed down the carriage and disappeared into the smoke and flames. It seemed like a long time before they saw him moving towards the end of the second carriage, clutching a bundle. He stood on the step, holding the wailing baby out in his hands.

'Here, take her, take her — I can't believe she's alive.' Edmund passed the baby down to Tobias, who took her gently and passed her over to Bunce, before reaching up to help Edmund climb down. 'Nay, there's her mother yet.' Edmund turned to go back into the carriage and, in that second, the gas from the carriage lanterns caught light. The gas pipes ruptured all along the carriages, exploding into flames, engulfing Edmund and the trapped passengers in a fireball that ripped along the length of the train.

Tobias and Bunce were thrown to the ground by the explosion. The baby in Bunce's arms screamed, as if she knew that her mother had died. Polly was further up the line, and she screamed along with the baby as she watched the train exploding. Then there was a deadly hush amongst the injured passengers straggling along the railway line. Suddenly not caring for the woman on her arm, Polly ran as fast as she could back down the line, past the injured and the dying, daring to take on the heat of the burning carriages. From out of the dark and flames walked Tobias with a baby in his arms, and Bunce a few feet behind him. They looked battered, scared and hardly able to stagger the length of the rail.

'Grandfather, Grandfather!' Polly yelled at the burning train and tried to brush past Tobias and Bunce.

'Polly, don't go there — he didn't stand a chance. He was trying to save this baby's mother. He wouldn't have known what had hit him.' Bunce held her arms as she fought to try and find her grandfather.

'Let me go. You can't leave him in there.' Polly screamed and tugged as Bunce held her tight.

'He's dead, Polly. Your grandfather's dead and there's nothing more we can do.'

17

The grey fingers of dawn crept over the scene of devastation, and with it came hoards of rescuers and onlookers to one of the worst train disasters that had ever happened on the Settle-to-Carlisle line.

Polly sat in the kitchen of one of the railway workers' houses at the junction. She felt numb. Her clothes were torn and her face and hands were filthy; but, most of all, her heart was broken. She looked out of the kitchen window, watching the firefighters and doctors rushing about. They were too late. Where had they been when her grandfather had tried to save the life of that young woman? Why hadn't he let old Bunce climb into that carriage? He'd no family — why had it been her grandfather? But, most of all, why hadn't Tobias tried harder to stop Edmund going back into the carriage in the first place? Polly's thoughts went back to Tobias restraining her from running down to the burning wreckage. She thought about how he'd held her tightly, stopping her from searching for her grandfather and making her punch his strong arms. She'd told him she hated him for not letting her go. He should have looked after her grandfather. It should have been Tobias who went into the wreckage for the baby.

'Looks like it's going to snow. That's all they need. What a terrible day this is, and it's

Christmas Eve.' Mrs Price looked out of the window and then at the young orphaned lass who was in her care. 'Are you all right, love? Do you need another cuppa? There's nothing like sweet tea for a shock.'

Polly shook her head. She'd had more cups of tea than she cared to mention, and it wasn't tea that she wanted, but a shoulder to cry on. Her world had been shattered and there was no one there for her.

'Aye, it's a sad day. All those folk on their way back up to Scotland for Christmas. And you, pet, what are you going to do without your grandfather? He was a good man, was Edmund; always talked to me, and was the same whenever you saw him. We often passed the time of day on an early summer morning when he delivered his milk.' Bessie Price folded her arms and peered out of the kitchen window again.

Polly looked at the nosy woman, who was nearly breaking her neck to see who they were bringing down the hill on stretchers towards the wagons, ready to journey to the makeshift mortuary at Hawes. She wished Matt would come back for her, as he had promised, when he'd rushed onto the station platform with men from the dairy, after hearing the news. She guessed that he'd become involved in the search for their grandfather, but she didn't hold out much hope of Matt finding anything of him remaining, as the heat had been so fierce.

'There's that Dawson lad, from the signal box. He's being walked down the road with a policeman on either side. The poor bugger, I

277

wouldn't want to be in his shoes. My Jack says he's not a bad lad, but still, he should have kept his mind on the job.' Bessie gave a running commentary on the comings and goings. 'Here's your brother — he's coming down the path now. He looks shattered. I'll put the kettle on.' She stood up and looked at the silent Polly, before reaching for the kettle as the back door opened.

Matt burst into the room, and Polly stood up as he reached his hand out to her. She crumpled into his arms as he wrapped them around her, and sobbed into his smoke-fumed jacket. She cried and cried, and then between the sobs she wiped the tears away and looked up at Matt as he caressed her hair, shaking his head in answer to the question he knew she was going to ask.

'They haven't got to that carriage yet, Pol, the flames are too fierce. They will find him — what's left of him. He will get a decent burial, we'll see to that. Don't worry.'

Bessie Price stood still with her cups and saucers of tea and placed them down quickly, to mop her eyes as she watched the young couple. 'If there's owt I can do, let me know. You can stop here as long as you want. Have your suppers while you wait on news.' She blew her nose on her apron and watched as Matt looked out of the window while holding Polly.

'He always was a stubborn old bugger. Why he couldn't have taken his milk to the dairy, I don't know,' said Matt as he looked down at Polly.

''Cause he did what he wanted, and wouldn't be bought by any man.' Polly smiled and wiped her cheek free of tears. 'I know one thing: my grandmother will be playing hell with him, if they are in heaven together. She'll be giving him a right what-for.'

'That's it, love, think of the good times.' Bessie patted Polly's arm.

'Tobias asked if you want to stop at Grouse Hall with him for a day or two, but I told him we were going home. I suppose the cows will need milking, and there's the dogs and hens to feed. Somebody will have to do it.' Matt looked at Polly.

'Why would I want to stay at Grouse Hall? He could have saved my grandfather, if he'd have shaped himself. I don't think I ever want to talk to Tobias Middleton again.' Polly grabbed her shawl from the back of the chair and glared at her brother. 'Are we going home then? Get me away from this terrible place. No doubt someone will tell us if they find Grandfather, and I can't stand another minute here, with everyone around me.'

'Of course, if that's what you want. I'll take you home, do the few jobs and then perhaps return to see if they've found him.' Matt looked at his sister. She was angry with the world, and she wasn't going to be pacified with anything other than getting her own way.

'Aye, I hope they find him for you, lass. You'll feel better if you know there's something of him in a coffin, when it comes to burying him.' Bessie opened the back door to see them both out, satisfied that she'd done her best for the young lass and her brother, but also wishing they were gone, so that she could walk out to see the accident and hear the gossip herself.

★ ★ ★

The drive back up to Paradise passed in silence; both Matt and Polly had run out of words to say to one another. Old Clover plodded, as if she knew she'd lost her master. Silently, snow began to fall.

'Bugger it, Polly, this is all we need.' Matt drove Clover into the farmyard of Paradise and helped his sister down from the cart. 'I'll sort Clover and make sure she's fed. Are you all right going into the house alone?'

Polly nodded. Paradise was home, with or without her grandfather and grandmother. It was all she knew, and all she wanted to know.

'Right, I'll feed the hens and dog, and then I'll come in. The sheep are down in the bottom pastures already. Grandfather must have known it was looking likely to snow.' Matt pulled on Clover's harness and the old horse lifted her head in obedience.

Polly watched as Matt took Clover into the stable and then she walked up to the porch, opening the kitchen door that was never locked and welcoming the warmth from the dying fire as she entered the kitchen. The fire was barely alight from their early-morning attentions, and she stared for a moment at the chair that Edmund had always made his own. What she wouldn't pay for him and her grandmother to be sitting there now, content in front of the fire. Why had she taken them for granted?

She removed the fire-guard and added a few dry kindling sticks from the hearthside, blowing gently on the fire to encourage the flames. Soon flames were licking up the chimney and she added coal to the fire, making it feel warm and welcoming again in the kitchen. She lit the paraffin lamps and put one on the kitchen table and another in the window. It was going to be dark soon tonight, and the sky was dark and heavy with snow. She looked out of the window and noticed that Matt had lit the storm lantern in the barn. He must be milking the cows early, in readiness for the snow, which was falling more heavily now. It was a good job he was here. She didn't know how she would cope on her own. The house had suddenly become full of memories and ghosts, and she needed someone to be there for her.

Matt opened the kitchen door and walked in with a full bucket of milk in his hands. 'I've milked the cows, and all's done for the night. This snow's coming down thick and fast. I'm going to get stuck here, if I don't get back. You said you were all right in the house, didn't you?' He put the bucket down, spilling some milk on the stone flags of the kitchen in his haste. 'I'll have to get back to my grandmother — she'll be bothering about me.' He looked out of the window at the snowflakes, which were falling faster and faster.

'But I thought you'd stay with . . . ' Polly looked at her brother, as he made for the kitchen door.

'You'll be right. I'll be back in the morning. Nowt will hurt you here. Besides, you must be jiggered. Get yourself to bed — it'll be morning before you know it. I've got to go, Polly, because

I've left my horse at the junction. If I don't go now, I'll not get there, because of the snow.'

Polly listened to her brother making excuses and hadn't the strength to argue. He was right; she was jiggered, exhausted by the day.

'You'll come back tomorrow?' she pleaded.

'Aye, I promise, and I might have some news of Grandfather.' Matt gave her a quick hug and then was out of the kitchen door, running down the snow-covered path to the main road and on up further, to Hawes Junction.

Polly stood in the kitchen. The rest of the house was silent, dark and empty. Shadows played on the wall and the steady tick of the grandfather clock echoed as she sat in the chair by the fire. She was alone. It would be Christmas Day in the morning, and she would probably have no one to share it with; most of her family were dead now, and the ones that were alive were uncaring. Matt couldn't be relied upon; he'd not move from his grandmother's side, not on Christmas Day. A tear ran down her cheek as she felt the warmth of the fire. Tonight she was a weak young lass, with no one. How things had changed in twenty-four hours.

★ ★ ★

The morning came all too soon and, with it, the reality of the previous day's events. Polly pulled her patchwork quilt up around her chin and lay in her bed, thinking of the crash, and of her loss. It was a disaster. She'd never thought about losing her grandfather; in her mind, he was always going to be there. Now she was on her own and, by the look of the ledge of snow on the outside of her bedroom window, she would be alone all day. She wiped a tear away onto her already soaked pillow. Tears would not bring anyone back. She'd got to get herself together.

She pulled the covers back on her bed and shivered in the cold of the badly lit bedroom. Rummaging through her wardrobe, she pulled out a warm, clean skirt and top, which she pulled over her undergarments, and then proceeded to brush her hair. It smelt of smoke, and memories of the screams and of people's desperate cries came flooding back to her. She'd wash her hair as soon as she could — wash the hurt out of her hair, just like she was going to throw out the clothes that lay in a pile next to her bed, where she had abandoned them in her tiredness.

She went to the window. All was white outside: the farmyard was a perfect blanket, and the dale lay still and at peace with itself. Smoke rose from the houses along The Street, and Polly thought of the people within them waking up and enjoying Christmas Day. Children would be opening presents from Father Christmas, and couples would be wishing one another well on this special day of the year. She wandered into her grandparents' room and sat on the double bed they had shared all their life, picking up a photograph that they had both cherished, taken at the photographer's in Hawes on their silver wedding anniversary. Polly rubbed her finger around the outline of their faces and whispered, 'I love you — happy Christmas', before putting it back in its place. It was funny, but she had never realized before that her grandmother had been quite a stunner when she was younger.

It was then that the small box caught her eye. It was wrapped in holly-covered paper and tied with a red ribbon with a tag on it. Polly picked it up and read the small brown label, recognizing her grandfather's handwriting:

Happy Christmas, Polly,
    Your grandmother would want you to
have this.
    Love, Grandfather

She couldn't stop the tears as she opened the box. Her grandfather wasn't there, and hadn't known when he'd wrapped it how much it would mean to her. No matter what it was in the box, she would treasure it forever. She held the label close to her heart and swallowed her tears as she carefully unwrapped the paper. Underneath was a velvet-covered ring box. She opened the lid and gazed upon her grandmother's engagement ring. It shone and sparkled in the poor morning light. Her grandmother had always worn it, and as a child Polly had played with it, pretending that she was a princess. It had been the only piece of jewellery Ada had, besides her wedding ring, and that she had worn to her grave.

Polly placed the ring on her finger and looked at it. What was she going to do? She couldn't manage on her own; even her grandparents had had one another. Her grandfather must have loved Ada, when he'd bought his bride-to-be the sparkling ring. She'd never be that lucky — never. As for Tobias, who knew what he thought of her? Surely he could have saved her grandfather. Could she ever forgive him, and would he ever forgive her for the hateful words she had spat at him in haste? She doubted it; all was lost.

★ ★ ★

'Polly, Polly, are you here, lass?' Len Brunskill looked up at the windows of Paradise, after trying the locked kitchen door. He shivered in the cold and waited for a reply.

Slowly the kitchen door opened and there Polly stood, waif-like.

'Oh, you are here! Martha said I should come up and see if you were, but we expected you to be up Gayle, with Matt and his grandmother. You've not spent the night alone here on your own?' Len walked up to her and opened the door wider and looked at the pale, ghost-like form.

Polly nodded her head.

'Aye, lass, I'm so sorry. By God, you're going to miss him — he was one in a million, was Edmund.' Polly stood and wept in Len's arms, as he held her tight in the cold light of the morning. 'Come on, lass, let's get something to eat in you, then I'll see to the stock outside and then you are coming home with me. Martha wouldn't have it any other way, and I owe it to your grandfather. He was the best friend any man could ever have, and I'm not going to let him down now.' Polly sat as Len lit the fire and buttered some bread, covering it with jam while waiting for the kettle to boil.

'Well, your bucket of milk will not be going anywhere. The road's blocked with snow and there's no trains running, because of the crash. I know Edmund would have cursed me for wasting it, but it's going down the drain.' Len looked at the untreated milk from the previous night, still standing in the bucket on the kitchen floor, and picked it up as he made towards the kitchen doorway. 'I'll milk the cows and see to them tonight, and every day until we can get something sorted. Perhaps you should think of sending the milk to Bill Sunter. It would be easier for you, if you decide to stop here.' Len wiped his brow with his cap. This wasn't for him to suggest, but what else could he do?

'No, it'll never go to Bill Sunter. My grand-father wouldn't want it to. I'll sort it myself.' Polly curled up in the armchair and gazed into the fire.

'All right, lass. Well, you warm yourself while I fodder up, and then we'll go down home for Christmas dinner, although we haven't much to celebrate this day.' Len shook his head as he went out into the yard. What the hell was going to happen to Paradise? That Matt wanted his arse kicking, leaving his sister alone, after losing her grandfather in such a way. He was just like his father. There was no doubting that.

☆ ☆ ☆

Matt sat across from his grandmother, enjoying every mouthful of his Christmas dinner.

'Do you think she'll have realized yet, that so-called sister of yours, that a slip of a lass can't run a farm?' Dora Dinsdale licked her fingers as she picked the last piece of meat from the turkey's wishbone and looked across at her beloved grandson.

'You should have seen her face, when I said I was coming home. She was frightened, Gran. She'll be begging to stay with us, if we leave her there alone for a night or two.' Matt grinned, leaning back in his chair, and burped.

'Aye, well, it should be yours, lad. Who's heard of a lass running a farm? They are always passed down to the man of the family. The sooner she realizes that, the better. It'll be nice to get out of this poky cottage. I miss my farmhouse. If that bloody useless husband hadn't died on me, we would still be up Dent.'

'Never mind. New year, new house, Gran, and I can give over working at that bloody dairy. Happy Christmas, Gran, may all our dreams come true!'

18

Polly lay in the comfortable bed in the spare room of the Brunskills' cottage. Martha and Len had shown her nothing but kindness all day, as they had fussed around her, trying to ease the pain of her loss. But it didn't make much difference. Christmas would never be the same again; she would always hear the cries of the injured and dying, as she thought about the night she lost her beloved grandfather.

Martha had broken down in tears as she carved the turkey at dinnertime, and the afternoon had been silent as the grave as they all thought about the loss of the previous night. There had been no parlour games, and no singing at the piano to the glory of Christmas, as no one had been in the mood. Len had been true to his word and had walked up the lane to Paradise to milk the cows, with the onset of evening, and Martha had insisted that at least for tonight Polly stayed with them. She hugged her pillow and warmed her toes on the earthenware bed-bottle that Martha had lovingly put in the bed for her. The bed was comfortable enough, but she wished she were back home. Even though Paradise was full of memories, it was home and her bed was more cosy. She sighed, feeling guilty that she had stopped crying, but the tears wouldn't come any more. They had been never-ending all day, but now she just felt sick and empty. Tomorrow she would go back up to Paradise. She'd take up Len's offer of milking the cows for her, but she needed to go home. The Brunskills didn't need her around the house, wailing like a spectre, and it was better that she kept herself to herself. It was time to prove to everybody that she was strong enough to look after herself and that she could run Paradise on her own.

Polly was brought back from her thoughts by hearing a knock on the front door of the Brunskills' home. It was too late for visitors, so she knew it must be important. She tiptoed out of bed and sat at the top of the stairs, trying to listen to the muffled voices down in the hallway. She recognized the deep voice of Bob Raw, the undertaker.

'We've found Edmund — that is, what's left of him. I've taken him into the chapel of rest, along with the others. I thought you might like to tell the lass. It might be easier, coming from you.' She heard him cough quietly and Martha stifle a sob.

'Aye, we'll tell her in the morning. Thanks for coming round and letting us know.' Len sighed.

'It's a bad do. There's twelve dead in all. What a bloody time for a crash. How's the lass taking it? It's not long since Ada died, so she'll be on her own now, except for that brother of hers. Does anyone know where Danny, her father, is?' Bob quizzed, as Len kept him in the hallway.

'She's bearing up well. I don't know about her brother. He didn't grow up with Edmund, so he's a separate kettle of fish. And Danny — only

289

God knows where he is. I suppose someone should try and find him. I bet Bill Sunter will know what he's up to; they were always close.' Len whispered something to Martha that Polly couldn't make out, and then Polly heard her crying again.

'Well, somebody will have to pay for the funeral, although there's talk of the railway paying for them all. It was that Dawson lad's fault — the poor bugger will have that on his conscience all his life. Right, I'm off, Len. I'd wish you and Martha happy Christmas, but it's not right under the circumstances; it's far from happy.'

'Aye, goodnight, Bob. Thanks for letting us know. I'll tell Polly in the morning. No good waking her up, only to upset her more tonight.' Len closed the door after his late-visiting guest.

Polly could hear Martha sobbing in Len's arms downstairs as she crouched at the top of the stairs. She shivered with cold and fear. So that was it: they'd found her grandfather. She stood up and made her way back to the warmth of her bed. On her mind was a burning question and worry. Did Bill Sunter know where her father was and, with her grandfather dead, would he now return? This was another reason for her to go home. Her grandfather wouldn't want her father in Paradise, of that Polly was sure. Tomorrow she must go home, be brave and plan for the future.

19

Boxing Day dawned bright and brash, with clear blue skies and a weak winter's sun, whose rays played and shined upon the crystals of the white, snow-covered fields. Polly breathed in sharply. The air was frost-filled, and her breath steamed up in front of her as she held up her long skirts and made her way up the field path to home.

Martha and Len had told her the news of her grandfather's body being found and had begged her to stay another day with them, just to get over the shock. But Polly's mind was made up. All her life her grandparents had been grooming her for this moment, and now it was time to prove that she was worthy of looking after the family farm. Once the snow had melted, she'd do as Edmund had done and take the milk to the station. She could do it; the kits weren't that heavy, and Clover was so placid she took no looking after. Until then, she'd milk the cows herself and turn the milk into butter. She'd sell it to Sam Allen or, failing that, hawk it around the market on a Tuesday.

She had written to her Aunt Evie while with the Brunskills, and had told her of the accident and that she would write again when she had a date for the funeral. Len had promised to post it once the snow had been cleared, so that was in hand. All she needed to do today was fodder the sheep, feed Clover, the hens and dog, then milk the cows and skim the milk for cream to make into butter. She could do that, no problem. Len had tried to persuade her to let him help, but had known it was a useless argument when he'd noticed the determined look on her face.

Instead of going straight into the house, Polly went into the stable. She patted old Clover on her hind-quarters and the horse turned and looked at her.

'We'll manage, won't we, lass? I know what to do, though I might take longer, so you'll have to be patient.' She patted Clover's neck, and the horse snorted and looked at Polly with her huge blue eyes, as if she understood what she was being told. 'Let's start with you: water and some hay. And you can shut up, Jip. I'll make your breakfast once I've got the fire going. In fact, you can come and join me in the house for company.' Polly freed the black-and-white collie dog that was prancing and barking on the chain, tied up next to Clover. She watched as he ran out of the stable and then sniffed and rolled in the covering of snow in the yard, before disappearing through the farmyard gate. Breakfast would be served sooner than Polly could make it, in the form of a rabbit from the fell side, if Jip had his way, and she didn't blame him.

She lifted the wooden water bucket and went out into the yard to the water trough, breaking a hole in the ice that covered it, to fill the bucket. Her hands tingled with the cold as she made several trips back and forth to the trough to fill Clover's and the cows' drinking troughs up. Then she climbed up to the hay-loft and pushed down enough hay to feed the horse, cows and sheep. She smelt the sweet smell of the hay from last summer, and with it the memories of the summer's hay-field, just after the death of Ada, came flooding back. She felt herself swallowing back the tears as she filled up Clover's hay-rack and then moved on to sort out the cows. Life was hard then, but she doubted it was going to get any worse. She picked up the three-legged milking stool and sat down next to the cows, with her bucket under the udder of the first cow while it ate through the hay. Her fingers gripped firmly around the teats of its udder, pulling gently, and slowly releasing the warm, creamy milk from its swollen bag. Her head rested gently on the cow's side and, as she milked it, tears ran down her cheeks and fell into the bucket of milk. This was her life now. She was beholden to the farm stock — all other dreams had to be forgotten. Grandfather had been right: this was her place in life, and she'd better get on with it.

* * *

Polly sat snoozing in front of the fire. Her hands were raw with the cold and frost, and every bone in her body ached with the rigours of the day. Jip lay down beside her on the pegged rug and twitched in his sleep, dreaming about the rabbits that he'd chased that day. The full moon beamed in through the kitchen, adding light to the dimly lit kitchen and a ghostly sheen to her surroundings.

All of a sudden Jip sat up, pricking his ears

293

and curling his lip into a growl.

'What's up, lad? What have you heard?' Polly pulled her shawl around her and patted Jip's head as he carried on growling and then broke into a stifled bark.

A heavy knock on the door made Polly freeze for a moment. Who would be visiting at this time of night? It couldn't be Matt; he wouldn't knock and neither would Len. They knew just to walk into the house.

Polly held onto Jip's collar and told him to be quiet as she shouted from behind the kitchen door, 'Who is it? Who's there?' Jip strained on his collar and barked louder, scratching at the door to get at the visitor.

'Polly, Polly, it's me — Tobias! I'm sorry if I've disturbed you.'

The deep voice she knew so well came through the door, and she sighed in relief and told Jip again to be quiet. She opened the door slightly with one hand as she held back the excited collie. The moonlight played on the outline of Tobias as she opened the door to him, letting the dog break free.

'I thought I'd come and make sure that you are all right. But I see you already have a guardian, and a good one at that.' Tobias looked gingerly at the sheep-dog that was baring its teeth at him.

'Jip, go to bed,' Polly shouted at the dog and pointed next to the fire, making the dog crouch and look slyly at the stranger against whom he was going to guard his mistress. 'I said: Bed!' The collie's ears went down and it crept slowly past the couple, before curling up on the rug. 'What are you doing here? How have you managed to get here?' Polly stood in the doorway and could only think what a mess she must look. She was thankful it wasn't daylight.

'I walked, my dear. It's a lovely night for a moon-light walk, and I was worried about you. We parted on bad terms. I didn't want us to part like that. I promised your grandfather I'd look after you, and I don't go back on my word. Besides, Polly, tonight was supposed to be our night at the Boxing Day Ball.' Tobias looked at her. Even by the dim light her face told him how tired and worn-out she was. 'Are you going to ask me in, or should I just freeze on your doorstep and be turned to ice by morning?' Tobias patted his arms with his hands, trying to get some warmth back into his frozen limbs.

Polly hesitated for a moment. She was alone, and even though she had feelings for Tobias and had always known him to be honourable, she knew she was just a vulnerable young woman. 'Len Brunskill might be calling, I wouldn't want him to think . . . '

'Think what, Polly — that I'm taking advantage of you? Polly, I was with your grandfather when he died. We were to meet tonight. I don't think that's taking advantage. Besides, Martha and Len are good people; if he does call in, we'll be the better for it.' Tobias smiled. 'Honestly, Polly, I'll behave.'

She held the door wide and bade him enter. She didn't really need a lot of persuading. Jip raised his head idly, as Tobias took off his coat and warmed his hands at the fire.

'Some defender of your honour, he is,' Tobias laughed, as the dog stretched out, enjoying the warmth of the fire.

'He's good company — at least I'm not on my own,' Polly sighed. 'And he doesn't answer back.'

Tobias stood in front of her as she reached for the kettle from next to the fire, to make her visitor a drink. 'Are you all right, Polly? You know I did all I could to stop your grandfather from going back into that burning carriage. As I said, he asked me to look after you, and that's what I aim to do.' Tobias reached his hand out to Polly as she brushed past him.

'You didn't try hard enough, though, did you? He's gone, and I've no one left except a brother who doesn't give a damn about me.' Polly could feel the tears welling as she brushed his hand from her.

'You've got me, Polly; you'll always have me. I promised your grandfather, and I knew from that first time we met that there was an invisible bond between us. I felt it so strongly when you flashed those blue eyes at me, on that wild, mist-filled spring day.' Tobias pulled her small frame towards him and felt Polly's body shudder as he held her tightly. It was the first true form of affection she'd had since the crash. He listened to her start to cry, and held her tightly as she wept openly in his arms. He stroked her long, black hair and whispered soothing words of sympathy and love, as he kissed her head gently, with heartfelt kindness. 'Shh, shh, it will be all right. I'm here, I'll look after you. I'll always be here for you, Polly of Paradise. Nobody's going to hurt you ever again.'

Polly looked up with dew-wet eyes at the dark figure of the man she knew she loved. This was the moment she had waited for, for so long, but it was tinged with such sadness. She reached up and kissed him gently on the lips. This was different from the forbidden kiss with Matt, and the unloving kisses of Joe. This was one of passion and lust, but also of tenderness. She loved Tobias with every inch of her body, and in that moment she was determined that she was going to show him her love for him, and keep him close to her forever.

★ ★ ★

'You brazen little slut!' Dora Dinsdale looked at the partly dressed Polly and then at Tobias, as he pulled his braces up over his shirt. 'Your grandfather's not even dead in his grave, and you're sleeping with the first man that comes calling.'

'It's not like that, Mrs Dinsdale. We didn't mean to take it that far, and you have no right to call Polly a slut. Believe me, she did not take going to bed with me lightly. She needed consoling, alone in the house by herself.' Tobias pulled his jacket on and glared at Mathew and Dora Dinsdale, who had entered the house while he and Polly had lain contentedly in one another's arms in bed. The weather had changed overnight and the rain that was now coming down steadily had unblocked the road, giving the

Dinsdales access to Paradise.

'And you thought you'd take advantage — just like your father would have done. Aye, it's a case of like father, like son. He was nowt and you are nowt, with your flash ways. And her — well, she's not fit with owt. Me and my lad will move in here, after Edmund's funeral, so you can forget about putting your mitts on her and Paradise. Things are going to change.' Dora Dinsdale looked at Tobias Middleton, standing in the kitchen of Paradise Farm. He was a quick mover, she'd give him that, but God, he'd played right into her hands. Now she and Matt could claim to be protecting Polly from his lecherous ways, as well as worming their way into owning Paradise. After the funeral she had every intention of contesting the will. If Edmund had just left it to Polly, that wasn't right; her Matt should be joint heir.

'You are wrong, Grandmother. He loves me, and we are to be wed,' Polly screamed across the kitchen as she tied her skirts.

'Don't be so bloody stupid, lass. What would he want with you, other than a bit of what he fancies? Look at you: you're a bloody mess. Even our Matt only looked at you because he was after what was rightly his. That's right; he knew you were his sister, when you were supposedly courting! Oh, don't look so shocked. We had to know how the land lay with Paradise, and if my lad had a chance of getting it.' Dora spat the words out like venom. Since the day the twins had been born she had vowed revenge for her daughter's death, and Paradise Farm would be just payment for the grief she had gone through.

Matt hung his head with shame, as his grand-mother went just that bit too far. He hadn't meant to hurt Polly that much, and it was only after talking about her to Dora that the penny had dropped about who Polly really was, and what could possibly be gained.

'Why, you bastards!' Tobias swore at the two devious, deceitful people that he now hated with every breath he took. As he watched, Polly crumpled up into a shivering mess.

'Aye, go on, lad. Hit a defenceless woman, and then I can get you locked up, out of the way.' Dora laughed as Tobias stepped forward.

'Tobias, no — she's not worth it. She can't get her hands on Paradise. Grandfather was going to leave it to me. He promised me he's been to the solicitors, so there's nothing they can do.' Polly jumped to her feet, pulled Tobias from her grandmother and looked at Matt with his shamed face.

'That's what you think, lass. My Matt here rightfully owns half of this place and we'll contest any will that there is. After all, he is the man, out of the two of you. Why do you think the law is going to favour a feeble young woman like you? And *he'll* not always be here — look, he's making for the door even now.' Dora tossed a look at Tobias, as he walked to the kitchen door and opened it wide.

'I'm opening the door because you two are no longer welcome. Now get out, and leave Polly in peace.' Tobias stood, dark and brooding, by the doorway. 'Out — get out now! — else by God I will not be responsible for my actions,' he bellowed like a madman, across the kitchen, making the mouthy Dora go quiet and Matt realize that Tobias was too powerful to be taken on, in the temper he was showing now.

'You'll not be throwing me out, once I've talked to the solicitor down in Hawes. He'll be taking you to court,' simpered Dora as she walked past him.

'Out! Get out, and don't bother coming back.' Tobias didn't even look at her, as Dora eyed him from beside the door.

'I'll fucking get you one day — you are nothing. This place is mine,' Matt whispered in Tobias's ear and grimaced as he walked past him.

'And good day to you. Please call again when you can prove the farm is yours. But for now, get out of this yard,' shouted Tobias from the porch, as the two angry Dinsdales climbed into their horse and trap and cracked the whip over the horse's head to set it into action.

'Ta. Fuck you, you cheeky bastard,' Matt yelled as Tobias closed the door upon them.

Tobias leaned against the closed kitchen door and sighed, looking at Polly, who was crying in the chair. 'Well, we know now where we stand. I'm a bastard, which if he did but know it is partly true, as my dear departed father used to always call me by that endearing name when I was a child. But you, my dear, are not a slut; you are ever the lady, and the woman I love.' He walked over to Polly and held her tightly. 'Don't let their words hurt you, my love. Wait until after we've buried your grandfather, and then I'll

300

come with you to old Winterskill. We'll see if there is indeed a will bequeathing Paradise to you, and tell him of this incident. He's a good friend of my mother. He'll do anything for her, and me. Don't you fret, my love, he'll not be bullied by your brother and grandmother.'

Polly held Tobias tightly. She had wanted to be this close to him for so long, but it didn't feel right under the circumstances. 'I don't think I can ever forgive Matt. I should have known he was using me. He was so cold towards me, once our grandfather told us both the truth about our parentage. I guessed then that he had already known.' She sniffed and looked up at Tobias.

'Families are strange things. Sometimes you are better off without them. Although I love my mother — she means everything to me. I'll take you to meet her, when we go and see Winterskill. It was he who told her that I was her son, after my father died; she had no idea, you know. All she knew was that, when she first saw me, she felt this inexplicable bond and a need to protect me. That is what she has done from the very first day I met her in the kitchen of Grouse Hall, and every day since. That is what I'm going to do for you, my love. No matter what worries come our way, I'll stand by you and protect, and love you always.'

Polly relaxed in Tobias's arms. He was a good man, and under the aloofness that some people felt about him lay a heart of gold, and a heart that had borne a lot of sadness. They were two souls thrown together through life's injustices, and with Tobias she knew she would be safe.

20

Christmas led into a new year and with it came the day of Edmund's funeral. The days had been long and hard since his death and Polly was relieved in some ways that her grandfather was finally being put to rest. The chapel at Garsdale was full, with folk paying their respects outside as well as in. Polly walked behind the hearse with her arms linked with Martha and Len Brunskill's. Behind her walked Matt and his grandmother, who refused to give Polly a second glance as she cried. The vicar started his sermon as the bearers carried aloft the few charred remains of Edmund in his coffin.

'You all right, lass? Take no notice of them; they'll not say owt while you're with me.' Len squeezed her hand tight, feeling Polly tremble. She'd told him about what had happened, straight after the argument between Tobias and Dora Dinsdale. He'd found her crying in the stable when he'd come to make sure she was all right, and had been shocked by her outburst. He hadn't thought highly of her sleeping with Tobias, but what Matt and her grandmother had done was worse. As for Dora Dinsdale, well, she had always been a manipulative woman. Poor old Bernard, her husband, had probably been hounded to his grave by her sour tongue.

Polly smiled up at Len. He and Martha had been her rock. She was thankful for their advice and support and thought the world of them. She looked around at the pews full of friends, neighbours and railway workers, who had come to show their respect to the old man who had risked his life for others. She blushed as she spotted Tobias at the end of a pew near the front. He was there with his mother, Daisy Allen. She looked graceful, covered from head to toe in black lace. Polly knew Tobias wanted her to meet his mother, but she thought it only proper to wait until after the funeral. She searched the pews again. She'd expected her Aunty Evie and Uncle Albert to attend, but she'd not had any correspondence from them since she told them of Edmund's death. She'd thought they might surprise her by coming to the funeral.

Bill Sunter stood at the end of one of the pews, and next to him stood Maggie, who looked blooming; another two months and she would be a mother. Maggie smiled and wiggled her gloved fingers at Polly, until her father told her to stop when the vicar and the cortège halted at the head of the chapel. Polly shuffled into the front pew and bowed her head in prayer between the two Brunskills. She wanted to cry, but nothing came out. She'd cried so much since the accident, and crying wasn't going to bring anyone back, so it was futile to do so.

'I am the way . . . ' The vicar gave his blessing and then led into the first hymn. 'Please rise and sing together 'The Lord is My Shepherd'. Edmund was known for loving his beloved flock of Swaledale sheep, and I believe in his later years for his love of a certain Herdwick. Which, I am told, he'd found a good home for, in *its* later years.' The vicar smiled down at Polly and she felt a lump rise in her throat.

It had seemed like only a few months ago that she was viewing the old Herdwick in lamb at Hawes, with Edmund and Ada joking about it. Len must have told the vicar. He'd organized everything with her, and had thought of all the personal little bits that she either hadn't known or had forgotten about. She stood, with her legs wobbling and her voice faltering, as she remembered both her grandmother and grandfather. She had no idea what was going to happen in the days after the funeral. But what she did know was that she had been lucky — so lucky that she had taken everything for granted. How she now longed for that love and security again; a simple thing like a meal ready on the table, a warming pan in the bed and, most of all, a smiling face that wished her well.

★　★　★

The funeral tea was held in the village hall. Mrs Armitage had organized sandwiches, cake and trifle, with tea to accompany them, and she wandered around each table, making sure everyone's needs were catered for. Polly sat between Martha and Len, with Tobias and his mother.

'So, Polly, Tobias tells me that you have been so brave since your grandfather's death. It's a terrible thing to be left on one's own. Although, of course, I know you've a brother.' Daisy Allen gazed across at the young slip of a lass, who looked like she would burst into tears at any moment. 'It's a pity we cannot choose our relations, like we choose friends; it would cause a lot less trouble.' She smiled as Polly bowed her head. 'Don't worry, my dear. Tobias will not let them get the better of you. He's told me how much he thinks of you, and that he will move heaven and earth to make you happy. You are in good hands, my dear.' Daisy smiled. Polly reminded her a lot of herself at that age, and she didn't want Polly to have the same heartache that she'd had.

Polly blushed. 'Thank you, Mrs Allen, I appreciate your concern. Tobias has been wonderful.' She raised her head and looked quickly across at the face she loved.

'Aye, they are a right pair of lovebirds, these two. A bit of hope out of a tragedy.' Len Brunskill smiled and squeezed his wife's hand and looked at her.

'Yes, I can tell my Tobias is smitten. It's about time; he wasn't getting any younger. I'm pleased for you both. You'll come to tea on Tuesday, won't you, Polly, when you go to the solicitor's? I would love to get to know you a little better.' Daisy rose from her seat. She'd earned the respect of the locals over the years, helping to build up her husband's business, and then financing Tobias as he ventured into farming. Gone were the days when she was whispered about by the local gossips, and now she had an air of self-confidence about her, and the respect of the local community.

Tobias offered his mother his arm as she stood up, gazing at Polly as he did so.

Polly looked at them both. Could they be her new family? She hesitated for a moment before answering. 'Yes, I'd love to, Mrs Allen, if you are sure.'

'Of course I am, my dear. I want to hear all about you. Come, Tobias, see your mother home and then the day is your own.' Daisy stepped away from the table and gracefully walked past both Matt and his grandmother, who glared at the couple.

'Now, that's a grand family, lass. Edmund might have had his doubts, but Daisy's a lovely woman and she's brought Tobias up well. Get him snapped up, lass. You'll not regret it.'

'Len, you hold your wind. We are at a wake, so stop your matchmaking,' said Martha.

Polly blushed at the bickering couple.

'You make your own happiness in this world, lass, and if he makes you happy, then what's wrong with that.' Len winked. Funerals were a time to think of life as well as death; and life went on. He smiled as Maggie came and sat next to Polly and kissed her tenderly on the cheek, and they both cried together over the death of Edmund. One in, one out, Len thought, as Maggie made Polly feel her unborn baby kick. That was the way of the world, and nowt would stop it.

★　★　★

Polly kissed both Martha and Len as she left them, to walk home up the field path. They'd begged her to stay with them overnight, but she was adamant that she wanted to go home. The truth was that, on the one hand, she half-expected Matt and his grandmother to come barging in; and, on the other, she secretly longed for Tobias to come and visit her. Whichever it was, they would find her exhausted and without argument, for the day had broken her and the one thing that was keeping her hanging on was the warm smile of Daisy Allen and the promise of tea with her and Tobias on Tuesday.

Len had made her smile with his teasing. He knew her and her secrets too well. A cloud came over her as she remembered the dark looks and whisperings of Matt and their grandmother. People had shunned them at the funeral, knowing something was wrong, but not knowing quite what. Gossip was rife, and every time folk talked about who was to be left Paradise after old Edmund's day, a little bit more speculation happened. Even she didn't know what would happen until Tuesday. Who had inherited it would then be made clear.

Polly pulled down the latch on the kitchen door and walked into the dim light of the room. She was startled when there was a movement in her grandfather's chair. Had he come back to haunt her? Was he not really dead? Perhaps they'd been someone else's remains in the coffin?

'Well, is the old bugger dead and buried then?' A tall middle-aged man stood up in front of her, the light from the fire giving him a holy glow as he asked his question.

'Who are you, and what are you doing here? I'll call my dog — he bites!' Polly stepped back and fumbled for the kitchen-door latch as she kept her eye on the man in her kitchen.

'Hold your noise. You must be Polly? Well, Polly, this might surprise you, but I'm your father. So you can shut that bloody door and sit down.' Danny Harper turned and spat into the fire.

'You can't be. Nobody knows where he is. He's even in America, for all we know.' Polly didn't believe a word from the stranger who knew her name.

'He's not; he's here in front of you, and I'm bloody starving, lass. I've had nowt to eat since I left Liverpool yesterday morning. Get on and make us something.'

Polly looked at the brash man talking with a slight accent. It was the same accent as that of her Uncle Albert, who was Liverpool-born and bred. Was this really her father? She couldn't help but stare with her mouth wide open. She'd never dreamed of him turning up out of the blue.

'For God's sake, lass, I'm not a ghost. Or are you a bit feeble-minded? Bill told me you were as sharp as needles, but then again he'd tell me owt, that rogue.'

'It's just I've never seen you before — it's a shock!' Polly gathered her thoughts and then went into the pantry. What did you give your father the first time you ever fed him? Not a lot, in Polly's case, for she'd not baked or bothered cooking since the crash. She'd even had to throw the sacrificial Christmas goose out, after forgetting that it was hanging there, well past Christmas. She looked round, picked up a loaf of bread and a slab of Wensleydale cheese, some onion pickle and the one slice of cooked ham that she was going to have for her supper. That should fill him. Well, it was going to have to, because she hadn't even collected the eggs that morning. She looked at the man she now knew to be her father, as she buttered the bread, moving close to him as she put the kettle on the fire to boil.

'Bill said you were like your mother, and he's right. You'd think you were her.' Danny looked up at Polly as she offered him the supper, placing it on the kitchen table. He ate as if it was his first-ever taste of food, and talked with his mouth full as Polly watched his every move. 'You don't say a lot, do you? I don't bite, you know.'

Polly's curiosity got the better of her. 'Where have you been until now, and why come home and not even show your face at the funeral?' She looked at him from the other side of the table. Even by the oil lamp's dim glow she could tell that he had weathered skin, and his face was hard, with a once-broken nose and sharp eyes.

'Now you are asking a question, lass. Why, indeed?' Danny sniggered. 'No matter how much that bloody old bugger of a father said he hated me, he could never forget I was his son. And I know that this spot is mine, now he's dead. He'd never leave it to anyone else but his lad. So that's why I'm back.' Danny leaned back in his chair and belched as he studied Polly's worried face.

She quickly remembered the deeds that she'd dared to look at, the night her grandfather was drunk. He was right: Paradise had always been passed to the male heir, and she'd been daft to think it would ever be hers.

'And as for where I've been, well, I'm surprised Bill Sunter's never told anyone. I've lived in Liverpool these past eighteen years, making my living on the docks and helping Evie and Albert out, when they needed a hand with their dairy. Thank God they never let on to my mother and father. They knew how tight the lead was that the old bugger kept me on, when I was at home. I'd never any money, and could never afford to stand my round in the pub with my mates. All he ever promised me was that one day I'd own this spot — Paradise.' Danny watched Polly's face. 'He told you that too, did he? You don't have to tell me, for your face tells me everything.'

Polly bowed her head. He was right, but deep in her heart she knew that Edmund and Ada had loved her.

'Anyway, I'm back. Happen not for long, just until this place is sold. I've instructed old Winterskill to put it up for sale next month, by auction in the Crown Hotel. The sooner it's sold, the better.' Danny took a long drink of his tea and watched as a tear ran down Polly's cheek. 'Winterskill wrote to me last week, telling me that I'd inherited this place. Not long after my father's death, Bill gave him my address.' Danny looked at his daughter. She was the spit of her mother — the mother who had nearly trapped him in a life he didn't want.

'I'd say you could come back to Liverpool with me, but I've a wife and six bairns already. We only live in a back-to-back in Everton; it's no life for a country lass. You'll have to go into service or something — at least that will get a roof over your head.' Danny had no intention of having Polly in tow with him, on his return to Liverpool. With the money from the sale of the farm, he could better his lot and not worry for once about how to feed his hungry brood.

Polly started to sob. She was losing everything because of this selfish man, who was her father. He'd walked out on her mother and now he was walking out on her, leaving her with nothing.

'For God's sake. Your mother used to do this and all she did was moan, and look where that got her.'

Danny went quiet as he was interrupted by a knock on the kitchen door. He got up out of his chair and opened it, to the surprise of Tobias Middleton. 'Who are you, and what do you want?'

Polly listened at the table and blew her nose hard, brushing away her tears as she realized it was Tobias at the door.

'I'm Tobias Middleton. I've come to see if Polly's all right.' He placed his foot in the doorway and peered at Polly, crying at the table. 'Who are you, and why are you making my Polly upset?' Tobias wasn't going to remove his foot, even though Danny was trying hard to push him out of the door.

'*My* Polly. Now that's interesting, because I'm her father, lad. And I'll not have any fancy fella courting my lass while I'm here. Tobias Middleton — now let's see. The only Middletons I remember are those at Grouse Hall. Um . . . Clifford, who broke his neck when out riding with the hunt, was he your father? You must be the thing he kept under his table. I remember the scandal now, when I think back. All grown-up now, are we? Well, you can bugger off. My lass is not seeing anyone, especially not you.' Danny put the heel of his, boot into Tobias's foot and slammed the door shut, as Tobias screamed in pain. 'You'll not be seeing him, lass, not while I'm here. He's worth nowt anyway.'

Polly sobbed as Danny warmed himself next to the fire, and Tobias could be heard shouting that he would return with help the next day.

Could things possibly get any worse? Polly didn't think so. All hope of a happy life at Paradise had vanished, along with Edmund's ashes.

21

Danny sat on the edge of his parents' double bed. He sighed as he dropped his braces from off his shoulders and then unbuttoned his tight shirt collar, placing the starched removable white collar and stud on the table next to the bed. It had been a long time since he'd been in this room. It hadn't altered at all; the bed was still in the same place, and the washstand and wardrobe, only now everything seemed smaller. He'd thought the same thing as he'd walked around the rest of the house. It was funny how the mind played tricks on you as you grew older.

Danny rubbed his brow and hung his head. He was knackered. He'd left Liverpool at break of dawn, with his wife Teresa yelling at him, begging him not to go, and their youngest bawling in her arms. The bloody woman, she was always yelling at him, with her mad Irish ways; and if she wasn't yelling at him, she wanted him in her bed. Danny smiled. She was a fair woman — enough to drive a man mad, one way or another. He unlaced his shoes, dropped his trousers and then lay on the top of the double bed, watching the shadows cast by the oil lamp on the wall. He had to sell the old spot, for he needed money to bring his brood up; besides, it meant nowt to him now.

He cast his mind back to the day he'd left Paradise. He'd slept all the way to Liverpool on the mail train, he'd been that tired with worry and guilt. It wasn't until he'd reached Liverpool station that he realized he was out of his depth, and what a green country boy he was. Folk had bumped into him, cursing him for getting in their way, as he looked around him at the number of people going about their business, and at the huge buildings, the trams and horses that filled the streets. He'd sought refuge in a pub called Rosie O'Grady's, where, after having a pint or two of ale, he'd sat in the corner of the snug watching a group of men playing cards. It had been then that one had shouted at him to join them and, like a fool, he'd accepted. At first all had gone well; he'd even won a hand or two, and the three men he was playing with seemed to be respectable. He hadn't noticed the sly looks they gave one another, as they watched him count out money from his father's life savings and place his treasured ticket to a better life in his other pocket. Like a fool he'd got drunk and staggered out into the dark alleyway of the pub to relieve himself, only to be set upon by his so-called new best friends. They had nearly beaten him to a pulp, breaking his nose and stealing his father's money and the golden ticket to America.

He'd lain in his own blood and pee, groaning and nearly half-dead, for the best part of an hour, until the lass from behind the bar had come across him as she made her way home. He'd never forget her screams when she saw his battered body, or the way she had helped him to his feet and the kindness she'd showed him, insisting that she took him to the infirmary and get the bobbies. When he'd said no, she'd taken him to her basement flat and given him her bed for the night, cleaning his wounds and listening to his woes. It turned out they were a lot alike. She'd escaped from her oppressive Catholic father in search of a better life in Liverpool, only to find that life was not as easy as she had thought for a woman on her own. Especially an Irish woman: 'No dogs, no Irish' was on every boarding house's door in Liverpool. Finally she'd got a job in Rosie O'Grady's, with the slum of a basement in part payment of her wage.

From the moment he'd been able to open his swollen eyes, Danny had known Teresa was a good woman. A night of sympathy had turned into nearly twenty years of happiness — a few ups-and-downs, and plenty of times with no money, but on the whole he was sure it had been a better life than staying in Garsdale. Those three bastards who had brayed him to within an inch of his life had done him a favour, for he'd never have met Teresa O'Shea if it hadn't been for them, or got a job on the docks. She'd also helped Danny find his Aunty Evie, who made him welcome and promised not to tell his father and mother where he was. There was no love lost between Edmund and Evie, after he inherited the farm and she had to make her own way in the world after their parents' deaths. The only unwritten condition was that Edmund sent his milk to Evie, to deliver on her doorstep rounds, just to give her a little income and not leave her in poverty.

Danny had thought about this a lot and had decided a long time ago to sell Paradise, if it ever became his. He would be best rid of it, for the bloody place had only caused bother. Besides, with the money from Paradise, his life would be complete, and his family would want for nowt. Danny yawned and listened to the silence, which he wasn't used to. Even in the middle of the night there was always some noise in the heart of Everton. He could faintly hear the sobs of Polly in the next bedroom. He sighed. She'd get a job somewhere; somebody would take her in. She and her brother had ceased being his headache the minute he'd left the dale, so why should he bother about her now?

★ ★ ★

Polly sat up in bed. She could hear men's voices out in the yard below her window. It was later than she'd thought; she'd not slept until the early hours of the morning and now, even though it was only just getting light outside, her bedside clock told her it was eight-thirty in the morning. She yawned and wiped her eyes. They still ached from the sobs of the previous evening and, even in the cold light of the morning, nothing seemed much better. She lay in bed listening to the voices. She recognized two: one was that of her so-called father, and the other was Bill Sunter's. She didn't know to whom the third voice belonged. Whoever he was, she didn't want to know him; if he was linked to Danny, she'd rather have nothing to do with him. She couldn't make out what they were saying, but one of them must have a horse and cart with them, as she'd heard the horses neighing as they waited impatiently.

Curiosity got the better of her as she sat on the edge of the bed, and she was about to pull the curtains when a shot rang out across the farmyard. The rebound echoed down the dale and startled Polly. She threw the curtains back and gasped with shock as she saw the dead body of Clover, the family horse, being dragged onto the knacker-man's cart. Clover, how could this happen to Clover! She was old, but she was the most trustworthy animal you could have wished for, so gentle, and Polly loved her so much. They had grown up together; she'd always been there to take the family everywhere. Now the heartless Danny had killed her in cold blood, and her carcass was being hauled about by men who didn't care about her devoted service.

Polly watched as her father patted Bill Sunter on the back, then tethered the three milk cows to the back of the cart, before the knacker-man whipped his team into action, slowly trundling with his cart of death down the field path and onto the road. She watched from the bedroom window with tears running down her face. She hated her father. He was no farmer, and he didn't love the place where he'd been born. He was nothing but a selfish bastard. It was no wonder he'd never been talked about since he left, for he was an embarrassment to her family name. She pulled her dress on. She didn't quite know how she was going to be civil to him — he was a murderer, in her eyes. Clover had been part of the family and was more than a means of transport, in Polly's opinion.

'Bloody hell, what time do you call this? It's a bloody good job the cows have gone this morning, or else they'd have gone mad, wanting milking. Not that they could have given a lot; they were bloody old things, not worth a lot. I think I probably swindled old Brookes when he paid me what he did for them. Still, he was happy with the price — more fool him.' Danny sat back in his chair and grinned at Bill Sunter, who was smoking a cigarette across from him.

Polly didn't say anything. She was in no mood to talk to this hard bastard of a man, but she had to keep a civil tongue in her head.

'What's up? Not talking to your old man? If I hadn't have sold them to Brookes, someone else would have done. They were as old as the hills. Besides, it's less work for us. I can't be bothered with bloody milking, and the horse was better gone before it dropped dead on us. The bloody bag of bones!' Danny knew Polly was upset, but he didn't care. Why should he, when all he wanted to do was to get back to Liverpool?

'And what are we to do for milk? And how do we get into Hawes?' Polly glared at her father.

'Bill here is going to drop us some milk off when his man does the rounds, and he's lent me a horse — it's in the stable. It's a bit more of a handful than that old nag, but it'll get me to Hawes in half the time.'

'Aye, it's a good horse. You are welcome to it, until you go back to your missus and bairns.

Stop fretting about the milk, Polly. Old Oliver will drop it off to you in a morning, until Paradise is sold.' Bill looked at the sulking Polly. Her mood was dark, like her raven-coloured hair.

'And how do I get to Hawes, or hadn't you thought of that?' Polly looked at her father as she examined the self-satisfied pair.

'You've legs. Shanks's pony — it'll not hurt you. Besides, why do you want to go into Hawes? I hear that even your best friend isn't there any more, and it isn't as if you are best mates with your brother, from what I hear.' Danny sniggered and looked at Bill Sunter, who leaned back in her grandfather's chair and looked like the cat that had got the cream.

'I'm off out, I need some air.' Polly grabbed her shawl and fought back her tears and the words she really wanted to say to her father. She didn't know where she was going, but she couldn't stay with these two nasty, self-centred men, who didn't give a damn about her.

'What about making us something to eat?' Danny shouted after her, but she was gone, slamming the door behind her.

Polly marched down the home field. She'd never felt so furious and upset in all her life. She hated her father. She couldn't abide the sight of him — him and that sniggering Bill Sunter. Her grandfather had been right: they were both worth nowt. She sniffed, stopping her nose from streaming and mixing with the tears that she was fighting back. Her heart pounded as she got to the gate that led onto the main road and she turned to close it, looking up at her home.

Smoke rose from the chimney and, to the outside world, everything appeared normal. She looked at the sheep grazing in the bottom field. They needed moving; the field was nearly bare — another day or two and they'd be going hungry. This wasn't a good thing to happen, with lambing time in another four months, for the ewes would need all the nutrients they could get.

She checked her thoughts. Why should she care? She wasn't going to see those lambs anyway. What did her father have in store for the ewes: surely not butchering them, when most were in lamb? She fastened the gate and walked onto the bridge top, gazing down into the River Clough below. As a child she had run back and forth across the bridge, watching sticks and twigs race one another in the swift currents. Now she just stared into the dark-brown winter waters and pondered what she was to do with her life. It wasn't worth a lot. There was only really Tobias who meant anything to her, and sometimes she was uncertain if his affections towards her were true.

'Now then, Polly, what are you doing down here? Were you coming to ours?' Len had crept up on her and stood standing next to her, the smell of his pipe tobacco reminding her of her grandfather, as he puffed in another lungful.

'I didn't hear you for the sound of the water.' Polly looked up at Len, who immediately saw that she'd been crying.

'Aye, lass, are you still crying for your grandfather? Come in and have a cuppa with the old lass and me. It's all right being independent

320

and being up there on your own, but sometimes you need someone to talk to, to get things off your chest, then things don't look so black.' Len put his arm around Polly's shoulders. He'd been worried when he'd spotted her from his front-room window, worried that she was going to throw herself into the river. Martha had told him to hurry and save the lass and, looking at her, they might have got it right.

'I'm not on my own — that's the problem,' Polly muttered. 'My father's come home, and Bill Sunter's up there with him. My grandparents would be turning in their graves, knowing what's going on at home.' She looked at Len's shocked face.

'Danny's back! But when? What does he look like? Where has he been? And how come that bloody Bill Sunter is always with him?' Len was as much in shock as Polly had been the previous night, as he walked her over the bridge and into his cottage.

'Here, sit down. You look done for, lass. Mother, put the kettle on. We've a visitor and she's fetched some news.' Len shouted through to the kitchen and Martha came running in to see if Polly was all right.

'Danny's back, he's up at Paradise!' Len gave Martha a knowing look.

'Well, I never! He didn't have the decency to come to his father's funeral. Or his mother's, come to think of it. So why turn up now?' Martha sat down on a chair arm and looked at Polly.

'Because he's been left Paradise. My grandfather's left it to him, not me.' Polly swallowed hard and looked at the faces of the elderly couple, as she told them her devastating news.

'But he was going to leave it to you, lass. He said he was off to see old Winterskill, after Ada died. He said he had to change his will, because his lad was worth nowt; and that Matt, your brother, was like his father and should never get his hands on it. The silly old bugger must have never got on with it.' Len sighed and looked at Polly. 'He meant it for you, Polly. He knew you were the farmer, and he was so proud of you.'

'Aye, well, my father is putting it up for sale. He wants nowt to do with it, so what can I do? I haven't a penny to my name and, after he's sold it, no roof over my head, either, because he's going back to Liverpool to his wife and family.'

'Oh, lass, you love that place. We can offer you a roof over your head, but we've no brass. We only just have enough to live on, let alone help you buy back your home.' Martha held Polly tight, and the warmth of her hand was a comfort against Polly's skin. 'We'll look after you the best we can — it's the least we can do. Ada and Edmund were good folk. I don't know what they did to deserve Danny.'

'Thank you. I just don't know what to do. The knacker-man came and took Clover and the cows away this morning. I saw Clover being loaded onto his cart and heard the shot as I lay in my bed. I loved that horse,' wept Polly.

'Your father never did have a bloody heart. I can always remember when Danny was a young lad, your grandfather had some pups from one of his sheep-dogs. Danny had tied one to the kitchen-table leg and teased it so much that it wound itself so tightly around the table leg that it choked itself to death, in fear of the young lad's taunts. Your grandfather found Danny laughing at what he'd done. I don't think he'd have been able to sit down for a day or two, after your grandfather had finished belting him. By God, your grandfather was mad with him.' Len stood and looked out of the window. 'Looks like there are some more visitors going up to your home. Your Matt and his mother are going to be in for a shock, if my eyes don't deceive me. I hope she hasn't given notice on her house, else she's going to be out on her arse as well.' Len stood by the curtains and looked across at the neighbouring farm.

'Father, language!' Martha chastised him.

'Couldn't happen to a nicer pair, if you ask me. They deserve all they get. Now, that one is like his father, and she's just a bitter old woman.' Len watched, interested to see how long the visitors stayed at Paradise.

'I'd rather Matt had Paradise than my father. At least he'd live in it and farm it,' sighed Polly.

'Aye, well, he's not stopping long today. He must have got short shrift, because he and his mother are coming down your home field a hell of a lot faster than they went up it. Your father must be a fearsome man, to have frightened that old witch and her lad. If we are going to take him on, we'd better find a good way to do it. And I think we all know someone who fits the job — someone who would do anything for you. Someone with enough brass to buy your father out, ninety times over, I think. We'll show the clever bastard that he never deserved that farm, and he knows it!'

22

'But I couldn't, Tobias, really. I'm sure your mother and Sam don't want me under their feet,' protested Polly, as Tobias helped her up into his trap.

'They will welcome you with open arms. Besides, you can hardly stay here with me. And I know Len would have you stay with him and Martha, but that's a bit too near to your father, for my liking. He's such a violent man.' Tobias had not stopped worrying about Polly since the confrontation with her father the previous evening, and had been saddling his horse to tackle him, when she and Len had entered the yard of Grouse Hall.

'Aye, Tobias is right. I wouldn't want to take Danny on if he came knocking on my door. I'm too old to take on a big bloke like him, and it'll take everything in me not to give him a piece of my mind, besides worrying about where you are. Daisy will look after you — she's salt of the earth, is Daisy.' Len looked up at the young lass of whom he'd become a protector.

'But I hardly know her, and I've no clothes with me. I should go home and gather some things,' said Polly.

Tobias grasped the reins and looked at her. 'You are not going back to that place until he is out of it. And we will get him out of it, one way or another. I am quite prepared to lay my

325

life down on that statement. I know what that farm means to you.'

'Go on — get on your way. Daisy will love to fuss over you, and Sam will fill your belly. He's a bloody good cook, you know; you'll not go hungry at Mill Race.' Len smiled as he watched Tobias squeeze Polly's hand. He would have struggled to have put together a better-looking couple, and they were so alike in their ways. He watched as the gig lunged out of the yard. Polly would be all right, Tobias would see to that. His job was to make sure the sheep were moved, until their rightful owner was restored; a job he was not looking forward to.

Tobias left Polly in the gig and went to talk to his mother. Polly didn't want just to impose herself on Daisy, by standing like a homeless orphan on her doorstep.

'Polly, my dear, come on in. I will not have you sitting out here a minute longer in this cold January wind. Tobias, put some more coal on the fire and the kettle on to boil. I'll place a warming bottle in the spare bed, just to air it.' Daisy put her arm around Polly and walked her down the path and into the main room of Mill Race cottage.

Tobias did as his mother told him. Polly was made to feel at home and given the chair nearest the fire; Daisy removed her shawl and hung it up on the cloak stand. Polly looked around the warm and cosy cottage. This was the home that Tobias had grown up in, after moving out of Grouse Hall with his mother. She smiled as he looked at the toy soldiers that his mother still kept on a whatnot, and which must have been Tobias's when he was a boy. Len was right: Daisy Allen was a lovely woman, who had indeed welcomed her with open arms.

'Sam won't be long. He's just gone into Hawes, to make sure everything's all right at the shop. He'll be back by four. Nobody will be out on a cold winter's night like this. Now what are we going to do about you and your home? Your father sounds like a dreadful man. Tobias and I know all about dreadful men, don't we, Tobias? Still, sometimes you can't choose who your father is!' Daisy sighed.

Tobias smiled at his mother, before plucking up the courage to speak his true feelings.

'Well, Mother, I know what I want to do, but I'll need your permission and blessing.' Tobias looked at Daisy. 'Mother, I love you with all my heart, but I need a partner in my life, and I think I've found her in Polly.' He reached out for Polly's hand. 'I know we've not known one another long, but, as you have virtually said, we are like peas in a pod and I love her.' Tobias paused as he saw Polly gasp and tears spring to her eyes.

Polly stared at him. She had no idea Tobias had been planning to spring this upon her; he'd not said a word, and they hadn't talked about marriage once. And now, if she was hearing correctly, he was seeking his mother's permission.

'Polly, I want to marry you. And as an engagement present I want to buy you Paradise Farm, to do with as you wish. I would of course

327

prefer you to live with me at Grouse Hall, in which case we would have to rent Paradise to a tenant.' Tobias kissed Polly's shaking hand and gazed into her eyes.

'Tobias, are you sure about this? Should you and Polly not talk about it first? Can your bank account stand it? You have bought several properties over the last few months! I'm not trying to dampen the love you obviously feel for one another, but looking at Polly, she is as shocked as I am.' Daisy looked at her son; sometimes he was so impulsive. It was a trait he got from his father.

'I'm sure. Polly, will you be my wife?' He waited and watched as she gasped for unutterable words.

Her heart beat fast. She'd dreamed of this moment — the moment she owned Paradise, and the day she would marry Tobias Middleton. His mother smiled across at her, but at the same time she could sense doubt in Daisy's smile. It would be a big step for his mother to lose Tobias to her, and for him to risk yet more money. She swallowed hard before she replied.

'Tobias, I do love you. I'm honoured to be asked to be your wife, and that you would buy Paradise for me. But this has come out of the blue, to both your mother and me. Can you give me just a few days — at the most a week — to think it over, and for your mother to get used to the idea?' Polly squeezed his hand tightly and smiled at her dark-haired lover. She did love Tobias; she just wanted time to adjust in her mind to the idea that she was going to be his wife.

'I thought you'd embrace my offer, Polly. I thought that if I bought you your home, you couldn't disown me — that you'd be mine forever.' He stood up and looked at both his mother and Polly.

'Tobias, I do love you. Just let me think about it; it's a big decision to make.' She pulled on his jacket sleeve.

'Tobias, calm down. As Polly says, she just needs time to think. She hasn't said no, has she?' Daisy looked at her impatient son. He couldn't handle the smallest rejection. The early years of being brought up by his father had taken their toll, despite all the love she'd shown him. 'Give us both time — say, a week? And in the meantime, go to the solicitor's and ask how much they expect to sell Paradise for. Winterskill will tell you, especially if you tell him the circumstances. Who knows: Danny Harper might even accept an offer before it goes to auction.' Daisy stood by her son and put her arm around him. 'Now come, sit down next to Polly. I'll go and fill that stone bed-bottle and place it in the bed, while you two lovebirds talk. You've a lot of plans to make, between you.' She urged her son to sit down next to Polly, who looked near to tears.

Tobias shrugged his shoulders and gave in to his mother's wishes, as he sat back down in his seat and watched as Daisy walked through to the kitchen.

'I do love you, Tobias,' Polly whispered. 'It's just that my life is moving so fast, and I need time to think. And no matter how much I love my home, it's a huge price to pay, just for my hand in marriage.' She leaned over and kissed him on the cheek.

'It's nothing — it means nothing to me, if I can't have you. I'm not bothered about Paradise, if I don't have you; but I know the two will never be separated. Marry me, Polly, please marry me. I'm lonely and I need you.' Tobias squeezed her hand again and looked into her eyes.

'Give me a little time, Tobias, that's all I ask. A week at the most, I promise.' She kissed him on the cheek again. Her dreams were about to come true, but she would have liked to have been courted just a little longer and not to feel that, along with the purchase of Paradise, she was just another deal.

'Very well, I'll wait. And, like Mother says, I'll visit the solicitor in the morning, along with the bank. Oh, Polly, you'll want for nothing, and we'll be good for one another. I need a wife who knows about livestock and farming, and an empty-headed society beauty is not for me. I love your country-fresh looks, and the wild look that you give me as you tease me. Please say you'll marry me — you'll not regret it.' Tobias got down on bended knee and begged Polly, as she smiled at him, not understanding why his need was so urgent.

'Give me a week, Tobias. Let me see what goes on at Paradise, and how your mother and stepfather feel about me, because you must admit this has come completely out of the blue.' She ran her hands through his long, dark hair and smiled. She did love him, but she loved Paradise just as much, and she wanted both.

Len Brunskill took Jip, the farm-dog, off its chain and walked out of the farmyard at Paradise, whistling instructions to the dog as it herded the flock of pregnant ewes up the field and into the higher pasture. They took no persuading; the offer of better eating had been denied them for so long that they jostled for position through the open pasture gate.

'What the hell do you think you're doing with my bloody sheep?' Danny Harper strode down the limestone-cobbled yard and swore at Len.

'I'm shifting them, lad. Or have you been away that long that you forgot sheep in lamb need something to eat?' Len looked at Danny. He'd changed; he used to be a bonny, open-faced lad. The man who stood in front of him was hard and rugged, with not an inch of feeling in his body.

'I didn't tell you to move 'em. They are my bloody sheep, and it's up to me whether they are fed or not.' Danny looked at the old man that he now recognized as his father's best friend.

'Well, it's up to thee, lad. But another day and they'd have been dying because of you, and I couldn't have that. I owe it to your father; his stock was his pride and joy, just like Polly was.' Len waited for a reaction, hoping that Danny had the decency not to tackle him, at his age.

'Well, she's buggered off, and you can, too. And take that bloody dog with you. I'll not want it now. Take it or I'll put a bullet through its head, like the horse.' Danny stared at the old man he'd known all his life.

'You are a hard bugger, Danny Harper. Your father and mother loved you, and you broke their hearts when you left. It's a good job they can't see you now, and see what you've done to your home. You don't deserve any luck, lad, and you will never have it, the way you carry on.' Len turned away from Danny's angry face and just hoped that the lad wouldn't stop him in his tracks.

'Aye, bugger off! You've got nowt, living in a rented house with not a penny to your name. You always were an interfering old bastard,' Danny shouted at him as Len walked down the field path.

Len turned. 'I tell you what, lad. I've got more than you'll ever have. Because I can walk down the streets of Hawes and talk to anyone, whereas you'll be shunned, like a leper. Life's not all about money, lad.' He strode out fast; he wasn't going to waste any more time on a useless bugger like Danny Harper. He whistled for Jip and patted the dog's head. 'Looks like you're coming to live with me, lad. You'll be a bit of company for me and the old woman. But I'll warn you now: she'll have you in that tin bath, as sure as eggs are eggs, because she won't be having you smelling in her house.' He glanced back as he closed the field gate, sighing and shaking his head. What a mess. His old mate would have been heartbroken.

23

'Tobias, I don't know if I dare lend you what you're asking for.' Simon Hodgkin leaned back in his chair and looked at the anxious young man. 'You've already bought two properties in as many years. We need some revenue *in* now, not out. It will be autumn before we see some significant income coming in, with the sheep sales. But, as it stands, you will be struggling to keep your head above water this year.'

'But I need to buy this property. My future depends upon it, and young Winterskill says that I can probably secure it at a reasonable price.' Tobias banged his fist down on the table and swore under his breath. 'For God's sake, man. I've four farms, and I'm nearly the biggest landowner in the area.' He sighed.

'That's the trouble — your money's all tied up. Times are changing, Tobias, and money is hard to come by.' Simon looked at the figures in front of him. 'You say that you think the property will make no more than two thousand?'

Tobias nodded, hoping that he had persuaded his cautious bank manager.

'Well, with the money you have in your savings, and the money we are hoping to accrue this next year, I can perhaps be persuaded to lend you half the value of the property. You'll have to curtail your spending, and perhaps ask your mother to lend you the rest.' Simon dropped his pencil on the desk and looked across at the anxious farmer. He admired Tobias's ambition, but the bank's money was not to be played with.

'That's better than nothing. I'll find the rest from somewhere; as you say, my mother might help me out.' Tobias rose from his seat. He couldn't argue any more. He'd just have to try and find the rest from somewhere. He held out his hand for Simon to shake.

'I'll draw up the paperwork, in readiness. Did you say the auction's at the end of the month?' Simon shook Tobias's hand.

'Yes. He won't accept a private offer, thinks he'll make more going to auction.' Tobias stood and looked at the man who had just given him hope.

'Silly man, there's no money out there. He should be thankful for what he gets. It's hard at the moment. Between you and me, Tobias, the dairy is struggling. I've had Bill Sunter in this morning and told him I can't support him any more. He spends money like water, and he's no business sense whatsoever!' Simon shook his head.

'Now that does surprise me. Not that I like the man, anyway.' Tobias couldn't curtail his interest.

'No, he's a bit too big for his boots. Better to keep your head down and know what you are doing, like us two, Tobias.' Simon slapped him on the back and ushered him to the door. 'Good luck with the auction. I'm sure your mother will support you.'

Tobias nodded as he closed the door behind

him. If only he didn't have to ask his mother for money. She'd helped him often enough, and he doubted she would help again.

★ ★ ★

Polly listened to the raised voices in the parlour of Mill Race. Tobias had asked her to leave the room and said he needed to talk to his mother in private. His face had been set firm, and she had guessed that it was over the matter of their coming wedding. She'd only been there two days, but already she felt like part of the family. Daisy made her feel so welcome, and Sam Allen kept the house running with surplus food from the family business. She'd never been so well fed and feared that her waistline was expanding by the day. She dried the lunch plates and then listened with her ear against the door.

'Mother, please, five hundred pounds or even two-fifty. I might not even need it and, if I do, I can pay you back in the autumn.' Tobias was nearly pleading with his mother.

'No, Tobias. I promised Sam that I would not give you any more of my savings, at least not until after my day.' Daisy's voice was firm. 'I know that farm means everything to the lass, but you'll both have to make do with what you've got; you've got to learn you can't have everything.'

'I don't think you want me to get wed. I promised Polly her family home, and I'm not going back on my promise. Even if I have to live on bread and cheese all year, it'll be worth it. I love her, Mother.'

'You might do, lad, and she is a grand lass — I'd be proud to be her mother-in-law — but there's nothing worse than being without money. I should know, and you should remember what it was like when you were a boy. Do you want to start married life off like that? Nine months is a long time, until you get your farm rents back in, and money from the back-end lamb sales.' Polly heard Daisy sigh. 'I suppose I can give you two-fifty, but don't tell Sam. He worries enough about takings in the shop at this time of year.'

'Mother, I won't let you down. We'll rent Paradise out to someone, and I'll pay you back with the first year's rent. Polly just needs to keep it in her family. I knew you'd understand, because you always say you'll have to be carried out of this place in a box. Well, Paradise has been in Polly's family for years, and she feels just the same. You know I can't thank you enough.'

'Aye, I know. There's always been Harpers at Paradise, just like there's always been Frasers here. That's why I'm soft enough to give you the money. Thinking about it: call it our wedding present to you, and then perhaps I don't have to go behind Sam's back. You shouldn't have secrets when you're married.'

'Thank you, Mother. Polly and I couldn't wish for anything better.'

'Just think on, Tobias, to look after her, and not treat her like your father did us. I know you never would, because I hope that I've brought you up to be a gentleman. Now go and tell Polly what you're up to. The poor lass will be worrying to death at the noise we are making.'

Polly quickly moved away from the kitchen door and started putting the dried dishes into the kitchen cupboard. She'd play ignorant of hearing the conversation in the adjoining room.

'Polly, I've been discussing purchasing your old home with my mother. Your father will not sell it privately; he's adamant that it has to be sold at auction. I'll be honest. I'm struggling to raise the money, but I think that, with the help of my mother's wedding gift to us, I can buy it.' Tobias looked at her, awaiting her response. He loved her so much he'd barter his soul for her, if she asked him to.

'Tobias, you don't have to buy Paradise, to marry me. Your family have welcomed me like one of their own, these last few days, and you know I love you. I just wanted some time to see how I fit in. I was frightened that things were moving so fast, and out of my control. So, my love, I'll be sad if we can't buy my home, but it won't make any difference to my answer to your wedding proposal. Which I can now say 'Yes' to, with all my heart.' She put her arms around Tobias. The last day or two, and the earwigged conversation, had made her sure that Tobias loved her, and that their love was not about possessions. She had to make sure of that, for she wasn't going to be used again. And now she knew just how far Tobias was prepared to go, to make her his.

'Polly, I do love you, but I promised you your home and we will buy it, and we will have the grandest wedding this dale has seen.' Tobias held her tight and kissed her, as he ran his fingers through her long, dark hair.

'Only if we can afford it, Tobias. A simple wedding will be just fine. I'm not one for finery.' Polly kissed him, feeling embarrassed that his mother was watching them.

Daisy made herself scarce. The young ones of today had no control over their feelings. If she had done that in front of old Mrs Allen, she would have thought Daisy so common. Still, as long as her Tobias was happy, it didn't matter. And Polly was just returning his love.

24

Polly stood outside the goldsmith's window in the centre of Hawes. She fingered her grandmother's engagement ring, which had never been off her finger since the day she'd opened her unexpected present, after her grandfather's death. Her heart was aflutter and she breathed in deeply as she entered the shop. Inside, it was adorned with glass-topped cases of shining jewels, and ticking clocks. She looked across at the little bespectacled man behind the counter and picked up her courage as he looked at her.

'Yes, what can I do for you?' He gazed at the young girl in front of him and noted her dress. She'd not be buying anything of worth, dressed in clothes like that.

'I . . . I have a ring for sale. My grandmother left me it, and it just doesn't suit me.' Polly stood in front of the old man and pulled her precious grandmother's ring off her finger. She held it within her two fingers for a second, thinking twice about parting with it and hoping that her grandmother would have understood.

'I see, well, pass it over to me. I only buy second-hand goods of decent quality. I'll not be interested if it's just glass.' The sharp-voiced man placed it in his hand and peered at it through his small purpose-made magnifying glass, taking his time examining the cut of the stones and the gold-carat markings, which spoke of the ring's quality.

'Well, it's certainly not glass. This is a quality piece. Your grandmother was a very lucky lady.' He looked again, before raising his head to look at Polly. 'Are you sure you should be parting with this? Once I've bought it, you can't have it back.' He looked at the young lass in front of him. She must be desperate to sell such an heirloom.

'Yes, I'm sure — it's of no use to me. I'd rather have the money to add to buying my home.' Polly fought hard to keep back the tears.

'Your home — where's that then?' The old man was filled with curiosity.

'Paradise, down Garsdale. It's up for sale tomorrow in the Crown, and I need every pound I can raise.' Polly bent her head, for she didn't like folk knowing her business.

'So you are Danny Harper's lass. I heard he was back. Your grandfather must be turning in his grave. I went to school with Edmund, you know.' The jeweller twiddled the ring in his fingers and looked at Polly. 'This is worth quite a bit, lass. Your grandfather had a good eye when he bought this. Now, what to offer you . . . ? If I send it down to London, it will make a nice sum.'

Polly felt sick as the old man looked at her and then at the ring. Please let him offer something decent, she thought, so that she could do her bit towards buying back her home.

'Can we say a hundred pounds? I can probably make a bit more, if I do send it down south.' He looked at her over his spectacles.

Polly looked at him, thinking about how her

grandfather had taught her to barter. 'Can you make it one hundred and twenty-five? I do need every penny!'

'Mmm . . . I don't know.' The diamonds twinkled in the dim light of the shop, as if enticing him to make the offer. 'Go on, then. Edmund was a good man, and I'll get my money back somehow.'

Polly breathed a sigh of relief. Now she could help Tobias at the auction tomorrow night.

*　*　*

The Crown was full with drinkers and with people who were interested in seeing just how much one of the oldest farmhouses and land was worth at auction. Polly entered with Tobias and took a seat in the corner of the snug, where the auction was to be held. There was a poster on the whitewashed walls, telling of the auction and of the designated two lots. Polly's stomach was churning. That was her home they were advertising; that was what she and Tobias had come for. She looked around the room. There were one or two farmers she recognized, and the auctioneer was flicking through the relative papers, with the solicitor by his side. She felt as if the whole room was looking at her, as Tobias bought her a gill of ale and squeezed her hand tightly.

'Thank you. Tobias, I'm going to give you this. I thought it might help towards the sale tonight.' Polly pulled her money out of a bag that Daisy had lent her. 'Just in case you need it. I know

341

you've struggled to raise the cash.' She bowed her head, as she didn't want him to be embarrassed by her knowing.

'Where did you get this from? We'll manage. So far there looks to be only me interested in it. Gerald Winterskill says it looks promising.' Tobias quickly flicked through the money. 'There's over a hundred here. How did you get it?' He looked worried.

'My grandmother's ring. I couldn't think of it going to a better cause than saving my home.' Polly looked at her bare finger.

'Then I'll buy it back tomorrow morning. We'll buy this farm tonight at a reasonable price, you'll see.' Tobias lifted his pint to his lips and then stopped in mid-flow as Danny Harper and Bill Sunter walked in through the doorway and sat up at the bar. The room went quiet as the drinkers looked at Danny, the lad who'd stolen money from his own father and then run away, disowning his own unborn children. One of the farmers spat onto the paved stone floor of the snug and announced that he 'was fussy who he drank with', then left to go and drink in the posh end, with a few more farmers following.

Danny laughed. 'Aye, bugger off. You always were a funny old bugger. And I should have guessed you'd be here, with that bastard there. Has he come to hold your hand, while I make you homeless?' he cried, glaring at Polly and Tobias. 'You should have been at home looking after me — your father — instead of rolling about in bed with him.'

Gerald Winterskill stood up. 'You are not

helping matters, Danny. The sooner we get this auction over, the better.'

'Huh! A man should say what he thinks, instead of skulking. Isn't that right, Bastard?' Tobias didn't rise to the taunt and just stared at the vulgar, self-centred man who reminded him of his own father, who had called him by the same name.

The auctioneer checked his pocket watch. He'd give it another minute and then he'd start the auction. He'd be glad when he was out of this hate-filled room, for the atmosphere was overpowering.

'Get yourself in there. You have to see what it makes.' Dora Dinsdale pushed her grandson Matt into the small room and sat next to him near the doorway. Matt glanced across at Polly and gave her a faint smile, but didn't dare say anything.

'Well, isn't this a nice family gathering?' bellowed Danny sarcastically. 'Could it be that you are all after my money. For God's sake, man, get a move on. Let's get the bastard of a place sold.'

The auctioneer looked at the solicitor, who gave him a reassuring nod, and then came the moment that Polly had dreaded all her life.

'Ladies and gentlemen, we have here today two lots. The sixteenth-century farmhouse known as Paradise, with four bedrooms, three downstairs rooms — including a kitchen — and various outbuildings. I'm sure you've seen the details. And lot two: the surrounding fifty acres of pasture and meadowland.' The auctioneer stood up with his gavel in his hand and looked at the peering faces. 'I'll start with the house. What are

343

you going to give me? How about seven-fifty? Anyone? Come on — it's worth that, at least?' He looked around the room at the faces he knew and they all shook their heads. 'Five hundred?'

Tobias raised one hand and nodded his head. Polly squeezed his other hand tightly.

'Five hundred to Mr Middleton, thank you, sir. Any more bids?'

'Aye, six hundred here.' Bill Sunter lifted his hand. Danny was standing next to him, grinning.

Polly's heart sank. Bill Sunter couldn't own her house. He just couldn't live there — her grandfather had hated him.

'Any more offers?' the auctioneer yelled.

'Six-fifty,' Tobias shouted.

'Seven hundred.' Bill Sunter leaned back on the bar and smirked at Tobias.

Tobias rose from his seat. 'Mr Winterskill, could you ask him if his bids are honourable. I believe Simon Hodgkin is in the next room, and I think you will find that Mr Sunter may not have the funds to cover his offer.' Tobias smiled as he sat down. He could tell by the look on Bill Sunter's face that he didn't want his affairs to be made public.

'Why, your father was right: you are a bastard in more ways than one,' said Bill.

'Aye, I may have been. But I'm right with folk, when you aren't.' Tobias liked the way Bill was squirming.

'Tell him, Bill. You could buy that bugger out, ninety times over.' Danny slapped his best mate on the back and laughed.

'Gentlemen, we are selling this house. Can I

344

have your attention, please!' The auctioneer tried to gain control as a buzz filled the room. 'We are at seven hundred pounds: is that bid still standing?' He looked at Bill, who nodded his head.

'Right, with you, Mr Middleton.'

Tobias shook his head and hesitated, looking into Polly's eyes, sensing her loss at losing her home to the man whom her grandfather had hated.

'Seven hundred and fifty.' He squeezed Polly's hand tight.

'And you, Mr Sunter?' The auctioneer looked at him.

Bill Sunter dropped his head and shook it. 'Nah! Let the bastard have it. I can do better than that, but I must have been mad, wanting to buy that bloody spot.' Danny Harper whispered in his friend's ear and didn't look best pleased with his friend's decision.

'Right, Paradise Farm House is sold to Tobias Middleton. Please see Mr Winterskill here, to go through the paperwork after the auction of the land. Before I go any further, who is interested in the land? I presume you are, Mr Middleton, as it always has belonged to the house?'

Tobias nodded his head as the auctioneer looked around the room for interest. There was none.

'Perhaps, Mr Harper, Mr Winterskill, yourself and Mr Middleton could come to an agreement on the price. I can hardly hold an auction for one man.'

Danny Harper slammed down his pint on the bar and swore.

'It's either that or withdraw it from sale.' The auctioneer waited.

'You've bloody won. Give me five hundred quid for the land and then it's yours.' Danny scowled. He needed the money more than the land, and as soon as it was in his hands, he was off.

Tobias stood up and offered him his hand to shake on it.

'Just fucking get it signed for.' Danny stood over Gerald Winterskill as he put the paperwork in place.

Polly watched as Tobias went through with everyone what he needed to do. Her head was light with relief. Paradise was safe, and hopefully her father would not hang about the dale much longer.

'He's bought it then. The wealthy bastard's bought it for you, I suppose?' Matt came and sat next to her.

Polly nodded. 'We are to be married, so he's bought that as my wedding present.' Polly blushed.

'You always have been the lucky one. You've landed on your feet, with that one. At least he's better than our father is. He isn't up to much, is he?' Matt bowed his head. 'I don't think things are good at the dairy. Bill hasn't paid the farmers for their milk this month. He likes his drink and women too much, that's his trouble.' He looked at his sister, who now appeared even more beautiful with a flush of true love on her cheeks. 'Did you know that Maggie has had a baby girl? She was early, but they are all fine. Her mother was full of it yesterday morning.' Matt smiled.

'Can you imagine Maggie in charge of a baby? She can hardly look after herself.'

'I hadn't heard. How lovely — she'll be thrilled. I must ask Tobias if we can go and visit on a good day, when he's not busy. I wonder what they are calling her?' Polly smiled at the thought of her friend and her newborn in her cottage in Swaledale, and hoped that Maggie's father had paid for it.

'I think they said she was called Ivy, but you know me: I might have got it wrong.'

'Matt, I hope you'll be all right. Do you think the dairy will close?' Polly was concerned. Even though Matt had hurt her in the past, he seemed low in spirits and not at all himself.

'I'll be fine. Look, now that Tobias is return-ing, I'll be on my way. I can't be his favourite person.' Matt sloped off back to his grandmother, who grabbed him by his arm and they walked out of the snug.

'There you go, Miss Harper. Paradise Farm is all yours, my dear. I've even asked old Winterskill to put the deeds in your name — that is, until we are married.' Tobias held both Polly's hands tightly for everyone to see.

'You make me sick. It'll not last, as you're both too much alike. Fuck you both! I hope that you've nothing but worries.' Danny sneered, then picked his coat up and left, with Bill Sunter following in his wake.

'Don't listen to him, my love,' Tobias said. 'We will be happy. We've got one another, and no worries. He's not worth calling your father — just like mine wasn't. I hope to prove an excellent father to our children. However, we had better start with an engagement first. We will pick up tomorrow the ring that you sold. Let's hope that the jeweller still holds it. Your grandmother and grandfather will not be at rest until we retrieve it.'

'How many children were you planning on us having, Tobias?' Polly blushed.

'Oh, at least three or four. It was no fun being an only child. Besides, Grouse Hall needs filling; all those rooms need some laughter in them, so let's brighten up the place.' Tobias squeezed her tightly.

'And Paradise — what do we do with that?'

'That's for you to decide, my dear.' Tobias smiled.

'Could I rent it to my brother? He's going to be out of work, from what he's just been saying. And he's so low in spirits.' Polly knew that was a lot to ask, but it would make the night complete.

'He is indeed out of work. The bank is foreclosing on Bill Sunter tomorrow; he's bankrupt. So I think your brother would make an ideal tenant. I'm not so sure about your grandmother, though, although she seems to keep him in line. Come, let's go home and tell my mother and Sam the good news. I can't wait to see their faces. Mother can organize the wedding banquet she's been planning for years.' Tobias took Polly's arm and walked out of the Crown, wishing everyone a good evening as they went.

Outside, snow had started to fall very lightly. The moon shone and illuminated the houses and streets of Hawes.

'Confetti from heaven, Polly. And it's for us two: we have your grandparents' blessing.'

Polly looked at Tobias. She loved him with every inch of her heart. And yes, they would have three or four children, or even more, because with him by her side they could do anything. Grouse Hall would be a home of happiness, and Paradise would always be hers, no matter what.

25

Polly stood outside the porch of Paradise. Her home was at last back in safe hands. She played with the engagement ring on her finger and thought about how tender Tobias's kisses had been, as he slipped the ring onto her finger. She smiled as she thought of the jeweller; his joy at their union had been obvious. He'd wiped his eyes, dismissing his tears, and then stood back and smiled at them, knowing they were deeply in love. There weren't many couples to whom he wished such good luck, but Hawes was abuzz with the news of Bill Sunter's downfall and of the Middleton lad from Grouse Hall buying Paradise for the love of young Polly.

She smiled. A few months ago she had thought everything was lost, and now she had everything she ever wanted. She might not be farming Paradise herself, but she was going to be living at Grouse Hall, which was even better. Instead of a few tens of acres of land, she'd have hundreds. She'd have the finest china to eat from, and purebred horses to ride on. With Tobias by her side, she'd want for nothing. They'd raise a family to be proud of and make a name for themselves. If only her grandparents were alive to see the outcome to all the times of grief.

She sighed as she turned the lock and opened the door into the kitchen that she knew so well. Tears filled her eyes as she looked around at the mess her father had left behind him: the table and chairs tipped over, and the ashes from the cold fire scattered beyond the hearth. He didn't deserve to be called her father; he was nobody to her and she was glad to see the back of him. He had cared for none but himself.

It was cold in the kitchen, with no fire lit in the grate, but Polly wasn't there to stay — just to pick up her belongings — so she quickly scouted around the house for treasured trinkets that reminded her of home. She sat on the edge of her grandparents' bed and lovingly ran her finger around the only photograph there of her grandparents, and thought about how much she missed and loved them. But Tobias would soon be here to take her back to his mother's: a house filled with love and joy at the upcoming wedding, and a new family who would love her once again. In return she would prove to them all that she was a strong Dales lass, who knew her own mind, but would also be faithful until the day she died to a husband and family she knew she would always love. Everything was in place to look forward to now; there was no need to look back. Polly sniffed. Enough, she told herself — she was strong. Nothing and nobody would ever make her cry again.

⋆   ⋆   ⋆

Tobias closed the farmyard gate behind him and lingered for a while. The hall's roof was white with snow, as was the surrounding countryside. He remembered the days of his youth when he shivered like a dog under the kitchen table, half-frozen and half-starved, black and blue from the beatings his father had given him. No child of his would ever be treated like that. No child — no matter what their parentage — deserved to be treated like an animal, unfed, unloved and unwanted. How he had hated his father, his father's friends and the dark, unwelcoming place that Grouse Hall had been then. It had been his prison, a place of despair. Now, with his beloved Polly by his side, they would turn it into a place of love, with children laughing in the passages and a welcome to whoever visited. The dark days were behind him; he had to bury his dark memories of the past and make a new life. Aye, it was time for change, and Tobias welcomed it with open arms. He was already being talked about with more respect, after challenging the honour of Bill Sunter, and buying Paradise for love. The memory of his father was already being eroded. Evil would not get the better of him and Polly — he'd see to that.

'Go home, Rex,' Tobias shouted at his dog as he climbed up into his trap. 'I'm off to collect the woman I love, and I hope she will always love me. A new life, Rex, that's what we'll make together; a new life, lad. You'll see.'

★   ★   ★

Danny Harper stood in the dark on the freezing-cold station at Hawes Junction. It was a case of déjà vu. He'd been there before, waiting for the early mail train, with his father's money

352

in his hands. He lit his fag and rubbed his hands together to keep warm. He'd be glad to see the back of this bloody spot; he couldn't call it home any more. He picked up his bag of belongings and heard the mail train coming over Maller-stang viaduct.

'Bloody hell, mate, I didn't think you were going to make it.' He turned round to hear the heavy breathing of Bill Sunter behind him.

'I wasn't going to stop and let the bloody bailiffs in. Bugger that! They can throw her on the street, but not me.'

Danny patted him on the back. 'Well, you've only just made it, because the old iron horse is here, and it won't wait.'

'By hell — a new life, just what we both want. Glad you've decided to come with me to America. You want nothing with being tied down with a wife and bawling kids.' Bill threw his kitbag on the train.

'Aye, Teresa will fetch them up and they'll fend for themselves. They'll soon be grown, like those two here.'

Danny looked around at the dale of his birth for one last time. This time he was going to go, and this time he never would return, of that he was sure. Why return to Liverpool and a life of misery, when he could do what he wanted? He was a free man with brass in his pocket, and that was all that mattered.

Other titles published by Ulverscroft:

FOR A FATHER'S PRIDE

Diane Allen

1872: Young Daisy Fraser is living in the Yorkshire Dales with her beloved family. Her sister Kitty is set to marry handsome, wealthy Clifford Middleton. But on the eve of the wedding, Clifford commits a terrible act that shatters Daisy's happy life. She carries her secret for the next nine months, but is left devastated when she gives birth and the baby is pronounced dead. Soon she is cast out by her family and has to make her own way in the world. When further tragedy strikes, she sets out for the bustling streets of Leeds. Daisy longs for a love of her own, but doesn't realize that the key to her happiness may be closer than she thinks . . .

FOR A MOTHER'S SINS

Diane Allen

1870. Railway workers and their families have
flocked to the wild and inhospitable moorland known as Batty Green to build a viaduct
on the Midland Railway Company's ambi-
tious new Settle-to-Carlisle line. Among them
are three very different women — tough
widow Molly, honest and God-fearing Rose,
and Helen, downtrodden by her husband and
seeking a better life. When tragedy strikes, the
lives of the three women are bound together,
and each is forced to confront the secrets and
calamities that threaten to tear their families
apart.

FOR THE SAKE OF HER FAMILY

Diane Allen

It is 1912 in the Yorkshire Dales. Alice Bentham and her brother Will have lost their mother to cancer. Money is scarce and pride doesn't pay the doctor, or put food on the table. Alice gets work at Whernside Manor, looking after Lord Frankland's fragile sister Miss Nancy. Will and his best friend Jack begin working for the Lord of the Manor at the marble mill. But their purpose there is not an honest one. For a while everything runs smoothly. But corruption, attempted murder and misplaced love are just waiting in the wings. Nothing is as it seems and before they know it, Alice and Will's lives are entwined with those of the Franklands — and nothing will ever be the same again.